KT-561-232

Sleepyhead

Mark Billingham

W F HOWES LTD

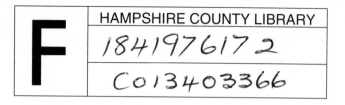

F

HAMPSHIRE COUNTY LIBRARY

1841976172

C013403366

This large print edition published in 2003 by
W F Howes Ltd
Units 6/7, Victoria Mills, Fowke Street
Rothley, Leicester LE7 7PJ

1 3 5 7 9 10 8 6 4 2

First published in 2001 by Little, Brown and
Company

Copyright © Mark Billingham 2001

The right of Mark Billingham to be identified as
the author of this work has been asserted by him
in accordance with the Copyright, Designs and
Patents Act, 1988.

All rights reserved

A CIP catalogue record for this book is available
from the British Library

ISBN 1 84197 617 2

Typeset by Palimpsest Book Production Limited,
Polmont, Stirlingshire
Printed and bound in Great Britain
by Antony Rowe Ltd, Chippenham, Wilts.

For Claire. For Everything. You're chocolate.

ACKNOWLEDGEMENTS

I owe a huge debt of thanks to a great many people, for a variety of reasons:

Dr Phil Coburn, for his expert advice, sick mind and champagne moments; Carol Bristow, for help with matters of police procedure; Professor Sebastian Lucas at St Thomas's Hospital; Nick Jordan, Bernadette Ford and David Holdstock at the Metropolitan Police Press Office; Caroline Allum; Hilary Hale, my brilliant editor, and all at Little, Brown for their boundless enthusiasm; Sarah Lutyens, my agent, for the furniture; Rachel Daniels at London Management; Peter Cocks for pictures; Howard Pratt for sounds; Mike Gunn for jokes; Paul Thorne for in-flight reading.

And my mother, Pat Thompson, for thirty-nine years. Remember what you said about shouting in bookshops . . .

PROLOGUE

Roger Thomas. F.R.C. Path.

Dr Angela Wilson,
HM Coroner,
Southwark.

26 June 2000

Dear Angela,

Following our recent telephone conversation, I write to summarise certain
concerns which you might like to include as an addendum to my post-mortem
report (PM2698/RT) on Ms Susan Carlish, a twenty-six-year-old stroke victim
discovered at home on 15 June.

The PM was performed at St Thomas' Hospital on 17 June. The deceased died as a
result of a brainstem infarction due to basilar artery occlusion from what would
appear to be spontaneous vertebral artery dissection. Examination being twelve
hours post mortem, I was unable to test for Protein C and Protein S deficiency.
This aside, and taking into consideration that Ms Carlish was an occasional
smoker, there would still appear to be an absence of conventional risk factors for
stroke. I also discovered some minor neck trauma with ligamentous damage at C1
and C2 vertebral level though this would not be inconsistent with some previous
whiplash or sporting injury. Traces of a benzodiazepine were discovered in the
blood. Enquiries have produced a prescription for Valium made out to Ms Carlish's
flatmate eighteen months ago.

While I remain in no doubt as to the cause of death, and concede that all police
enquiries have drawn a blank, I am consulting a number of colleagues and copying
this letter to all pathology departments and Coroners Courts in the Greater
London area. I would be interested to confer with anyone who may have dealt with
the body of a stroke victim (prob. female 20–30) displaying any or all of the
following peculiarities:

Absence of conventional risk factors
Torn ligaments in neck
Benzodiazepines in the bloodstream

If you wish to discuss my findings, with a view perhaps to a second post-mortem
examination, I would of course be delighted to chat with you further.

Yours sincerely,

Dr Roger Thomas FRC Path, Consultant Pathologist

P.S. The condition of the body (which honked like a pair of freshly scrubbed
wellies!), was as I told you, of no concern to the authorities and delighted the
morticians, but it was, to say the least, a little disconcerting!!

PART ONE

THE PROCEDURE

'Wake up, Sleepyhead . . .'

And lights and voices and a mask and sweet fresh oxygen in my nostrils . . .

And before?

Me and the girls are linking arms to belt out 'I Will Survive' and scare the shit out of every white-sock-wearing Camberwell Casanova in the club . . .

And now I'm dancing on my own. At a cashpoint, for God's sake! Unfeasibly pissed. Top night.

And I'm struggling to get the key in the door.

And there's a man in a car with a bottle of champagne. What's he celebrating? One more can't hurt on top of a bucketful of tequila.

And we're in the kitchen. I can smell some sort of soap. And something else. Something desperate.

And the man is behind me. I'm kneeling. If he wasn't holding me up I'd flop on to the floor. Am I that far gone?

And his hands are on my head and on my neck. He's very gentle. Telling me not to worry.

And . . . nothing . . .

CHAPTER 1

Thorne hated the idea of coppers being hardened. A hardened copper was useless. Like hardened paint. He was just . . . resigned. To a down-and-out with a fractured skull and the word SCUM carved into his chest. To half a dozen Girl Guides decapitated courtesy of a drunken bus driver and a low bridge. And the harder stuff. Resigned to watching the eyes of a woman, who's lost her son, glaze over as she gnaws her bottom lip and reaches absently for the kettle. Thorne was resigned to all this. And he was resigned to Alison Willetts.

'Stroke of luck, really, sir.'

He was resigned to having to think of this small girl-shaped thing, enmeshed in half a mile of medical spaghetti, as a breakthrough. A piece of good fortune. A stroke of luck. And she was barely even there. What was undeniably lucky was that they'd found her in the first place.

'So, who fucked up?' DC David Holland had heard about Thorne's straight-for-the-jugular approach, but he was unprepared for the question so soon after arriving at the girl's bedside.

'Well, to be fair, sir, she didn't fit the profile. I mean, she was alive for a kick-off, and she's so young.'

'The third victim was only twenty-six.'

'Yes, I know, but look at her.'

He was. Twenty-four and she looked as helpless as a child.

'So it was just a missing-persons' job until the local boys tracked down a boyfriend.' Thorne raised an eyebrow.

Holland instinctively reached for his notebook. 'Er . . . Tim Hinnegan. He's the closest thing there is to next-of-kin. I've got an address. He should be here later. Visits every day apparently. They've been together eighteen months – she moved down here two years ago from Newcastle to take up a position as a nursery nurse.' Holland shut his notebook and looked at his boss, who was still staring down at Alison Willetts. He wondered whether Thorne knew that the rest of the team called him the Weeble. It was easy to see why. Thorne was . . . what? five six? five seven? But the low centre of gravity and the very . . . breadth of him suggested that it would take a lot to make him wobble. There was something in his eyes that told Holland that he would almost certainly not fall down.

His old man had known coppers like Thorne but he was the first Holland had worked with. He decided he'd better not put away the notebook just yet. The Weeble looked like he had a lot more questions. And the bugger did have this knack of asking them without actually opening his mouth.

'Yeah, so she walks home after a hen night . . . er, a week ago Tuesday . . . and winds up on the doorstep of A and E at the Royal London.'

Thorne winced. He knew the hospital. The memory of the pain that had followed the hernia operation there six months earlier was still horribly fresh. He glanced up as a nurse in blue uniform put her head round the door, looking first at them and then at the clock. Holland reached for his ID, but she was already shutting the door behind her.

'Looked like an OD when she came in. Then they found out about this weird coma thing, and she gets transferred here. But even when they discovered it was a stroke there was no obvious link to Backhand. No need to look for benzos and certainly no need to call us.'

Thorne stared down at Alison Willetts. Her fringe needed cutting. He watched as her eyeballs rolled up into their sockets. Did she know they were there? Could she hear them? And could she remember?

'So, if you ask me, the only person who's fucked up is, well, the killer really. Sir.'

'Find us a cup of tea, Holland.'

Thorne didn't shift his gaze from Alison Willetts and it was only the squeak and swish of the door that told him Holland had gone.

Detective Inspector Tom Thorne hadn't wanted Operation Backhand, but was grateful for any

11

transfer out of the brand spanking new Serious Crime Group. The restructuring was confusing everybody and at least Backhand was a straight-forward, old-fashioned operation. Still, he hadn't coveted it like some he could mention. Of course it was high profile, but he was one of that strange breed reluctant to take on any case he didn't seriously think could be solved. And this was a weird one. No question about that. Three murders that they knew about, each victim suffering death due to the constriction of the basilar artery. Some maniac was targeting women in their homes, pumping them full of drugs and giving them strokes.

Giving them strokes.

Hendricks was one of the more hands-on pathologists, but a week earlier, in his laboratory, Thorne had been less than thrilled at having those clammy hands on his head and neck as Hendricks tried to demonstrate the killing technique. 'What the bloody hell d'you think you're doing, Phil?'

'Shut your face, Tom. You're off your face on tranquillisers. I can do anything I like. I just bend your head this way and apply pressure to this point here to kink the artery. It's a delicate procedure this, takes specialised knowledge . . . I don't know. Army? Martial arts, maybe? Either way he's a clever bastard. No marks to speak of. It's virtually undetectable.'

Virtually.

Christine Owen and Madeleine Vickery both had risk factors: one in middle age, the second

12

a heavy smoker on the pill. Both were discovered dead at home on opposite sides of London. That they had recently washed with carbolic soap was noted by the pathologists concerned, and though Christine Owen's husband and Madeleine Vickery's flatmate had considered this odd, neither could deny (or explain) the presence of a bar of carbolic in the bathroom. Traces of a tranquilliser were found in both victims, and were attributed in Owen's case to a prescription for depression, and in Vickery's, to an occasional drugs habit. No connection between these tragic yet apparently natural deaths was ever made.

But Susan Carlish had no generally accepted risk factors for stroke, and the tranquillisers found in the one-room flat in Waterloo, in a bottle with no label, were something of a mystery. It was down to the torn ligaments in her neck and one bloody clever pathologist that they'd even got a sniff of it. Even Hendricks had to admire that particular bit of path. work. Very sharp.

But not as sharp as the killer.

'He's playing a percentage game, Tom. Loads of people are walking about with high-risk factors for stroke. You for a start.'

'Eh?'

'Still got a gold card at Threshers, have you?'

Thorne had started to protest but thought better of it. He'd been out on the piss with Hendricks often enough.

'He picks three different areas of London knowing there's a hell of a slim chance that the victims will ever be connected. He goes about his business and we're none the wiser.'

Now Thorne stood listening to the persistent wheeze of Alison's ventilator. Locked-in syndrome it was called. They didn't know for sure but she could probably hear, see and feel. Alison was almost certainly aware of everything going on around her. And she was completely and utterly unable to move. Not the tiniest muscle.

Syndrome wasn't the right word. It was a sentence. And what about the bastard who'd passed it? A martial-arts nutcase? Special Services? That was their best guess. Their only guess. None the wiser . . .

Three different areas of London. What a mess that had been. Three commanders sitting round a table playing 'Whose Knob's the Biggest?' and putting Operation Backhand together.

He had no worries as far as the team was concerned. Tughan was efficient at least, and Frank Keable was a good DCI, if at times a little too . . . cautious. Thorne would have to have a word with him about Holland and his notebook. He never put the bloody thing down. Couldn't the division take on a single detective constable with a memory span greater than the average goldfish?

'Sir?'

Goldfish Boy was back with the tea.

'Who put us on to Alison Willetts?'

14

'That would be the consultant neurologist, er . . . Doctor . . .'

Holland cleared his throat and swallowed. He had a plastic cup of hot tea in each hand and couldn't get out his notebook. Thorne decided to be nice and reached out to take a cup. Holland groped for the notebook.

'Dr Coburn. Anne Coburn. She's teaching over at the Royal Free today. I've made you an appointment for this afternoon.'

'Another doctor we've got to thank.'

'Yeah, and another bit of luck as it goes. Her old man's a consultant pathologist, David Higgins. He does a bit of forensic work. She tells him about Alison Willetts and he goes, "That's interesting because . . ."'

'What? And he says and she says? Bit of a casual post-nookie chinwag, was it?'

'Don't know, sir. You'll have to ask her.'

Standing aside to let a pale ginger-haired nurse through to change Alison's feeding line, Thorne decided there was no time like the present. He thrust his untouched tea back at Holland.

'You stay here and wait for Hinnegan to show up.'

'But, sir, the appointment isn't until four-thirty.'

'So I'll be early.'

He trudged along a maze of cracked red linoleum-floored corridors in search of the quickest way to the exit and an escape from the smell that he and every right-minded person in the world

15

hated so much. The Intensive Therapy Unit was in a newer wing of the National Hospital for Neurology and Neurosurgery, but it still had the smell. Disinfectant, he reckoned. They used something similar in schools but that just took him back to forgotten gym kits and the horror of PE in underpants. This was a different smell.

Dialysis and death.

He took the lift down to the main reception area, whose imposing Victorian architecture made a surprising contrast with the modern, open plan style of the hospital's newer parts. There was a faded grandeur about the stone tablets that lined the walls and the dusty wooden plaques inscribed with the names of the hospital consultants. Pride of place went to the full-length portrait of Diana, Princess of Wales, a former patron of the hospital. The painting was accomplished, unlike the bust of the Princess that stood on a plinth next to it. Thorne wondered if it had been sculpted by a patient.

As he neared the exit, the muttered curses and dripping umbrellas coming towards him through the main doors told him that summer was at an end. A week and a half into August and it was over. He stood beneath the hospital's elaborate red-brick portico and squinted through the downpour towards where his car was parked, tight against the railings that ran around Queen Square. People scurried through the rain, heads down, across the gardens or towards Russell Square tube station. How many were doctors or nursing staff? There were a dozen hospitals or specialist units within a mile of him. He could just see Great Ormond Street Children's Hospital from where he stood.

He turned up his collar and prepared to make a dash for it.

At first he thought it was a parking ticket and he pulled it roughly from beneath the wiper blade. As soon as he removed the single sheet of A4 from the polythene wrapper and unfolded it, he saw it was something else. He carefully inserted it back into its protective wrapping, wiped off the rain and peered at the neatly typed message. After the first four words he was no longer aware of the rainwater running down the back of his neck.

DEAR DETECTIVE INSPECTOR THORNE. WHAT CAN I SAY? PRACTICE MAKES PERFECT AND DON'T YOU JUST ENVY HER THAT PERFECT . . . DISTANCE? I INVITE YOU TO CONSIDER THE CONCEPT OF FREEDOM. TRUE FREEDOM. HAVE YOU EVER REALLY CONSIDERED IT? I'M SORRY ABOUT THE OTHERS. TRULY. I SHALL NOT INSULT YOUR INTELLIGENCE WITH PLATITUDES ABOUT ENDS AND MEANS BUT OFFER IN MITI-GATION THE THOUGHT THAT A MASSIVE UNDER-TAKING OFTEN HAS AN APPROPRIATE MARGIN OF ERROR. IT'S ALL ABOUT PRESSURE, DETECTIVE INSPECTOR THORNE, BUT THEN YOU'D KNOW ALL ABOUT THAT. SERIOUSLY, THOUGH, TOM, MAYBE I'LL CALL YOU SOMETIME.

Pressure . . .

Thorne looked around, his heart thumping. Whoever left the note must be close – the car hadn't been there long. All he could see were grim-set, rain-soaked faces, and Holland dodging the puddles as he loped across the road towards him.

'Sir, the boyfriend's just arrived. You must've passed him on your way out.'

The look on Thorne's face stopped him dead in his tracks.

'Alison is not a fuck-up, Holland.'

'Of course not, sir. All I meant was—'

'Listen. This is what he wants.' He pointed back towards the hospital. 'Do you understand?' His shirt was plastered to his back. Rain and sweat. He could barely understand it himself. He could hardly believe what was struggling to come out of his mouth. Holland stared at Thorne open-mouthed as he spoke the words that would cost him so much. Words which even as they formed on his lips, told him he should never have agreed to become part of this.

'Alison Willetts is not his first mistake. She's the first one he's got right.'

Tim's not handling this very well. He had that funny choke in his voice when he was talking to Anne. Anne? First-name terms and we've never met. She sounds nice, though. I like our chats in the evening. Obviously a bit one-sided but at least somebody knows there's something going on in here. There's still some*body* going on in here.

Did I mention the tests by the way? Absolutely fucking excellent. Well, some of them. Basically there's some sort of kit, literally a kit, in a special case, which tests if you're a complete veggie or not. To see if you're in Persistent Vegetative State. PVS. Which I keep mixing up with VPL but PVS is a bit more serious. They just test all your senses. Banging bits of wood together to see if you can hear, to see if you react. Not quite sure what I did, really, but they seemed pleased. I could have done without the pinpricks and that stuff they waft under your nose that's like the stuff you inhale if you've got a really bad cold. But the taste test makes up for it. They give you whisky. Drops of whisky on your tongue. This is my kind of hospital.

Anne did the tests. She looks dead attractive for somebody quite old. I can't see her very well but that's the image I get of her. I'm not even seeing shapes, really. More like the shadows of shapes. And some of those shadow-shapes are definitely policemen. Tim sounded really nervous when he was talking to one of them. He was pretty young, I reckon.

The man outside the house with the bottle of champagne did . . . what? Turned me into a pretty dull conversationalist but what else? Hurt me somewhere but nothing feels like a wound.

Everything feels like a scar.

Did he touch me? Will he be the last one ever to touch me?

Come on, Tim. I'm alive. It's still me. More or less. You're cracking up and I'm the one singing 'Girlfriend In A Coma' to myself . . .

It was nice that Carol and Paul came in. Christ, I hope all this business didn't bugger up the wedding.

CHAPTER 2

'Are we looking at a doctor?'

As soon as he had asked the question, Thorne knew what Holland would be thinking. It was undeniable that Anne Coburn was the sort of doctor most men would look at. About whom most men would contrive painful jokes about cold hands and bedside manners. She was tall and slim. Elegant, he thought, like that actress who was in *The Avengers* and plays the old slapper in that sitcom. Thorne put her in her early forties, maybe a year or two older than he was. Although the blue eyes suggested that her hair might once have been blonde, he liked it the way it was now – short and silver. Perched on the edge of a small, cluttered desk, drinking a cup of coffee, she seemed almost relaxed. By comparison with the day before at any rate.

She'd sent him away from the Royal Free with a flea in his ear. Thorne could still hear the laughter of thirty-odd medical students as he'd trudged away up the corridor. It was evidently a treat to take a short break from brain scans to watch the teacher give a high-ranking police officer a thorough bollocking. Anne Coburn did not like to be interrupted. She'd apologised for the incident over the phone when Thorne rang to rearrange their appointment back at Queen Square where she worked. Where she treated Alison Willetts.

She took another swig of coffee and repeated Thorne's question. Her speech was crisp, efficient and easy on the ear. It was a voice that could certainly wow impressionable medical students or frighten middle-aged policemen. 'Are we looking at a doctor? Well, certainly someone with a degree of medical expertise. To block off the basilar artery and cause a stroke would take medical know-how. To cause the kind of stroke that would induce locked-in syndrome is way beyond that . . . Even if someone knew what they were doing, the odds are against it. You might try it a dozen times and not succeed. We're talking about fractions of an inch.'

Those fractions had cost three women their lives. Thorne flashed on a mental image of Alison Willetts. Make that four women. Perhaps they should count their blessings and thank God for this lunatic's expertise. Or, more likely, worry that now he thought he'd perfected his technique he'd be eager to try again. Dr Coburn hadn't finished. 'Plus of course, there's the journey to consider.'

Thorne nodded. He'd already started to consider it. Holland looked confused.

'From what I can gather, you're presuming that Alison had her stroke at home in south-east

22

London,' said Coburn. 'He would have had to keep her alive until he could get her to the Royal London, which is at least . . .'

'Five miles away.'

'Right. He'd have passed any number of hospitals on the way. Why did he drive all the way to the Royal London?'

Thorne had no idea, but he'd done some checking. 'Camberwell to Whitechapel, he'd have passed three major hospitals, even on the most direct route. How would he have kept her alive?'

'Bag and mask's the most obvious way. He might have had to pull over every ten minutes or so for half a dozen good squeezes on the bag but it's fairly straightforward.'

'So, a doctor, then?'

'I think so, yes. A failed medical student possibly – chiropractor, perhaps . . . a well-read physiotherapist at a hell of a stretch. I've no idea where you'd even begin.'

Holland stopped scribbling in his notebook. 'A hypodermic needle in a haystack?'

Coburn's expression told Thorne that she'd found it about as funny as he had.

'You'd better start looking for it then, Holland,' Thorne told him. 'I'll see you tomorrow. Get a cab back.'

Every step that he and Dr Coburn took towards Alison's room filled Thorne with something approaching dread. It was a terrible thought

23

but he would have found it easier had Alison been one of Hendricks's 'patients'. He couldn't help but wonder if it might not have been easier for Alison too. They walked through to the Chandler Wing then took the lift to the second floor and Medical ITU.

'You don't like hospitals, do you, Detective Inspector?'

An odd question. Thorne couldn't believe that anybody liked hospitals. 'I've spent too much time in them.'

'Professionally or . . . ?' She didn't finish the question because she couldn't. What were the right words? 'On an amateur basis?'

Thorne looked straight at her. 'I had a small operation last year.' But that wasn't it. 'And my mother was in hospital a long time before she died.'

Coburn nodded. 'Stroke.'

'Three of them. Eighteen months ago. You really *do* know how brains work, don't you?'

She smiled. He smiled back. They stepped out of the lift.

'By the way, it was a hernia.'

The signs on the walls fascinated Thorne: Movement and Balance; Senility; Dementia. There was even a Headache Clinic. The place was busy but the people they passed as they moved through the building were not the usual walking wounded. He saw no blood, no bandages or plaster casts. The corridors and waiting areas seemed full of people

24

moving slowly and deliberately. They looked lost or bewildered. Thorne wondered what he looked like to them.

Much the same, almost certainly.

They walked on in silence past a canteen filled with the casual chatter that Thorne would have associated with a large factory or office building. He wondered if they ever got that smell out of the food.

'What about doctors? Are we on your shit list?'

For a ridiculous second he wondered if she was coming on to him. Then he remembered the faces of those bloody medical students. This was not a woman about whom he could presume anything. 'Well, not at the moment anyway. Too many of them responsible for putting us on to this. You for a start.'

'I think my husband can take credit for that.' Her tone was brisk, without an ounce of false modesty.

She caught Thorne's fleeting glance towards where a wedding ring should have been. 'Soon to be ex-husband, I should say. It was a chance remark, really. One of the more civilised moments in a rather bloody how-shall-we-handle-the-divorce session.'

Thorne looked straight ahead, saying nothing. Christ, he was so English!

'What about the china? Who keeps the cat? Did you hear about the lunatic who's stroking out women all over London? You know the sort of thing . . .'

25

Phobia. Death. Divorce. Thorne wondered if perhaps they should move on to the crisis in the Middle East.

'Forty-eight hours after she was brought in we gave Alison an MRI scan. There was oedema around the neck ligaments – bright white patches on the scan. You see it in whiplash victims, but with Alison I thought it was unusual. On top of what my husband had told me—'

'What about the Midazolam?'

'His benzodiazepine of choice? It was a very clever choice, as a matter of fact, especially as there was every chance it would be the same drug given to Alison in A and E. How's that for muddying the waters?'

Thorne stopped. They were outside Alison's room. 'Can we check that?'

'I did. And it was. I know the anaesthetist who was on duty at the Royal London that night. The toxicology report showed Midazolam in Alison's bloodstream but it would have done anyway – that's what was used to sedate her in A and E. But we also take blood routinely, on admission, so I checked. Midazolam was present in that first blood sample too. That's when I decided to contact the police.'

Thorne nodded. A doctor. He had to be. 'Where else do they use Midazolam?'

She thought for a moment. 'It's pretty special-ised. ITUs, A and E, Anaesthetics, that's about it.'

'Where's he getting it from? Hospitals? Can't you get this sort of stuff over the Internet?'

'Not in these quantities.'

Thorne knew that this would mean contacting every hospital in the country for recorded thefts of Midazolam. He wasn't sure how far back to check. Six months? Two years? He'd err on the side of caution. Besides, he was sure Holland could use the overtime.

Coburn opened the door to Alison's room.

'Can she hear us?' Thorne asked.

She brushed Alison's hair off her face and smiled at him indulgently. 'Well, if she can't, it's not because there's anything wrong with her hearing.'

Thorne felt himself redden. Idiot. Why *did* people whisper at hospital bedsides?

'To be honest, I'm not sure. The early signs are good. She blinks to sudden noises but there are still tests to be done. I talk to her anyway. She already knows which registrar is an alcoholic and which consultant is doing it with three of his students.'

Thorne raised an inquisitive eyebrow. Coburn sat and took Alison's hand.

'Sorry, Detective Inspector, girls' talk!'

Thorne could do little but watch her among the mess of wires and machinery. Wires and machinery with a young woman attached. He listened to the hiss of Alison's ventilated lungs and felt the throb of her computerised pulse, and he thought about

27

the one doctor out there somewhere who was most definitely on his shit list.

He sat on the tube trying to guess how much longer the businessman opposite him had to live. It was a game he greatly enjoyed.

It had been such a wonderful moment the day before when Thorne had looked straight at him. He hadn't really seen him: it had been no more than half a second and he was just a passer-by with his hood up, but it had been a lovely bonus. The look on the policeman's face had told him that he'd understood the note. Now he could relax and enjoy what had to be done. He'd lie in the bath when he got home and think about it some more. He'd think about Thorne's face. Then he'd grab a few hours' sleep. He was working later on.

The man opposite looked flushed. Another tough day at the office. He had a smoker's face, pale and blotchy. The broken veins on his cheeks were probably a sign of bad circulation and excessive drinking. The small, creamy blobs on the eyelids, the xanthelasma, almost certainly meant that his cholesterol was way too high, and that his arteries were well furred up.

The businessman gritted his teeth as he turned the pages of his newspaper.

He gave him ten years at most.

As his battle-scarred blue Mondeo moved smoothly through the early-morning traffic on the Marylebone

Road, Thorne nudged the Massive Attack tape into the stereo and leaned back in his seat. If he'd wanted to relax and switch off he'd have plumped for some Johnny Cash or Gram Parsons or Hank Williams, but there was nothing like the repetitive, hypnotic thud of music he was twenty-five years too old for, to concentrate his thoughts. As ever, when the mechanised beat of 'Unfinished Sympathy' started thumping from the speakers he pictured the incredulous look on the face of the teenage assistant in Our Price. Smug little git had looked at him like he was some old saddo trying to pretend he still had his finger on the pulse.

The spotty teenage face became the infinitely more attractive one belonging to Anne Coburn. He wondered what sort of music she liked. Classical, probably, but with a Hendrix album or two stashed away behind the Mozart and Mendelssohn. What would she make of his penchant for trip-hop and speed-garage? He guessed that she'd go for the saddo theory. He stopped at the lights and rolled down the window to let the beat blast out at the snooty-looking woman in the Saab next to him. Thorne stared straight ahead. When the light hit amber, he turned, winked at her and pulled gently away.

And when he got back to HQ? There would be a convincing babble of efficient-sounding voices, a scurrying back and forth with files, and the buzzing and beeping of faxes and modems. Thorne smacked out the rhythm on his steering-wheel. And as a backdrop to this montage of proper procedure there would be the wall; a blackboard detailing names, dates and ACTIONS, and lined up above it there would be the pictures: Christine, Madeleine and Susan. Their unmarked faces sharing a pallid blankness, but each, to Thorne, seeming to capture a dreadful final instant of some unfamiliar emotion. Confusion. Terror. Regret. All *in extremis*. He turned up the music. In factories and offices across London, workers were copping furtive glances at calendar girls – Saucy Sandra, Naughty Nina, Wicked Wendy. The days, weeks and months that lay ahead for Thorne would be counted off by the reproachful faces of Dead Christine, Dead Madeleine and Dead Susan.

'How's it going, Tommy?'

Christine Owen. Thirty-four. Found lying at the bottom of the stairs . . .

'Shake 'em up, will you, Tom, for fuck's sake?'

Madeleine Vickery. Thirty-seven. Dead on her kitchen floor. A pan of spaghetti boiled dry . . .

'Please, Tom . . .'

Susan Carlish. Twenty-six. Her body discovered in an armchair. Watching television . . .

'Tell us what you're going to do, Tom.'

They would make lists, no question, long lists they would cross-reference with different ones. DCs would ask hundreds of different people the same questions and type out their notes and DSs would take statements and make phone calls and type out *their* notes, which would be collated and indexed and, perhaps, several thousand fields full of cows' worth of shoe leather later, they might get lucky . . .

'Sorry, girls, nothing yet.'

They weren't going to catch this bloke with procedure. Thorne could feel it already. This wasn't the convenient copper's hunch of a thriller writer – he knew it. The killer might get himself caught. Yes, there was a chance of that. The profilers and psychological experts reckoned that, deep down, they all wanted to be caught. He'd have to ask Anne Coburn what she thought about that the next time he saw her. If that turned out to be sooner rather than later he wouldn't be complaining.

Thorne pulled into the car park and killed the music. He stared up at the dirty brown building in which Backhand had made its home. The old station on Edgware Road had been earmarked for closure months ago and was now all but deserted, but the vacant offices above had been perfect for an operation like Backhand. Perfect for the lucky buggers who didn't have to work there every day. An open-plan monstrosity – one enormous fishtank for the minnows with a few smaller bowls around the edges for the bigger fish.

For a moment he was deeply afraid to go in. He got out of the car and leaned against the bonnet until the moment passed.

As he trudged towards the door, he made a

decision. He wasn't going to let anyone put a picture of Alison on the wall.

Fourteen hours later Thorne got home and rang his dad. They spoke as often as Thorne could manage and saw each other even less. Jim and Maureen Thorne had left North London for St Albans ten years before, but since his mum had died Thorne felt the distance between him and his dad growing greater all the time. Now they were both alone and their telephone conversations were always desperately trivial. His dad was always keen to pass on the latest dirty story or pub joke, and Thorne was always pleased to hear them. He liked to let his old man make him laugh – he liked to hear *him* laugh. Aside from the forced lightheartedness of these phone calls, he suspected that his father wasn't laughing a great deal. His father knew damn well that *he* wasn't.

'I'll leave you with a couple of good ones, Tom.'

'Go on then, Dad.'

'What's got a one-inch knob and hangs down?'

'I don't know.'

'A bat.'

It wasn't one of his best.

'What's got a nine-inch knob and hangs up?'

'No idea.'

His dad put the phone down.

He sat down and, for a few minutes, he said nothing. Then he began to speak softly. 'Perhaps, in retrospect, the note on the windscreen was a little . . . showy. It's not like me, really. I'm not that sort of person. I suppose I just wanted to say sorry for the others. Well, if I'm being truthful, I must admit that a part of me wanted to boast just a little. And I think Thorne's a man I can talk to. He seems like a man who will understand how proud I am about getting it right. Perfection is everything, isn't it? And haven't I been taught that? You can believe it. I have been well taught.

'I mean, it's been a struggle and I'm certainly not saying that I won't make any more mistakes, but what I'm doing gives me the right to fail, wouldn't you say? The one . . . frustration is that I can only imagine how good it feels on the machines. Safe and clean. Free to relax and let the mind wander. No mess. And if I feel proud at liberating a body from the tyranny of the petty and the putrid then I can't be condemned for that, surely. It's the only real freedom left that's worth fighting for, I'd say. Freedom from our clumsy movement through air. Our bruising. Our . . . sensitivity. To be released from the humdrum and the everyday. Fed and cleaned. Monitored and cared for. All our filthy fluids disposed of. And, above all, to *know*. To be aware of these wonders as they are happening. What does a corpse know of its washing? To know and to feel all these things must be wonderful.

'God, what am I thinking? I'm sorry. I don't have to tell *you* any of this.

'Do I, Alison?'

Sue and Kelly from the nursery came to see me yesterday. My vision's a lot better already. I could see that Sue was wearing far too much eyeliner as usual. There's plenty of gossip. Obviously not as much as usual with me in here, but still good stuff. Mary, the manageress, is really pissing everybody off, sitting on her arse and correcting the spelling on the happy charts. Daniel's still being a little sod. He cried for me last week, they said. They told him I'd gone to Spain on my holidays. They told me that when I came out we'd all go and get completely pissed and that they'd rather be in here any day than changing shitty nappies on three pounds sixty an hour . . .

There wasn't much else after that.

And, at last, a bit of real excitement. Some bedpan-washer or something got blocked up. I know it doesn't sound earth-shattering, but there was water everywhere and all the nurses were sloshing round and getting really pissed off.

Excitement is relative, I suppose.

I dreamed about my mum. She was young, like she was when I was at school. She was getting me dressed and I was arguing about what I was going to wear and she was weeping and weeping . . .

And I dreamed about the man who did this to me. I dreamed that he was here in my room, talking to me. I knew his voice straight away. But it was also a voice I recognised from after it happened. My brain has gone to mush. He sat by my bed and squeezed my hand and tried to tell me why he'd done it. But I didn't really understand. He was telling me how I should be happy. That voice had told me to enjoy myself as he handed me the champagne bottle and I took a swig.

I must have invited him in. I must have. I suppose the police know that. I wonder if they've told Tim?

Now that dreams are the closest thing I have to sensation, they've become so vivid. It would be fantastic if you could press a button and choose what you were going to dream about. Obviously someone would have to press the button for me, but a selection of family and friends with a healthy degree of filth thrown in would be nice.

Mind you, once you've been fucked to this degree, a shag is neither here nor there, really, is it?

CHAPTER 3

Thorne had been wrong about the summer: after a fortnight's holiday of its own, it had returned with a sticky vengeance, and the siren call of the launderette could no longer be ignored. He was horribly aware of the smell coming off him as he sat sweltering in Frank Keable's office. They were talking about lists.

'We're concentrating on doctors currently on rotation in inner London, sir.'

Frank Keable was only a year or two older than Thorne but looked fifty. This was more due to some genetic glitch than any kind of stress. The lads reckoned he must have started receding at about the same time he hit puberty, judging by the proximity of his hairline to the nape of his neck. Whatever hormones he had left that stimulated hair growth had somehow been mistakenly rerouted to his eyebrows, which hovered above his bright blue eyes like great grey caterpillars. The eyebrows were highly expressive and gave him an air of wisdom that was, to put it kindly, fortunate. Nobody begrudged him this bit of luck – it was the least you could hope for when you looked like an overfed owl with alopecia.

Keable put one of his caterpillars to good use, raising it questioningly. 'It might be best to look a bit further afield, Tom. We'd be covering our bases, should the worst happen. We're not short of manpower.'

Thorne looked sceptical but Keable sounded confident.

'It's a big case, Tom, you know that. If you need the bodies to widen things out a bit, I can swing it.'

'Let's have them anyway, sir, it's an enormous list. But I'm sure he's local.'

'The note?'

Thorne felt again the heavy drops of rain that had crawled inside his shirt collar and trickled down between his shoulder-blades. He could still sense the polythene between his fingers and thumbs, as he'd read the killer's words while the water ran down into his eyes, like tears coming home.

The killer had known where Alison was being treated. He was obviously following the case closely. Theirs as well as hers.

'Yes, the note. And the locations. I think he'd want to be around to keep an eye on things.'

To monitor his work.

'Is it worth putting a watch on the hospital?'

'With respect, sir, the place is crawling with doctors . . . I can't see the point at the minute.' His eyes drifted to the calendar on the dirty yellow wall

– views of the West Country. Keable was originally from Bristol . . . The heat was making it hard to concentrate. Thorne undid another button on his shirt. Polyester. Not clever. 'Is there any chance of moving that fan round a bit?'

'Oh, sorry, Tom.'

Keable flicked a switch on his black desktop fan, which started to swing backwards and forwards, providing Thorne with a welcome blast of cold air every thirty seconds or so. Keable leaned back in his chair and puffed out his cheeks. 'You don't think we're going to crack this, do you, Tom?'

Thorne closed his eyes as the fan swung back in his direction.

'Tom, is this about the Calvert case?'

Thorne looked at the calendar. Two weeks now since they'd found Alison, and they were nowhere. Two weeks of banging their heads against a wall, and getting nothing but headaches.

Concern, or what passed for it, crept into Keable's voice. 'Cases like this, it's completely understandable . . .'

'Don't be silly, Frank.'

Keable leaned forward quickly. In charge. 'I'm not insensitive to . . . moods, Tom. This case has a taste to it. It's not . . . in the run of things. Even I can sense it.'

Thorne laughed. Old colleagues. 'Even you, Frank?'

'I mean it, Tom.'

'Calvert is ancient history.'

'I hope so. I need you focused – and focused is not fixated.'

Keable wasn't sure but he thought that Thorne nodded. He continued as if the exchange had never happened.

'I think we'll make a case if we get him. We should be able to match up the note to the typewriter for a start.'

Keable sighed and nodded. The old fashioned typewriter was a bit of luck, a lot easier to identify than a laser printer, but still, they needed a suspect first. He'd been in the same position plenty of times. It was hard to sound enthusiastic about evidence which was only of any use when someone was in custody. The procedure had to be followed, but at the end of the day they had to catch him first. Keable knew that procedure was his strong point. He was a good facilitator. It was this self-awareness that had allowed him to leapfrog other officers, Thorne included. It also ensured that those officers didn't resent it. He recognised the talents of others and the lack of them in himself. He was a forger of team spirit. He was well liked. He helped where he could and left the job at the office at the end of the day. He slept well and had a happy marriage – unlike other officers. Thorne included. 'He'll make a mistake, Tom. When we get a hit on a drugs theft we can start narrowing things down a bit.'

Thorne leaned in close to the fan. 'I'd like to get over to Queen Square, if that's okay. It's been a while and I'd like to see how Alison's doing.'

Keable nodded. This hadn't been his most successful attempt at one-on-one morale-building but, then, he hadn't expected a backslapping gagfest from Tom Thorne. He cleared his throat as Thorne stood up, walked to the door and then turned.

'That note was spotless, Frank. It was the shortest forensic report I've ever seen. And he doesn't wash the bodies in a ritualistic way. He's just very, very careful.'

Keable turned the fan back on himself. He was unsure exactly what Thorne expected him to say. 'I'd been wondering whether we should get the boys to chip in for some flowers or something. I mean, I thought about it but . . .'

Thorne nodded.

'Yes, sir, I know. It hardly seems worth it.'

'These are really lovely. It was a very nice thought.' Anne Coburn finished arranging the flowers and closed the blinds in Alison's room. The sun was streaming in through the window, causing the girl's face to flush a little.

'I meant to come in sooner, but . . .'

She nodded, understanding. 'You could have written a note to say congratulations, though.'

Thorne looked down at Alison and immediately understood. It was difficult to notice one less machine amid the confusion of life-preserving hardware. She was breathing. The breaths were shallow, almost tentative, but they were her own.

Now a tube ran into a hole in her windpipe, covered with an oxygen mask.

'She came off the ventilator last night and we performed the tracheostomy.'

Thorne was impressed. 'Exciting night.'

'Oh, it's non-stop excitement in here. We had a small flood a while ago. Have you ever seen nurses in wellies?'

He grinned. 'I've seen the odd dodgy video . . .'

It was the first time he'd heard her laugh: it was filthy.

Thorne nodded towards the flowers, which he'd picked up at a garage on the way in. They weren't quite as lovely as Anne Coburn had said. 'I felt like such an idiot last time, you know, whispering. If she can hear I thought she must be able to smell so . . .'

'Oh, she'll smell these.'

Suddenly Thorne was aware again of the stickiness beneath his arms. He turned to look at Alison. 'While we're on the subject . . . sorry, Alison, I must really hum.' He was embarrassed at the silence where a response should have been. He hoped he could get used to talking to this woman with a tube in her neck and another up her nose. She was unable to clear her throat. She was unable to lift the hand that lay pale and heavy on the pink flowery quilt. She was . . . unable. And yet, selfishly, Thorne hoped that she thought well of him, that she liked him. He wanted to talk to her. Even now he sensed that he would *need* to talk to her.

41

'Just fill in the gaps yourself,' Coburn said. 'It's what I do. We have some cracking chats.'

The door opened and an immaculately suited middle-aged man walked in with what at first glance appeared to be candyfloss on his head.

'Oh . . .' Thorne saw Coburn's features harden in an instant. 'David. I'm busy I'm afraid.'

They stared at each other. She broke the uncomfortable, hostile silence. 'This is Detective Inspector Thorne. David Higgins.'

The soon-to-be-ex-husband. The helpful pathologist.

'Pleased to meet you.' Thorne held out a hand, which the immaculate suit shook without looking at him – or at Alison.

'You did say that this would be a good time,' said the suit, half smiling.

He was obviously trying hard to be pleasant for Thorne's benefit but clearly it did not come naturally. On further inspection the candyfloss was in reality a teased up and hairsprayed dyed vanilla quiff – a ridiculous affectation in a man who was at least fifty-five: he looked as if he'd walked off the set of *Dynasty*.

'Well, it would have been,' said Coburn frostily.

'My fault, Mr Higgins,' said Thorne. 'I didn't have an appointment.'

Higgins moved towards the door, adjusting his tie. 'Well, I'd better make sure I have an appointment in future, then. I'll call you later, Anne, and we can arrange one.' He closed the door soundlessly behind him. There was a muffled exchange outside and the door was opened again by a nurse. It was time for Alison's bedbath.

Anne Coburn turned to him. 'What do you usually do for lunch?'

They sat in the back of a small sandwich bar on Southampton Row. Ham and Brie on a baguette and a mineral water. A cheese and tomato sandwich and a coffee. Two busy professionals.

'What are Alison's chances of regaining any significant . . . ?'

'Nil, I'm afraid. I suppose it depends a little on your definition of "significant" but we have to be realistic. There have been documented cases of patients regaining enough movement to operate a sophisticated wheelchair. They're doing a lot of work in the States with computers operated by headsticks, but realistically it's a bleak prognosis.'

'Wasn't there somebody in France who dictated an entire book with an eyelash or something?'

'*The Diving Bell and the Butterfly* – you should read it. But it's pretty much a one-off. Alison's gaze reacts to voices and she seems to have retained the ability to blink, but whether she has any real control over it is hard to say at the moment. I can't see her giving you a statement just yet.'

'That wasn't the reason I asked about . . . It wasn't the *only* reason.' Thorne took an enormous bite of his sandwich.

Anne had done most of the talking but had

already finished hers. She looked at him, narrowing her eyes, her voice conspiratorial. 'Well, you've been privy to my disastrous domestic situation. What about yours?' She took a sip of mineral water and watched him chew, her eyebrows arched theatrically. She laughed as, twice, he tried to answer and, twice, had to resume his efforts to swallow the sandwich.

Finally: 'What – you mean is it disastrous?'

'No. Just . . . is there one?'

Thorne could not get a fix on this woman at all. A vicious temper, a filthy laugh, and a direct line of questioning. There seemed little point in going round the houses.

'I've moved effortlessly from "disastrous" to just plain "bleak".'

'Is that the normal progression?'

'I think so. Sometimes there's a short period of "pitiful" but not always.'

'Oh, well, I'll look forward to that.'

Thorne watched as she reached into her bag for a cigarette. She held up the packet. 'Do you mind?'

Thorne said no, and she lit up. He stared as she blew the smoke out of the side of her mouth, away from him. It had been a long time since his last cigarette.

'More doctors smoke than you'd imagine. And a surprising number of oncologists. I'm amazed that more of us aren't smackheads to be honest. Do you not, then?' Thorne shook his head. 'A policeman who doesn't smoke. You must like a drink, then?'

He smiled. 'I thought you worked too many hours to watch television.'

She groaned with pleasure as she took a long drag.

Thorne spoke slowly but was still smiling when he answered the question. 'I like more than one . . .'

'Glad to hear it.'

'But that's pretty much it, as far as the clichés go. I'm not religious, I hate opera, and I can't finish a crossword to save my life.'

'You must be driven, then? Or haunted? Is that the word?'

Thorne tried to hold the smile in place and even managed to produce a chuckle of sorts as he turned away and looked towards the counter. When he'd caught the eye of the woman at the till he held up his coffee cup, signalling for another. He turned back as Anne was stubbing out her cigarette. She exhaled, enjoying it, running elegant fingers through her silver hair.

'So, does "desperate" and "bleak" involve children?'

'No. You?'

Her smile was huge and as contagious as smallpox. 'One. Rachel. Sixteen and big trouble.'

Sixteen? Thorne raised his eyebrows. 'Do women still get upset if you ask how old they are?'

She plonked an elbow on the table and leaned her chin on the palm of her hand, trying her best to look severe. 'This one does.'

45

'Sorry.' Thorne tried *his* best to look contrite. 'How much do you weigh?'

She laughed loudly. Not filthy, positively salacious. Thorne laughed too, and grinned at the waitress as his second cup of coffee arrived. It had barely touched the table when Coburn's bleeper went off. She looked at it, stood up and grabbed her bag from the floor. 'I might not be a smackhead, but I do an awful lot of indigestion tablets.'

Thorne lifted his jacket from the back of his chair. 'I'll walk you back.'

On the way towards Queen Square things became oddly formal again. Small-talk about Indian summers gave way to an awkward silence before they were half-way there. When they reached her office, Thorne hovered in the doorway. He felt like he should go, but she held up her hand to stop him as she made a quick call. The bleep had not been urgent.

'So how is the investigation going?'

Thorne stepped into the office and closed the door. He had thought this was coming over lunch. His capacity to bullshit members of the public had once been endless, but he spent so much of his time exercising that particular skill on superior officers that he couldn't be bothered trying it on with those who had no axe to grind.

'It's a . . . bleak prognosis.'

She smiled.

'Every day there's some stupid story in the paper about armed robbers tunnelling into the shop next door to the building society or burglars falling asleep in houses they've broken into, but the simple fact is that most people who break the law give serious thought to not getting done for it. With murderers, you've got a chance if it's domestic, or when there's sex involved.'

She leaned back in her chair and took a sip from a glass of water.

Thorne watched her. 'Sorry, I didn't mean to make a speech.'

'No, I'm interested, really.'

'Any sort of sexual compulsion can make people sloppy. They take chances and eventually they slip up. I just can't see this bloke slipping up. Whatever's been driving him isn't sexual.'

Her eyes were suddenly flat and cold. 'Isn't it?'

'Not physically. He's perverse . . . but he's—'

'What he's doing is grotesque.'

There was a matter-of-factness about the statement that Thorne had no argument with. What shook him was her use of the present tense. There were those who thought or hoped (and, by Christ, he hoped) that perhaps there'd be no need for new pictures on the wall. But he knew better. Whatever mission this man thought he was on, whatever it was he hoped to achieve, he was *actually* stalking women and killing them in their own homes. And he was enjoying himself. Thorne could feel himself start to redden.

'There's no conventional pattern to this. The ages of the victims seem unimportant to him, as

47

long as they're available. He just picks these women out and when he doesn't get what he wants he just leaves them. Shiny and scrubbed and slumped in a chair or lying on a kitchen floor for their loved ones to stumble across. Nobody sees anything. Nobody knows anything.'

'Except Alison.'

The awkward silence descended again, more stifling than the air trapped inside the tiny office. Thorne felt the retort of his outburst bouncing off the walls like a sluggish bullet. There was none of the usual irritation when his mobile phone rang. He grabbed for it gratefully.

DI Nick Tughan ran the Backhand office: an organiser and collator of information, another embracer of procedure. His smooth Dublin brogue could calm or persuade senior officers. Unlike Frank Keable, though, Tughan had the self-awareness of a tree-stump and little time for characters like Tom Thorne. The way the operation had been going up to now, meant that it was very much his show and he ran it with an unflappable efficiency. *He* never lost his temper.

'We've got a fairly major Midazolam theft. Two years ago, Leicester Royal Infirmary, five grams missing.'

Thorne reached across the desk for a piece of paper and a pen. Anne pushed a pad towards him. He began to scribble down the details. Maybe there had been a slip-up, after all.

'Right, let's send Holland up to Leicester, get

all the details, and we'll need a list of everyone on rotation from, say, ninety-seven onwards.'

'Ninety-six onwards. Already sorted it. It's been faxed through.'

Tughan was well ahead of him and thoroughly enjoying it. Thorne knew what he would have done next. 'Obvious question then . . . any matches?'

'A couple in the South-East and half a dozen in London. But there's an interesting one. Works at the Royal London.'

Interesting was right. Anne Coburn had spotted it straight away. Working on the assumption that Alison had been attacked in her home, then why the Royal London? Why not the nearest hospital? Thorne took down the name, kept the compulsory, if distasteful, back-slapping brief and hung up.

'Sounded like good news.' She didn't apologise for eavesdropping.

Thorne was starting to like her more and more. He stood up and reached for his jacket. 'Let's hope so. Five grams of Midazolam. Is that a lot?'

'That's a hell of a lot. We'd use anywhere up to *five milligrams* to sedate an average-sized adult. That's intravenously, of course.'

She stood up and moved round the desk to see him out. As she walked to the door she glanced at the scrap of paper, which Thorne had not yet picked up, and stopped dead in her tracks.

'Oh, God!' She reached for it just as Thorne did – he should never have let her see it, but a tussle would have been . . . unseemly. What harm could it do? He opened the door. 'Is this man your . . . match, Detective Inspector?' She moved back to her side of the desk and sat down heavily.

'I'm sorry, Doctor, I'm sure you understand. I can't really—'

'I know him,' she said. 'I know him extremely well.'

Thorne hovered in the doorway. This was starting to get awkward. Procedure dictated that he leave straight away and send someone back to get a statement. He waited for her to continue.

'Yes, he certainly worked in Leicester, but there's no way he'd have anything to do with stealing drugs.'

'Doctor—'

'And he's got something of a cast-iron alibi as far as Alison Willetts is concerned.'

Thorne shut the door. He was listening.

'Jeremy Bishop was the anaesthetist on call at the Royal London A and E the night Alison was brought in. He treated her. Do you remember? I told you I knew him. He told me about the Midazolam.'

Thorne blinked slowly. Dead Susan. Dead Christine. Dead Madeleine.

'Come on, Tommy, you must have something to go on?'

He opened his eyes. She was shaking her head. She'd seen the date on the piece of paper. 'I'm sorry, Detective Inspector, but much as you dislike Detective Constable Holland . . .'

50

Thorne opened his mouth and closed it again.

'. . . it's a waste of time to send him to Leicester. The man you're looking for is certainly clever, but there's no guarantee he ever worked at Leicester Royal Infirmary.'

Thorne dropped his bag and sat down again. 'Why am I starting to feel like Dr Watson?'

'August the first is rotation day. Normally it would be a reasonable assumption that in order to steal a large quantity of drugs from a hospital you'd have to work there. Yes, hospital staff are overstretched and occasionally inefficient, but as far as dangerous drugs are concerned there *is* a procedure in place.'

Thorne's favourite word again.

'But on rotation day, things can get a bit lax. I've worked in hospitals where you could walk out pushing a bed and carrying a kidney machine on August the first. I'm sorry, but whoever took these drugs could have come from anywhere.'

Susan. Christine. Madeleine. *'Something, Tommy. A lead. Something . . .'*

Thorne took out his phone to call Tughan back.

It was Helen Doyle's first round of drinks, but already she was worrying about how much she'd spent. A few designer bottles and a couple of rum and Cokes and it was three times what she earned in an hour.

Sod it. It was Nita's birthday and she didn't do this very often.

She loaded the drinks on to a tray and looked across to where her mates were sitting at a corner table. She'd known three of them since school and the other two for almost that long. The pub wasn't busy and the few people in there were probably pissed off with the noise they were making. On cue the gang began to laugh, Jo's high-pitched cackle the loudest of all. Probably another one of Andrea's filthy jokes . . .

Helen walked slowly back to the table, the other girls cheering when she put the tray down and diving on to their drinks as if they were the first of the night.

'Didn't you get any crisps?'

'Forgot, sorry . . .'

'Dizzy bitch.'

'Tell her the joke . . .'

'How much fucking ice has he put in here?'

Helen took a swig and looked at the label on the bottle. It didn't actually say what was in it. She'd got through plenty already. Hooch, Metz, Breezers. She was never really sure what she was drinking, what the booze was, but she liked the colours and she felt fashionable with the slim, cold bottle in her hand. Sophisticated. Nita drained half of her rum and Coke. Jo emptied the remains of a pint of lager and belched loudly.

'What do you drink those for? It's like pop!'

Helen felt herself blush. 'I like the taste.'

'It's not supposed to taste nice, that's the point.'

Nita and Linzi laughed. Helen shrugged and took another swig. Andrea nudged her. 'Like you know what!'

There was a groan. Jo stuck two fingers down her throat. Helen knew what they were talking about, but part of her wished they wouldn't. Sex was pretty much all Andrea ever talked about.

'Tell us how big his cock was again, Jo.'

The strippergram had been Andrea's idea and Nita had seemed to like it. Helen thought he was really fit, all covered in oil, and he made her go very red, but the poem about Nita hadn't been that good. She could tell that he'd been as embarrassed as her when Jo grabbed his crotch, and for a second he'd looked really upset. Then he'd smiled and grabbed his clothes from off the floor while everybody whistled and cheered. Helen had whistled and cheered too, but she wished she'd been a bit more pissed.

'Big enough!'

'More than a mouthful's a waste.'

Helen leaned across to Linzi. 'How's work?'

She was probably closest to Linzi, but they hadn't spoken properly all night.

'Shit. I'm going to chuck it in . . . do some temping or something.'

'Right.'

Helen loved her job. The money was poor, but the people were nice and even though she had to give her mum and dad a bit, it was still cheap living at home. She couldn't see the sense in moving out, not until she met someone. What was the point in renting a grotty flat like Jo or Nita? Andrea still lived at home anyway. God knows where she was having all that sex she was always on about . . .

'Let Me Entertain You' came on the jukebox. It was one of her favourite songs. She nodded her head to the rhythm and sang the words quietly to herself. She remembered a fifth-form disco, and a boy with an earring and sad brown eyes and cider on his breath. When the chorus came, the rest of the girls joined in and Helen shut up.

The bell rang and the barman shouted something incomprehensible. Andrea and Jo were all for another round. Helen grinned but she knew she should be getting back. She would feel bad in the morning and her dad would be waiting up for her. She was starting to feel woozy and knew that she should have gone home and had her tea before she came out. She could have changed too. She felt frumpy and self-conscious in her black work skirt and sensible blouse. She'd grab a bag of chips on the way home. And a piece of fish for her dad.

Andrea stood up and announced that they'd all put in for one more. Helen cheered along with the rest of them, drained the bottle and reached into her purse for a couple of pound coins.

Thorne sat with his eyes shut listening to Johnny Cash. He rolled his head around on his neck, enjoying every crack of cartilage. Now the Man in Black with the dark, dangerous voice was insisting that he was going to break out of his rusty cage. Thorne opened his eyes and looked around at his neat, comfortable flat – not a cage, exactly, but he knew what Johnny was talking about.

The one-bedroom garden flat was undeniably small, but easily maintained and close enough to the busy Kentish Town Road to ensure that he never ran out of milk or tea. Or wine. The couple in the flat upstairs were quiet and never bothered him. He'd lived here less than six months after finally selling the house in Highbury, but he already knew every inch of the place. He'd furnished the entire flat during one wretched Sunday at IKEA, spent the next three weeks putting the stuff together and the succeeding four months wishing he hadn't bothered.

He couldn't say he'd been unhappy since Jan had left. Christ, they'd been divorced for three years and she'd been gone nearly five, but still, everything just felt . . . out of kilter. He'd thought that moving out of the house they'd shared and into this bright new flat would change things. He'd been optimistic. However close to him the objects around him were, he had no real . . . connection to any of them. It was functional. He could be out of his chair and in his bed in a matter of seconds but the bed was too new and, tragically, as yet unchristened.

He felt like a faceless businessman in a number-less hotel room.

Perhaps it would have been better if Jan had

gone because of the job. He'd seen it often enough and it was the stuff of interminable TV cop shows – copper's wife can't stand playing second fiddle to the job, blah blah blah. Jan had never been an ordinary copper's wife and she'd left for her own reasons. The only job involved in the whole messy business was the one she'd been on every Wednesday afternoon with the lecturer from her creative-writing course.

Until he'd caught them at it. In the middle of the day with the curtains drawn.

Candles by the bed, for Christ's sake . . .

Jan said later that she never understood why Thorne hadn't hit him. He never told her. Even as the scrawny bastard had leaped from the bed, his cock flapping, scrabbling for his glasses, Thorne knew that he wasn't going to hurt him. As he let the pain wash over him, he knew that, reeling and raw as he was, he couldn't bear to hear her scream, see the flash of hatred in her eyes, watch her rushing to comfort the little smartarse as he sat slumped against the wardrobe, moaning and trying to stop the blood.

A few weeks later he'd waited outside the college and followed him. Into shops. Chatting with students on the street. Home to a small flat in Islington with multi-coloured bicycles chained up outside and posters in the window. That had been enough for him. That simple knowing.

You're mine if I ever decide to come and get you.

But after a while even that seemed shameful.

56

He'd let it go. Now it was the stuff of late nights and red wine and singers with dark, dangerous voices.

Yes, he'd brought the job home – especially after Calvert, when things had slipped away from him for a time – but they'd got married far too young. That was all, really. Perhaps if they'd had kids . . .

Thorne scanned the TV pages of the *Standard*. Tuesday night and bugger all on. Even worse, Sky had shown the Spurs-Bradford game at eight o'clock. He'd forgotten all about it. At home against Bradford – should be three points in the bag. Teletext, the football fan's best friend, gave him the bad news.

She was slumped, her back against his legs, buttocks pressing down on her heels and knuckles lying against the polished wooden floorboards. He stood behind her, both hands on the back of her neck, readying himself. He glanced around the room. Everything was in place. The equipment laid out within easy reach.

Her mouth fell open and a wet gurgling noise came out. He tightened his grip, ever so slightly, on her neck. There was really no point in trying to talk and, besides, he'd heard quite enough from her already.

An hour and a half earlier, he'd watched as the group of girls had begun to thin out. A couple had wandered off towards the tube and a couple more to the bus stop. One tottered off down the

Holloway Road. Local, he guessed. Perhaps she'd like to join him for a drink.

He'd taken a left turn and driven the car round the block, emerging on to the main road twenty yards or so ahead of her. He'd waited at the junction until she was a few feet away then got out of the car.

'Excuse me . . . sorry . . . but I seem to be horribly lost.' Slurring the words ever so slightly. Just the right side of pissed. And so well-spoken.

'Where are you trying to get to?'

Wary. Quite right too. But nothing to worry about here. Just a tipsy hooray lost on the wrong side of the Archway roundabout. Taking off his glasses, looking like he's having trouble focusing . . .

'Hampstead . . . sorry . . . had a bit too much . . . Shouldn't be driving, tell you the truth.'

'That's OK, mate. Hammered meself as it goes . . .'

'Been clubbing?'

'No, just in the pub – mate's birthday . . . really brilliant.'

Good. He was glad she was happy. All the more to want to live for. So . . .

'I don't suppose you fancy a nightcap?' Reaching through the car window and producing it with a flourish.

'Blimey, what are you celebrating?'

Christ, what was it with these girls and a bottle of fizz? Like a hypnotist's gold watch.

'Just pinched it from a party.' Then the giggle. 'One for the road?'

About half an hour. Thirty minutes of meaningless semi-literate yammering until she'd started to go. She was full of herself. Nita's boyfriend . . . Linzi's problems at work . . . a couple of dirty jokes. He'd smiled and nodded and laughed, and tried to imagine how he could possibly have been less interested. Then the nodding-dog head and the sitcom slurring, and it was time for the innocuous-looking man to tip his paralytic girlfriend into the back of his car and take her back to his place.

Then he'd made the phone call, and put her in position.

And now Helen wasn't quite so gobby.

Again the gurgling, from somewhere deep down and desperate.

'Ssh, Helen, just relax. It won't take long.'

He positioned his thumbs, one at either side of the bony bump at the base of the skull and felt for the muscle, talking her through it . . . 'Feel these two pieces of muscle, Helen?'

She groaned.

'The sternocleidomastoid. I know, stupidly long word, don't worry. These muscles reach all the way down to your collar-bone. Now what I'm after is underneath . . .' He gasped as he found it. 'There.'

Slowly he wrapped his fingers, one at a time around the carotid artery and began to press.

He closed his eyes and mentally counted off

the seconds. Two minutes would do it. He felt something like a shudder run through her body and up through the thin surgical gloves into his fingers. He nodded respectfully, admiring the Herculean effort that even so tiny a movement must have taken.

He began to think about her body and about how he might have touched it. She was his to do with as he pleased. He could have slipped his hands from her head and slid them straight down the front of her and beneath her shirt in a second. He could turn her round and penetrate her mouth, pushing himself across her teeth. But he wouldn't. He'd thought about it with the others too, but this was not about sex.

After considering such things at length he'd decided that his was a normal and healthy impulse. Wouldn't any man feel the same things with a woman at his mercy? So easily available? Of course. But it was not a good idea. He did not want them . . . classifying this as a sex crime.

That would be easy, would throw them too far off the scent. And he knew all about DNA.

A growl came from somewhere deep in Helen's throat. She could feel everything, was aware of everything and still she fought it.

'Not long now . . . Please be quiet.'

He became aware of a drumming noise and, without moving his head, glanced down to where her fingers were beating spastically against the floorboards. Adrenaline staging a hopeless rear-guard action against the drug. She might make it, he thought, she wants to live so much.

One minute forty-five seconds. His fingers locked in position, he leaned down, his lips on her ear, whispering: 'Night-night, Sleepyhead . . .'

She stopped breathing.

Now was the critical time. His movements needed to be swift and precise. He eased the pressure on the artery and pushed her head roughly forward until chin was touching chest. He let it rest there for a few seconds before whipping it back the same way so that he was staring down at her face. Her eyes were open, her jaw slack, spittle running down her chin. He dismissed the urge to kiss her and moved her head back into the central position. Back into neutral. Then he took a firm grip and entwined his fingers in her long brown hair before twisting the head back over the left shoulder.

And holding it.

Then the right shoulder. Each twist splitting the inside of the vertebral artery. Now it was up to her.

He laid her down gently and placed her body in the recovery position. He was sweating heavily. He reached for a glass of cold water and sat down on the chair to watch her. To wait for her to breathe.

His mind was empty as he focused, unblinking, on her face and chest. The breaths would be short and shallow, and he watched and willed the smallest movement. Every few seconds he leaned forward and felt for a pulse.

Helen's body was unmoving.

He reached for the bag and mask. It was time to intervene. Ten minutes of frantic squeezing, shouting at her: 'Come on, Helen, help me!' Screaming into her face. 'I need you to be strong.'

She wasn't strong enough.

He slumped back into the chair, out of breath. He looked down at the lifeless body. A button was missing from her shirt. He looked across at the plain black shoes, neatly placed one next to the other by her side. The small pile of jewellery in a stainless-steel dish next to them. Cheap bracelets and big, ugly earrings.

He mourned her and hated her.

He needed to move. Now it was just about disposal. Quick and easy.

He began to strip her.

Thorne picked up the bottle of red wine from the side of his chair and poured another glass. Maybe forty-year-old men were better off on their own in neat, comfortable but small flats. Forty-year-old men with bad habits, more mood swings than Glenn Miller and twenty-odd years off the market had very little say in the matter. A taste for country-and-western hardly helped.

Johnny was singing about memories. Thorne made a mental note to programme the CD player to skip this track next time. Had Frank been right

when he'd asked if the Calvert case was still part
of the equation?

Take one fresh and tender corpse . . .

Fifteen years was too long to be lugging this
baggage around. It wasn't his anyway. He couldn't
recall how it had been passed on to him. He'd only
been twenty-five. Those far above him had carried
the can, as it was their job so to do. He'd never had
the chance to take the honourable way out. Would
he have done it anyway?

One man, released . . .

He'd had no say in letting Calvert go after the
interview. The fourth interview. What happened in
that corridor and later, in that house, seemed like
things he'd read about like everybody else. Had he
really felt that Calvert was the one? Or was that a
detail his imagination had pencilled in later, in the
light of what he had seen that Monday morning?
Once everything started to come out, his part in it
all was largely forgotten anyway.

Four girls, deceased . . .

Besides, what was his trauma – God, what a stupid word – compared with the family of those little
girls who should still have been walking around?
Who should have had their own kids by now.

Memories are made of this.

He pointed the remote and turned off the song.
The phone was ringing.

'Tom Thorne.'

'It's Holland, sir. We think we've got another
body.'

'You think?'

His stomach lurching. Calvert smiling as he walked out of the interview room. Alison staring into space. Dead Susan, dead Christine, dead Madeleine, crossing their fingers.

'Looks the same, sir. I don't think they'd even have passed this one on to us but she hasn't got a mark on her.'

'What's the address?'

'That's the thing, sir. The body's outside. The woods behind Highgate station.'

Minutes away, this time of night. He downed the rest of the glass in one. 'You'd better send a car, Holland. I've had a drink.'

'Best of all, sir . . .'

'Best?'

'We've got a witness. Somebody saw him dump the body.'

I could sense that Tim really wanted to know who the flowers were from. He didn't say anything, but I know he was looking at them. He didn't ask me. Maybe that's because it was a question he actually wanted an answer to, and not just a pointless conversation with his ex-girlfriend who's now a retarded mong.

Sorry, Tim. But nothing can prepare you for this, can it? I mean, you go through all the usual stuff, holidays together, meeting each other's friends. He never had to deal with meeting the parents, jammy sod. His were a nightmare! But this was never part of the deal, was it? 'How would you cope if I was on a life-support machine and completely unable to move or communicate?' never really comes up in those early intimate little chats, does it?

Oh, and I've got an air mattress now, to stop me getting bed sores apparently. It's probably hugely comfy. Makes a racket, though. Low and electrical. Sometimes I wake up and lie in the dark thinking that somebody's doing a bit of late-night vacuuming in the next room.

Anne's got the hots for that copper, I reckon. He does seem nice, I grant you. Nicer than her ex anyway, who sounds like a tit. The copper's funny, though. I was pissing myself when he apologised for being a bit whiffy. I heard Tim asking one of the nurses about the flowers. There was no card and the nurse went away to ask one of her mates. Now I think Tim suspects I'm having an affair with a policeman. Obviously, he must be a fairly strange policeman with a taste for cheap yellow nighties and extremely compliant girlfriends who never answer back.

What's that old joke about the perfect woman? If I was a nymphomaniac and my dad owned a brewery, he'd be quids in . . .

CHAPTER 4

The Sierra pulled up behind the operations van. As soon as Thorne stepped out of the car he could see that things were going to be difficult. Even at two o'clock in the morning it was still muggy but there was rain coming. Valuable evidence would be lost as the scene turned quickly to mud. The various photographers, scene-of-crime-officers and members of the forensic team were going about their business with quiet efficiency. They knew they didn't have very long. Anything useful was usually found in the first hour. The golden hour. Tughan would still have everything covered anyway: he'd have rung for a weather forecast. This was their first sniff of a crime scene, and nobody was taking any chances.

Thorne set off down the steep flight of steps that led to Highgate tube station and gave access to Queens Wood – the patch of woodland bordering the Archway Road. As he walked he could see the glare of the arc lights through the trees. He could see the figures of forensic scientists in white plastic bodysuits, crouched over what he presumed was the body, in search of stray fibres or hairs from the girl's clothing. He could hear instructions being barked out, the hiss of camera flashes recharging and the constant drone of the portable generator. He'd been at many such scenes in the past, far too many, but this was like watching the A-team work. There was a determination about the entire process that he'd seen only once before. There was a distinct absence of whistling in the dark. There was no gallows humour. There wasn't a flask of tea to be seen anywhere.

It was only when he ducked under the handrail and began to pull on the plastic overshoes provided by a passing SOCO that Thorne realised just how difficult a crime scene this would be to examine. He also saw at once how callous the killer had been in his choice of dumping ground. The body lay hard against the high metal railings that bordered the pavement all the way down the hill. On one side lay the main road and, on the other, some hundred feet of dense woodland on a steep hill leading down to the underground station at Highgate. The only access to the body was up the hill and through the trees. Though a well-trodden path had already emerged, it was still a slow process negotiating the route to the body. The ground was hard and dry but it would take only ten minutes of rain to turn it into a mud chute. By the time they'd got the scene protected with polythene tents it would hardly have been worth the effort. He hoped they got what they needed quickly. He hoped there was something to get.

Dave Holland came jogging down the slope towards him. He was backlit beautifully by the arc lights. Thorne could quite clearly make out the silhouette of a notebook being brandished. He doesn't look like a policeman, thought Thorne, he looks like a prefect. Even with a hint of stubble, his tidy blond hair and ruddy complexion made him the obvious target for comments of the aren't-policemen-looking-younger-these-days variety. Pensioners adored him. Thorne wasn't sure. Holland's father had been in the force and, in Thorne's experience, that was rarely without problems. He doesn't even move like a copper, he thought. Coppers don't skip down hills like mountain goats. Coppers move like . . . ambulances.

'Cup of tea, sir?'

OK, perhaps he'd been a bit naïve. There was always tea.

'No. Tell me about this witness.'

'Right, don't get too excited.'

Thorne's heart sank. It was obviously not going to be earth shattering.

'We've got a vague physical description, not a lot.'

'How vague?'

'Height, build, a dark car. The witness, George Hammond . . .'

That fucking notebook again. He wanted to ram it up the cocky little gobshite's arse.

69

'. . . was at the top of the path a hundred yards further up the main road. He thought the bloke was chucking a bag of rubbish over.'

That was what Thorne had already worked out. He must have pulled up and heaved the body over the railings. She might just as well have been a bag of rubbish.

'And that's it? Height and build?'

'There's a bit more on the car. He says he thinks it was a nice one. Expensive.'

Thorne nodded slowly. Witnesses. Another thing he'd had to become resigned to. Even the more perceptive ones gave conflicting accounts of the same event.

'Mr Hammond's eyesight isn't brilliant, sir. He's an old man. He was only out walking his dog. We've got him in the car.'

'Hang about, those railings are six feet high. How big did he say he was?'

'Six two, six three. She's not a big girl, sir.'

Thorne squinted into the lights. 'Right, I'll have a word with the optically challenged Mr Hammond in a minute. Let's get this over with.'

Phil Hendricks was crouched over the body, his pony-tail secured beneath his distinctive yellow showercap. The scientists had finished their scraping and taping, and Hendricks was taking his turn. Thorne watched the all-too-familiar routine as the pathologist took temperature readings and conducted what, until the body was removed, would be a cursory examination. Every minute or so he would heave himself on to his haunches with a grunt, and mumble into his small tape-recorder. As always, each tedious detail of the entire procedure was being immortalised on film by the police cameraman. Thorne always wondered about those characters. Some of them seemed to fancy themselves as film-makers – he'd actually had to bollock one once for shouting, 'That's a wrap.' Some had a disturbing glint in their eye that said, 'You ought to come round to my place and have a look at some of the footage I'll be showing the lads at Christmas.' He couldn't help wondering if they were all waiting to be headhunted by some avaricious TV company eager for more mindless docusoaps. Maybe he was being too harsh. He was too harsh about Holland as well. Perhaps it was just the perfectly pressed chinos and loafers he didn't like. Maybe it was just that Holland was a young DC eager to please.

Hadn't *he* been like that? Fifteen years ago. Heading for a fall.

Hendricks began to pack away his gear and looked up at Thorne. It was a look that had passed between them on many occasions. To the untrained eye this 'handing over of responsibility' might have seemed as casual as two pool-players exchanging a cue. Pathologists were supposed to be colder than any of them but despite the Mancunian's flippant, nasal tones and dark sense of humour, Thorne knew what Hendricks was feeling. He'd watched him crying into his pint often enough. Thorne had never reciprocated.

'He's getting a tad fucking casual, if you ask me.' Hendricks began fiddling with one of his many earrings. Eight the last time Thorne had counted. The thick glasses gave him an air of studiousness but the earrings, not to mention the discreet but famous tattoos and the penchant for extravagant headgear, marked him out as unconventional to say the least. Thorne had known the gregarious goth pathologist for five years. Ten years his junior and horribly efficient, Thorne liked him enormously.

'I didn't, but thanks for the observation.'

'No wonder you're touchy, mate. Two – one at home to Bradford?'

'Robbed.'

'Course you were.'

Thorne's neck was still horribly stiff. He dropped his head back and gazed up into a clear night sky. He could make out the Plough. He always looked for it: it was the only constellation he knew by sight. 'So, it's him, then, is it?'

'I'll know for sure by the morning. I think so. But what's she doing here? That's a hell of a busy road. He might easily have been seen.'

'He was. By Mr Magoo, unfortunately. Anyway, I don't think he was here very long. He just stopped and chucked her out.'

Hendricks moved aside and Thorne looked down at the woman who in a few hours would be identified as Helen Theresa Doyle. She was just a girl. Eighteen, nineteen. Her blouse was pulled up,

72

revealing a pierced belly-button. She was wearing large hoop earrings. Her skirt was torn, revealing a nasty gash at the top of her leg.

Hendricks clicked his bag shut. 'I think the wound's from where she got caught on the railings as the bastard hoicked her over the top.'

Something caught Thorne's eye and he glanced to his right. Standing twenty or so feet away, staring straight at him, was a small fox. A vixen, he guessed. She stood completely still, watching the strange activity. They were on her territory. Thorne felt a peculiar pang of shame. He'd heard farmers and pro-hunt lobbyists ranting about the savagery of these animals when they killed, but he doubted that a creature killing to feed itself and its young could enjoy it. Bloodlust fed off a particular kind of intelligence. There was a shout from the top of the hill and the fox prepared to bolt but relaxed again. Thorne could not take his eyes from the animal as it stared into the artificially lit reality of a warped kind of human bloodlust. Of a genuine brutality. Half a minute passed before the fox sniffed the ground, its curiosity satisfied, and trotted away.

Thorne glanced at Hendricks. He'd been watching too. Thorne took a deep breath and turned back to the girl.

Conflicting emotions.

He felt revulsion at the sight of the body, anger at the waste. Sympathy for the relatives, and terror at the thought of having to confront them, their rage and grief.

But he also felt the buzz.

The rush of the crime scene. The first crime scene. The thing that might smash the investigation wide open might be under their noses, waiting, asking to be found.

If it was there, he'd find it.

Her body . . .

There were leaves in her long brown hair. Her eyes were open. Thorne could see that she had a nice figure. He tried to get the thought out of his mind.

'He's always taken a bit of time before, a'n't he?' mused Hendricks. 'Nice and easy. Taken the trouble to lay them down like they'd stroked out watching telly or cooking dinner. He didn't really seem to care this time. Bit of a rush job.'

Thorne looked at him, asking the question.

'An hour or two at the most. She's not even cold yet.'

Thorne bent down and took the girl's hand. Hendricks pulled off his showercap then snapped off his rubber gloves, releasing a small puff of talcum powder. As Thorne leaned forward to close the girl's eyes, the hum of the generator filled his head. Hendricks's voice seemed to be coming from a long way away.

'I can still smell the carbolic.'

Anne Coburn sat in the dark room at the end of a horrible day that by rights should have ended three hours earlier. The papers were forever banging on about the intolerable hours worked by junior doctors but senior ones didn't exactly have it easy. A meeting with the administrator that should have taken an hour, and lasted three, had given her a headache that was only just starting to abate. It had raged through two lectures, a consultation round, an argument with the registrar and a mountain of paperwork. And David was still on the warpath . . .

She sat back in the chair and massaged her temples. Christ, these chairs were uncomfortable. Had they been designed that way deliberately to encourage visitors to deposit their fruit and bugger off?

Maybe if David had still been at home she'd have left the paperwork, but not any more. The house would be quiet. Rachel would be tucked up in bed by now, watching some emaciated drug casualty with too much eyeliner prancing about on MTV.

She thought about her daughter for a while.

They hadn't been getting on very well recently. The GCSEs had put them both under a lot of strain. Rachel was just letting off steam, that was all, having slogged her guts out. Anne had decided to buy her a present when she got her results, to say well done for working so hard. A new computer, maybe. She thought about getting it now instead.

And then she thought about Tom Thorne.

She looked at the flowers he'd brought with him and smiled as she remembered his apology to Alison for . . . what was the word he'd used?

Humming. She'd thought he'd smelt good. She thought he smelt honest. He wasn't a hard man to find attractive. She probably had a few years on him, but knew instinctively that he wasn't the type that would be bothered by that. He was chunky. No . . . solid. He looked like he'd been round the block a few times. He was the sort of man to whom she'd found herself drawn since things had begun to fizzle out with David – many years ago, if she was being honest with herself.

It was odd that there was more grey in Thorne's hair on the left-hand side. She'd always liked brown eyes as well.

Anne was suddenly aware that she was voicing her thoughts. These late-night conversations with Alison were becoming routine. Nurses were used to discovering her wittering away in the middle of the night. She had begun to look forward to talking to Alison. Engaging with Alison's brain was vital as part of her treatment but Anne found it therapeutic too. It was strange and exciting to be able to speak your mind and not be . . . judged. It was confession without the spooky stuff. Perhaps somewhere Alison *was* judging her. She was probably full of opinions – 'Sod the crusty copper! Find yourself a tasty young medical student!'

One day Anne would find out exactly what Alison had been thinking. Right now, the hum of the machinery was making her sleepy. She stood up, reached across and gently squeezed the lubrication drops into Alison's eyes before taping them shut for the night. She took off her jacket, scrunched it up and put it beneath her head as she sat down again. She closed her eyes, whispered goodnight to Alison and was immediately asleep.

By seven thirty the next morning the body had been formally identified. Helen Doyle's parents had rung to report that she hadn't come home at about the same time as George Hammond was watching her tumble over the railings into Queens Wood. Within hours of that first concerned phone call, Thorne was leaning against a wall, watching them walk slowly down the corridor, away from the mortuary. Michael Doyle sobbed. His wife, Eileen, stared grimly into the distance and squeezed her husband's arm. Her high heels click-clacked all the way down the stone steps as they walked outside, to be greeted by the dazzling, crisp and completely ordinary dawn of their first day without a daughter.

Now Thorne stood with his back to a different wall. Dead Helen had taken her place alongside the others. She hadn't spoken up yet but it was only a matter of time. Now, forty or so officers of assorted rank, together with auxiliaries and civilian staff, sat waiting for Thorne to speak to them. As ever, he felt like the badly dressed deputy headmaster of a run-down comprehensive. His audience exchanged bored pleasantries or swapped laddish insults. The few women on the team sat together, deflecting the casual sexism of colleagues for whom 'harass' was still two words. The wisps of smoke from a dozen or more cigarettes curled up towards the strip-lights. Thorne might as well have been back on twenty a day.

'The body of Helen Doyle was discovered this morning in Queens Wood in Highgate at just after one thirty a.m. She was last seen leaving the Marlborough Arms on Holloway Road at eleven fifteen. The post-mortem is being carried out this morning but for now we're working on the assumption that she was killed by the same man responsible for the deaths of Christine Owen, Madeleine Vickery and Susan Carlish . . .'

The dead girls: *'Oh, come on, Tommy. You know it was him.'*

'. . . as well as the attempted murder of Alison Willetts.'

But it *wasn't* attempted murder, was it? The killer was actually attempting to do something else. Thorne didn't know the word for it. They'd probably have to invent one if they ever caught him. He cleared his throat and ploughed on.

'George Hammond, who discovered the body, has given us a vague description of a man seen removing the body from his car and dumping it at the scene. Six feet one or two, medium build. Dark hair possibly. Glasses maybe. The car is a blue or possibly a black saloon, no make or model as yet. The victim was abducted at some point on her journey from the pub to her home on Windsor Road, which is no more than half a mile away,

78

sometime between eleven fifteen and eleven thirty. Nobody's reported seeing anything but somebody did. I'd like them found, please. Let's get a make on that car and a decent description . . .'

Thorne paused. He could see one or two officers exchanging glances. It had taken him less than a minute to impart the essential information, the paltry scraps of fact that were supposed to shift the operation up a gear.

Frank Keable stood up. 'I don't really need to tell you, but the usual press blackout, please.' The media hadn't got hold of the killings, not as the work of one man at any rate. The fact that the murders hadn't been concentrated in one area and had been so well disguised had made it hard for them. It had taken the police long enough to put it together themselves. Still, Thorne was surprised: Backhand had been up and running for weeks now and they usually had sources within most high-level operations. In time there would be a leak and then the usual buck-passing would begin. The tabloids would come up with a lurid nickname for the killer, publicity-hungry politicians would bleat about law and order, and Keable would give him a speech about 'pressure being brought to bear'. But so far so good.

Keable nodded at Thorne. He was free to continue.

'Helen Doyle was eighteen years old . . .' He stopped and watched his colleagues nod with due disgust. He had not paused for effect. He was

79

feeling the knot in his stomach tighten, slippery and undoable.

Helen was not much older than Calvert's eldest.

'Unlike the other victims she was not attacked in her home. It's a fair bet he didn't do it on the street and the method of killing would suggest that he couldn't do it in a car. So where did he take her?' Thorne talked some more. The usual stuff. Obviously they were still waiting on the results from the forensic team. These were the first real tests they'd been able to carry out and he was hopeful. They should all be hopeful. This might be the breakthrough. It was time to pull their fingers out. They were going to get him. Come on, lads . . .

The house-to-house was allocated. There was talk of a television reconstruction. Then chairs were scraped back, sandwiches ordered, and Frank Keable was summoned to the office of the detective superintendent.

'What's the point? He knows I'll have sod all to tell him until this afternoon.'

'Maybe he just wants to share a power breakfast with you. Mind you, you've already had yours.' Thorne pointed at the ketchup stain on Keable's shirt.

'Bollocks.' He spat on a finger and tried to rub out the bright red splodge.

'He got it wrong again last night and he doesn't like it,' Thorne said.

Keable looked up at him, still rubbing, reaching into his pocket for a handkerchief.

'The way he dumped the girl's body so quickly. He just wanted shot of her, Frank. He thought he'd cracked it after Alison and when he botched it again I think it really pissed him off. He's getting impatient. And he's getting arrogant. He took a big risk snatching this one off the street. These women, these girls, are just bodies to him, dead or alive. He's just carrying out a procedure on them and I think he blames them when he gets it wrong. There's no real violence, but he's angry.'

'If he's in such a hurry to get rid of them, what's the washing all about?'

'I don't know. It's . . . medical.'

'The fucker probably scrubs up.' Keable snorted. Thorne stared over his head. 'Oh, come on, Tom. Listen, isn't this what we want? If he's getting impatient or whatever, he's far more likely to screw up somewhere and give us what we need to get him.'

'Or just start killing faster. It's been twenty two days since Alison Willetts was attacked. Susan Carlish was six weeks before that . . .'

Keable stroked the top of his head. 'I know, Tom.' It was a declaration of efficiency, a statement of competence, but Thorne saw something else: a quiet instruction to calm down. A warning. So often he glimpsed the same thing concealed behind a gentle enquiry or a concerned stare. He'd see it most, of course, when there was a suspect. Any suspect. It scalded him, but he understood. The Calvert case was part of a shared history.

Folklore almost, like Sutcliffe. A guilt they all inherited at some level or other. But he'd been part of it and they hadn't. He'd been . . . in amongst it.

Keable turned and marched away towards the lift. A car would be waiting to take him across town for the meeting. He pressed the button to go down and turned back to Thorne. 'Let me know as soon as Hendricks gets in touch.'

Thorne watched Keable get into the lift and each shrugged their way through the fifteen seconds of dead time waiting for the doors to close. Keable would tell the chief superintendent that while they were obviously waiting on the results of all the tests, there was the distinct possibility of a breakthrough. Somebody must have seen the killer taking the girl. This was definitely the break in the case that they needed.

Thorne wondered if they would bother broaching the subject that had hung in the air since the note was discovered on his car. It might have been saying 'come and get me', and dumping Helen Doyle's body so clumsily may well have been a taunt, but one thing was obvious: the killer was no longer bothering to disguise what he was doing because he knew they were on to him. If knowing the police had put it together was making him careless, then Thorne was happy that he knew. What really bothered him was how.

Why can't they fucking well fix this? They can stick a human ear on a mouse and clone a fucking sheep. They clone sheep, for Christ's sake, which is the most pointless thing ever since how the bloody hell are you supposed to tell when every sheep looks like every other sodding sheep and there's NOTHING REALLY WRONG WITH ME!

Nothing really . . . wrong.

A stroke. It sounds so soothing, so gentle. I don't feel like I've been stroked by anything. I feel like I've been hit with a jackhammer. My nan had a stroke, but she could talk afterwards. Her voice was slurred and the drugs made her go a bit funny. Up to then she'd just wittered on about . . . you know, old people's stuff. She never went as far as telling complete strangers how old she was at bus stops, but you know the sort of thing. The drugs they put her on turned her into a geriatric performance poet. She'd lie there ranting about how motorbikes were driving through the ward at night and how the nurses all wanted to have sex with her. Honestly, it was hysterical – she was eighty-six! But at least she could make herself understood.

This man gave me a stroke. Anne told me what he did. Twisted some artery and gave me a stroke. Why can't they just untwist it, then? There must be specialists or something. I'm lying here screaming and shouting, and the nurses wander past and coo at me like I'm taking a lazy afternoon nap in the sun. They must have finished all the tests by now. They must know that I'm still in here, still talking to myself, ranting and raving. It's doing my head in! See? I've still got a sense of humour, for fuck's sake.

I was right about Anne and the copper. Thorne. I've met women like Anne before. Always go for the two types of men – the ones that spark something off in their brains or the ones that get it going in their knickers. A man who does both? Forget it. I think it's fairly obvious which category her ex falls into. Time to ring in the changes. So the copper's luck's in, if you ask me.

I reckon I might have to stick to the brain-boxes from now on.

Tim just sat by the bed this morning and held my hand. He doesn't even bother talking to me any more.

CHAPTER 5

Thorne sat perched on the edge of Tughan's desk in the open-plan operations room. As Tughan's hands manoeuvred his mouse and flew across his keyboard, Thorne could almost see the Irishman's back stiffen. He knew he was annoying him.

'Isn't there something you should be doing, Tom?'

Phil Hendricks had worked through the night, and even before Keable had settled down to coffee and croissants with the chief superintendent, Thorne had received the information he'd wanted. Helen Doyle had been heavily drugged with Midazolam and had died as a result of a stroke. In spite of the body's location and the apparent break with his routine, there was no doubt that she had been the killer's fifth victim. That was pretty much all they knew, other than that Forensics had gathered some fibres from Helen Doyle's skirt and blouse. Thorne got straight on the phone.

'Any joy on these fibres?'

'Give us a bloody chance.'

'All right, just give me your best bloody guess, then.'

'Carpet fibres, probably from the boot of the car.'

'Can you get a make?'

'Where do you think this is? Quantico?'

'Where?'

'Forget it. Look, we'll get on to it. Something to match it to would help . . .'

The change in the pattern bothered Thorne, but they were left trying to answer the same questions. How had he talked his way into these women's houses and perhaps, in Helen Doyle's case, talked her into getting into his car? Helen Doyle's body, like that of Alison Willetts and Susan Carlish, was unmarked yet full of drink and drugs. The tranquilliser had to have been administered with alcohol. But how? Had the killer been watching Helen all night and spiked her drink before she left the pub? That would have been difficult – she was with a large group of friends and, besides, to have got the timing of it right would have been near impossible. How could he have known exactly when the drug would start to take effect? It was still the best guess, so Thorne had set about rounding up as many people as possible who had been in the Marlborough at the time. This, on top of the general canvassing along Helen's route home, meant that they were going to need every extra body that Frank Keable could deliver. If he could deliver. Thorne was hopeful of finding somebody who'd seen Helen after she'd left the pub. He still couldn't fathom why the killer was being so brazen but it made him more optimistic than he'd felt in a long time.

'Is there something I can help you with?'

Tughan smiled a lot but his eyes were like something on a plate. He was as skinny as a whippet and fiercely intelligent, with a voice that could cut through squad-room banter like a scalpel. It was always Tughan's thin lips Thorne imagined whispering into the mouthpiece whenever some lunatic phoned Scotland Yard with a coded warning. It wasn't that Thorne didn't appreciate what Tughan was capable of or what he brought to the investigation: Thorne could just about find his way into a file, if he had to, but he couldn't type to save his life and always found himself strangely hypnotised by the screensavers. When new evidence came in, Tughan was the man to make sense of it with his collation programmes and filefinders. Thorne knew that if they'd had a Nick Tughan fifteen years earlier instead of a thousand manilla folders . . . if they'd had a Holmes computer system instead of an antiquated card index, then Calvert might not have done what he did.

'Hey, Tommy, bugger the Calvert case, what about our case?'

'Tom?'

'Right . . . sorry, Nick. Have you got a copy of the Leicester/London matches handy?'

Tughan grunted, scrolled and double clicked.

The printer on the far side of the office began to hum. Thorne had actually been hoping that Tughan might have had a hard copy lying about. It would have been quicker to walk across to his own little goldfish bowl and fetch the copy on his desk, but he couldn't begrudge Tughan his little triumphs of efficiency. He begrudged him virtually everything else, and the feeling was entirely mutual.

Thorne stared at the list. Half a dozen doctors who had been on rotation at Leicester Royal Infirmary at the time of the Midazolam theft and now worked in local hospitals. Anne Coburn's information about the significance of the date had somewhat dampened any enthusiasm for this line of enquiry, and the discovery of Helen Doyle's body had rightly demanded everybody's attention, but Thorne still sensed that it might be important. It was possible to look at the date of the drugs theft as significant in quite the opposite way. Might not the killer (if indeed it *was* the killer) have chosen that date to make it look as if he might have come from anywhere when in fact he *was* working at the hospital? Besides, they were still working through the far bigger list of all doctors currently on rotation locally so they'd have to get round to this lot eventually.

Jeremy Bishop's name was second on the list.

Thorne was aware of what could only be described as a smirk on Holland's face as they rode the lift down to the car park. 'Isn't he Dr Coburn's friend?'

'She knows him, yes. And his alibi certainly checks out theoretically, yes.'

Jeremy Bishop had unquestionably been responsible for treating Alison Willetts in A and E.

'But Alison Willetts was taken to the Royal London for a reason,' Thorne explained, as if talking to a child. 'I want to check exactly when Bishop came on duty in relation to when she was brought in.'

The smirk stayed on Holland's face. He knew all about Thorne's visit to Queen Square. Was he visiting Alison Willetts or the doctor who was treating her? He was well aware that they could have checked out Bishop with a phone call or, at the very least, sent somebody else.

Thorne felt no compulsion to explain himself to Holland any further. As they stepped out at the ground floor and walked towards the car, he tried to convince himself that Bishop's friendship with Anne Coburn, about whom he was thinking more than he should, wasn't the main reason he was keen to eliminate him from the enquiry as quickly as possible.

As he tucked into a late breakfast, he thought about how tired Thorne had looked at eight o'clock that morning arriving at work. He'd watched him from the greasy spoon opposite as the policeman leaned against his car for a moment before plodding towards the door. He hadn't considered Thorne the plodding type at all. That was why he'd been so delighted when he discovered that he was on the case. That, and the other obvious reason. Thorne, he'd decided, was definitely dogged. And stubborn. These were qualities he required. Plus, of course, the capacity for being too clever for his own good. He certainly needed that. All in all, Thorne was perfect. But it had troubled him to see Thorne looking so worn out. He hoped that the fatigue was just physical and that the detective inspector wasn't burning out. No, he was justifiably exhausted after the . . . demands of the night before. They'd found her quickly. He was impressed. So Thorne had had a rough night. That made two of them.

One out of five. Down from twenty-five to twenty per cent. He'd known straight away, of course. He'd made the necessary phone call then gone about his business, but it was obvious within a minute or two that she'd let him down. Stupid drunken sow. His heart, which had been pounding with the oncoming rush of the dash to hospital with another one for the machines, had quickly slowed to its habitual steady thump. *Her* useless, cholesterol-soaked heart couldn't be bothered to thump at all. What an opportunity he'd given her. But she'd let her sad, silly little life ebb away. Oh, he'd almost certainly have been seen getting rid. They'd have a description of sorts by now. So what? They might even have seen the car. So much the better.

He chewed his toast and stared out of the window at the view across London. The mist was starting to lift. It would be another glorious day. Helen had been just as easy as the others to prepare. Easier. He was getting better at it. There had been those couple of disastrous attempts earlier on, but he was more relaxed about it these days.

Christine and Madeleine had been cautious at first. They were naturally reluctant to let him in but they were lonely women and he was an attractive man. They wanted to talk. And more. And he was very persuasive. Susan and Alison had both invited him in almost instantly and happily drunk themselves into oblivion. Literally. He giggled to himself. The champagne had been an inspired idea. He'd thought about a jab but it would have been messy and he didn't want any sort of struggle. The wait was a little longer with the champagne, naturally, but he liked watching them go slowly. He savoured the frisson of their impending malleability. The other one – the one whose name he hadn't had time to find out – had positively guzzled it down. But then he'd had to leave because the timing had not been . . . judicious. Still, he felt sure that she'd said nothing about it. She would have had a hard enough time explaining to her husband or boyfriend or girlfriend why she was so utterly out of it when they got home. She certainly wouldn't have mentioned inviting a strange man into the house.

It had been such a relief to be able to work on

Helen in his own home. He so hated dissembling. He'd hated creeping about in those dreary houses. It had made his flesh crawl to leave the bars of soap and bottles of pills in those dirty, greasy bathrooms. Rolled-up tights and shit stripes in the lavatory bowls. He hated putting his hands on them. On their heads. Even through the gloves he could feel the dirt and grease in their hair. He could swear he almost felt things . . . moving. But now he could work in clean, comfortable surroundings. Now *he* knew that *they* knew that *he* knew that . . .

He whistled his own invented melody to accompany this comforting refrain as he tried his best to stay awake. Thorne wasn't the only one feeling the strain. He needed more coffee. For a moment he closed his eyes and thought about Alison. She hadn't let him down. She'd wanted to live. He thought about going to visit her again, but it was perhaps a little risky. Security in ITUs was fairly tight, these days. The flood had been an inspired idea but could only be a one-off. He began to drift away. Yes, he'd need to think of something else if he wanted to go and see Alison again without getting caught.

Without bumping into Anne Coburn.

'Are you in any pain, Alison?' Doctors Anne Coburn and Steve Clark watched the pallid, peaceful face intently. There was no response. Anne tried again. 'Blink once for yes, Alison.' After a moment there was the tiniest movement – the ghost of a twitch around Alison's left eye. Anne looked across at the occupational therapist who scribbled notes on his clipboard. He nodded at her. She carried on. 'Yes, you are in pain? Was that a yes, Alison?' Nothing. 'Alison?' Steve Clark put his pen away. Alison's left eyelid fluttered three times in rapid succession. 'OK, Alison.'

'Maybe she's just tired, Anne. I'm sure you're right. It's just a question of her gaining sufficient control.'

Anne Coburn had a lot of time for Steve Clark. He was a brilliant therapist and a nice man, but he lied very badly. He wasn't at all convinced. But she was. 'I feel like somebody who's called out the TV repairman and then there's nothing the matter, only the other way round . . . oh shit, you know what I mean, Steve.'

'I just think that maybe you're rushing things a bit.'

'I'm following well-established guidelines, Steve. The ECG shows normal brain activity.'

'Nobody's arguing with that but it doesn't mean she's got the ability to communicate. I agree that there is movement but I've seen nothing to convince me that it isn't involuntary.'

'This isn't just me, Steve. You can talk to the nursing staff. I'm sure she's ready to communicate.'

'She might be ready—'

'And she's able. I've seen it. She indicated to me

that she was in pain, that she was tired. She . . . greets me, Steve.'

Clark opened the door. He was eager to be on his way. 'Maybe she's not comfortable with the pressure of . . . performing.'

Later, when she felt calmer, Anne would realise that he'd been trying to be genuinely sympathetic. At that moment she was angry and frustrated, for herself and for Alison. 'She isn't a performer and these are not cheap theatrics . . .'

But that's exactly what it felt like.

As Holland steered the unmarked Rover into a quiet tree-lined street in Battersea, he took a deceptively vicious speed bump just fast enough to take several layers off the underside of the car and to awaken his boss somewhat rudely.

'Jesus, Holland . . .'

'Sorry sir . . .'

'I know it's only a company car, but for Christ's sake!'

The sunshine was dazzling and Thorne felt every one of the twenty-eight hours since he'd last slept. Holland actually held the car door open for him! Thorne felt that it wasn't so much in deference to his rank as a subtle reminder that the fifteen years he had on the younger man were starting to show.

Jeremy Bishop lived in an elegant three-storey house with a small but well-maintained front garden. Probably four bedrooms. Probably tastefully decorated Thorne guessed, and crammed with what the slimier estate agents, if you could quantify slime, would refer to as 'periods'. Probably worth a piffling half a million. All this, and a nice Volvo parked outside. Clearly Bishop was not struggling.

Holland rang the bell. Thorne looked up at the windows. The curtains were still drawn. After a minute or two the door was opened, Holland made the introductions and he and Thorne were ushered into the house by a sleepy-looking Jeremy Bishop.

While Holland stood efficiently with his note-book at the ready, Thorne slumped into a chair, gratefully accepted a cup of coffee and racked his brain as to why Jeremy Bishop looked so familiar. He was, Thorne guessed, in his mid- to late-forties and, despite the stubble and redness round the eyes, looked ten years younger. He was tall, six two or three, and he reminded Thorne of Dr Richard Kimble, the character played by Harrison Ford in *The Fugitive*. There was plenty of grey in the short hair, but along with the wire-rimmed glasses, it served only to make him look 'distinguished'. This irritated Thorne enormously: his own grey hair simply made him look 'old'. Bugger prob-ably didn't even have grey pubes. Bishop would, without question be a regular performer in student nurse fantasies – 'Oh, Doctor! Here in the sluice room!?' He thought about Anne Coburn. He tried not to think about her stripping in the sluice room. Weren't doctors ugly any more? He remembered the rancid old GP he'd been dragged to see regularly as a boy: a hideous crone with a man's haircut and moustache, who smelt of cheese and always had a Craven A dangling from the corner of her mouth as she mumbled in an incomprehensible eastern-European accent. No such worries with Jeremy Bishop. His modulated tones would have calmed a thrashing epileptic in an instant.

'I presume this is about Alison Willetts,' he said.

Holland looked at Thorne, who sipped his coffee. Let the constable handle it.

'And why would you presume that, sir?'

Thorne stared at Holland through the steam from his coffee-cup. Nice start: sarcasm, superiority and a hint of aggression. Make your subject feel at ease.

Bishop wasn't fazed at all. 'Alison Willetts was attacked and seriously injured. I treated her, and they don't send detective inspectors round when you haven't paid your parking fines.' He smiled at Holland who could do little else but move on to item two in the do-it-yourself guide to interviews.

'We are investigating a very serious crime, which—'

'Has he done it again?'

Thorne almost spilt his coffee as he sat bolt upright in his chair. Holland looked across at him, thoroughly nonplussed. Bishop's amusement at the look on Holland's face was not lost on Thorne. He guessed that Bishop had seen that look many times as a junior doctor found themselves suddenly out of their depth and sought reassurance, or preferably hands-on assistance, from a senior colleague. Thorne decided that the hands-on approach was best. 'Done what again, sir?'

'Look, I'm sorry if I'm not supposed to know about the other victims. As far as I'm concerned it's simply a question of putting my patient's condition in context. I was informed that there had been other attacks. Anne Coburn and I are very old friends, Inspector, as I'm sure you're well aware.'

Thorne was very well aware that, despite Frank Keable's best intentions, the lid was not going to stay on this case for very long. Not that he ever really thought of cases as having lids . . . saucepans had lids . . . cases had . . . what? . . . locks? . . . well, only open and shut ones. Mind you, was there any point in a case that didn't open and shut. God he was tired . . .

'I'm sorry if we got you out of bed, sir.'

Bishop spread his arms across the back of the sofa. 'Oh, well, I obviously look as rough as you, Inspector.' Thorne raised an eyebrow. 'I spend a lot of time with people who don't get much sleep for one reason or another. The eyes give it away instantly. I've been on call all night. What's your excuse?' His laugh was somewhere between a chuckle and a snort.

Thorne laughed back at him through a good impression of a yawn. 'Yep . . . busy night. What about you, sir?'

Bishop stared at him. 'Oh . . . no, not really. Went in to treat an overdose at about three o'clock and got home about five thirty. But even when you're not called in, it's hard to relax when you're bleeper-watching. Thank God for cable TV.'

'Anything good on?'

'I'm a confirmed channel-hopper, I'm afraid. A lot of old sitcoms, the odd black-and-white film and a fair bit of smut.' He looked up and grinned in disbelief at Holland. 'Are you actually writing all that down, Constable?'

Thorne had been asking himself the same question. 'Only the bit about smut. Detective Constable Holland's life lacks excitement.' Thorne was astonished to see Holland actually blush.

Bishop stood up and stretched. 'I'm going to get another coffee. Anybody else?'

Thorne followed him into the kitchen and they chatted over the growing grumble of the kettle.

'So what time did you go in the night you treated Alison Willetts?'

'I was bleeped at about three o'clock, I think. One sugar, wasn't it?' Thorne nodded and waited for Bishop to continue. 'The patient was found outside by a service entrance . . . I'm sure you know all this . . . and brought straight into A and E.'

'Did you call in when you were bleeped?'

'No need. It was a message saying red trauma. You just go. Sometimes you might get an extension number to ring, or sometimes it's just a message to phone in, but with a trauma call you just get in the car.'

'And when Alison Willetts was brought in, you were the first person to treat her?'

'That's correct. I checked her pupils – they were reacting. I bagged and masked her, intubated her, Midazolam to sedate her, ordered a CT of her head and an ECG, and handed it over to the junior anaesthetist.' Bishop took a sip of his coffee. 'Sorry, I must sound like an episode of *Casualty*.'

Thorne smiled. 'More like *ER*. On *Casualty* it's usually a cup of sweet tea and a couple of aspirin.'

Bishop laughed. 'Absolutely right. And the nursing staff aren't quite so attractive.'

'So if you were bleeped at three o'clock you got there, what, about half past?'

'Something like that, I suppose.'

'And Alison, the patient, was brought in about quarter to four?' Bishop sipped and nodded. 'So why were you bleeped in the first place?'

'I really couldn't tell you, I'm afraid. It isn't unusual – sometimes you can spend ages trying to find out why you've been called in. I've been bleeped before when I shouldn't have been. As for that particular night, I've never really thought about it. I mean, if I'd known exactly what had happened – or, rather, what we'd later discover – I might have a better grasp of the sequence of events that night. It was just a routine emergency at the time. Sorry.'

Thorne put down his coffee-cup. 'Not to worry, sir. I'm sure we can find out.'

Bishop smiled as he picked up Thorne's cup, poured the unfinished coffee into the sink and opened the door of the dishwasher. 'Why I might have been bleeped four Tuesdays ago? Good luck, Inspector.'

As the car moved slowly through the traffic on Albert Bridge, Holland chose not to ask his superior officer a number of questions. Why did we bother driving all that way? Do you think Jeremy Bishop is giving Anne Coburn one? Why do you take the piss out of me all the time? Why do you think you're so much better than everybody else?

He looked across at Thorne, who was slumped in the passenger seat with his eyes shut. He was wide awake.

Thorne spoke only once, to tell Holland that they weren't going back to the office just yet. Without opening his eyes he told him to turn right and drive along the river towards Whitechapel. They were going to call in at the Royal London Hospital first, to see just how cast-iron this alibi of Jeremy Bishop's really was.

Just call me the Amazing Performing Eyelid Woman! Only I can't sodding well perform, can I?

I went out with this actor once. He told me about a recurring dream where he was onstage ready to do his luvvie bit and then all the words just tumbled out of his head like water running really fast down the plughole. That's what it felt like when Anne was asking me to blink. Christ, I wanted to blink for her. No . . . I wanted to blink for me. I can do it, I know I can. I've been doing it all the fucking time when there's nobody there and I've been blinking when Anne's asked me to before. She asked me if I was in pain and I blinked once for yes. One blink. A fraction of a movement in one poxy eye and I felt like I'd just won the lottery, shagged Mel Gibson and been given a year's supply of chocolate.

Actually, I felt like I'd just run the London Marathon. A couple of blinks and I'm knackered. But when that therapist was watching I couldn't do it.

I was screaming at my eyelids inside my head. It felt like the signal went out from my

101

brain. But slowly. It was like some dodgy old Lada beetling along the circuits, or whatever they're called. Neuro-highways or whatever. It was on the right road and then it just got stuck at roadworks somewhere. Like it lost interest. I know I can do it but I haven't got any control over it. When I'm not trying I'm blinking away like some nutter, but when I want to I'm as good as dead.

If blinking's all I've got left, I'm going to be the greatest fucking blinker you've ever seen. Stick with me, Anne. There's so much I want to tell you. I'll be blinking for England, I swear.

I could feel the disappointment in her voice. I wanted to cry. But I can't even do that . . .

CHAPTER 6

'Where to, sir?'

'Muswell Hill, please.'

'No problem, sir. Where is that, please?'

Thorne sighed heavily as the simple journey from his flat in Kentish Town suddenly became an altogether trickier proposition. It was his own fault for calling a minicab. Why was he such a bloody cheapskate?

He was trying not to think about the case – this was a night off. He fooled himself for about as long as it took the cab to reach the end of his road. He would have loved to spend an evening without his curious calendar girls, but it was going to be hard, considering where he was going and who he was going to see. The subject of Jeremy Bishop might be strictly off limits with Anne Coburn. It was becoming clear that they were extremely close. Were they perhaps more than that? Thorne tried not to think about that possibility. Whatever, their relationship made things awkward in every sense, not least procedurally.

Thorne hated the cliché of the instinctive copper

as much as he hated the notion of the hardened one. But the instinctive copper was only a cliché because, he knew, it contained a germ of truth. Hunches were nothing but trouble. If they were wrong they caused embarrassment, pain, guilt and more. But the hunches that were right were far worse. Policemen . . . good policemen, weren't born with these instincts. They developed them. After all, accountants were only good with numbers because they worked with them every day. Even an average copper could spot when someone was lying. A few developed a feel, a taste, a sense about people.

They were the unlucky ones.

'Here you go, sir.'

The minicab driver was thrusting a tattered *A–Z* at him. Christ on a bike, thought Thorne, do you want me to drive the bloody car for you?

'I don't need the *A–Z*. I'll give you directions. Straight up the Archway Road.'

'Right you are, sir. Which way is that?'

Thorne looked out of the window. Another warm late-August evening and a T-shirted queue of eager Saturday night concert-goers was waiting to go into the Forum. As the cab drove past he strained his head to see the name of the band but only caught the word '. . . Maniacs'. Charming.

He now lived no more than half a mile from where he'd grown up. This had been his adolescent stamping ground. Kentish Town, Camden, Highgate. And Archway. He'd worked out of the

104

station at Holloway for six months. He knew the road Helen Doyle had lived in. He'd drunk in the Marlborough Arms. He hoped she'd enjoyed herself that night . . .

Jeremy Bishop.

Yes, it had started as a strange familiarity, which he still couldn't fathom, but it had become more than that. In the few days since he'd first laid eyes on the man, his feelings had begun to bed themselves down on more solid foundations.

Thorne had found out quickly why Bishop had smiled when he'd told him he was going to check out why he'd been bleeped the night that Alison had come in. He was amazed to find that the calls put out to bleep doctors were untraceable. There were no official records. The call could have been made from anywhere by all accounts. It was even possible to bleep yourself. None of the likely candidates could recall bleeping Bishop on the night that Alison Willetts came in. He'd spoken to the senior house officer, the registrar and the junior anaesthetist and their recollection of events that night was as fuzzy as Bishop had known it would be. He was certainly there when she was brought into A and E but his alibi, as far as when she was attacked and when she was dumped at the hospital, was not quite as solid as Anne Coburn had first thought.

He couldn't put any of it together yet, nowhere near, but there were other . . . details.

The canvas of the area in which Helen Doyle

105

had disappeared had started to yield results. She had been seen by at least three people after leaving the pub. One was a neighbour who knew her well. All the witnesses described seeing her talking to a man at the end of her road. She was described variously as 'looking happy', 'talking loudly' and 'seeming as if she was pissed'. The descriptions of the man varied a little but tallied in a number of areas. He was tall. He had short, greying hair and wore glasses. He was probably in his mid- to late-thirties. They thought he was Helen Doyle's new boyfriend. Her older man.

All the witnesses agreed on something else. Alison was drinking from a bottle of champagne. Now they knew how the drug was administered. So simple. So insidious. As the victims' capacity to resist had melted away they'd each felt . . . what? Special? Sophisticated? Thorne sensed that the killer thought of himself in exactly those terms.

The driver turned on his radio. An old song by the Eurythmics. Thorne leaned forward quickly and told him to switch it off.

The cab turned right off the Al towards Highgate Woods.

'It's just off the Broadway, OK?'

'Broadway . . .'

Thorne caught the driver's look in the mirror. Apologetic yet not really giving a toss.

'If black cab drivers do the Knowledge, what do you lot do?'

'Sorry, mate?'

'Doesn't matter.'

He'd waited a day before talking to Frank Keable. Stepping into the DCI's office he'd been thoroughly prepared to outline his suspicions – the details that pointed towards Bishop. Ten minutes later he'd walked out feeling like he'd just left Hendon.

'I have to be honest, Tom. No, he doesn't have a rock solid alibi but . . .'

'Not for any of the murders, sir. I checked with—'

'But all you've got is a lot of stuff that, well, it doesn't rule him out, and what about the description? Two of the witnesses say he's early- to mid-thirties.'

'The height's right, Frank, and Bishop looks a lot younger than he is.'

It was at that point that Thorne had become aware that it was all starting to sound unconvincing. He decided to stop before he said something that might make him look vaguely desperate. *'And he's a doctor! And I don't really . . . like him very much . . .'*

The same night he'd walked into his flat and heard a woman's voice coming from the living room.

'. . . at the office. God, I hate these things – sorry. Anyway, please give me a call, I'm very excited about it.'

He grinned. How could a woman who probed about in people's brains be so out of her depth

with an answering-machine? He found it endear-
ing, then knew that she'd think he was being
patronising. He picked up.

'Tom?'

What was she asking? '*Is* that Tom?' Or 'Is it
OK if I *call* you Tom?' Either way his answer was
the same.

'Yes. Hi . . .'

'This is Anne Coburn – sorry, I was just waffling
away. I tried to get you at the office, I hope you
don't mind.'

He'd written his home number on the back of
the card he'd given her. He threw his coat on to
the sofa and dragged the phone over to the chair.
'No, that's fine. I've just this second walked in the
door. So, what are you excited about?'

'Sorry?'

'You said you were excited. I heard it on the
machine as I was coming in.'

'Oh, right. It's Alison. I think she's really starting
to communicate.'

He was bending to retrieve the half-empty bottle
of wine by the side of the chair but instantly sat up
again. 'What? That's fantastic.'

'Listen, I do mean *starting*, and I have to say
there are people who aren't quite as convinced as
me that the movements aren't involuntary but I
think you should see it.'

'Yes, of course . . .'

'He's killed another girl, hasn't he?'

Thorne leaned back in the chair. He wedged

the phone between ear and shoulder and started to pour himself a hefty glass of wine. Had it made the papers? He hadn't seen anything. Even if it had, there was no link to the other killings. So how did she . . . ?

Bishop. He'd obviously told her they'd been round. And just how much had *she* told *him* about the other killings? He'd need to ask her about that, tactfully.

'Look, I understand if you don't want to discuss it. Tom?'

'No, I was just thinking about something. Yes. We've found another body.'

It was her turn to pause. 'I know I said that Alison wouldn't be giving you any statements and she won't, I mean not in any conventional sense, but perhaps . . . Listen, I don't want to raise any false hopes.'

'You think she might be able to respond to questions?'

'Not just yet, but I think so, yes. Simple ones. Yes and no. We could work out a system maybe. Sorry, I'm waffling again. Obviously we need to talk about it but I just wanted to let you know . . .'

'I'm glad you did.'

And then she invited him to dinner.

He proffered the plastic bag containing a bottle of his favourite red wine as soon as she opened the door.

'Thanks, but there was no need.'

'Don't get excited, it's only a plastic bag.'

She laughed and stepped forward to kiss him on the cheek. Her perfume was lovely. She was wearing a rust-coloured sleeveless top, cream linen trousers and training shoes. He was struck, not unpleasantly as it happened, by the fact that she was an inch or two taller than he was. He was used to that. He felt like he was going to enjoy himself. His good mood evaporated in an instant as he glanced over her shoulder and saw a man in the kitchen at the other end of the hall.

Jeremy Bishop was leaning against the worktop, opening a bottle of champagne.

Anne stepped aside to usher Thorne in and caught his look. 'Sorry,' she mouthed, shrugging.

As Thorne removed his leather jacket and made approving noises about the original coving, he was wondering what she meant. Sorry? She couldn't possibly have any idea what he really thought about Bishop, so what was she sorry for? As he walked towards the kitchen he came to the heartening conclusion that she was sorry they weren't going to be alone. Bishop held out a hand, smiling at him. Thorne smiled back. Sorry? Thinking about it, he wasn't sure that *he* was sorry at all.

'Perfect timing, Detective Inspector.' Bishop offered him a glass of champagne. Thorne felt a chill pass through him as he took it. Bishop looked thoroughly at home, moving easily around a kitchen with which he was obviously familiar.

He wore pressed chinos and a collarless shirt. Silk by the look of it. He probably called it a blouse. Thorne felt instantly overdressed in his tie, and instinctively reached up to undo the top button of his shirt, which he definitely called a shirt.

Bishop drained his glass. 'Has the hernia been giving you any more trouble?'

'Sorry?'

'It came to me just after you and your constable left. Come on – don't tell me it hasn't been driving you mad as well. Your hernia op last year . . . I was your gas man.' Without waiting for a response – he would have been waiting for some time – he turned to Anne. 'I've given your sauce a stir, Jimmy, and I'm off to the loo.' He handed Anne his glass and moved past Thorne towards the stairs.

They stood in silence until they heard the bathroom door close.

'Is this awkward for you, Tom? Tell me if it is.'

'Why should it be?'

'I didn't invite him.'

Some good news. Thorne smiled graciously. 'It's fine.'

'I had no idea he was coming. He just dropped by and it would have been rude not to ask him to stay. I know you've questioned him, which is bloody ridiculous . . .'

Thorne took a sip of champagne. It wasn't a drink he was fond of.

'So?'

'So what?'

'So is it awkward?'

Awkward was putting it mildly. Thorne couldn't recall the last time he'd had a cosy dinner with a prime suspect.

He remembered the scene in Keable's office. Make that *his* prime suspect.

Still, it might be interesting. He already knew the basic facts. The two children, the wife who'd died. But there was no question that it would be valuable to get another . . . slant on things. Anne was looking intently at him. He hadn't answered her question. So he asked one instead: 'Jimmy?'

'A nickname from med-school days. James Coburn. You know, *The Magnificent Seven*. He was the one with the knives.'

'Right. Was he any good with scalpels?'

She laughed. 'Whatever misguided reasons you had to question Jeremy, I can fully understand that this might be putting you in a compromising position, but there are two very good reasons why you should stay and have dinner.' Thorne had no intention of going anywhere, but was perfectly happy to let her persuade him. 'One, I would very much like it if you did, and two, I make the finest spaghetti carbonara in North London.'

Dinner was fantastic. It was certainly the best meal Thorne had eaten in a while, but that was to damn it with faint praise. That his eating habits had become a trifle sloppy had been brought home to him on receipt of his BT family and friends list.

They might just as well have sent an embossed calling card saying, 'You Sad Bastard'. Thorne's ten most frequently dialled numbers had not exactly been what he'd call kith and kin. He could only hope and pray that he didn't win the holiday. Two weeks in Lanzarote with the manager of the Bengal Lancer and a posse of spotty pizza-delivery boys on mopeds was hardly a prospect that appealed.

'I hope my grilling proved useful, Detective Inspector.' The way Bishop emphasised Thorne's rank, he might have been reading the cast list of an am-dram whodunnit. His evident glee at the situation told Thorne that he was more than willing to play his part but Anne was quick to discourage his interest in the case.

'Come on, Jeremy, I'm sure Tom doesn't want to talk about it. He probably can't, even if he wanted to.'

This was fine with Thorne. He had no need to talk about the case. He wanted to let Bishop talk, and once the boundaries had been established he wasn't disappointed. Bishop was full of stories. He seemed permanently amused, not only at his own patter but at the peculiarity of their cosy little threesome. Again, fine with Thorne. The anaesthetist dominated the conversation, occasionally making an effort to engage the policeman in trite chit-chat.

'Where do you live, then, Tom?'

'Kentish Town. Ryland Road.'

'Not my side of London. Nice?'

Thorne nodded. *No, not particularly.*

Bishop was a witty and entertaining raconteur – probably. Thorne did his best to laugh in all the right places, although he felt clumsy and cack-handed as he watched his fellow diners twirl spaghetti with professional deftness and delicacy.

'. . . and the two old dears were sat talking about the beef crisis and how they were going to exercise their rights as consumers and stick it to the French.'

'Politics in A and E?' Anne turned to Thorne. 'It's usually non-stop babble about football or soap operas or "I know it's a nasty cut but he's never hit me before, honest."'

'But get ready for the killer . . .' Bishop drained his wine glass, letting them wait for the punchline. 'I heard them saying how they were going to boycott French fries!'

Thorne smiled. Bishop raised his eyebrows at Anne and they both giggled before saying as one, 'NFN!'

Stifling her laugh, Anne leaned across to Thorne. 'Normal For Norfolk.'

Thorne smiled. 'Right. Stupid or inbred.' Bishop nodded. Thorne shrugged. *I'm just a copper. Thick as shit, me.*

Anne was still giggling. They'd already polished off two bottles of wine and hadn't finished the pasta yet. 'Somewhere there's a doctor with too much time on his hands thinking up these jokes. There's loads of them, not very nice usually.'

'Come on, Jimmy, they're just a bit of fun. I bet Tom's had to deal with a few JP FROGs in his time, haven't you, Tom?'

'Oh, almost certainly. That would be . . . ?' Thorne raised his eyebrows.

'Just Plain Fucking Run Out of Gas,' Anne explained. 'When a patient is going to die. I hate that one . . .' She poured herself another glass of wine and leaned back in her chair, retiring momentarily as Bishop warmed to his theme.

'Jimmy gets a bit touchy and squeamish at some of the more ghoulish jokes that get us through the day. Seriously though, some of the shorthand is actually a useful way to communicate quickly with a colleague.'

'And keep the patients in the dark at the same time?'

Bishop pushed up his glasses with the knuckle of his index finger. Thorne noticed that his finger-nails were beautifully manicured. 'Absolutely right. Another of Jimmy's pet hates, but by far the best way if you ask me. What's the point of telling them things they aren't going to understand? If you do tell them and they do understand, chances are it's only going to frighten the life out of them.'

Anne began to clear away the plates.

'So better a patient who's in the dark than a JP FROG?'

Bishop raised his glass to Thorne in mock salute. 'But that's not the best one. I get to deal with a lot of JP FROGs, but Jimmy, specialising as she does

115

in lost causes, is very much the patron saint of TF BUNDYs.' He grinned, showing every one of his perfect teeth. 'Totally Fucked But Unfortunately Not Dead Yet.'

Thorne could hear Anne in the kitchen loading the dishwasher. He remembered the smug look on Bishop's face as he'd put the coffee cups in his dishwasher a few days before. He wore the same expression now. Thorne grinned back at him. 'So what about Alison Willetts? Is she a TF BUNDY?'

Thorne saw at once that if he'd thought this would throw Bishop then he was seriously understimating him. The doctor's reaction was clearly one of undisguised amusement. He raised his eyebrows and shouted through to the kitchen. 'Oh, Christ, Jimmy, I think I'm outnumbered.' He turned back to Thorne and suddenly there was a glimmer of steel behind the flippancy. 'Come on, Tom, is the moral indignation that was positively dripping from that last comment really meant to suggest that you care about your . . . victims, any more than we care about our patients? That we're just unfeeling monsters while the CID is full of sensitive souls like your good self?'

'Christ, Tommy, what a smug bastard . . .'

Susan, Maddy, Christine. And Helen . . .

'I'm not suggesting anything. It just seemed a bit harsh, that's all.'

'It's a job, Tom. Not a very nice one at times and, yes, it's quite well paid after you've slogged

116

your guts out training for seven years then spent a few more kissing enough arses to get to a decent level.' That certainly rang a bell. 'We're paid to treat, we're not paid to care. The simple truth is that the NHS can't afford to care, in any sense of the word.'

Anne put an enormous plate of cheesecake in the centre of the table. 'M and S, I'm afraid. Great with pasta. Crap at puddings.' She went back through to the kitchen leaving Bishop to start divvying it up.

'I always tell students that they have a choice. They can think of the patients as John or Elsie or Bob or whatever and lose what little sleep they get . . .'

Thorne held out his plate for a slice of cheese-cake. 'Or . . . ?'

'Or they can be good doctors and treat bodies. Dead or alive, they're bodies.'

What had Thorne said earlier to Keable?

'Are you going to let him get away with this shit, Tommy?'

'I'm not sure what I'm going to do. Why don't you help me? Is it him? Is he the one?'

The one question they never answer.

Thorne started to eat. 'So, what do most of your students decide?'

Bishop shrugged and took a mouthful. He chuckled. 'There's another one.'

'What?'

'CID. Another acronym.'

Thorne smiled at Anne as she sat back down

and helped herself to a slice. Bishop grunted, demanding the attention of the audience. He'd obviously come up with something wonderful. Thorne turned to him and waited. Get ready for the killer . . .

'Coppers In Disarray?'

Bishop was the first to leave. He'd shaken Thorne's hand and . . . had he winked? Anne led him into the hall to get his jacket, leaving Thorne on the sofa with a glass of wine listening to them saying their goodbyes. Their obvious intimacy disturbed him in every way he could think of. The next part of the evening, whatever that was, would have to be handled very carefully. Their voices were lowered, but there was no mistaking Bishop's low hum of contentment as he kissed Anne goodbye. Thorne wondered how witty and garrulous he'd be with a detective constable's fist half-way down his throat. He wondered how smug he'd be in an airless interview room. He wondered what he'd have to do to get him into one.

He heard the front door shut and took a deep breath. Now he wanted to be alone with Anne and not just because of what she could tell him about Bishop.

She came back into the living room to find Thorne staring into space with a huge smile on his face. 'What's so funny?' Thorne shrugged. He didn't want to get off on the wrong foot by telling her that he'd just come up with his own little acronym for Jeremy Bishop. A highly appropriate one as it happened. GAS.

Guilty As Sin.

'Where's Rachel this evening? Have you locked her in her room with a Spice Girls video?'

'She's out celebrating her GCSE results.'

'God, of course, it was today.' The papers had been full of it. The increase in pass levels. The ever-widening gap between girls and boys. The six-year-old with an A* in maths. 'Celebrating? She must have done well?'

Anne shrugged. 'Pretty well, I suppose. She could maybe have tried harder in one or two subjects, but we were pretty pleased.'

Thorne nodded, smiling. *We?* 'Hmm . . . pushy mother.'

She laughed, flopping into the armchair opposite him and picking up her glass of wine. Thorne leaned forward to refill his own glass.

'Tell me about Jeremy's wife.'

She sighed heavily. 'Are you asking me as a policeman?'

'As a friend,' he lied.

It was a good few seconds before she answered. 'Sarah was a close friend. I'd known them both at medical school. I'm godmother to their kids, which is why I'm sure that your interest in him is a complete waste of time and I don't want to harp on about this, but it's starting to feel a bit . . . insulting actually.'

119

Thorne did not want to lie to her, but he did anyway. 'It's just routine, Anne.'

She kicked off her shoes and pulled her feet up underneath her. 'Sarah was killed ten years ago . . . you must know all this.'

'I know the basic facts.'

'It was a horrible time. He's never really got over it. I know he seems a bit . . . assured, but they were very happy and he's never been interested in anyone else.'

'Not even you?'

She blushed. 'Well, at least I know that *this* isn't an official question.'

'Completely unofficial and horribly nosy, I know, but I did wonder . . .'

'We were together once, a long time ago when we were both students.'

'And not since? Sorry . . .'

'My husband thought so, if that makes you feel a little less nosy. David always had a thing about Jeremy, but it was really just professional rivalry, which he liked to tart up as something else.'

Like his hair, thought Thorne.

He'd tried to pace himself and Anne had drunk far more than he had, but he was definitely starting to feel a little lightheaded.

'What do his kids do?'

James, twenty-four, and Rebecca, twenty-six, another doctor. These facts and many others filling three pages of a notebook in his desk drawer.

'Rebecca's in orthopaedics. She works in Bristol.'

Thorne nodded, interested. *Tell me something I don't know.*

'James, well, he's done all manner of things over the last few years. He's been a bit unlucky, if I'm being kind.'

'And if you're being unkind?'

'Well, he does sponge off his dad a little. Jeremy's a bit of a soft touch. They're very close. James was in the car when the – they had the accident. He was a bit screwed up about it for a while.' She blew out a long, slow breath. 'I haven't talked about this for ages . . .'

Suddenly Thorne felt terrible. He wanted to hug her, but instead volunteered to make another cup of coffee. They both stood up at the same time.

'Black or . . . ?'

'Listen, Tom, I've got to say this.' Thorne thought she was starting to sound a bit pissed. 'I don't know what you think about Jeremy, I don't know why you had to go and question him . . . I dread to think, actually, but whatever it is I wish you'd stop wasting your time. This is one of my oldest friends we're talking about, and I know he likes to play the hard-bitten, cynical doctor but it's just a party piece. I've heard it hundreds of times. He cares very much about his patients. He's very interested in Alison's progress . . .'

Alison. The one person they were supposed to talk about and hadn't.

'I meant to have a word with you about that,

actually. You know we're trying to keep some things out of the papers?'

Her face darkened. 'Am I about to get told off?' She wasn't remotely pissed.

'He seems to know a lot about the case and I just wondered if . . .'

She took a step towards him – not afraid of a fight. 'He knows a lot about the medical case, yes. We've spoken about Alison regularly and obviously he knows about the other attacks because that has a direct bearing on things.'

'Sorry, Anne, I didn't mean—'

'He's a colleague whose advice I value and whose discretion you can count on. I'd say take my word for it, but obviously there wouldn't be much point.'

She stared at him, his first reminder since that morning in the lecture theatre of just how scary she could look. Evidently he didn't have quite the same capacity to intimidate her. Something in his face, he had no idea what, suddenly seemed to amuse her and her expression softened.

'Well, what's it been? A few weeks? And we're already on to our second major row. It doesn't bode well, does it?'

Thorne smiled. This was highly encouraging. 'Well, I'd actually categorise the first one as more of a bollocking, if you want to be accurate.'

'Are you going to get that coffee or what?'

As he filled the mugs from the cafetière, she shouted through to him from the living room, 'I'll stick some music on. Classical? No, let me try and guess what you're into . . .'

Thorne added the milk and thought, never in a million years. He shouted back, 'Just put whatever you want on . . . I'm easy.' As he walked back in with the coffee, he almost laughed out loud as she turned round brandishing a well-worn and wonderfully vinyl copy of *Electric Ladyland*.

As the taxi – a black one, he wasn't going to make that mistake again – ferried him back towards Kentish Town, the evening's conversation rattled around in his head like coins in an envelope. He could remember every word of it.

Bishop had been laughing at him.

The cab drove down the Archway Road towards Suicide Bridge and he looked away as they passed Queens Wood. He pictured the fox moving swiftly and silently through the trees towards its earth. A rabbit still twitching in its jaws, trailing blood across leaves and fallen branches as the vixen carries its prey home. A litter of eager cubs tearing their supper to pieces – ripping away pale chunks of Helen Doyle's flesh while their mother stands frozen, watching for danger . . .

Thorne stared hard at shopfronts as they flashed past. Bed shop, bookshop, delicatessen, massage parlour. He shut his eyes. Sad, soggy men and cold, brittle women, together for a few minutes that both would try later to forget. Not a pleasant image but . . . a better one. For now.

He knew that Helen and Alison and the rest of it would be with him again in the morning, lurking inside his hangover, but for now he wanted to think about Anne. Their kiss on the doorstep had felt like the beginning of something and that, together with the reliably pleasant sensation of being moderately off his face, made him feel as good as he had in a long time.

He decided that, late as it was, he'd ring his dad when he got in. It was ridiculous. He was forty. But he wanted to tell him about this woman he'd met – this woman with a teenage daughter, for God's sake. Rachel had arrived back just as he was leaving. He'd said a swift hello before making a quick escape once the inevitable argument started about how late she'd got back.

He wanted to tell his dad that 'maybe', with a large dollop of 'perhaps' and a decent helping of 'forget it, never in a million years', one of them might not be spending quite so much time alone any more.

He added a two-pound tip to the six-pound fare and headed up the front path, grinning like an idiot. It was always a risky business for cabbies, wasn't it, picking up pissed punters? A healthy tip or vomit in the back of the cab? That was the gamble. Well, one had just got lucky.

Thorne was humming 'All Along The Watchtower' as he put the key in the lock, and was only vaguely aware of the dark figure that emerged from the shadows and ran up the path behind him. He turned just as an animalistic grunt escaped from the mouth behind the balaclava and the arm came down. He felt instantly sick as a bulb blew inside his head.

And suddenly it was much later.

The objects in his living room were at the bottom of a swimming-pool. The stereo, the armchair, the half-empty wine bottle shimmered and wobbled in front of him. He tried desperately to focus, to get a little balance, but all his worldly goods remained upside down and stubbornly unfamiliar. He looked up. The ceiling inched towards him. He summoned every ounce of strength to roll himself over, face down on the carpet and vomit. Then he slept.

A voice woke him. Hoarse and abrasive. *'You look rough, Tom. Come on, mate . . .'*

He raised his head and the room was full of people. Madeleine, Susan and Christine sat in a line on the sofa. Their legs were neatly crossed. Secretaries waiting for a job interview. Not one of them would look at him. To one side Helen Doyle stood staring at the floor and chewing nervously at a hangnail. Huddled into the single armchair were three young girls. Their hair was neatly brushed and their white nightdresses were crisply laundered. The smallest girl, about five years old, smiled at him but her elder sister pulled her fiercely to her breast like a mother. A hand reached towards him and dragged him to his knees.

His head pounded. His throat was caked in bile. He licked his lips and tasted the crusty vomit around his mouth.

'Up you come, Tom, there's a good lad. Now, eyes wide open. Nice and bright.'

He squinted at the figure leaning against the mantelpiece. Francis Calvert raised a hand in greeting. *'Hello, Detective Constable.'* The dirty blond hair, yellowed by cigarette smoke, was thinner now, but the smile was the same. Warm, welcoming and utterly terrifying. He had far too many teeth, all of them decayed. *'It's been ages, Tom. I'd ask how you were doing but I can see . . . Bit of a session, was it?'*

He tried to speak but his tongue was dead and heavy. It lay in his mouth like a rotting fish.

Calvert stepped towards him, flicking his cigarette towards the carpet and producing the gun in one horribly swift movement. Thorne looked frantically round at the girls on the armchair. They were gone.

At least he was to be spared that.

Knowing what would inevitably follow, he turned his attention back to Calvert, his head swinging round on his hunched shoulders with the ponderous weight of a wrecking ball. Calvert grinned at him, those rotten teeth bared as he clattered them theatrically against the barrel of the gun.

He tried to look away but his head was yanked upwards by the hair, forcing him to watch.

'*Ringside seat this time, Tom. All in glorious Technicolor. I hope that's not a new suit . . .*'

He tried to close his eyes but his eyelids were like tarpaulins, heavy with rain.

The explosion was deafening. He watched as the back of Calvert's head attached itself to the wall and began a slow, messy descent like some comical, slimy child's toy. He moved an arm to wipe away the hot tears that stung his cheeks. His hand came away red, the bits of brain between his fingers. As he slumped towards the floor he was vaguely aware of Helen moving across to join the others on the sofa and lead them in a round of polite but sincere applause.

It was like being horribly drunk and massively hung-over at the same time. He knew he mustn't drift off again. The faces were still jumping around in his head like pictures in a child's flick book, but the speed was decreasing. The equilibrium had almost returned but the pain was beyond belief.

He was alone, he was himself, and he was crawling across the puke-ridden carpet, inch by agonising inch. He had no idea what time it was. There was no light coming through the window. Late night or early morning.

His fingers grasped at the nylon fibres of the cheap shagpile. He took a deep breath. Gritting his teeth and failing to stifle a cry of agony, he willed his knees to shuffle another few inches across the vast and merciless eight feet of carpet that separated him from the telephone.

PART TWO

THE GAME

Not spoken to Anne for a couple of days. Not really spoken, I mean. Well, let's get this straight. Perhaps I'm making these conversations sound like bouts of non-stop banter, full of juicy gossip and cracking gags. Let's not be stupid. Basically she spills her guts and I just blink occasionally. Don't get me wrong, they're fucking dynamite blinks, but I don't think I'm chat-show material just yet.

She's probably spending every free moment she's got getting it from her tame copper and his trusty truncheon. There are so many jokes I could make about taking down her particulars and policeman's helmets but I am far too classy.

'Tits first, I'm not a slag.' That's me.

My head is full of corny jokes but, come on, what else have I got to do? I've got shitloads of time on my hands and I'm hardly up to my eyeballs, am I?

I can't even kill myself. Joke!

I hope she hasn't lost faith in me. Anne, I mean. I'm not exactly sending the doctors scurrying about with talk of medical miracles. I know that. There's days when I feel so together it's just like I've got pins and needles or something, and as soon as they wear off I can get up and get dressed and go and call Tim.

And there's other days.

I used to do this thing years ago when I'd lie in bed and try really hard to think of a new colour. One that didn't exist. Or a completely new sound that you've never heard before. I think I read about it in some wanky women's magazine thing about inner calm or some such crap. It's really weird. You start to get dizzy after a while and then feel a bit stoned. I feel like that quite a lot now. Or sometimes I'd lie on my back and stare for ages at the ceiling and try to convince myself that it was the floor. If you concentrate really hard you can actually do it and you start holding on to the sides of the bed in case you fall. It's like that in here, only all the time. And I can't hold on to the side of the fucking bed, can I?

I'm falling . . .

CHAPTER 7

Thorne would later classify the minor physical injury as the easiest of the ways in which he became a victim during the Backhand case. Not that he put himself anywhere near the top of the list. His life was not erased with the twist of a skilful finger or put on hold by the deadly and delicate touch of a hand on his neck. He never felt the sob catch in his throat as a sheet was lifted to reveal the expressionless face of a girlfriend or wife or daughter.

He saw them buried, but they were not his blood.

But still he suffered . . . losses. It was, of course his own doing, but he could only watch as, one by one, they fell away. This process, the honing down, the shedding of those around him was a long and painful journey for all concerned, but it began the moment Thorne opened his eyes and saw David Holland at his bedside, reading a copy of *FHM*. The first thing his brain told his mouth to do was swear, but all it could manage was a gulp and some half-hearted lip-smacking. He closed his eyes; he'd try again in a minute.

133

Holland was engrossed in a pictorial. The model, a quiz-show hostess, was gorgeous, but he reckoned that actually she wasn't that stupid. He couldn't help but be impressed by quotes like 'The main reason I had breast implants was that I wanted bigger tits.' He wondered what Sophie would look like with bigger tits. He flinched mentally at the tirade of abuse that would surely be heaped upon him were he ever to bring it up.

Hearing a noise he lowered the magazine. The Weeble was awake and trying to say something.

'Do you want a drink of water or . . . ?' Holland reached towards the jug on the bedside table, but Thorne was already closing his eyes.

Holland dropped the magazine and rummaged in a plastic bag beneath his chair. He produced a CD Walkman and, unsure exactly where to put it, placed it on the edge of Thorne's bed.

'I picked this up from your place after you were brought in. Thought you might be . . . you know . . . and I got this from Our Price . . .' He produced a compact disc and struggled manfully with the Cellophane wrapping. 'I know you're into that country-and-western or whatever. I don't know much about it as it goes – more of a Simply Red man myself. Anyway . . .'

Thorne opened his eyes again. Music. It was a nice thought but some sunglasses would have been better. Or a Bloody Mary. His vision was blurred. He squinted at the CD Holland was brandishing and tried to focus on the sleeve.

After a second or two he was able to make out the words *Kenny Rogers*. Before he had a chance to laugh he was asleep.

And Hendricks came. Filled him in on the details. Smacked over the head and drugged. Oh, and Spurs were already thinking about sacking their manager.

Then Keable. They'd got nothing from the flat. They'd fill him in when he was back on his feet. Oh, and the lads sent their best.

And finally Anne Coburn.

Thorne was perched on the edge of the bed putting on his shoes when the curtains were pulled aside. She was grinning. 'Fair enough – if I was in the Whittington I'd want to make a quick getaway.'

Thorne smiled for the first time since he'd last seen her. 'Why couldn't it have been the Royal Free, for Christ's sake? I could have done with a day or two with my feet up.'

Anne sat down next to him and gazed around the ward. 'This place isn't that bad, actually. It's just got a bit of a dodgy reputation.'

'I don't think people stick around long enough to find out. As soon as I saw the name on the blankets I started feeling much better.' He took what he hoped would be a final look around. Perhaps they *had* made an effort but there was something a bit desperate about it. The eastern-European eau-de-Nil on the walls had been replaced by a more optimistic orange, and there was even the odd pair of floral curtains, but it was still a hospital. He had spent the previous night failing to sleep through a cacophony of rattling trolleys, humming floor polishers and anonymous screeching. He would have felt only slightly less miserable in a private room with cable television, intravenous red wine and dancing girls.

Anne reached across towards his head. 'Can I?' Thorne lowered his head and she gently traced a finger along the stitches. 'They'd be happier if you stayed another night. I know you don't like hospitals but concussion is unpredictable . . . and when you've been shot full of Midazolam on top of it . . .'

'He wasn't very gentle about that either. I've got a bruise the size of a cricket ball on my arse. He could have tried the champagne – I might have gone for it, state I was in.'

'Perhaps you're not his type.' The filthy laugh . . .

Thorne finished tying his laces and stared straight ahead. 'Oh, he'll find out exactly what type I am.'

Anne looked away briefly at nothing in particular. She was starting to get a pretty good idea herself. 'He gave you a big dose, Tom. It can't have been . . . pleasant.'

'It wasn't.'

'It might sound strange but that's exactly why we use it. Midazolam fries your short-term memory and detaches you from reality. You go into a dream state. We can stitch up a ten-year-old while they stare at a blank wall and look at the lovely pictures.'

'Mine weren't particularly lovely.' He turned to look at her and tried his best to smile. 'How's Jeremy?'

She tried to look stern, but couldn't manage it. 'He's fine. He seemed rather concerned when I told him what had happened, considering that you two didn't really seem to hit it off.'

'He got home all right, then?'

She stared at him. He knew he was pushing it. He was being stupid and *she* was anything but. 'I mean, if he was half as pissed as I was, he might have had trouble.' The chuckle was forced and he knew she could see it. There was only one other way to go. He reached across and took her hand. 'I don't suppose we did hit it off, but the two of you *were* involved at one time.'

'It was twenty-five years ago.'

'Still, I'm hardly likely to invite him down the pub, am I?'

She squeezed his hand and smiled. They said nothing. Not telling the truth wasn't the same as lying and he *would* be jealous of Bishop if he didn't feel something a whole lot stronger. Better that she thought it was jealousy. Much better.

Thorne blinked slowly and held his breath. The smell . . . and creaking mattresses, and squeaky shoes, and the uncomfortable smile on the faces of people at bedsides. Was it the same smile he'd given his mother all those times he'd sat by her bed and squeezed her hand and looked into her milky blue eyes and tried to figure out where the fuck she'd gone?

'Tom . . .'

The curtains moved again and Dave Holland appeared. Thorne let go of Anne's hand. 'My taxi's here . . .'

Anne stood up and moved towards the curtain. Before she turned, Thorne saw her smile at Holland and put her hand on his arm. What the hell was that about? *Look after the poor old bugger?*

'Give me a ring, Tom.'

She left and Thorne stared hard at Holland. He looked for the smirk but didn't see it. He couldn't see a notebook either. His vision obviously wasn't back to normal yet.

As they walked towards the car Thorne could feel the chill in the air. August had finally thrown in the towel and now there would be bad weather coming. He preferred it that way if he was honest. He was happier in an overcoat. A security blanket that covered a multitude of sins. The warm night when he'd stepped out of that taxi, pissed and singing, seemed a long way away. If it hadn't been for the wine he'd guzzled while he and Anne had flirted and talked about Jimi Hendrix and failed marriages, he knew that the whole, hideous thing would be over by now. He might even have been what's laughably called a hero. If he hadn't been pissed he might have seen it coming. He might have turned round a second earlier and he'd have had him. He might, at the very least, have avoided the blow. But the man in the balaclava with the iron bar and the needle had had a distinct advantage, of course.

He'd known Thorne was pissed, hadn't he?

Holland held the car door open but Thorne didn't resent it. They pulled out on to Highgate Hill.

'Have you got any food in? I had a quick look and I couldn't see much.'

'Are you inviting yourself round for a meal, Holland?'

'Do you want to stop somewhere? There's a Budgens on the way, isn't there?'

'You can get me a sandwich when we get to the office.'

'Sir?'

Holland looked across at Thorne whose head lay against the car window, his eyes half shut. He'd been wrong about the Weeble. He looked distinctly wobbly.

'There's not much happening at the moment, to be honest. The DCI said it would be best if—'

'Office.'

Holland put his foot down.

He'd stood at a bus stop and watched as Thorne and the young DC had climbed into the car and driven away. Thorne had been in hospital less than thirty-six hours. He was impressed.

So, now what?

Things would pick up a bit, wouldn't they? Thorne would be on the warpath for sure. They'd all have taken it personally, he knew that. That was the copper's way. Once you involve one of their own, watch out! Like a piss-poor bunch of Masonic East-Enders. Thorne wasn't one of their own, though, was he? He'd hate that idea. He was getting to know the man, little by little, but he knew that for sure. He just needed to get him riled up a little, that was all.

The bus came, and he stood back and watched as people with no place to go hopped on and off, all of them pale and in pain. He turned away in disgust and started to walk down towards the underground station at Archway.

They'd probably see what he'd done to Thorne as a warning. Let them. Thorne would know it was something . . . other than that. He'd know a challenge when he saw one. When he felt one. He'd been personally involved since the first time he'd laid those big brown eyes on Alison. The sentimental idiot had felt sorry for her, hadn't he? He couldn't see beyond the machines. He couldn't smell the freedom. And he really cared about the dead ones. Oh, he really minded about those.

All in all it had worked out quite well and the business with Anne was a lovely bonus.

He stopped to look through the window of a bathroom shop. Mock antique mixer taps and other such shit. Baths with seats in and handles for the old and infirm.

Stupid.

He thought about Thorne's tiny flat. There was the home of a lonely man for sure. No, not a home. Neat and tidy, though, he'd give him that – apart from the empty wine bottles. He knew he'd have the edge on him that night on the doorstep. If Thorne had been sober he wouldn't have fancied his chances.

It was starting to get cold. He pulled down his hat and moved towards the entrance to the tube. Now he wanted some progress. He'd shaken things up for sure and they had to have come up with something. And let the profilers or whatever those over-qualified ponces called themselves, talk about a 'cry for help' or a 'desire to be stopped', if that's what paid their mortgages. Not that Thorne would have any time for psychobabble, he was pretty sure of that. And now that he knew what it felt like, now he knew how those women had felt before he'd laid hands on them, he'd be committed.

He'd known kids like Thorne at school. They just needed to be provoked and there'd be no containing them. Mad kids who would throw a desk out of the window or kill squirrels in the playground if you pushed them a bit – if you punched the right buttons. Thorne was no different. And now he'd kicked him in the shins. He'd rabbit-punched him. Now Thorne wouldn't stop.

A tall skinny woman with a pushchair beat him to the ticket machine. He stared at the back of her slender neck as she fumbled for change in her cheap plastic purse and stared at the station names as if they were printed in Chinese. Single mother, probably. The poor cow wrung out and desperate for a little comfort. Forty fags a day and a couple of Valium to numb the pain and get her through the afternoons.

He thought about any woman he saw now. He considered them all. He could see what each of them needed. Every one was . . . feasible.

'Good to have you back, Tom.'

Tughan's thin lips arranged themselves into what might pass as a smile. Thorne thought he looked like a gargoyle. Holland made himself scarce and Thorne settled into a chair opposite his fellow DI. The comments of other officers were acknowledged with a nod and a light-hearted comment, and some of the smiles were undoubtedly sincere, but there were other faces he was less pleased to see again.

'How's the head, Tommy? Now you know how it feels, mate . . .'

His calendar girls.

Yes, he knew what it felt like to have the power over your own body taken away. He'd been out of control so many times that it was almost familiar, but *that* loss went hand in hand with a warm, sleepy feeling that the booze threw in for good measure. The wine came with a little something special to ease the pain of smashed furniture or grazed knuckles. But the drug had taken him to places he never wanted to see again.

'He took away everything we had, Tommy . . .'

'I wanted to struggle . . .'

'We all did . . .'

'. . . to fight for my life, Tommy.'

Tughan's mouth was moving but the sound was coming from a long way away.

Christine. Susan. Madeleine. And Helen. Drugged into oblivion and confronted by a monster. He'd confronted nothing but ghosts. The memories of ghosts. He thought about Alison. He needed to see her. He was still around and he wanted her to know that. He was still around only because that had been what the fucker wanted. He'd realised that straight away and hated the fucker for having the power to spare him. He'd chosen to give him his life.

He had made a mistake.

'He should have killed me.'

'Don't say that, Tommy. Who would we have left to talk to?'

'Tom? Are you feeling all right? You shouldn't have come in.'

Thorne turned his eyes from the wall. He stood up and walked around the desk, catching Holland's eye as he put his hand on Nick Tughan's shoulder. 'Not caught him yet, then, Nick?'

Tughan laughed. Nails on a blackboard. 'I'll leave that to you, Tom. You're the one with the instincts, aren't you?' Thorne stiffened. 'The one

143

with experience.' He spoke the word as if he were naming a child molester. 'We're just getting on with the job, following leads. One or two of them yours, as a matter of fact.'

'Tom . . .'

Keable was speaking from the doorway of his office. Thorne looked up and he retreated, the invitation to join him unmistakable.

'I'll catch up with you later, Nick. Why don't you e-mail me what you've got?'

Thorne walked across to Keable's office. He could hear Holland and one of the other DCs laughing as he went. Business as usual. But not for him.

Anne wanted to talk to Alison. Her workload meant that it was becoming increasingly difficult to spend a significant amount of time with her every day and they had stuff to catch up on.

He joined her a second or two after she stepped into the lift.

'David.'

'On the way up to see your locked-in case, I suppose. Any developments?'

'Do you care?'

He pressed the button and the doors started to close. There really wasn't a great deal to look at as a tactic to avoid what was sure to be an unpleasant encounter. She wondered instead if it was possible to escape from a lift using a trap-door in the roof as she had seen people do so often in films.

'I was sorry to hear about the attack on your policeman friend.'

They'd certainly done it in *The Towering Inferno*.

'Just after your cosy dinner *à trois* with Jeremy, wasn't it?'

And Hannibal Lecter did it in *Silence of the Lambs*. Just after he'd cut that man's face off. Hmm.

'Anne?'

'Yes, it was, and no, you're not sorry, you're just a twat.'

The lift reached the second floor and Anne stepped out the moment the doors opened. Higgins stood preventing them from closing. 'Hanging around with police officers is obviously doing marvels for your vocabulary, Anne.'

'You're awfully well informed about what I'm up to, David. Using our daughter as a spy is rather pathetic, though.'

'Oh, I thought you two had no secrets?'

Not usually, but maybe it was time that changed. She'd need to talk to Rachel. He was now wearing that hideous smirk she remembered him reserving for tiny triumphs or the expectation of dutiful sex. She smiled at him, feeling nothing but pity.

'Why are you here, David?'

'Just because we're divorcing doesn't mean that I'm not interested in your life. I am.'

She stepped towards him. Did she see him actually flinch? 'There was an *Oprah* or a *Ricki*

Lake recently about divorcing couples, did you catch it? This woman said that it was only when she was divorcing Duane or Marlon or who-ever, that she realised how much she loved him. It's weird, because all it's making me realise is how much I wanted to divorce you in the first place.'

The smirk had gone and she could see that the quiff was beginning to wilt slightly, but she could still feel the sharp tingle of the slap in a parked car, and picture the look in his eye after he'd spat at her in an Italian restaurant. Now he tried hard to look world-weary, but just looked old.

'You've become bitter, Anne.'

'And your hair is utterly ridiculous. I'm busy, David.'

The lift doors moved to close again, and Higgins was finding it hard to retain his balance. 'Aren't you at all interested in my life, Anne? What I'm doing?'

He was getting rusty – dollying up the ball like that. She couldn't wait to smash it home. 'OK, David. Are you still fucking that radio-therapist?'

She heard the doors closing as she walked away up the corridor. She knew that he'd never be certain if she'd heard his pathetic parting 'Give my love to Jeremy,' but it didn't matter either way.

She couldn't wait to tell Alison.

★　　★　　★

146

'Sit down, Tom.'

Thorne moved to take the uncomfortable brown plastic seat so generously offered. 'Fuck, this sounds a bit serious. Am I going to get a bollocking for being whacked over the head and pumped full of shit?'

'Why are you here, Tom? Do you think we can't manage without you?'

'No, sir.'

'Stop pissing about, Tom.' Keable passed a hand across his face. He was probably trying to appear thoughtful, thought Thorne, or maybe he was just tired. All he had succeeded in doing was roughing up his voluminous eyebrows and making himself look like a bald wolfman. Keable puffed out his cheeks. 'Do you feel rough?'

'What are these leads that Tughan's talking about?'

'There was a note, Tom.'

Thorne was out of his chair in a second. 'At the flat? Show me . . .'

Keable opened a drawer and produced a dog-eared photocopied sheet of A4. He handed it to Thorne. 'The original's still at Lambeth.'

Thorne nodded. The Forensic Science Services Laboratory. 'Waste of time . . .'

'I know.'

Thorne sat down and read. Typed as before. The same smug familiarity in every sentence. The same enjoyment and belief in a unique and wonderfully detached sense of humour. The same sickening self-love . . .

147

TOM. I'M NOT A VIOLENT MAN. (HE PAUSES
FOR HOLLOW LAUGHTER AND TO LET THE DETEC-
TIVE INSPECTOR TOUCH HIS SORE HEAD.) DID
YOU NEED STITCHES? I'M SORRY. I HOPE
THE HEEBIE-JEEBIES WEREN'T TOO INTENSE.
BOOZE AND BENZOS AREN'T THE MOST HARMO-
NIOUS OF BEDFELLOWS. SADLY DIDN'T STAY
TO WATCH. I SIMPLY WANTED YOU TO FEEL
SOMETHING OF WHAT IT'S LIKE TO SURRENDER
YOURSELF. I KNOW IT WASN'T A SURRENDER IN
THE TRUEST SENSE OF THE WORD BUT WHO'S GOT
TIME TO BE PEDANTIC? YOU'VE GOT MURDERERS
TO CATCH AFTER ALL. A LITTLE PAIN WAS
NECESSARY TO BRING YOU UP TO SPEED. AND
THE GIRLS FELT NOTHING. REMEMBER THAT. I
MUST APOLOGISE FOR HELEN BUT SHE REALLY
DIDN'T WANT TO LIVE. ALISON WAS THE ONLY
ONE WITH ENOUGH FIGHT TO MAKE IT. WHAT
WAS THAT OLD ADVERTISEMENT 'IT'S THE FISH
JOHN WEST REJECTS . . .' THAT'S RATHER PAT
BUT I'M SURE YOU'LL GET MY POINT. I KNOW
YOU'RE ANGRY, TOM, BUT DON'T LET IT EAT
YOU UP. USE YOUR ANGER GOOD AS I HAVE AND
THERE'S NOTHING YOU CAN'T ACHIEVE. THERE,
I HAVE THROWN DOWN A GAUNTLET . . . OR AT
THE VERY LEAST A SURGICAL GLOVE!!
SPEAK SOON.
P.S. I HAVE A PERFECTLY HEALTHY SEX DRIVE
AND I WASN'T LOCKED IN A CELLAR AS A SMALL
CHILD, SO DON'T WASTE VALUABLE MONEY OR
RESOURCES ON CHARLATANS.

Thorne felt sick. He took a deep breath and slid the piece of paper back across the desk. Frank Keable raised his head and Thorne looked him straight in the eye. 'It's Bishop.'

Keable put the note into a drawer and slammed it shut. 'No, Tom, it isn't.'

Thorne couldn't look at him. His gaze drifted away to the green metal wastepaper bin, the cheap black plastic hatstand and expensive Barbour jacket. It floated across the dirty yellow walls and settled gratefully on the calendar. September. A particularly uninteresting view of Exmoor in the mist. A two-dimensional and probably long-dead stag the most animated thing in the room.

'So how did you and Dr Bishop enjoy dinner?'

Thorne was irritated that they'd put it together so quickly. He rather felt that he'd had his thunder stolen. He nodded, impressed. And curious.

'There was a message from Dr Coburn on your machine. She hoped you enjoyed your evening. We called her.'

'Right.'

'Did you, by the way? Enjoy your evening?'

'Yes.'

'Was the spaghetti good?'

'How the fuck . . . ?'

'You threw up all over your carpet, Tom. Spaghetti, and a fair amount of red wine . . .'

Thorne sensed that he might have only the one chance and he needed to perform better than he had last time. A matey tone was best. Conspiratorial. Us against him.

'He's a slimy piece of shit, Frank. He left before I did and waited.'

'He predicted your every move, then? He toddled off with the note he'd already prepared, tucked in his pocket, did he? And an iron bar and a syringe hidden inside his overcoat?'

Thorne was thinking quickly. Did Bishop have a bag with him? Had he seen a briefcase in Anne's hall? He couldn't remember. He was pretty sure Bishop had come by car anyway.

'He would have left the stuff in his car.' Standing his ground.

'Come on, Tom . . .'

Thorne stood up a little too quickly. He felt dizzy and casually reached out a hand to steady himself. He looked. Keable had seen it. It didn't matter. 'Surely he's worth looking at, Frank.'

'Yes, and Tughan's done it. We're not completely stupid. There's nothing there.'

'Tughan hates the idea because it's mine . . .'

'Nick Tughan's a professional . . .'

'Bollocks.'

Thorne was trying hard to sound controlled but he knew that by now the rest of the team would be eavesdropping without much difficulty.

Keable raised a hand. 'Go steady now, Detective Inspector.'

'Sir.' Thorne met Keable's eye. He pushed himself away from the wall and lowered his voice.

'I know what you think and I'm well aware of a certain reputation that I may have . . .'

'Let's not get into that, Tom.'

Thorne stared hard at him, breathing heavily. 'No, let's.'

Keable wouldn't hold the stare. 'There's no evidence, Tom.'

'Dr Jeremy Bishop has to be considered a major suspect. He worked at the hospital from which the Midazolam was stolen. He now works at the hospital where Alison Willetts was taken after she'd been attacked. I think he took her there after he'd attacked her to try, unsuccessfully, to give himself an alibi. He has no alibi for any of the murders and he fits the general description of the man seen talking to Helen Doyle on the night she was killed.' He'd said his piece.

Keable cleared his throat. He was going to say his. 'Bishop was involved with Dr Coburn, wasn't he?'

'Some years ago I believe . . . yes.'

'Are you?'

They couldn't confuse what he thought about Bishop with his feelings for Anne, could they? It was necessary to let Anne think that Bishop got to him on that level but Keable would see beyond that surely . . .

'Tughan isn't the only professional . . . sir.'

'Let's talk sensibly, Tom. Everybody agrees we're looking for a doctor.'

'But?'

'The Leicester connection is a red herring due to the date of the theft, if, in fact, the drug stolen was that used on the victims in the first place. Your reasoning as far as the Willetts alibi goes seems to me fanciful at best, and what he was or wasn't doing when the first three victims were killed is irrelevant.'

'What?'

'You know the game, Tom. The CPS isn't even going to look at the first three if we make an arrest. It was all pieced together too long after the event. We've got to go for Willetts and Doyle if we want to secure a conviction. We don't even have an accurate time of death for the first three victims.'

'When he decided it was time, Tommy. That was when.'

'Bishop was on call every one of those nights. He's only on call one night a week, it's a hell of a fucking coincidence.' He was almost whispering. 'I know it's him, Frank.'

'Listen to yourself, Tom. This isn't police work, this is . . . obsession.'

Thorne was suddenly very hot. Here it was, then. Calvert. His mark of Cain. Keable was going to pick away the scab.

'I'm sorry, but you were the one who talked about reputations. I'm not interested in reputations, but I wouldn't be doing my job if I wasn't aware of . . . recurring patterns.'

'You're talking like I'm a basket case. How many murderers have I put away in the last fifteen years?'

'You were right fifteen years ago. I know that.'

'And I've paid for it ever since. You've got no idea.'

'You've been right lots of times since then, but it doesn't mean you're always right.'

A minute or so earlier he'd felt like a fight. He'd wanted to get into it, but now he was suddenly exhausted, beyond it. 'Most of those times I was lucky. I could just as easily have fucked it up. I didn't always "know". But I knew fifteen years ago. And I know now.'

Keable shook his head, slowly, sadly. 'There's nothing there, Tom.' Then, an afterthought: an attempt to damp down the flames a little. He waved towards the main operations room. 'And you know full well that half the men in that office fit the general description.'

Thorne said nothing. Jesus, Exmoor looked bleak. Even the majestic stag looked deeply pissed off about the whole thing. Thorne saw himself walking into the mist, a tiny, distant figure leaving this shit behind him and disappearing. He felt the curtain of fog closing behind him, clammy on his shoulders as he marched across the damp, mossy ground with the voices of the girls echoing far behind him. He knew they'd be the only ones who would care about where he'd gone.

'Now, sit down, Tom, and let's talk about the things we can do. The reconstruction's already been shot. It's going out in a couple of days.'

'Let Tughan do it.'

Thorne was walking quickly towards the door. He'd lost Keable. He didn't care. He opened the door then turned back to the DCI. '*If*, you said.' Thorne shook his head. Keable stared at him. '*If* we make an arrest. Not *when*! You really are an inspiration to us all, Frank.'

'DI Thorne—' Keable was on his feet, shouting, but Thorne was already half-way across the operations room. Those with the imagination picked up conversations where they hadn't left off and those that couldn't be bothered stared at their shoes. As Thorne passed him, Tughan looked up, smiling, from his computer screen. 'I don't know what you're getting so worked up about, Tom. He's a doctor not a lecturer.'

Thorne kept moving. He would make the bastard pay for that one day, but now was definitely not the time.

Holland stood in the corner brandishing a sandwich and watching his boss stride towards him without looking left or right.

'Sir?'

'Right, Detective Constable Holland,' said Thorne. 'Now you can take me home.'

Rachel Higgins lay on her bed, listening to her mother moving about in the bathroom. She had the sound turned down on the TV but every so often she glanced at the screen and tried to figure out exactly what was happening plotwise. It was a trashy late-night Channel 5 skinflick so it wasn't difficult. She heard the toilet flush. Mum was on her way to bed.

She reached over for her Walkman and swept her long brown hair behind her ears before putting on the headphones. The Manic Street Preachers would take her mind off the fight with her mother. It was so stupid the whole thing. It had started with the usual argument about the bloody resits. So what if her grades for IT and chemistry were not what they'd been expecting? She wasn't doing any science subjects in the sixth form anyway. They'd knocked that around for a while and got on each other's nerves and then she'd started on about her 'privacy'. Her right to have a life! Jesus Christ . . .

Maybe she and her mum should stop pretending they were mates in that wanky *Ab Fab* middle-class way. If that was what her mother wanted, that suited her just fine. She'd only been talking to her dad, for fuck's sake. It wasn't like she'd been told not to.

On TV a flabby sound engineer was trying to get some session-singer's bra off. Or maybe he was her manager. He was ugly and she had saggy old tits.

She quite liked the copper, actually, and didn't give a toss if her mum wanted to shag his brains out, but now all of a sudden her mum was moving the goalposts. Certain things were 'her business' and she was allowed to have a private life.

It was obvious that the flabby bloke wasn't going to get his dick out. She picked up the remote, flicked off the TV and lay there in the dark trying not to cry.

The volume on her Walkman was turned up as high as it would go. The noise would send her to sleep eventually and the row would be forgotten in the morning.

It didn't really matter anyway. Her mum could have her secrets if she wanted.

Rachel had plenty of her own.

It sounds as if Anne gave that tit of a husband as good as she got by the lift. She's definitely well shot of him. I wish I could tell her to stop pissing about and make a move on that chunky copper. They've done dinner, now she should go for it, no question. Especially now some nutter's smacked him over the head. Get 'em while their resistance is low. Give him one while he's still dizzy!

I've always been good at getting people together. It was me who got Paul to go and chat Carol up. I wonder if they're back from their honeymoon yet. Presumably not or they'd have been in.

We had a really good laugh, actually, me and Anne. Well, she had a good laugh and I just thought about laughing. It's fucking freaky to tell you the honest truth. When I'm half out of it, which is most of the time (did I mention that the drugs in here are fantastic?) I imagine that all the nurses are actually inside me instead of outside in the real world. I try and pretend that they're like these little munchkins running about inside my body and doing all the things that my brain tells them to do. Sweet little mobile body parts. Nursey to open my eyes. Nursey to wipe away the sweat. Nursey to scratch an itchy tit (well, once I've mastered telling them it's itchy). Remember the Numskulls in that old comic? A funny bunch of dwarfs that lived inside this bloke's head. I think 'hungry' and this little thing in a blue uniform with a stiff cap and an upside-down watch comes and sticks something yummy in my feeding tube. I think 'piss' and, Bob's your uncle, the next little slave empties my catheter. Well, fuck it, you've got to get through the day.

That's another thing. I've got no bloody idea what time of day it is. Anne makes a point of telling me but ten minutes after she's gone I'm confused again. There's a lot of dizziness as well ('No change there, then,' the girls at the nursery would say). I wonder how all the kids are doing? Some of them will have moved up into the next room. A new lot for Daniel to start biting. I really miss them.

I wonder if I could still get pregnant?

CHAPTER 8

Hendricks had arrived laden down with cheap lager and by nine fifteen the pair of them were having trouble staying awake. The reconstruction would be shown in ten minutes. Hendricks, who was far too opinionated for his own good, ranted all the way through the news, while Thorne worked his way quietly through another can of beer and wondered why he hadn't called Anne Coburn.

Of course, he knew full well why he hadn't called her. The real question was how much longer he could maintain the pretence of integrity. Of actually having any.

His resolve was crumbling, can by can.

The most formal of contact, the most banal conversation would, he knew, be tainted by what he wasn't telling her. What he was choosing carefully and deliberately not to tell her. Of course, he was right on a procedural level not to involve her, he knew that. Well done him. But he wanted to see her. He wanted to tell her all sorts of things.

So . . . options.

He could continue to see her and simply not talk

about the case. Or about Alison. Or about how he felt every hour of the day . . . but he really wouldn't be giving very much of himself in return for what he needed from her, would he? Or he could tell her the truth. If, however, he confided in her that he thought her oldest friend was a multiple murderer then the relationship might well get off to an iffy start. If he told her that her medical-school chum – and former lover, let's not forget that – was a sociopathic killer then she was hardly going to see him as a prime candidate for getting into her pants, was she?

From the sofa Hendricks let out a long, contented belch. There was nothing like alcohol for bringing out the northern bloke in the southern professional. Or the testosterone-fuelled lad in the tired old man.

And now he'd have to deal with this . . .

It was not a programme he usually watched. He couldn't deny that it often provided useful leads and bumped up the arrest rates. At work they called it *Grass Up Your Neighbour* and it was truly astonishing how many people were only too pleased to do just that. It was the reconstructions that bothered him, and the grainy CCTV footage. He couldn't help but find the whole concept vaguely hilarious. It was usually about the time the orange-coloured presenter talked about 'anything that's jogged your memory' that Thorne stopped paying attention. The city, after all, was chock-a-block with members of the public happily toddling about having completely forgotten that they'd been caught in the middle of a vicious armed robbery a fortnight earlier. That sort of thing can easily slip your mind . . .

They always saved the reconstructions for the really nasty ones. He knew it was down to the tight budgets in both policing and television but there was still something so . . . last gasp about it all. There was a mawkishness to the whole process which made him uncomfortable. Every 'Sleep well', each 'Don't have nightmares' seemed desperately forced. One minute they'd be showing you your neighbour being battered, raped, murdered, and the next they were reassuring you that crimes such as this were 'extremely rare'. The false security of wonderfully malleable crime figures.

Sleep well, if you're a statistician.

Despite the taste, sensitivity and sombre tones it was still television. It was still, at bottom, entertainment or, at its very best, journalism, and it niggled him.

He thought about those police photographers getting Helen Doyle into focus.

'Here we go . . .' Hendricks sat up and grabbed the remote. The presenter and the specially selected media friendly officers outlined the menu of mayhem on offer for the next forty minutes. Backhand was up first. After a photogenic female DI had looked into the camera and assured him that attacks by complete strangers were very, very rare, Thorne was taken inside the Marlborough Arms.

He watched a young actress sitting with a group of girls, laughing. He watched her go to the bar and buy a round of drinks as the voiceover informed the viewer exactly who she was and what she was doing there and hinted darkly at what was about to happen to her. He watched as the young actress picked up her coat and walked towards the door with several other girls.

And he saw Helen Doyle step out on to the Holloway Road, say goodbye to her friends and stroll away to meet the man who would murder her. He saw the colour reappear in her face and the leaves fall from her hair. Beneath her blouse and skirt he knew that the scar from Hendricks's Y-shaped incision had faded and that her young skin was smooth again and smelling of talcum powder. His throat tightened as the blood pumped around the pallid, crumpled legs that carried Helen Doyle down past Whittington Park towards a house where her parents were waiting for her.

Now Helen is laughing and talking to a man and swigging from a bottle of champagne. The man is tall with greying hair. He is in his mid-thirties. Could he be a little older? Now Helen is starting to get a little wobbly. She all but falls into a dark-coloured car, which moves away to an unknown location where its driver will quietly, and with great skill, rob Helen Doyle and all those that love her of everything she is.

Then there was Nick Tughan at his most user-friendly. Thorne couldn't deny that he came across well. The jacket and tie were sober. That lilting voice sounded good, no question. The appeal for information was simple and heartfelt. Make a difference and come forward. For Helen. For Helen's family. The operations-room number was given out, and it was on to a series of armed robberies in the West Midlands. Thorne closed his eyes.

'*What d'you reckon, Tommy?*'

'*We'll have to wait and see what the calls bring in.*'

'*No . . . I mean . . . was I pretty, Tommy? Tell me. Did I look all right?*'

'*Yes, love. You were gorgeous.*'

'Tughan's got a touch of the Wogan about him, if you ask me.'

'I didn't. And you're pissed. Now, much as I hate to sully my expensive Scandinavian sofabed with Gooner scum such as yourself, you're welcome to stay.'

Hendricks was already clambering to his feet and reaching for his leather jacket. A half-empty can of lager was kicked across the room in the process.

'Sorry . . .'

'Clumsy bastard. Try and make it to the tube in one piece, will you?'

Hendricks waved and pulled a face as he walked past the front window. Thorne mopped up the spilt lager with kitchen towel, stuck on a George Jones CD and settled back in his chair. He was glad

Hendricks had gone. He wanted to sit on his own and wait for Holland's call.

Anne turned off the television and moved around the room, switching off the lamps. Thorne had told her about the champagne, about how the killer had drugged that poor girl. And Alison. Seeing it acted out in the places where it had happened had been chilling. Somehow she felt a connection with Helen Doyle, and through her she suddenly felt connected to Alison in a different way. She knew that she was being fanciful, dramatic even, but she knew she wanted to give Alison her life back for more than just professional reasons. She wanted the man who had attacked her and who had killed those other girls to have failed. She wanted to be the reason he failed.

She stood in the darkened living room and wondered why Thorne hadn't been on the programme. Perhaps he hadn't fully recovered yet. He'd seemed on the mend when she'd seen him in hospital, but maybe he shouldn't have checked himself out so quickly. He was pig-headed, but perhaps he was soft-headed as well. She thought about calling him, but she knew it would be a long call. She needed to get some sleep.

Brushing her teeth, she thought about David and pictured him being knocked over by the lift doors. The image made it easy for her to check her laughter lines in the mirror as she rubbed in night cream. She turned off the bathroom light and saw

Tom Thorne in the shadows, sitting on the edge of the bed in the hospital ward and staring across the room, a million miles away.

She'd call him tomorrow at work and suggest a drink.

As she went into her bedroom she heard the muffled chirp of the mobile from Rachel's room next door. She heard her daughter mumble a hello before pushing her door firmly shut. Anne was annoyed, but didn't want to challenge her about it. Not so soon after that stupid argument. All the same, she had to be up early for school in the morning.

It was a ridiculous time for her friends to be calling.

Holland called just after eleven thirty. Caller ID told Thorne that he was using his mobile. 'A lot of people saw her walking down the main road. One bloke rang up to tell us that she was singing when she walked past him.'

She'd been happy walking home. Was that a good thing?

'What was she singing?'

'Sir?'

'I can't remember, Tommy. Robbie Williams, maybe . . .'

'What about the killer?'

'Well, obviously there were fewer witnesses once she'd turned off the Holloway Road, but we've had a couple come forward. Nothing really new on a description. Three people rang to say that they thought the car might be a Volvo . . . Can you hear me?'

'Has Keable gone home yet?'

'Yeah, he left a couple of hours ago. Sir?'

Thorne grunted. Was it too late to ring?

'One other thing. We think the killer might have called.'

Thorne had thought it was possible, but it still took the breath out of him. 'Who took the call?'

'Janet Noble. We had the usual load of nutters, but she said this bloke sounded pretty convincing. She was a bit upset, to tell you the truth.'

'Go on.'

'A deepish voice, well spoken . . .'

Thorne knew what he sounded like. 'What did he say?'

'He said he was better-looking than the actor, that Helen Doyle was a lot plainer and that it was a far better brand of champagne.'

Of course. He'd care about details like that.

'And he asked where you were.'

'What did Noble tell him?'

'She said you'd been taken ill, sir.'

Thorne knew how well that would have gone down. If he'd believed it.

'Thanks, Holland, I'll catch up with you tomorrow . . .'

'Goodnight, then, sir . . .'

'. . . and thanks for that CD by the way. I never got a chance to . . .'

'That's all right. Is it any good?'

He felt a twinge of guilt. Kenny Rogers' *Greatest Hits* lay in a box at the bottom of his wardrobe along with a collection of battered paperback books and a self-assembly bathroom cabinet that had got the better of him. He was planning to take it to the charity shop at the weekend.

'Is that it on in the background? Sir?'

Dave Holland clipped his phone to his belt, said goodbye to the officers still taking calls and waited for the lift. He'd known this sort of thing might happen, especially with Thorne, but none of it was making his life any easier. He wasn't sure exactly what was going on, but you would have had to be stupid not to see that lines were being drawn. He knew what Sophie would tell him to do. Keeping your head down hadn't done the likes of Keable or Tughan any harm over the years, had it?

Or his father.

No harm. Just a nice little pension and some stories and not an ounce of anything like satisfaction in thirty-five years. He'd spoken proudly about 'keeping his nose clean' right up until the day he'd keeled over, stone dead at sixty.

Tom Thorne had never kept his head down in his life. Perhaps he was just . . . losing it. He'd been on the beer when Holland had called, no question about it.

As the ambulance had taken him away from his flat four days earlier, delirious, and Holland had

167

done his best to clear up, he realised that Thorne didn't consider himself better than anyone else. Not Keable or Tughan or ex-Detective Sergeant Brian Holland, four years dead. He was just a different sort of copper. A different sort of man. Maybe the sort of man whose approval meant something. If Holland could get that and still play it safe, then maybe that would be the way to go.

He took out his phone again. If Sophie was still up he'd grab them a curry on the way home. He let it ring four times and hung up. Finally the lift arrived and he stepped inside, knowing deep down that, in the coming days and weeks, playing it safe would not really be an option.

'Frank?'

'What is it, Tom?'

'Bishop drives a Volvo.'

'Right . . .'

'A dark blue Volvo sedan. I didn't put it in my initial report but there was one parked outside his house.'

'It's in Nick Tughan's report.'

'Tughan knew?'

'I told you, he's already looked into all that.'

'All that!'

'Can we talk about this in the morning?'

'And the calls tonight don't make a difference?'

'It's one more thing in the plus column, but there are still too many minuses.'

'You've spent too long talking to Tughan . . .'

'Goodnight, Thorne . . .'

'I'm making a formal request to be taken off this case, sir.'

'We'll definitely talk about this in the morning . . .'

'Anne? It's Tom Thorne. Sorry, did I . . . ?'

'Hello?'

'I'll call you tomorrow.'

'It's OK – funny, I was angry about Rachel being on the phone a minute ago. Is it a minute ago? I must have gone out like a light.'

'Rachel's on the phone? I'm—'

'On her mobile. Hate the whole idea of it, really, but . . .'

'It's a safety thing.'

'Hmm.'

'I was just wondering about Alison, really . . . and obviously how are you?'

'Alison's . . . hang on, let's get sat up. That's better . . . Alison's making progress, slowly. I don't want to bring the occupational therapist back just yet, but things are moving. And I'm fine . . . thanks.'

'I'd like to see her. To see how she's getting on. You said about her communicating more.'

'She is, but it's just not . . . reliable, I suppose. I'm putting together a system, which will probably be a complete disaster but anyway . . . How's the head?'

'So, what do you think? Can I come in and see you?'

'Her or me? You said—'

'Sorry?'

'Both of us . . . yep. What about Friday?'

'Fine.'

'I'm up to my eyes in it at the minute.'

'I know . . . That's great. I'm sorry for ringing so late. I've had . . . just . . .'

'A couple of drinks?'

'I've had all sorts of things.'

'Sounds interesting.'

'Not really. I'll let you get back to sleep . . .'

Past midnight. Sitting in an uncomfortable chair with an unpronounceable Swedish name and rearranging his life. Or screwing it up completely. Why did he only ever feel like he was achieving anything if he was pissing someone else off? He was the loudmouth in the pub quiz shouting at the questionmaster until he's proved wrong. He was the irate driver effing and blinding until the other driver points to the sign showing who has right of way. He was the stupid copper who couldn't conceive of being wrong. The idiot whose feelings were written all over his face. That face sent messages. It whispered, 'You're making a mistake.' It murmured, 'I'm right.' It screamed, 'I *know*.' It had got backs up for as long as he could remember. It had alienated colleagues and wound up superior officers.

It had told Francis Calvert to kill children.

There was one can of beer left. He put his favourite track from the George Jones album back on and turned it up. Jones's duet with Elvis Costello . . .

'There's a stranger in the house no one will ever see . . . but everybody says he looks like me.'

He'd have to play it carefully with Keable. However much he discredited Thorne's theories about Jeremy Bishop, Keable knew that the killer and Thorne had a connection. That first note had been written before Thorne had even met Bishop. There was a link. The killer wanted Thorne close. So, whatever Thorne did, he knew that Keable would be watching. The truth was that Thorne didn't really know *what* he was going to do and, more disturbingly, he had no idea what Bishop was going to do either. How would he react to Thorne leaving the case? Would he be . . . insulted? Would he do something to demand the attention he thought he deserved?

Thorne tried not to think about those things that might make him bitterly regret what he had chosen to do. He told himself that he'd been given very little choice. They wouldn't listen. Worse, they were judging him. Putting it down to Calvert. Fifteen years, and still he was tainted, any instinct called an obsession. Every observation, every thought weighed up and judged and found wanting.

He couldn't bear that judgement any longer. He didn't need the judgement of the living.

He was being judged every day by the dead.

He needed to be outside an operation that was stifling him. He had to get out and make things happen. While he dicked about following leads and smiling the right smiles, Jeremy Bishop was making a fool of him.

It was time to turn things round.

He had to go to bed. The following morning was not going to be pleasant and he'd need to be as sharp as he could be. But he still needed to make one more call. He got up and went to the mantelpiece for his address book. He couldn't remember the numbers of many pornographers offhand.

I'm glad Anne's spending more time with me again. I'd sort of started thinking that she'd moved on a bit, that the novelty had maybe worn off. I wouldn't have blamed her, but I can't believe she's got many like me. She told me her workload had built up and that the administrator was an arsehole, so fair enough. Mind you, if I don't start making some progress I might find myself out on my ear. Somebody's bound to need the bed.

We've pretty much got 'yes' and 'no' sussed, and 'in pain' is one of my specialities but blink-ing is hardly Esperanto. One for yes and two for no is all very well in theory but it's the control that's letting me down. And the gaps between the blinks are all over the shop. I try to blink twice but it's hard for Anne to know if I'm saying 'no' or saying 'yes, yes'. There's a lot of 'Is that a yes, Alison? No? Is that a no, then?' We're like a pair of comical foreigners on *Benny Hill*. This chicken is rubbery! Dad used to piss himself at that. Mum was never much for comedy shows, but he loved it. Maybe the old sod just fancied the women in bikinis. I caught Mum watching one of the videos a couple of weeks after my dad died. She must have got it out of the video shop. I was doing my NVQs, I think, and I came back from college early one day. She was sitting there watching this sad old fat bloke chasing these dolly-birds round and round a garden and crying her eyes out.

Tim had better buck up his sodding ideas as well. He just sits there holding my hand. I know he can't come much in the daytime because of work but he should make more of an effort in the evenings. I don't know anything. He doesn't tell me. What's happening on *Brookside*? Is he still playing football on Sundays? Has he put that shower curtain up yet? If Dad was here he'd kick him up the arse.

He's stupid, really, because the weight's dropping off me and if everything else is knackered then there's every chance I might actually have stopped ageing! I'll be walking out of here a slim and sexy shadow of my former self. There's one very tasty male nurse. Probably gay, but fit as fuck. If Tim's not careful I might have to start looking elsewhere.

CHAPTER 9

When he woke up he was still angry. The previous night's amateur dramatics had been hugely disappointing. And where the hell was Thorne? At least it confirmed what he'd suspected for a while – that the rigorous, high-priority investigation had got precisely nowhere. Perhaps they'd have the car by now, or a slightly better description, but it was still painfully slow. There wasn't even a sniff of the number plate. It was stolen, of course, but come on! It was nearly a fortnight since he'd given them Helen's body to play with and they were still begging for the help of the general public.

Useless wankers.

Thorne. Nowhere to be seen when he should have been grabbing his bit of televisual glory. He hadn't believed for a second that Thorne had still been recovering. No, there was something afoot among the jolly coppers for sure. This was unforeseen but easily dealt with. If all that his thuggish theatrics and beautifully arch little note had done was cause the boys in blue to have some sort of queeny tantrum, then he'd just have to find another way to chivvy them along, wouldn't he?

It was about time anyway. Maniacs were supposed to speed up as the frenzy took hold, weren't they? They'd expect nothing less. He'd considered livening things up a little. Perhaps a gay man or an old person next time. No . . . that would be bound to confuse them and he didn't want them confused. All things considered, he was ready for another bash. Keen as mustard to try, try, try again.

He'd tried kicking Thorne in the shins. It was time to aim for the heart.

Thorne looked around the pub. Businessmen in shirtsleeves using a basket of scampi or a microwaved chilli con carne as an excuse to sink a couple of pints at lunchtime. It was probably as good a place as any. Informants didn't like to meet too close to home and as it was, of all the people upstairs in the Lamb and Flag, Thorne looked the most likely villain. He was comfortable with that. He knew he looked . . . useful. It hadn't done him any harm by and large, though he would've liked to be taller.

A surly Australian barman emptied the ashtray Thorne wasn't using. 'Are you eating, mate? We need the table.'

Thorne opened his wallet. 'I'll have another mineral water.' He made sure his identification was visible. With a tut the barman wiped the table and went to fetch Thorne's drink.

The Perrier was the one thing slightly at odds

with the image he knew he was presenting, but the booze was, as yet, strictly confined to Little IKEA. Besides, he could do with getting straight back to work afterwards. He didn't think rolling in bladdered on his first day would go down too well.

The meeting with Frank Keable the day before hadn't been as prickly as he'd expected. Keable had wanted him to stay on the investigation, but for none of the right reasons. He talked about the integrity of the case, whatever that was, and how he could ill afford to lose an officer with Thorne's outstanding record. As far as the notes and the attack on Thorne, which Keable assured him was being viewed as an attempted murder, were concerned, Keable was predictably vague. He was adamant that this facet of the case would be monitored closely, but Thorne could sense a real fear on Keable's part that, were he to leave, Keable himself might become the object of the killer's bizarre attention.

Thorne knew that this was never going to happen.

The simple truth was that, if Thorne left, Keable was terrified of the press getting hold of it and understandably he did not relish explaining to the detective superintendent why one of his senior officers was jumping ship. Thorne had told him to put it down to a clash with Tughan. Or him. Anything he liked.

Keable asked him to reconsider. Thorne had

looked into the bored brown eyes of the Exmoor stag and stood his ground.

By lunchtime he'd been transferred back to the Serious Crime Group (West) out of Hendon, effective from nine o'clock the following morning.

He hoped things were a little clearer than when he'd left.

The Met was in a serious state of flux. Not only was it now under the direct auspices of the GLA and Mayor Livingstone, it was also undergoing major operational restructuring. NHS red tape was impressive, but it didn't even come close.

The old area system had gone. Five areas of London (NW, NE, SW, SE and Central), each with its own Major Incident Team (AMIT), which had in turn replaced the Area Major Incident Pools (AMIPs) and all now superseded by three Serious Crime Groups (East, West, South) encompassing all existing OCUs as well as the old Organised Crime Department, the Fraud Squad and the Firearms Unit.

The result? Hundreds of officers without a clue what was happening. Or indeed, why. The official line was that the new SCGs were supposed to be more proactive. The Met would no longer sit back and wait for crime to happen.

It was a good theory.

But you couldn't anticipate the likes of Jeremy Bishop.

As the DI on Team 3 out of Beck House in Hendon, Thorne had landed on his feet. He'd worked with DCI Russell Brigstocke for six months at Serious Crime and he knew that, barring anything major going down, Brigstocke wouldn't kick up a fuss should Thorne be unavailable from time to time.

Like since nine o'clock that morning.

'Kodak!'

If Thorne looked useful, the man in his early forties nodding and strolling over to join him was positively indispensable. Six feet four and built like a barn, with bleached blond hair, a nose-ring and, today, a bright yellow puffa jacket. But it wasn't all good news. Dennis Bethell's voice could start a fight at a hundred yards. It was a spilt pint waiting to happen.

'Can I get you one, Mr Thorne?'

Thorne always smiled the first time he heard the incongruous, high-pitched squeak. Whoever was responsible for these things had screwed up big-time or else had a great sense of humour. Somewhere there was an extremely irate cartoon mouse who sounded like Frank Bruno.

He pointed to his water. 'No, I'm fine.'

Bethell nodded for about ten seconds.

Thorne emptied his glass as the barman finally brought over a new one and took the money. Bethell, if anything, was even bigger than the last time he'd seen him.

'Steroids give you cancer, you know, Kodak.'

'Bollocks,' squeaked Bethell. 'They make you infertile. Anyway, this all right for you, Mr Thorne?

179

I know it's a bit busy, but coming up West is handy for me. I do a lot of business round here.'

'Course you do, Kodak . . .'

As porno merchants went, Dennis Bethell was among the least unpleasant. For twenty years Thorne had monitored his career with interest. He was purveyor of everything from soft-focus glamour snaps for car magazines to the more brightly lit and clinical stuff for those publications a little harder to reach. In the eighties his top-quality cumshot work had been much in demand, and his occasional foray into blackmail had caused the abrupt termination of at least one prominent political career. Dennis was old school. In an age where hard-core videos were a tenner and any mug punter with a PC could watch dwarfs doing it with donkeys at the drop of a hat, or the click of a mouse, he was still a firm believer in the power, the truth, of the single still photograph. Deep down, Thorne admired the filthy piece of pondlife.

'This boozer used to be the Bucket of Blood you know.'

Thorne did know. Two hundred and fifty years earlier this had been a brawler's pub. Whores and cut-throats doing business and slicing each other up for pennies while Hogarth sat in the corner jotting it all down and doing sketches. Thorne looked around him. He couldn't help but wonder if he might not have felt a little more at home.

'Business going well, then, is it?'

Bethell was lighting a Silk Cut. 'Oh, not too shabby. I've got a website, you know . . .'

'You're shattering all my illusions.'

'You've got to move with the times, haven't you? Have you seen the stuff that's out there?'

Thorne had. Plenty of it. 'And you think the stuff you do is any different?'

'I don't do anything with kids, Mr Thorne, you know that. I won't be doing with that filth. Besides, my stuff's a bit more exclusive, I reckon. It's harder to get hold of.'

'Yeah. You've got to stand on tiptoe in the newsagent.'

Bethell looked uncomfortable. Stubbed out the fag long before it was finished. Lit another. 'Can we get this over with, Mr Thorne?'

'Of course. I'm sorry to have kept you.'

'Listen, Mr Thorne, I don't really hear a great deal these days. I've been getting this webcam thing off the ground and apart from that it's just the usual stuff with the models. I don't hang around as much as I did . . .'

The barman returned with Thorne's change. From the table behind him Thorne could hear muffled sniggering. He really hoped it wasn't aimed at the big man sitting opposite him.

Bethell mistook Thorne's silence for disappointment.

'There's a bit of drugs business I could put your way. These young girls are dropping Es and putting

Charlie up their beaks like there's no tomorrow. They don't want to eat, see . . .'

More sniggering, and this time Bethell heard it too. Thorne turned round. Four media types. Short hair, square glasses and training shoes that probably cost more than his suit. They wouldn't look at him. He turned back round, lowering his voice as a cue for Bethell to do the same.

'I don't need information, Kodak.'

'Right.'

'I wish to avail myself of your high-quality professional services, which you will provide in return for me not sending Vice to go trampling through your darkroom.'

Bethell thought for a moment or three. 'You want me to take some photos?'

'Simple black and white portrait from as close as you can get. The subject will be unaware that he is being photographed.' Bethell was hardly inconspicuous, but Throne knew that the man had a great deal of experience in maintaining a low profile. In a parallel universe he might have been a highly paid *paparazzo*.

'No sweat, Mr Thorne, I've got this blinding new three hundred mil Nikon zoom.'

Thorne leaned in close. 'Listen, Bethell, this is a piece of piss, all right? A simple head shot. Coming out of his house, getting into his car, it doesn't matter. Should be simple for you. No beds. No animals. No drugged-up teenage girls.'

He thought about Helen Doyle, sitting in the pub, laughing.

'I never did anything like that, Tommy. Strictly a Bacardi Breezer girl . . .'

He gave Bethell the address and finished his drink while the photographer enthused a little more about lenses before lumbering off towards the gents'. As he went, Bethell gave the quartet on the table behind them a good hard look.

Thorne felt pretty sure that Bethell would do a decent job for him. It wasn't just because he'd make his life hell if he didn't, he could sense that the man would take pride in the work. Not for the first time Thorne thought about how much better he functioned with professional criminals. It was a game he was good at. Even the really nasty bastards he had squared up against in his eighteen months on the Flying Squad weren't hard to figure out. Some he caught and some he didn't, but he never had to waste his time wondering why they were doing it. Money, usually. Sex, occasionally. Because they couldn't be arsed doing anything else, often. But the rules of the game were simple: stop them doing it and let somebody else work out why afterwards.

Bishop and those like him were not playing by the same rules. Thorne knew that if he was going to catch Jeremy Bishop he'd have precious little help. He knew that he had to take things carefully, a step at a time. Bethell was the first step, but after that he'd be making it up as he went along. Whatever this new game was, Bishop had a distinct advantage. Thorne was certain that the 'why' was important. The 'why' was probably crucial. But this was where he was up against it.

Thorne didn't give a shit about 'why'.

When Bethell arrived back at the table Thorne stood up and started putting on his coat. 'Are we sorted, then?'

Bethell picked up his cigarettes. 'Yeah. No point me asking how soon you want these photos, is there?'

'Not really, no.'

The laughter from behind them told Thorne that he really should get out, straight away. Bethell was already taking a step towards them.

'Something funny?'

The biggest of the four stood up and stared at Bethell through designer glasses. It was not an aggressive move so much as a reflexive one, but it didn't really matter to Bethell. The thick finger he prodded into the man's chest must have felt like a battering ram. 'Something about how highly I speak of you, was it? Go on, tell me.' Square Glasses moved to swat away the finger; Short Hair moved to protect his friend and it went off.

As Bethell swung a fist bristling with signet rings into Square Glasses' face, Thorne stepped forward and backhanded his friend across the mouth. He fell backwards across the table, the expensive training shoes sending bottles and glasses flying in all directions. It was now two on two and all

184

over very quickly. The third man reached for a large metal ashtray but Thorne was on him in a second, bringing his forehead down across the bridge of the man's nose as casually as if he were bending to tie a shoelace.

It was only as the fourth man backed away in such a hurry as to knock a plate of vividly orange chicken tikka massala into a young woman's lap, that the screaming began in earnest. As the Australian barman hovered nervously, a fearsome-looking landlady with vanilla-coloured hair and a broken pool cue marched from behind the bar. 'Right. Call the police.'

The barman pointed an accusing finger at Thorne. 'They're already here.'

Thorne rubbed his forehead and looked around. Three men lying, kneeling, crawling across a wooden floor glittering with broken glass, blood splashing on to designer combat trousers, the horrified yet excited faces of two dozen onlookers . . .

He guessed that it was not the right time to mention to the landlady that Hogarth would probably have approved.

Ten minutes later Thorne and Bethell were on the pavement outside the Garrick Club. The landlady had taken a bit of mollifying and those with smashed teeth and shattered noses were predictably aggrieved until Thorne dropped the word 'cocaine' into the conversation and everything was hastily forgiven and forgotten.

Bethell placed an unwelcome hand on Thorne's

shoulder. 'Thanks for that, Mr Thorne. Laying into those wankers, that was good of you.'

Thorne could feel the headache starting to kick in. 'I didn't do it for you.'

He stuck out an arm to hail a cab.

And it wasn't them I was laying into . . .

They waited for Alison's boyfriend to leave before they wheeled in the blackboard. Bishop thought that Anne was being a trifle over-sensitive. After all, she'd kept him well appraised of Alison's progress, hadn't she? He'd hardly be expecting her to sit up and start singing.

Anne just wanted to wait a little before she got Tim involved. If all went well then she'd want to bring him in. He'd need to work with Alison himself anyway. She just needed to know that the basic frame-work was right. Once they were up and running it would be second nature to all of them. She felt that not understanding exactly what her responses signified would give him a skewed idea of Alison's condition.

If he wasn't thinking it already, he would be sure he'd lost her.

The wheels squeaked as the orderly moved the blackboard into position at the foot of the bed. Optimistic as she was, Anne could sense the enormity of the task that lay ahead of her. Alison was twenty-four. This was her first day at kindergarten.

'I wonder what my patients would think if I suggested anaesthetising them with a lump hammer?'

Bishop sipped his coffee and stared at the blackboard.

Anne said nothing. It was hardly state of the art, but at this stage it was adequate. She took off her coat and put on her glasses. She picked up the remote control hooked over the head of the bed and pressed a button. With a deep, resonant hum, the bed began to move and Alison was raised up until she was virtually sitting.

'Alison, I've got Dr Bishop with me this afternoon. You might remember him. He treated you the night you were brought in.' She turned to look at Bishop. He was studying the lines of letters, drawn in chalk.

Anne moved up to the top of the bed and took Alison's hand. 'Right, let's see if we can speed things up a bit. Can you see the black-board, Alison?'

Alison's right eyelid crinkled immediately. She half shut the eye then opened it. Then, five seconds later, a blink. Anne squeezed her hand.

'Good. A to Z in two lines and I've listed a few other things along the bottom. Later on we can increase the list as I get better at this but for now just the basics. "Tired", "in pain", "hungry", "thirsty", "nauseous". You'll have to bear with me, I'm afraid, until we get used to the speed of your responses. I know it'll be frustrating at first, but I think it's going to be worth it. OK, Alison?'

The vein on Alison's forehead was standing out. Ten seconds. A blink.

Anne moved round to the other side of the bed

and closed the blind. 'Right, let's just make things as comfortable as possible for you. Can you get the lights, Jeremy?'

Bishop moved to the door and turned out the lights. The room was in semi-darkness. From her pocket Anne produced what looked like a large fountain pen as she moved to the blackboard.

'Right, Alison, this is a laser pointer. It should make it easier to define the letters for you and it makes me feel a little bit less like I'm giving a military briefing. Let's just start at the bottom, make sure you're feeling all right.' She moved the laser pointer until the dot of light lay directly below 'in pain'. 'Don't bother with no if you're not. Just yes if any of them apply.'

Slowly she moved the pointer along the bottom row of words, highlighting each one for nearly a minute. As she waited Anne looked intently at Alison. She could hear the drone of the traffic outside. There was no reaction. She glanced across at Bishop. He nodded.

'Right, let's have a crack at this, shall we?' She began to move the pointer. Bishop removed a small pad from his top pocket and sat holding a pencil, waiting. Anne held the pointer under each letter for nearly a minute but after the first five or six she began to speed up a little. P . . . Q . . . R . . . S.

A blink.

Anne wanted to cheer. 'S. OK . . .'

She reached the end of the alphabet without any further reaction.

Bishop cleared his throat. 'It's a shame there aren't more words in alphabetical order, Jimmy.'

Anne turned to face him, the light from the pointer passing across his chest like the laser dot on a sniper's rifle. He was busily scribbling. 'Almost . . .'

'Almost what?' She could feel herself starting to get snappy.

'*Almost* is one. A word where the letters occur in alphabetical order. And *billowy*. *Aegilops* is actually the longest, which, amazingly enough, is an ulcer in part of the eye, though I can't see her bringing that up.' He smiled. 'Back to the beginning, I think.'

Anne felt stupid for not having considered this. Perhaps there was a more efficient way of laying out the letters. She'd have to work on it later. A second pass added H, O and R.

Anne tried to help. 'Short? Alison . . . short?'

Alison blinked. Anne waited. Alison blinked again. Back to the beginning.

On the third pass Alison blinked as the laser pointer reached M. Anne looked across at Bishop, who was scribbling in his notebook. He stood up, smiling, and moved towards the bed. 'I think she's being a bit over-eager. She's blinking in advance of some of the letters in case she misses them.'

Anne looked at him. There was a hint of impatience when she spoke. 'And?'

'If the S is a T and we go one letter on from the M . . .'

Anne thought for a moment, worked it out,

and blushed. Bishop smiled mischievously at her. 'She's asking how our friend the detective inspector is. If I were you I'd add a question mark to the board.' He was standing at the head of the bed. He looked down at Alison. 'And you might want to draw a smiley face on there somewhere as well. There's a definite twinkle in that eye.'

Anne picked up a piece of chalk, a little irritated. Perhaps she shouldn't have asked Jeremy to come along. She'd wanted a colleague who was also a friend to back her up and he'd been only too glad to help, but fond as she was of him, he could be awfully smug. She began to write on the blackboard. 'I'm glad all that time doing *The Times* crossword hasn't been wasted, Jeremy . . .'

Bishop wasn't listening. He was leaning down, his face close to Alison's. 'Do you remember me, Alison?'

A blink.

'From when you were admitted?'

Nothing. Then, a blink.

Bishop nodded. His voice was low and eminently soothing. 'That's good. Now what about before, Alison? Can you remember anything from before?'

A blink.

Anne turned back from the board.

Another one.

Bishop walked back towards Anne, shaking his head. He held out the notepad to her with a grin. Around the single word *THORNE* he'd drawn a heart with an arrow through it. Anne snatched it from him with part-mock, part-genuine annoyance and moved to open the curtains.

'Mr Thorne is very well, thank you, Alison. I'm frankly disturbed that my private life is of such immediate concern to you.' She walked to the bed and looked down. Alison's eyes were still locked on the blackboard. 'Not that I should expect a great deal else from a shameless Geordie hussy with a one-track mind!' She put her hand gently on the girl's shoulder. Her smile was huge and just for Alison.

She turned to look at Bishop, who was staring at the blackboard and smiling at something. She felt sorry for being irritated with him. 'Do you want to pop over for something to eat later?'

He answered without turning round. 'Sorry, Jimmy, I have a date.'

She moved to join him, her eyes wide at the prospect of intrigue. 'Sounds mysterious?'

'Not really.'

'Suit yourself. I'll get it out of you later, though, you know I will. What's so funny anyway?'

Bishop was snorting as he stared at the letters on the blackboard. Anne stared at him, still smiling. 'What?'

'Remember that night in your flat twenty-odd years ago?'

'No . . .'

'Raising the dead, me, you and David. And that girl from Leeds, what was her name?'

'Oh, God, that was freaky.'

'No, it wasn't. David was moving the glass.'

Anne pretended to shudder but felt a genuine chill at the memory. She turned to include Alison, pointing at the blackboard. 'He thinks this looks like a Ouija board.'

The smile on Bishop's face died a little, as he muttered to himself, 'Might just as well be.'

Thorne picked up the Backhand contact list from the kitchen table and walked through to the living room to call Dave Holland. *The Bill* was on with the sound turned down. As good a situation comedy as ITV would ever have.

'Hello . . .'

Holland's girlfriend. Christ, what was her name?

'Oh, hi, is that Sophie?'

'Who's this?'

'Oh, sorry, it's Tom Thorne, I work with Dave. Is he around?'

He heard the distortion in sound as she put her hand over the phone. He couldn't make out what she was saying. As Holland came to the phone he could hear the television being turned down.

'Holland, it's DI Thorne . . .' Best not to be too matey. 'I hope I'm not keeping you from your homework.'

'Sorry, sir?'

'*The Bill* – I heard it in the background. It's not real, you know.'

Holland laughed. 'Yeah, but that one they all take the piss out of is an awful lot like DI Tughan.'

The joke told Thorne a great deal. Holland knew the way things stood. As it happened, Thorne also knew which character he was talking about – he was spot on. He had seriously underestimated this young man. 'Listen, obviously you know I'm back at Hendon now, but I'd still be interested in any developments on the case. Who's come in, by the way?'

'Roger Brewer. Scottish bloke – seems nice enough.'

Thorne hadn't heard of him. Probably just as well. 'So, you know, anything comes up . . .'

'I'll let you know straight away, sir.'

'Anything and everything, Holland . . . please.'

Rachel looked at her watch. He was only five minutes late but she didn't want to miss the trailers. She thought about the nutter who'd sat behind her on the bus from Muswell Hill and decided she'd get a cab back. She checked her purse. If she paid for her own ticket she'd need to ask him to lend her the money. Mum would be happier with a taxi anyway, although she'd wonder why Claire's dad hadn't given her a lift. He usually did after she'd been round there for the evening. Maybe she could say his car was in the garage. But she might see him driving around. Or talk to Claire's mother on the phone. She decided it was probably easier to ask the cab to stop somewhere away from the house. Too many lies weren't a good idea. She wasn't very good at it and she didn't like lying to her mum anyway. She'd just have to pray her mum didn't run into Claire in the next few days.

She was starting to get cold. She did up another button on her denim jacket and stared at the corner of the street, willing him to appear.

She wasn't really lying about him, after all. She just wasn't telling. There'd only be a row and it would be a damn sight bigger than the one they'd had the other night.

These fucking resits that she didn't want to take were the problem. It was so unfair that the time when you started to get serious with people was the same time you had so-called important exams.

Were the two of them serious? It felt like it. They hadn't slept together yet, but not because she hadn't wanted to. It was him. He didn't seem in any hurry. He was obviously waiting for the right time. He was being nice and sensitive because he'd obviously already done it and she hadn't, and he didn't want her to feel like he was putting her under any pressure if she didn't want to . . .

Rachel knew that this would be the big thing with her mother. His experience. The thing that would send her mum ballistic . . .

Her hand flew to her hair as she saw him coming round the corner. He waved and started to jog towards her. He was really fit. In good condition. Claire would be so jealous. But Mum would not be impressed at all.

Not with him being so much older.

A blackboard! For fuck's sake. Anne brought in a brochure one day with these computers that they were developing in America that you can work with your eyelid or something. They can virtually tell what you're thinking, like something in a film. I've got a mobile phone which predicts what letters you're going to type in when you're sending somebody a text message. Bloody useful, actually, when your spelling is as bad as mine. That cost £29.99 as far as I can remember. And I get a poxy blackboard. Everyone goes on about the cuts in the NHS but this is really taking the piss, isn't it?

And there I was thinking that maybe they might be able to fix up some system so I could read or watch the telly. Nothing too fancy, just a few mirrors and stuff so that I wouldn't have to lie here all day staring at the piece of plaster that's about to fall off the manky grey ceiling up there. Well, there's no chance of that, I suppose. All these machines are probably on their last legs as well. The big one on the left is definitely making a few dodgy noises. I hope they give the nurses enough change to feed the meter. I wouldn't want to pop off in the middle of the night because somebody didn't have a fifty-pence piece.

I know this isn't Anne's fault and I know that you only ever think about these things when you're on the receiving end of it and everything. But still . . .

I was pretty chuffed with myself actually, when it came down to all the alphabet business. We just need to sort out a system so I can tell Anne to go back instead of forward. Otherwise it's sodding interminable. I'm sure she'll work it out.

That doctor she had with her was a right clever sod, mind you, working out that I'd blinked too early. I just had to go for it. If I'd waited and then not been able to blink in time and missed the letter I really wanted, the whole thing would have been cocked up. I'd've ended up spelling out the Czechoslovakian for chemist or something.

I suppose I should be grateful to that doctor if he was the one who sorted me out when I first came in. I do remember his face looking down at me. I remember him telling me to wake up, but I just drifted away. Before that I can only remember bits and pieces. Bits and pieces of a voice. Not the words. Not yet.

Just the sound. Smooth and gentle like Dr Bishop.

And there I was, worried that my mobile phone was going to give me cancer . . .

CHAPTER 10

Thorne got off the train at Clapham Junction. He came out of the station, checked his *A–Z* and began to walk up Lavender Hill. The house was only ten minutes' walk away. He was knackered after five. Carrying the briefcase didn't help.

Not that there was anything in it.

He'd spent precisely an hour at Beck House that morning, not listening as Brigstocke brought him up to speed on a caseload of assorted rapes and robberies-with-menace. He'd picked up the address of a security guard who needed questioning and headed straight for Hendon Central station. He'd have to find time to fit in the interview before he went to Queen Square. Well, he'd see a bit of London today anyway.

He didn't know this part of the city very well but you'd've had to be blind not to see that it was affluent. Wine bars on every corner, delicatessens, restaurants and, of course, more estate agents than you could shake a shitty stick at. Out of curiosity he stopped briefly to peer into a window. An oily-looking article with bad skin and a widow's peak smiled at him from behind a computer terminal. Thorne looked away and took in a few of the details on a revolving display in the window. Kentish Town wasn't cheap but he could have bought a big two-bedroom place with a garden there for the price of a toilet cubicle in leafy Battersea.

His breath back, he started plodding on up the hill. He was already panting again when his phone rang. The squeak was unmistakable. 'Bethell here, Mr Thorne.'

'I know. Are they ready?'

'Oh . . . you recognised my voice, eh?' Bethell laughed.

Thorne had to hold the phone away from his ear. Half the dogs in the area were probably rushing towards him already.

'How did it go, Kodak?'

'Could have gone better, as it goes . . .'

Fucking idiot. He should have brought a camera and done it himself.

'Listen, Bethell . . .'

'Don't worry, Mr Thorne, I got the photos. Good ones too. He was standing on his door-step pissing about with a hanging basket. What's this bloke do anyway? Some sort of business-man, is he?'

'Why could it have gone better?' Bethell said nothing. 'It could have gone better, you said.'

He could hear Bethell take a long drag on a cigarette.

'Yeah, nothing that I couldn't handle, but after he'd gone back inside this other bloke pulls up outside and when he gets out of his car he looks around and, I don't know, maybe the sun was glinting off the lens or something but he saw me anyway.'

'What was he like?'

'I don't know – tall, in his early twenties, I suppose. Bit of a student type, I reckon – you know, a bit grungy.'

The son. Popping round to borrow a few quid, if what Anne had said was true.

'What did he say?'

'You're breaking up, Mr Thorne . . .'

'What did he say?'

'Oh, you know, he asked me what I was doing. I told him I was composing a portfolio of common urban birdlife and I just stared at him until he pissed off. No sweat. Got a picture or two of him as he buggered off, actually.'

Thorne smiled. He'd sent the right man for the job.

'So when can I have them?'

'Well, they're just drying at the minute. Couple of hours?'

That would work out perfectly.

'Right. Bucket of Blood about one-ish.'

'Is that a good idea?'

Bethell was right. Thorne doubted his welcome would be a warm one.

'Outside, then. Try not to talk to anybody.'

'I'll be there, Mr Thorne.'

'Kodak, you're better than Boots.'

He'd rung the Royal London to check and found out that Bishop's night on call was still Tuesday. He wasn't due in until lunchtime. With a bit of luck Thorne would catch him at home. He certainly looked well rested when he came to the door wearing an expensive-looking lemon sweater and a winning smile.

'Oh . . . Detective Inspector. Should I have known you were coming?'

Thorne could see him looking over his shoulder, searching for a colleague or a car.

'No, sir, this is purely an on-spec sort of thing. Bloody cheeky, if I'm honest.'

'How's the head?' Bishop was relaxed, his hands in his pockets. They were going to have a cosy chat on the doorstep. Fine.

'Much better, thanks. Good job I'm hard-headed.'

Bishop leaned back against the front door. Thorne could see through to the kitchen, but there was still no invitation to come in.

'Yes, I rather got that impression that night round at Jimmy's. Thoroughly enjoyed myself by the way and I hope you didn't mind my being somewhat spiky.'

'Don't be silly.'

'I can't help myself sometimes. I do love a little verbal sparring.'

'As long as you keep it verbal, sir.'

Bishop laughed. He didn't have a filling in his mouth.

Thorne shifted the briefcase to the other hand. 'I had a good time too, which is sort of why I thought I could be a bit pushy and ask you an enormous favour.' Bishop looked at him, waiting. 'I've been to see somebody just round the corner from you, on a totally different case coincidentally, and my constable needed to rush off because his girlfriend's had some sort of accident . . .'

'Nothing serious?'

'I don't think so, trapped her hand in a door or something, but anyway I'm a bit stranded. I've got another interview to do and I'm running late, and as you were only round the corner and seeing as we've already had dinner together . . .'

Bishop stepped forward past Thorne, bent down and began to pull the brown leaves from a large pot on the driveway. 'Ask away.'

'Could I ponce a lift to the station?'

Bishop looked up and stared at him for a few seconds. Thorne could sense that he saw through the lie and was looking to see if it was there in his face. He'd be amazed if it wasn't. Thorne broke the stare and turned his attention to the dying flowers. 'They look as if they were probably lovely a few weeks ago.'

'I'm going to plant evergreens next year I think. Dwarf conifers and Ivies. This is such a lot of work for something that dies so quickly.' He crumpled the dead leaves into his hand and stood up. 'I'm actually going into town. Is that any good to you?'

'Yes. Fantastic. Thanks a lot.'

'I've just got to grab my keys and stuff. Come in for a minute.'

Thorne followed Bishop into the house and stood waiting in the hall. Bishop shouted to him from the kitchen, 'There was a photographer hanging about round here yesterday. Bloody nuisance. I wondered if you knew anything about it.'

So the son had obviously come straight inside and told him about Bethell lurking in the undergrowth or wherever he'd been hiding himself.

'Probably the press just sniffing around. They've been getting worked up since the Helen Doyle reconstruction. Did you see that?'

'No.' Had Thorne detected the hint of a pause before he'd answered? 'I didn't know they'd made any connection to the attack on Alison Willetts.'

They hadn't.

'No, but somebody may have leaked a list of people we'd interviewed or something. These things happen, unfortunately. I'll look into it if you like.'

Bishop came striding up the hall pulling on a sports jacket. He grabbed his keys from the hall table. 'I wouldn't like to see myself splashed across the front page of the *Sun*.' He opened the front door and ushered Thorne out. 'Mind you,' he shut the door behind him and put a hand on

Thorne's shoulder as they walked towards the car, 'a discreet photo on page three of the *Daily Telegraph* is a different matter. Might impress a few young nurses.'

Bishop climbed into the car and Thorne walked round towards the passenger side. He stopped behind the car and held up the briefcase. 'Can I chuck this in the boot?' He saw Bishop glance into his rear-view mirror and smiled as he heard the clunk of the boot being opened from the inside.

As the Volvo cruised along the Albert Embankment, Bishop slid a CD into the player. The sound system was certainly a step up from the tinny rattlebox in Thorne's Mondeo. Some people probably thought country music sounded better that way. Bishop glanced across at him. 'Not a classical man?'

'Not really. This is fine, though. What is it?'

'Mahler. *Kindertotenlieder*.'

Thorne waited for the translation – which, amazingly, didn't come. The car was immaculately clean. It still smelt new. When they stopped at lights, Bishop drummed on the wooden gear lever, his wedding ring clicking against the walnut.

'You've known Anne a long time, then?'

'God, for ever. We were pushing beds around the streets together when we were undergraduates. Me and Anne, Sarah and David.' He laughed. 'I'm sure that's why hospitals are so short of beds. They all get pushed into rivers by high-spirited students.'

'She told me about your wife. I'm sorry.'

Bishop nodded, checking his wing mirror although there was nobody behind them.

'I can't believe the time has gone so quickly, to be honest. Ten years ago next month, actually.'

'I lost my mother eighteen months ago.'

Bishop nodded. 'But it wasn't your fault, was it?'

Thorne clenched his teeth. 'I'm sorry?'

'The crash was my fault, you see. I was pissed.'

Anne hadn't mentioned that. Thorne stared at him.

'Don't worry, Inspector, I wasn't driving, there's no case to reopen. But Sarah was tired, and she was driving because I'd had one too many. I have to live with that, I'm afraid.'

You must live with a lot of things.

'It must have been hard bringing up two kids, though? They can't have been very old.'

'Rebecca was sixteen and James was fourteen and, no, it was a bloody nightmare actually. Thank God I was already doing quite well by then.' He stepped on the brakes sharply as the car in front decided against jumping a red light. Thorne jolted back in his seat. Bishop looked across at him, a strange expression on his face. 'Her chest was completely crushed.'

They sat in silence until the lights changed.

Why should I feel sorry for you?

'I saw Alison yesterday. Anne was testing out a communications device. I'm sure she'll tell you all about it . . .'

And then small-talk across Waterloo Bridge and into the West End.

Bishop stuck his hazards on as he pulled over on Long Acre to let Thorne jump out. 'How's that?'

'That's perfect. Thanks again.'

'No problem. I'm sure we'll run into one another soon.'

Thorne slammed the door. The electric window slid down.

'Don't forget your briefcase . . .'

He drove slowly through Covent Garden, up to Holborn, then doubled back towards Soho. Cutting through small streets lined with newly opened shops, their chrome-cluttered interiors bathed in the glow of lava lamps. 'Scouting for locations', he believed this was called in the film world. Locations where he might find the next one. There were many to choose from and he'd have a better selection once it was dark, but he was just getting the feel of things.

He tightened his grip on the steering-wheel. He was still unsure what game Thorne was playing. He was making it all so easy for him and still things were far from satisfactory. The one thing he hadn't bargained for was ineptitude. He should have. He knew what was going on most of the time, and the control he felt at those moments was what would keep everything moving towards the correct and proper outcome. But there were seconds of doubt too. Then he felt as if the unexpected might be round the corner and come rushing at him and send everything spinning into confusion. He did not like surprises.

He hadn't liked them for years.

He'd decided to stick to roughly the same pattern but he fancied a bit of a change. Pubs had proved successful and, of course, the discothèque in south London, but he wanted to adjust the demographics. Perhaps he'd move upmarket a little. Somewhere beset with lacquered wood and polished steel, where decibels inhibited conversation to bellowed soundbites. Set about treating some young thing full of pills and alcopops. Half the job would be done for him already.

All he'd need to do would be to cruise along behind the night bus . . .

Yes, she would probably be very young. Younger than Helen, even. And so much luckier. Success would mean relief from many more years of struggle and stretchmarks. He would get this one right, like Alison. If her heart had the strength, even near death, to keep pumping the blood around the body, then she would be cared for.

He looked around at the other drivers drowning in their cars, the pedestrains choking, the shopworkers being slowly suffocated. All of them dying a little, day by day. He couldn't help all of them, but one was going to be given a fighting chance very soon.

Then Thorne might start doing his job properly.

The kiss, when Anne opened the door to her

office, felt awkward. The smiles were genuine and unprofessional. They both wanted more. They'd have to wait.

The blackboard stood against the wall. Thorne took a step towards it. 'This would be the communications device that Jeremy was telling me about?'

She looked stunned. 'You've seen him?'

He shrugged. 'He gave me a lift into town this morning.' *Now he had one or two bits and pieces in his briefcase.*

'Oh.' She walked over and self-consciously rubbed out some of the scrawlier chalk marks. Now, under the lines of letters, there were two small arrows, one pointing forwards, the other backwards.

'It's . . . evolving. I'm hopeful.'

He wished he'd made a move on her that night after dinner. For all sorts of reasons. Now things were so difficult. 'I got one of the blokes at work to have a look on the Internet for me,' he said. 'There were all sorts of . . . gizmos.'

She smiled. 'Oh, there are. If Alison ever recovers significant movement there are powerchairs that are incredibly sophisticated. Even as she is now there's the Eyegaze system, which can be operated by the tiniest eye movement. She could manoeuvre a mouse and type into a computer with vocaliser software. She could speak. She could control virtually any element within her immediate environment.'

'All horribly expensive, I suppose?'

'Believe me, I was lucky to get the blackboard. Do you want a coffee?'

Thorne wanted all manner of disgusting things. Right there on her desk. He wanted to be pushed backwards across it scattering notes on to the floor. He wanted to unzip himself and watch as she walked towards him smiling, hitching up her skirt . . .

'I'd really like to go and see Alison.'

'Well, you go on up and I'll grab us a couple of coffees from the canteen. You remember where it is, don't you?'

The room was not so cluttered with hardware as the last time he'd seen it. It still felt as if he'd taken the lift to the basement and stumbled into the generating room, but there was a lot less of it. Alison seemed less attached. There were fresh flowers – from her boyfriend, he supposed. It suddenly struck him that he'd never met Tim Hinnegan. He had no idea what he looked like, what he did for a living. He'd ask Holland.

Fuck that. He'd ask Alison. When he had time.

He needed a piss and hurriedly availed himself of Alison's *en-suite* facilities. A low metal pan, a sink, a sharps bin. Handles screwed at a variety of heights and angles into the insipid yellow walls. He flushed the toilet and splashed cold water on to his face.

Thorne sat in the chair nearest the bed and

looked at her. Her eyes were wide open, the right eye flickering. The smallest movement but seemingly constant. It was incredibly difficult to maintain eye-contact with her. There was a challenge in that unflinching stare – he was imagining it, he knew, but he still felt embarrassed. How long did you ever hold eye-contact with anyone? Even someone with whom you were intimate? A few seconds? Alison would look deep into his eyes for as long as he was comfortable with it. He quickly realised, with something like shame, that this wasn't very long.

He took her hand and held it tight against the blanket. To have lifted it clear of the bedclothes would have felt like . . . taking advantage.

'Hi, Alison. It's Detective Inspector Thorne.' He reddened, remembering that she'd just been staring at him for nearly a minute. He was starting to sweat. He shuffled the chair a little closer to the bed and squeezed her hand. 'You must be sick of people being as stupid as me.'

Alison blinked. The sluggishness of the eyelid's downward movement was probably normal but, to Thorne, it implied a weary amusement in her answer. He thought he felt a split-second tremor in her fingers and looked into her eyes for confirmation. There was none. How many of her friends had sat where he was and felt the same things? How many had shouted for a nurse and gone home feeling stupid?

He was actually starting to feel genuinely relaxed.

The low hum of the machines was soothing and soporific. It wasn't unlike being pissed. There was an enjoyable conversation to be had. But he knew that Anne would arrive with the coffee at any time and there was one question he couldn't ask with her in the room.

Letting go of the small, warm hand was difficult but he needed to open the briefcase. From the stiff-backed manilla envelope he produced the ten-by-eight black-and-white photo, and held it down by his side wondering how best to phrase the question.

She'd recognise Bishop, of course she would. He'd been in the room with Anne the day before, hadn't he? He wasn't really looking for anything like an identification. He just hoped he might learn something else. Get a sense of something else. A recognition beyond the one he knew would be there anyway.

He knew that nothing that happened in this room would ever be admissible as evidence. He also knew instinctively that he couldn't ask her straight out if the face she was about to see belonged to the man who'd put her here. Christ alone knew how fragile she was feeling. She was almost certainly confused, disoriented, even now. He'd have to take it slowly.

Much as he wanted this, he couldn't hurt her.

'Alison, I'm going to show you a picture.' He held up the photo. For a moment he said nothing.

There was just the relentless hum. 'You've seen this man before, haven't you?'

His eyes didn't shift from hers for an instant.

She blinked.

His phone rang.

Anne didn't want the coffee to go cold and had tried to keep the conversation with the administrator as brief as possible. He'd collared her at the till and even the few fragments of his monologue that had got through to her had bored her rigid instantly. He was a pathologically dull individual who, were he ever to become a hospital visitor, could set back the treatment of coma patients by decades. She'd smiled and nodded. God knows what she'd actually agreed to.

Now, as she walked towards Alison's room, she wondered if Thorne felt as she did – as though this was some sort of bizarre date, sharing a cup of coffee with Alison as a chaperone.

It was kind of him to have looked into Alison's condition on the Internet. She'd have to check it out for herself: she was well briefed, of course, on all the technological advancements that were making the lives of those with permanent disabilities easier – at least, those with a substantial private income. Things were moving quickly, though, and she was likely to be better informed by the Net than she would be by current medical literature.

She had no idea whether or not Thorne was good at what he did. It was obvious that he cared, that he got involved. As far as his job was concerned, caring might not necessarily be a good thing. She knew what Jeremy would say about it.

Holding a cup in each hand she pushed open the door to Alison's room with her backside and nudged it shut with her hip. She turned to see Thorne standing by the window, staring into space. She looked at the empty chair by Alison's bed and knew instantly that something was wrong.

'Tom?'

She could see the tension in his jaw. His face was the colour of a corpse.

'Someone has contacted my office . . . my former office, anonymously.'

He turned his head slowly towards Alison, but Anne could see that he was looking at a space on the back wall, above her head. His eyes dropped to the girl's face and stayed there for a second or two before he turned and walked slowly out of the room.

Anne put the coffee on the table next to Alison's bed and followed him. He was waiting outside the door. The moment the door was closed, he took a small step towards her and spoke calmly, the fury just held in check.

'I have been accused of molesting Alison.'

The screaming, hypnotic pulse of the music had focused Thorne's mind and steered his thoughts into the dark places in his head that were usually best avoided. He was sitting on the floor, his back

213

resting against the sofa, the beer can cool against his cheek.

Keable had tried to set his mind at rest. 'Don't worry, Tom, it's obviously nothing. Just some nutter who claimed to have heard it from somebody in the hospital. Nobody's taking it seriously – it's not like he could have heard it from Alison Willetts, is it?'

Insensitive to the last, but Thorne was relieved that he couldn't argue with the reasoning. He let his head fall back on to the sofa cushion and stared at the ceiling.

He thought about touching Alison.

He thought about hearing Jeremy Bishop beg.

The doorbell rang. He got slowly to his feet. He opened the door and went straight back to his spot on the floor by the sofa. Formalities seemed pointless. Anne walked in and stood by the fireplace. She dropped her bag, took off the thin raincoat and spent five seconds taking in the room. The first thing she noticed was the beer. 'Can I?'

She walked over, smoothing down her long black skirt. Thorne handed her a can of lager from the broken four-pack by his side. 'Not a brand I'm familiar with.'

'I know. Expensive wine and cheap, piss-weak lager. Don't ask me why.'

'So you can enjoy the drinking without the sensation of being drunk.'

'That's definitely not the reason.'

She sat down on the sofa behind and to his right. 'Tom, that phone call. It's just a crank.'

He half crushed his empty can then stopped and put it down gently next to the others. 'I know exactly who it is.'

'Well, it's stupid to let it upset you.'

He turned and looked at her over his shoulder. 'No. Not upset.'

Anne could see in his eyes that the nice side of him, the side that bought Alison flowers, was far from being the whole story. Though it was difficult to contemplate such a thing, she would not want this man as an enemy.

She took a long swig of beer and gestured towards the stereo. 'Who's this?'

'Leftfield. The track's called "Open Up".'

She listened for a minute. Hated it.

'That's John Lydon doing the vocal,' Thorne said, as if it made a difference.

'Right . . .'

'Johnny Rotten . . . the Sex Pistols?'

'Sadly, I was a little too old even for them. What are you, then? Forty?'

'Forty a few months ago. I was seventeen when "God Save The Queen" came out.'

'God. I was already a third-year med student.'

'I know. Pushing beds into rivers.'

She gave him what his dad would certainly have described as an old-fashioned look. 'So what were *you* doing?'

Not going to university, thought Thorne. For so

many reasons, he wished he had. 'I was about to join the force, I suppose, and managing my acne.' Wanting to be a policeman more than anything. Trying to make his mum and dad proud. Wanting to do good, and all the other stupid ideas of which he'd been so brutally disabused.

Anne drained her can and Thorne passed her another. They sat in silence for a minute, remembering, or pretending to remember.

'Thanks for coming over by the way. Did you drive?'

'Yes. Bugger to park, though.' Thorne nodded. 'It's good to get out actually. Rachel and I are getting on each other's nerves a bit at the moment.'

'Yeah?'

'She's got a couple of resits to do and she thought the whole exam thing was behind her. So she's being a bit . . . spiky.'

Thorne remembered his first encounter with Anne Coburn in a lecture theatre at the Royal Free. Spiky obviously ran in the family.

Anne took another long slug of beer. Enjoying it. 'Just run-of-the-mill teenage angst, I suppose. She hasn't pierced her belly-button or painted her room black yet, but it's probably just a matter of time.'

'It'll sort itself out.'

'And so will this business with Alison.'

'It's all right, there won't be an investigation or anything. Nobody's taking it seriously.'

'Except you.'

'If that's what he wants.' The *he* spat out like something sour.

'Why don't you talk about it, then?'

'Anne, I don't need a doctor. Or a mother.'

She shuffled forward to the very edge of the sofa and leaned forward, her head down.

'Fine. Do you want to go to bed, then?'

Thorne had always thought that spluttering your drink out when somebody surprised you only ever happened in *Terry and June*, but he succeeded brilliantly in snorting a decent amount of cheap lager into his lap. The sitcom moment made him laugh uncontrollably.

Anne laughed, too, but she was also blushing to her toenails.

'Well, fuck . . . I don't know what you're supposed to say . . .'

'I think you just said it.'

She slid off the sofa on to the floor next to him. 'So?'

'Well, these trousers have got Tesco's own lager all over them now. They'll have to come off . . .'

He leaned across and kissed her. She put down her lager and placed a hand on his neck. He broke the kiss, looked at the floor. 'Now, this carpet has unhappy memories and I'm still not a hundred per cent sure I've got the smell of vomit out of it . . .'

'You smooth-talking bastard.'

'So, the palatial bedroom suite?'

She nodded and they stood up. There was still a hint of awkwardness between them. Nothing had yet been abandoned, but taking hands would have seemed a little silly all the same. Thorne held open the bedroom door. 'I have to warn you, I've got a Swedish virgin in here.'

Anne raised her eyebrows and looked into the room, seeing only a small fitted wardrobe, a chest of drawers and a neatly made bed. She didn't get it. 'Eh?'

'The bed . . .' Thorne pulled her to him. 'It doesn't matter . . .'

Thorne woke and looked at the clock. It was nearly two thirty in the morning and the phone was ringing. He was instantly wide awake. He slipped out of bed and hurried naked into the living room where the handset was recharging on the base unit just inside the front door. The heating couldn't have been off for very long but the flat was already freezing.

'Sir, sorry it's so late. It's Holland.'

Thorne pressed the phone tight to his ear and wrapped an arm around his shoulder. He could still hear Leftfield. The CD was on repeat and they'd forgotten to turn it off.

'Yes?'

'We might have something here. A woman rang through. She'd seen the reconstruction – waited a couple of days wondering whether to call.'

'Go on.'

'Nine months ago a man knocked on her door claiming to be looking for a party. She thought he looked all right – you know, friendly enough. She invited him in. He was carrying a bottle of champagne.'

Thorne stopped shivering.

'I haven't got much more than that at the minute, sir. For some reason he left, and she didn't really think anything of it until the programme. She reckons she can give us a pretty good description, though.'

'Does Tughan know about this?'

'Yes, sir. I've already called him.'

Thorne felt a twinge of annoyance, but he knew that Holland couldn't have done anything else. 'What did he say?'

'He thought it sounded hopeful.'

'Anything about me?'

He could hear Holland thinking.

'Don't spare my feelings, Holland, I haven't got any.'

'There was some crack about you and Miss Willetts, sir. I don't really remember – just a joke, really.'

Nobody was taking it seriously.

'When are you going to interview her?'

'Myself and DI Tughan are going to see her tomorrow morning.'

Thorne took down the details, scribbling the woman's name and address on a Post-it note next to the phone. The initial buzz was wearing off a little and he could feel the cold again. He wanted to get back to bed.

'Thanks for that, Holland. One quick thing . . .'

'Don't worry, sir, I'll call you as soon as we've seen her.'

'Great, thanks. But I was going to say, if anybody should ask, your girlfriend trapped her hand in a door this morning . . .'

He realised as soon as he'd hung up on Holland that he was terribly awake. He turned off the music and scurried around the living room with a bin liner, picking up empty beer cans. For a second he was tempted to look inside Anne's bag, which still lay where she'd dropped it. Had she brought a change of clothes with her?

He thought better of it and instead grabbed the spare duvet from the cupboard in the hall and sat on the sofa in the dark.

Thinking.

Things were moving quickly. There had been cases before where he'd felt like an outsider – he would come at things from a different angle – but he was still, if only nominally, part of a team. This time it was different. He'd felt good marching out of Keable's office but within minutes he was wondering if he'd done the right thing. He still wondered.

He knew why he'd walked away. Whatever Keable had told his bosses about politics and personality clashes, it still came down to judgement.

Their passing of it; his lack of it.

His judgement and theirs, and that of those long gone. But even the judgement of the dead could not always be trusted. Any conviction based on such testimony would surely be flawed. Only one man could judge him.

And Tom Thorne was the harshest judge of all.

He thought about the woman asleep in his bed. Anne wasn't the first woman he'd slept with since Jan. There had been some drunken fumbling with an ambitious young sergeant and a short fling with a legal secretary – but this was the first time he'd felt frightened afterwards.

Once upon a time Anne had been involved with Bishop. Thorne still wasn't sure to what extent, but that hardly mattered. The killer who had all but turned his life upside down had once had sex with the woman who was now, at least for the moment, sharing his bed. He suddenly wondered if Bishop might be jealous. It made sense. The anonymous phone call, the accusation, had seemed a little . . . beneath him. Could the attack here in this room have been, at least in part, a warning to stay away from Anne? On top of everything was there actually a sexual rivalry? The idea was comforting. It began to give him back a sense of control. He'd felt it slipping away as the anger had swept over him after the accusation about Alison. Now he was calmer.

Back in the hospital. *Oh, he'll find out exactly what type I am . . .*

A man trained to save life was taking it in the name of something Thorne could never under-stand. Didn't care about understanding.

If Thorne was going to stop him, it was important to maintain the initiative.

He went to fetch the phone, curled up on the sofa and dialled 141 . . .

A few minutes later, he crept back into the bedroom, slid under the duvet and lay there blinking, unable to sleep.

Around four o'clock Anne woke up and did her best to help him.

'How do you feel?'

A question I'm asked every day. Sometimes more than once. It's not that I don't understand why. It's that I'd-better-say-something kind of thing. Better than sitting there looking at the clock and wondering which nurse gets to wipe my arse, I suppose. It's hospitals. It makes people feel strangely compelled to buy fruit and breathe through their mouth and ask ridiculous questions. But why questions, for fuck's sake? Don't ask me questions. Tell me things, if you like. I'm a good listener. Getting to be very, very good. Tell me anything you like. Bore me rigid. Sit there and waffle on about how your boss doesn't understand you, or your husband's not interested in sex any more or you want to travel or nursing's badly paid, or you like to drink in the afternoons but don't – ask – me – things.

How do you feel?

It's not like you're actually expecting an answer, is it? You'd be bored off your tits if I decided to play along. If I wanted to respond with a pithy 'Not too bad, thank you for asking, and how are you?' that would take, at present levels of blinking proficiency and taking into account the fatigue factor, approximately forty-five minutes. Sorry you asked? Well, don't, then.

How do you feel?

Grateful that you're there, don't get me wrong. All of you. Visitors, nurses popping heads round the door, cleaners. Say hello. Come in and tell me lies. Just don't be predictable. The only reason you're asking, really, is that you can't tell precisely just by looking at me. Not exactly. I mean, you could take a wild stab in the dark. You could make a pretty good guess. You wouldn't need to phone a friend, would you? I'm lying in hospital. Utterly fucked. I'm hardly going to be over the moon. But most of the time you don't have to ask people how they feel. It's obvious. You can see if someone's happy, or tired, or pissed off because it's there in their face, but my face doesn't give a lot away. It must say something, I suppose, but I can only guess, really. If there's an expression that says, 'Closed,' or 'Gone to lunch,' it's probably there or thereabouts.

How do you feel? OK, then . . .

Angry. Stupid. Optimistic. Bored. Tired. Awake. Frustrated. Grateful. Irritated. Violent. Calm. Dreamy. Shit. Confused. Ignorant. Ugly. Sick. Hungry. Useless. Special. Horny. Pessimistic. Ashamed. Loved. Forgotten. Freaky.

Mislaid. Relieved. Alone. Frightened. Stoned. Dirty. Dead . . .

Horny? I know, sorry, very strange. But I'm lying here on a sexy mattress that hums and there's that very gorgeous nurse who actually might not be gay after all. So . . .

Did I say confused? Yes.

A lot of the time. Like why did Thorne show me a picture of Dr Bishop? I had a feeling he was leading up to something. Maybe it's like when you go deaf or blind and your other senses get better to compensate. Because most of me's knackered maybe I'm becoming a bit witchy or something. I know he wanted to ask me things but then his phone rang and he talked quietly and went a bit funny.

Nobody's told me anything yet about what happened. Not really. About the crime, I mean. I know what he did to me . . .

But I still don't know why.

CHAPTER 11

He got on to the tube at Waterloo. Eight stops, direct, on the Bakerloo line. The carriage was absolutely packed, just the way he liked it. Sometimes he needed to let two or three trains go and wait for the right one. There was no point in squeezing on when the carriage was empty of interest. He watched as the train roared into the station, ignoring his fellow travellers as they inched towards the edge of the platform. He scanned each carriage as it moved past him, making his choice.

It might take a few stops before he'd got to where he needed to be but he moved easily through the crowd of commuters. He enjoyed the build-up. He loved negotiating that sweaty knot of pent-up anger and rustling newspapers to get himself into the right position.

It didn't usually take long to find her.

Today she was tall, only an inch or two shorter than he was. She had dark hair in a bob, and glasses through which she tried to take in as much of her copy of *The Beach* as she could under the circumstances. There was always the danger, of course, that she might get off the train before he did. Before he'd had a chance to get close to her. So many of them got off at Oxford Circus or Baker Street. He wasn't too disappointed when that happened. There was always tomorrow. The rush-hour was wonderfully predictable.

He made his first contact as the train stopped at Piccadilly Circus. That wonderful jolt as the train came to a standstill. Thirty seconds later he would get another chance when they pulled away again. He was behind this one. Sometimes he liked to be face to face. To see their expression as he half looked away or shrugged apologetically. And he loved the breasts, of course. But this was his favourite. He liked the feel of their behinds against his groin. He could place a sweaty hand in the small of their backs to steady himself. He could smell their hair. Best of all, he could turn and look at the person behind him if he needed to, starting a small wave of accusatory looks and sighs as his excitement mounted.

She'd washed her hair this morning. He wondered whether she'd had sex last night. If she'd showered she would have washed the smell away, which was a shame, but he loved the smell of her hair all the same. And a hint of something else at the nape of her neck. The train slowed and came to a halt in the tunnel between Oxford Circus and Regent's Park. Another lovely little push.

With the train motionless, he thought for a minute about what he had to do today. An interview

227

this morning. He enjoyed those. He liked to run things. He could read people well, he knew that. But they could never read him.

The train moved off again with a useful jerk. Only four stops to go. Perhaps one more before the big one. She was looking intently at her book, but he knew she was thinking about him. Despising him. That was fine. Let her think it was over. Let her relax, thinking he'd moved or got off without her seeing. She wouldn't want to look over her shoulder to check. He'd wait until they left Marylebone.

The train moved towards his final destination. He was sure that she'd felt every inch of him that time. It was a second, no more, but he'd felt the crack in her buttocks, the cotton of her long black skirt against the polyester of his work trousers. He'd felt her tense up.

Only once had one of them confronted him. She'd moved away and stepped off the train before turning back and screaming at him. Other passengers looked, but he smiled indulgently and held up his hands and let himself get lost in the mêlée of others getting on the train. Only once. They were pretty good odds. Of course, if it ever came to it, he had a pretty good defence up his sleeve.

This was his favourite moment. One last good one and then away. In that second or two before the doors opened he leaned against her and took everything in. The feeling of his erection against her arse, his face against the back of her head.

The intimacy was breathtaking. They might have been lovers, curling up together in bed at night, the sheets damp and smelly . . .

Then off and pushing through the crowd towards the door. As he sidled past her he saw her glance up from her book. Close up she was far from gorgeous but he didn't care. The tension in her face and the heat in his groin were all that really mattered. It was only a game, after all. It was part of the hustle-bustle, wasn't it? He smiled and thought the same thing he always did after such a lovely start to the working day: So don't live in London, love.

Doing up the buttons of his jacket to hide the tiny bulge, Nick Tughan stepped off the train at Edgware Road, and turning his mind towards the day ahead, began moving quickly towards the escalator.

Anne had left early saying she needed to get home before Rachel was awake and Thorne had slept until well after nine. He'd phoned Brigstocke to say he'd be in late. Not that he had anything planned – he was waiting on Holland. He was just plain knackered.

He was enjoying his fourth piece of toast and looking forward to the rare, illicit thrill of *Richard and Judy* when the doorbell rang.

He recognised James Bishop straight away from Kodak's photo. Bethell's appraisal had been about right, he thought: grungy was the word. He was tall and skinny, wearing a long dark coat over

T-shirt, jeans and grubby training shoes. What looked like very short, bleached-blond hair was hidden beneath a black pork-pie hat, and he carried a dirty green bag slung across one shoulder.

'Are you Thorne?'

The same well-modulated tones as his father, despite the sad attempt at the oikish London accent, and the same chiselled features, albeit camouflaged by several days of light stubbly fuzz. It was like looking at Dr Jeremy Bishop as a student.

'Yes, I am, James.' That put the cocky little sod on the back foot. Thorne couldn't help smirking. 'Could I ask how you got my address?'

'Yeah. You told my dad which road you lived in . . . I've knocked on virtually every door in the street.'

You should have just asked him, James. He knows exactly where I live.

'I see. Woken up many of my neighbours?'

Bishop smiled. 'A couple. A very tasty housewife asked me in for a cup of tea.'

'We're pretty friendly round here. Fancy a bit of toast?'

Thorne turned from the front door and strolled back into his flat. There was a pause before he heard the young man close the outer door, and another before he shut the door to the flat and came sloping into the living room.

'Not bothered about the toast, but I wouldn't mind a coffee . . .'

230

Thorne went into the kitchen and watched as his visitor hovered in the middle of the living room. 'James is it, then? Or Jim?'

'James.'

Right, thought Thorne, spooning the coffee into a mug. Jim to your trendy mates but James when you're trying to borrow money off Daddy. He carried the coffee through and handed the mug to him. 'So?'

Bishop looked disarmed. Evidently, this wasn't how he'd wanted things to go. He tried to sound as dangerous as he could, which wasn't very. 'I want you to leave my old man alone.'

Thorne sat down on the arm of the sofa. 'I see. What is it you think I'm doing exactly?'

'Why are you hassling him?'

'Hassling?'

'There was a bloke taking photos outside his house the other day, then when you turn up with some bollocks about scrounging a lift you tell him it was probably reporters. He might have fallen for that, but I think it's crap. What were you doing there anyway?'

'I'm a policeman, James, I can go pretty much wherever I want.'

Bishop was starting to enjoy himself a little. That made two of them. He took a step towards the mantelpiece then turned to Thorne, smiling. 'Shouldn't you call me "sir"?'

Thorne returned the smile with interest. 'If this conversation formed part of an investigation then

231

perhaps I might, yes. But it doesn't, we're in my flat and you're drinking my fucking coffee.'

Bishop's hands tightened around his mug. Wondering what to say next. Thorne saved him the trouble. 'I think your father's overreacting somewhat.'

'He doesn't even know I'm here.'

Right. No. Course not.

'He got these phone calls.'

'When?'

'Last night. In the middle of the night. Four or five, one after the other. He phoned me up in a right panic.'

'What sort of phone calls?'

'You tell me.'

The cockiness had started to return. He needed slapping down harder. 'Listen, I questioned your father as part of an investigation that I'm no longer even part of, all right?' As Bishop's mouth fell open, Thorne felt a twinge of something approaching sympathy. 'Now tell me about the phone calls.'

'Like I said, in the middle of the night. He could hear somebody there. Whoever it was had withheld their number and that was it. One after the other. He's upset – no, he's frightened. He's fucking shit-scared.'

I seriously doubt it.

'So what are you going to do about it?' Bishop was starting to sound genuinely angry.

'I'll tell you what I told him about the photographer. I'll look into it. That's the best I can do.'

232

'Are you seeing Anne Coburn?'

It was Thorne's turn to be genuinely angry. 'Behave yourself, James . . .'

'Seeing as you're off the investigation it could be that, though, couldn't it?'

'What?' Thorne took a deep breath. Trying not to lose it, knowing it was the father, not the son, he needed to save it for.

'If you and Anne were . . . you know . . . it would be a reason to get at my father.'

Thorne stood up and moved towards Bishop. He saw the slightest flinch, but only shook his head and reached for the empty coffee cup.

'As far as I can remember, Dr Coburn, as your godmother, was responsible for your spiritual well-being. Looking at you, she's obviously failed miserably but that is, I believe, where your relationship with her ends. You probably got a silver christening spoon and the odd birthday present, but who she's sleeping with is not part of the deal.'

Bishop nodded, impressed. Then he broke into a grin. 'So you are, then?'

Thorne smiled as he carried the empty mugs through to the kitchen. 'What do you do, James, when you're not worrying about your father?'

Bishop moved aimlessly around the living room. He stopped to study the pile of CDs. 'I always worry about my father. We're very close. Are you and yours not, then?'

Thorne grimaced. 'Well?'

233

'I move about a lot. Bit of writing. Tried being an actor. Anything that pays the rent, I suppose.'

Thorne was starting to feel that he understood this young man. Not that he understood many of them any more. This one wasn't quite the good-for-nothing he'd thought Anne had described. Beneath the attempts at nonconformity there was almost certainly an inherited conventionality, which he was trying desperately to escape. Which was *why* he was trying to escape. He was misguided for sure, but essentially harmless. James Bishop had no idea of the poisonous gene pool in which he was splashing around. He could piss in the water as much as he liked, but in all the ways that didn't matter, the poor sod was his father's son.

'Did you study?'

'I wasted a couple of years at college, yeah. I'm not the ivory-tower type.'

Thorne came back into the living room and picked up his jacket. 'Tower Records type, though?'

'Oh, yeah . . .' Bishop self-consciously fingered the T-shirt that carried the shop's logo. 'I'm working there at the moment.'

Thorne gestured towards the hallway. It was time to go. Bishop moved quickly towards the front door, in no hurry to hang about.

'Well, maybe I'll see you in there,' said Thorne. 'What's your country section like?'

Bishop laughed. ''Fuck should I know?'

Thorne opened the front door. It was starting to rain.

'Stupid question. What – you more into ambient? Trance? Speed-garage? Could you get me a discount on the new Grooverider twelve-inch?'

Bishop looked at him.

Thorne pulled the door shut. 'You've had quite a few surprises this morning, haven't you?'

Margaret Byrne lived on the ground floor of a small terraced house in Tulse Hill. She was not what Holland and Tughan had been expecting. A plain and prematurely grey-haired woman, she was probably in her late forties and considerably overweight. Tughan could not conceal his surprise as she peered round her front door at them, one foot held in place against the jamb to prevent a large ginger cat escaping. Once the IDs, which she'd asked to see, had been produced, she was happy to invite them in. She insisted on making them tea, leaving Tughan and Holland to negotiate a route round at least three more large cats before arriving at comfortable chairs in her front room.

Holland was thinking it, but it was Tughan that said it. 'This place fucking stinks,' he hissed, before adding drily, 'No wonder he changed his mind and pissed off.'

After the tea, and a good selection of biscuits, had appeared, Holland sat back, as he'd been instructed to do, and let Tughan run things.

'So you live alone then, Margaret?'

She pulled a face. 'I hate Margaret. Can we stick to Maggie?'

Holland smiled, thinking, Go on, don't make it easy for him.

'Sorry. Maggie . . .'

'My husband left a couple of years ago. Don't know why I call him that, he could never be arsed to marry me, but anyway . . .'

'No children?'

She wrapped her grey cardigan tight across her chest. 'Got a daughter. She's twenty-three, lives in Edinburgh, and I haven't got the first idea where her father is.'

She took another biscuit and began stroking the black-and-white cat that had jumped on to her lap. She muttered to it softly and it settled down. Holland thought she was a bit like his mum. He hadn't seen her for ages. Maybe he'd talk to Sophie about asking her down to stay for a bit.

'Right, tell us about the man with the champagne, Maggie.'

'Didn't you write it down when I phoned up?'

Holland smiled. Tughan didn't.

'We just need a few more details, that's all.'

'Well, it was about eight o'clock, I think. I answered the door and this bloke was standing there waving a bottle about. He asked me if this was where Jenny was having a party?'

'Have you got a neighbour called Jenny?'

'I don't think so. He said he was sure he'd got the right address and we had a bit of a laugh about something or other and he started being a bit naughty, you know, saying how it was a shame

236

to waste a bottle of champagne. He was flirting . . . I think he was a bit tipsy.'

'You said when you called that you could give us a very good description.'

'Did I? Oh, bloody hell. Right, well he was tall, definitely over six feet, glasses, and very well dressed. He had a very nice suit on, you know, expensive . . .'

'Colour?'

'Blue, I think. Dark blue.'

Holland was jotting it all down and keeping his mouth shut like a good boy.

'Go on, Maggie.'

'He had short, greyish hair . . .'

'Greyish?'

'Yeah, you know, not silver, just greying, but he wasn't that old, I don't think. Well, not as old as me at any rate.'

'How old?'

'Thirty-six . . . thirty-seven? I've always been rubbish at that. Well, I think most people are, aren't they?' She turned and looked at Holland. 'How old d'you reckon I am?'

Holland could feel the colour coming to his cheeks. Why the hell had she asked *him*? 'Oh . . . I don't know . . . Thirty-nine?'

She smiled, acknowledging the kindness of the lie. 'I'm forty-three, and I know I look older.'

Tughan, anxious to get back on track, cleared his throat. The cat, startled, shot off Margaret Byrne's lap and flew out of the door. This, in turn, made Tughan jump, which Holland would later remember as the only amusing thing about the entire interview.

'What did he sound like? Did he have an accent?'

'Pretty posh, I'd say. A nice voice . . . and, you know, very good-looking. He was handsome.'

'So you invited him in?'

She brushed more cat hair than there was from her skirt. 'Well, I think he was dropping hints. Like I said, he was waving this bottle around.' She looked at Tughan and held eye-contact. 'Yes. I invited him in.'

Tughan smiled thinly. 'Why?'

Holland was starting to feel uncomfortable. This woman could help them. She might well be the only person who *could* help them. Why she had invited the man who might have killed her into her home was information they didn't need now. This woman wasn't mad or desperate or sex-starved, for Christ's sake. Loneliness was not a crime, much as Tughan seemed to be enjoying touching the tender spot of it. She hadn't answered him anyway. He let it go.

'What happened then?'

'Like I said on the phone, this was the funny part. He opened the champagne – I remember being disappointed because there wasn't a pop – and I said I'd go and get some glasses. He said great and he was just going to make a quick phone call.'

Tughan looked at Holland then back at Margaret. 'You didn't mention that when you called.'

'Didn't I? Well, he did.'

Tughan sat forward in his chair. 'He made a call from here? From your phone?'

'No. Just as I was going off to the kitchen I saw him take out one of those horrible little mobile things. I hate them, don't you? Always beeping and playing daft tunes when you're sitting on a train.'

'And you were in the kitchen?'

'And I was in the kitchen, and I'd just got the glasses down and given them a wipe out because they were a bit dirty, and I heard the front door slam. I came back out and he'd buggered off. I opened the front door but I couldn't see him. I heard a car pull away up the road, but I didn't really see it.'

Tughan nodded. Holland had finished writing.

Margaret Byrne looked quickly from one to the other. 'You reckon he was the bloke who killed that girl up in Holloway, then?'

Tughan said nothing. He stood up and threw Holland a look, telling him to do the same. 'If we send a car for you tomorrow could you come down to Edgware Road and work with one of our computer artists?'

She nodded, and picked up a passing cat as she got to her feet.

When they reached the front door Tughan stopped and looked at her. She smiled nervously at him.

239

'Why did you wait so long before reporting this matter?' Tughan said. 'I mean, you even waited for four days after the reconstruction went out on TV.'

She pulled the cat close to her neck. Holland stepped forward, putting a hand a little too forcefully on Tughan's shoulder.

'We'd better get going. Thanks for all your help.'

The gratitude in her eyes was obvious. She took hold of his sleeve. 'Was it him?'

Tughan was already on his way to the car. Holland watched him deactivate the alarm, climb in and slam the door. He turned back to her. 'I think you were very lucky, Maggie.'

She smiled and gripped his sleeve a little tighter as her eyes began to fill with tears. 'It would be the first time . . .'

I'm in a much better mood now. I don't mean generally, that's still up and down. Tim said I was moody before and he's probably right. But now, in here, I can be a right bitch. I think that's fair enough, though. I think I deserve a medal for the few nice moods I do have.

Anyway . . .

Even in here there's always something that can cheer you up. It's not exactly *Carry On Doctor* but there's laughs to be had if you look for them. Sick ones, usually, but you can't be too fussy. There's this nurse, Martina, who's taken it upon herself to make sure I look pretty all the time. Under normal circumstances, of course, I'd tell her that you can't improve on perfection, but granted, she's got a job on her hands. To be honest, I think she's doing it to get a break from the catheter and arse work, which is hardly brimming with job satisfaction, is it? At first I didn't mind when she was trimming my hair and cutting my toenails but she's started getting a bit ambitious. I think she's a failed beauty therapist or something. She painted my nails the other day and the colour was fucking revolting and yesterday afternoon she decided that a bit of lippy might cheer me up. Putting lipstick on somebody else is like trying to have a wank with your left hand. Forget it. I looked like a clown in a coma, or a tit in a trance, as my nan used to say.

I think she was trying to make me look like one of those hideous women who work on the makeup counters in department stores – you know, the ones who spend all day surrounded by cosmetics and haven't got a fucking clue how to put them on. Here's a tip. Don't use a trowel. I always want to creep up behind them and shout, 'Mirror! Use a mirror!'

I didn't plan what happened this morning, I swear, but I quite wish I had. Obviously some of the other nurses had noticed that Martina was spending all her time tarting me up instead of doing any of the dirty work and she got lumbered with cleaning out my breathing tube. I can fully understand not wanting to do it, it's bloody foul. So Martina is supposed to pull it out and clean out all the muck or something so it doesn't get blocked. Imagine somebody was waggling a tube around in your mouth. Well, it's pretty much the same when it's straight into your neck. You'd want to cough, wouldn't you? Coughing isn't one of my best things, these days, but I must have been saving it up. There's

Martina trying to be all efficient and I just let one go. I couldn't help it. I coughed out of my neck, for Christ's sake!

Like I said, it wasn't on purpose and she didn't help by screaming the place down, but this enormous lump of phlegmy glop just splattered on to her forehead.

I hope she might stay away for a bit now. Or maybe just stick to the rearend stuff. At least you know what's coming at you! Come on, though, pearl nail polish?

Everything's moving along on the blink front. Another small complication is that sometimes I screw things up by blinking just because my brain thinks it's high time I did. Same reason you do. That doesn't help. I'm spelling away, then I suddenly throw in an X or a J for no good reason. Like suddenly shouting, 'Bollocks,' in the middle of a conversation.

It's like Newcastle on a Saturday night.

CHAPTER 12

Rachel sat at the desk in her room, the chemistry textbook in front of her long since invisible. She knew that this was what being involved with someone was about. Highs and lows. She'd gone out with a boy for nearly six months when she was a fourth-former and still remembered the dull ache of the phone that didn't ring and the stabbing agony of the undelivered note. This was much worse, though.

She had her own locker now in the sixth-form common room, and had to fight the urge to run and open it every five minutes to check her phone. By the end of the day there would always be at least a text message. She saved them all and reread them constantly. A voice message was always better, though. She loved his voice especially.

She walked over and slumped down on the bed, picking up her phone from where it was recharging as she went. She listened to the message again, that strange part of her that she knew was common to everybody, savouring the pain of it.

Like gnawing at a mouth ulcer.

He wasn't sure if he could make it tonight. He

might be able to but he didn't want to let her down at the last minute. He was sorry. It was a work thing he couldn't get out of. They'd better cancel. He'd call tomorrow.

As always, she was offered the option to delete the message. She saved it, although it was saved, anyway, in her head. She lay there endlessly pulling to pieces every phrase and analysing every nuance. Had he sounded distant? Was this the start of letting her down gently? He'd call tomorrow, he said, not later tonight. She wanted to call him but knew she wouldn't. The idea of being clingy made her sick. But she knew that if it came to it she would be.

She desperately wanted a cigarette but couldn't risk it. She'd had a couple in the garden the night before when her mum had been out screwing the policeman. She sometimes climbed up on the desk and opened a window to blow the smoke out but her mum would be coming to bed any time. Her mum who smoked, but said that *she* couldn't. Very fucking fair.

She'd speak to him tomorrow and everything would be fine and she'd feel like a pathetic sad cow.

She wasn't a stupid little girl any more. That was why he wanted her.

The carpet fibres that Thorne had scraped from the inside of Bishop's boot were in a small plastic bag. He knew he couldn't take them to Forensics himself and he didn't feel he could ask Holland yet. But there was somebody he could ask.

When the plastic bag dropped on to the pool table, Hendricks didn't shift his gaze a millimetre as he lined up the shot, the cue sliding easily back and forth along the cleft of his chin. He casually potted the eight ball and straightened up. 'That's another fiver.' His eyes shifted to the bag and its contents. 'Where did you get 'em?'

Thorne handed over the money and put his cue down on the table. 'Where d'you think I got them?'

'All right, smartarse, *how* did you get 'em?'

'The less I tell you, the less chance there is of you opening your big Manc gob.'

'I haven't said I'll do it yet, and you're not exactly asking very nicely.'

Thorne knew Hendricks would do it, but still felt bad about asking him. He'd put him up plenty of times, they'd done each other favours, lent each other money, but this was work. This was asking a lot. Hendricks was sharp. If he agreed to do it, he'd do so knowing the risks. He wouldn't lose his job, but he might find himself having to take on a bit more lecture work. He was also sharp enough to see that it was a lot of effort for what would probably be precious little reward.

'If you're so sure it's him, then why are you bothering?'

Two teenagers who had been hovering, waiting for a game, stepped forward. One slapped a fifty-pence piece down on the edge of the table. Thorne moved to the bar. Hendricks picked up the plastic bag and followed him. He was chuffed at the thought of the two teenagers watching them go, convinced they were witnessing a deal in some strange new drug.

'Well?'

'Because it's *only* me that's sure.'

'Fair enough, and when they do match up what does that tell you? Fuck all. We're pretty sure the killer drives a Volvo and I don't think the carpet in the back of each one is individually produced. I know they're nice cars, but come on . . .'

'Tickets to Spurs–Arsenal, on me.'

Hendricks took a long slow drink of Guinness. 'I want a box.'

'How am I supposed to do that?'

'How am I supposed to march into the forensics lab with a plastic bag full of carpet fibres I've produced out of the sodding ether?'

'I'll see what I can do. Listen, Phil, you know that lot, they won't ask questions. They're scientists not taxmen. Just tell them you're trying to help and you've got a mate who drives a Volvo. In fact, take in some other fibres from the back of your car or something – you know, like a comparison.'

'I don't recall a single witness seeing a beige Nissan Micra, do you?'

Hendricks had a point. He did perhaps own the single most repellent vehicle on the road in Greater London.

'Thanks, Phil.'

'Remember, a box!'

'Yeah, yeah . . .'

'Did you know that the Volvo is the only commercially produced car you can't kill yourself in? I mean, obviously you can drive one into a wall if you fancy it, but it has a cut-out device, you know, so that you can't tie a hose to the exhaust, and sit inside and asphyxiate yourself.'

Thorne grunted. 'Pity.'

Thorne had left the pub twenty-five pounds poorer but without the plastic bag that had been burning a hole in his pocket. He'd had a good night.

He hadn't drunk a thing.

Ten minutes after he got in, Holland rang. The DC spoke quietly, almost in a whisper. He told Thorne that Sophie was asleep in the next room and he didn't want to wake her.

He didn't want her to know who he was calling.

Thorne listened as Holland told him about Margaret Byrne. She might have been his first victim if the killer hadn't panicked for some reason. He told him what she'd said about the killer's voice. Nice, she thought. Posh. And soothing, probably, thought Thorne. Gentle.

When he heard about the phone call, Thorne pressed the receiver against his ear so hard that it hurt. Bishop bleeping himself? He dismissed the idea. It didn't make any sense. It was possible, he knew that, but what was the point? There was no record anyway, so why go through the motions?

Dave Holland shrugged off Thorne's question about how he'd got on with Tughan. A flippant remark did the job. He had been trying to forget the discomfort, the unease that had permeated every corner of Margaret Byrne's front room whenever the Irishman had opened his mouth. He wasn't sure whether the unease had been his or Margaret's, but it was stifling. It had stayed with him, following him around for the rest of the day like something rank.

Thorne didn't seem particularly interested in Margaret Byrne herself. When he announced that he'd phoned and arranged to see her the following morning, Holland understood why. He tried to dissuade him. What was the point? They'd already spoken to her and she was coming in anyway to knock up an e-fit.

Thorne was well aware that they'd already seen her.

But they hadn't got a picture of Jeremy Bishop in their pocket.

Anne enjoyed the drive home in the dark. There was usually a play on the radio or a short story or something. Often, in the forty-five minutes or so from Queen Square to Muswell Hill, she'd become so engrossed that she'd have to sit in the car outside the house and wait for it to finish.

She kept the radio off tonight. She had enough to think about.

That morning, in Alison's room, she'd found the photograph of Jeremy. It was lying on the small table in the corner of the room, probably put there by a nurse. It was obvious to her what Thorne had been doing in Alison's room the day before while she was fetching them coffee and she couldn't bring herself to think about what it might mean. She knew somewhere, of course, what it *might* mean. It could hardly mean very much else, but she couldn't bring herself to even try to deal with it.

Not now.

Feelings for two men. For one man those feelings had been shifting, settling into something else over a period of time. For the other they'd changed overnight.

Her relationship with Jeremy had not been the same since Sarah was killed. They'd always shared everything, which she knew had been the cause of so much tension between herself and David, but since the accident Jeremy had become reserved. His aloofness could be amusing, but had begun to wear her down a little. And recently he had become arrogant . . . more arrogant, and occasionally unpleasant. The work seemed a chore to him. He was going through the motions. He would always be a fixture in her life, she knew that, and so would the children, but there was no joy in it any more. She felt . . . dutiful.

Even so, the things Thorne must be thinking were so shocking. They were unimaginable.

She drove along Camden High Street. She was five minutes from his flat.

If she'd found that photograph twelve hours earlier there would have been a confrontation. She would have demanded to know the answers to questions she could no longer ask. And she would not have slept with him. Might not. The sex had changed everything. She knew it was a horribly old-fashioned outlook on things but it was hers. It always had been and it had cost her too many years of unhappiness to remember.

Now she had to . . . compartmentalise. She needed to ignore a side of the man she was sharing a bed with. It seemed to threaten everything. Her feelings for Thorne gave her little option and those she was losing for Jeremy might just make it possible. For the time being at least she had to make a choice. She could not think about a future with Thorne while having to reconcile herself to the damage he seemed determined to do to her past. And a future with him, however short, was what she felt she should go for.

She would put her fingers in her ears and scream. She had no choice.

She thought about Alison, so removed from everything. More than anything she wanted to bring her back. But with the fear and hate and mistrust that seemed to be so much part and parcel of everything, she couldn't help but wonder if Alison might be better off where she was.

She turned the radio on. There was nothing

worth listening to, but she was nearly home anyway.

The bath was starting to get cold.

Thorne sat up and looked at his watch, which was lying next to his mobile phone on the toilet lid. Nearly one o'clock in the morning.

He'd been lying, completely still, with his head under the water. His eyes were open and he stared up at the ceiling swimming above him, waiting for the water to stop moving around him and seeing how long he could hold his breath. It was a game he had played as a kid, lying in a steaming bath in that big old, echoey bathroom, pretending to be dead. He had stopped the night his grandmother came in, saw him, and took a bit of a turn. He'd sat bolt upright the second she screamed, but he would never forget that look on her face.

It was a look he'd seen many times since.

He'd usually have a glass of wine in the bath, but tonight he had thought better of it. It wasn't that he was on the wagon. He'd clambered aboard that particular vehicle a couple of times and it was a very dull ride. He just didn't think he should have a drink.

Not on a Tuesday night.

It felt, in so many ways, like the beginning of something. Since last night he'd thought about Jan a few times, but not in a maudlin or sentimental way. Being with Anne hadn't made him think about what he was missing. On the contrary, he realised finally that he hadn't been missing it. Missing Jan.

And it might be the beginning of the end of the sweat-stained nightmare that was this case. He thought about Holland and Hendricks out on a limb for him and hoped that what might happen the next day would save them the trouble. It could all be that easy. He wouldn't march back into Keable's office like Charlie Big Potatoes, full of himself, but it would be close.

Thorne got out of the bath, towelled himself off and threw on his dressing-gown. Ignoring the plastic Thresher's bag in the kitchen, he walked across to the stereo and stuck on *Grievous Angel* by Gram Parsons. Now, there was a man who couldn't say no to a drink.

'*You can, though, Tommy.*'

'*Best not tonight, eh?*'

'*Please, not tonight . . .*'

He lay down on the sofa, thoughts buzzing around in his head like a swarm of fat black flies.

He wanted to ring Anne but thought she'd be in bed by now. His dad would still be up. Or was Anne working late? He couldn't remember. Had James run home and told Daddy all about their little chat? Probably. Had Alison overheard the phone call in her room? Holland's girlfriend didn't like him, that was obvious. How the fuck was he going to organise a box at White Hart Lane?

What would the eldest Calvert girl have been now? Twenty-four? Twenty-five?

The wine would fuzzy up his thinking a little for sure, but it might at least slow things down. He stayed on the sofa and the wine stayed in the bottle. Tomorrow, who could say? There might be cause to celebrate.

Tonight Jeremy Bishop was on call.

There was no way he was going to sleep without calling, so he did. Bishop picked up almost immediately. As the smooth tones gave way quickly to impatience then anger, Thorne flicked the switch that terminated the call, and lay there, relieved, holding the phone. The tension eased in an instant and an overwhelming tide of fatigue began to creep over him. He crossed his arms over the phone on his chest and closed his eyes.

He got into the car and sat for a moment, steadying himself. He'd had a tough day. Things had come up that needed dealing with and had almost upset his plans for the evening. It was going to be OK, though.

The courtesy light faded away and he began to relax, satisfied that he'd left everything ready at home, should he be lucky enough to bring a guest back. He placed the things he would need on the passenger seat. All could be easily hidden in his pocket when the time came. He was sad that he'd had to dispense with the champagne, but she might have seen that stupid reconstruction. There was no need for it now anyway, but there had been something stylish about it. He'd never skimped:

it had always been Taittinger. He'd believed in making their last taste a good one – their last taste in any conventional sense.

The conversations while he'd been waiting for the drug to kick in, though tedious in the main, had at least given him a sense of who he was treating. That was important. The thirty minutes with Alison had made him feel even better about the new life he'd given her. In that half an hour or so of drunken drivel, he'd come to understand the old life he'd be saving her from. From now on it was something of a lottery in that respect.

He smiled. It could be you!

He hoped that the police would be able to see past what were purely practical reasons for this change in his working methods. He didn't want time wasted on irrelevancies. Champagne last time, needle this time, it didn't really matter. Thorne would understand. He might not be involved officially any longer, but that was neither here nor there.

He turned the ignition and switched on his headlights. He felt confident and capable. Once he was back at home and performing the procedure he would not consider the possibility of failure. With the others, it had only been when the light had finally died in their eyes that the word had even entered his head.

He took out his glasses and began to clean the lenses, setting his mind to the immediate task of preparing a new patient. There would need to be some force, unfortunately, as there had been with Thorne, but once he'd found the vein it would be over quickly. Then he just had to keep her quiet for a few minutes and there were ways of doing that. Something sharp would do it nicely. Once the drug began its work she would not be able to cry out anyway, so he shouldn't have too many problems.

The car pulled away and he thought for a while about what he might do when it was all over. There were so many ways that it might end but he wondered how he might look back on what he was doing now. What he'd been forced to do. It would be strange, beginning again, but he would be able to remember certain things with fondness. There would always be Alison and however many other successes time allowed him. He could revel in that. And he would certainly remember and enjoy the symmetry of a punishment justly meted out. Such a fitting punishment. He grinned and began to hum the tune. Someone would certainly wish they'd never dragged him along to Gilbert and Sullivan . . .

He pointed the Volvo towards the West End and leaned back in his seat, feeling as good as he had in a long time.

He'd accomplished so much with skill and rage.

Like I said, some days are a lot better than others . . .

This is the first joke I'm going to tell Anne.

There's this really tasty and sexy young potato and she's walking home from the disco one night, after a top night out with her best friends the parsnip and the runner bean, when she's attacked by this mad carrot. The carrot does all sorts of horrible stuff to her and she winds up in hospital. All her skin's been peeled off and she's been all mashed up and she's just lying there and the only thing that's undamaged are her eyes. The eyes of this potato. So the next day this potato's boyfriend, who's a tall, good-looking swede, comes to the hospital and talks to the doctor and, with tears in his eyes, he says, 'What are her chances, Doc?' The doctor looks down at the poor, sad potato lying in the bed and says to him, 'I'm sorry . . . but she's going to be a vegetable for the rest of her life.'

CHAPTER 13

Brigstocke had presumed it was a hang-over. 'Sleep it off' was not the traditional response to somebody phoning in sick but Thorne couldn't really argue. Brigstocke had worked with him before and it was a reasonable assumption. It wouldn't be too long before his patience gave out, though, and he went higher up. Thorne knew he didn't have much time. He didn't think he'd need much.

One look at the good weather had made up his mind. He decided to take the Thameslink overground from Kentish Town to Tulse Hill. It was direct, and an attractive alternative to sitting in the car for as long as it might otherwise take him to drive to Birmingham, or getting tense and sweaty on the underground. He'd never seen the attraction of the tube. For Thorne it inevitably meant the Northern line – interestingly the line of choice for most people who chose to jump in front of a tube train. He guessed that they were probably choosing to think of others in their own moment of deepest despair. If you're going to fuck up commuters, then why not fuck up those to whom chaos and delay are barely noticeable any more?

Thorne had decided long ago that, should he ever feel the need, he would be a handful-of-pills-bottle-of-red-wine-lie-on-the-bed-and-drift-away-to-Hank-Williams kind of bloke. Anything else was just showing off.

Though it had to be said, a gun in the mouth looked good on some people.

He looked out of the window as the train rumbled across the Blackfriars rail bridge. If it was a different world south of the river, it was one with its own dividing line. South-west was definitely the more gentrified, Clapham and Richmond and, of course, Battersea. There were *nice* areas of South-east London – he was fond of Greenwich and Blackheath – but, on the whole, that part of the city was as close as London got to a war-zone. South-east . . . *Sarf*-east London didn't need coppers, it needed United Nations peacekeepers. At that very minute in Bermondsey and New Cross there were characters propping up bars in dodgy boozers that would have made Slobodan Milosevic shit himself.

He opened his case and looked at the pictures again. They looked like stills captured in any undercover police operation. A career opportunity for Bethell should he ever decide to hang up his dirty mac for good. Bishop was photogenic, Thorne had known he would be, though when the smile he wore in company was absent, the face was considerably harder, severe even.

Thorne went through the pictures one by one. There was the photo of James walking back towards the house after the confrontation with Bethell. He was glancing back over his shoulder, trying to look tough. He hadn't managed it. Thorne wondered if he had a girlfriend. Probably some horsy type called Charlotte, who called herself Charlie, wore black and hung about in Camden Lock on a Sunday afternoon popping pills. He was looking for the best photo – the one in which Bishop was looking virtually straight at the camera. Perhaps he'd heard Bethell moving about or caught a glimpse of bleached hair bobbing about in the bushes. The photo wasn't there and Thorne realised where he'd left it. The phone call he'd taken in Alison's room had thrown him so completely that he'd all but forgotten why he was there in the first place. Maybe a nurse had found it and thrown it away. Unlikely. Anne had almost certainly come across it by now, which meant that he'd have some explaining to do. By then, of course, it would all have been worth it and she'd realise he'd been right. Who was he kidding? Right or wrong, the deceit involved would probably ensure that what had happened between them two nights earlier would turn out to have been a one-night stand.

The old man next to him had been pretending to be reading his newspaper but had been sneaking furtive looks at the photos on Thorne's lap at every opportunity. Maybe he thought Thorne was some kind of spy or sleazy *paparazzo*. Maybe he thought

Thorne had killed his Princess. Either way he was becoming annoying. Thorne turned one of the photos round and held it up so that the old man could have a good look. He quickly glanced back down at his newspaper. Thorne leaned over and whispered conspiratorially, 'It's all right, he's a doctor.'

The old man didn't look up from his paper for the rest of the journey.

Margaret Byrne's house was a five-minute walk from the station. He didn't know the area well but it seemed amazingly calm and suburban, considering that Brixton was two minutes away. Thorne had been on the streets there in 1981. He had never felt so hated. He and many fellow officers had comforted themselves with the thought that it was no more than police bashing. An excuse to torch some flash cars and nick a few TVs. Events since then had made him realise he'd been wrong. And Stephen Lawrence had changed everything.

Thorne rang the doorbell and waited. The curtains in the front bay windows were drawn. The bedroom, he guessed. He looked at his watch; he was ten minutes or so late. He rang the doorbell again. He looked around in the hope of seeing a woman hurrying up the road, having popped out to grab a pint of milk, but saw only a woman in the house opposite, eyeing him suspiciously. He eyed her back.

Thorne pressed himself against the window and peered through a small crack in the green curtains but the room was dark. He turned to see the woman across the road still staring at him. He began to feel uneasy.

'Calm down, Tommy. She's probably just nodded off or something.'

'Oh, Jesus, not now.'

There was a small passage on the right-hand side of the house all but blocked by a couple of black plastic dustbins. Thorne climbed over them and walked slowly down the passageway. The high gate at the end was locked. He dropped his case over the gate and trudged back to grab one of the bins, having decided that the Neighbourhood Watch co-ordinator over the road would probably have called the police by now anyway.

He tried to lower himself down as far as possible on the other side of the fence but the drop to the patio on the other side still made his teeth rattle. The small garden was neat and tidy. There were blouses and slacks hanging on a washing-line.

The back door had been forced open.

He knew he should unlock the gate and get back to the front of the house.

He knew he should phone for back-up.

He knew the phone was staying in his pocket.

The rush was instant, and breathtaking. There was fear too, pumping round his body, tightening his fists and loosening his bowels. This was the fight-flight reflex at its most basic.

Fight or flight. It was never going to be any contest.

Thorne felt his skin slipping off and falling to the ground like an old overcoat. He felt his nerve-endings vibrate, raw and bloody, his senses painfully heightened. The wind in the trees was a cacophony. A face in a faraway window, an oncoming juggernaut. He could taste the air. Tinfoil on a filling.

There was no theatrical creak as he pushed open the door and tensed every muscle. He stepped into a small kitchen. The surfaces were spotless, a tea-towel folded over a chair, washing-up stacked neatly on the draining-board. Thorne fought the impulse to reach for the breadknife and stood still, trying to control his breathing. To his left was an open door that he could see led on to the living room. He moved soundlessly across the linoleum and scanned the room. It was empty. The brown carpet looked new but was presumably the first stage of improvements – the suite was saggy and threadbare. Thorne hurried across the room, took a deep breath and opened the door at the far end.

He was in a dimly lit hall just inside the front door. There were two more rooms opposite him. The one on the right nearest the front door had to be the bedroom; the other, he guessed, a toilet.

It was worth a try. 'Mrs Byrne?'

Nothing.

From behind the second door he heard a small, muffled thud. The thumping in his chest was anything but.

'It always comes down to the final door, Tommy.'

'Open it . . .'

'She'll come walking through the front door in a minute and you'll feel like a right tit . . .'

Thorne opened the door.

He cried out, staggering backwards in sudden shock as something flew, hissing, out of the room and into his legs. He pushed himself off the wall and watched, his heart smashing against his chest as a cat careered into the living room. He heard the bang as it clattered through the cat-flap in the kitchen door.

Then he could smell it.

Cat shit and something else. Something more familiar and far more disgusting. Tangy and metallic, and so strong he could have licked it out of the air. His tongue on a dying battery.

Resigned to the harder stuff . . .

Resigned to the inevitability of what he was going to see, Thorne stepped forward into the darkened room and reached for the light switch.

There were four more cats. One stared down at him from the top of the wardrobe while a second hopped lazily from a highly polished dressing-table. Two more were on the bed. Curled up across the body of Margaret Byrne.

She lay straight, down the edge of the left-hand side of the bed, her hands by her side, her head back and turned towards him. One eye was half open but not as wide as the scarlet smile across her neck, the incision made gaping by the angle of her head on the pillow.

'*Sweet Christ . . .*'

The blood was pooled beneath her collar-bone and had overflowed across her left side and on to the duvet, from where it still dripped slowly on to the patterned blue carpet. One side of her pink blouse was sopping red. A foot or so from where Thorne was standing, frozen to the spot, there was another bloodstain, already sunk in and brown. Spatter patterns snaked away across the carpet, reaching as far as the wall on the opposite side of the bed. He could see straight away that this was where she'd been attacked, before being laid out on the bed to die, he guessed, a short time later. While her killer watched.

Something glinting on the carpet near the end of the bed caught his eye. An earring, perhaps. He could see a necklace too, and rings, and a wooden jewellery box on its side by the wall.

Margaret Byrne had tried to save the few things she had which were precious. But the man she had tried to save them from had not come to rob her.

Once again the nagging voice of procedure. He was contaminating a crime scene. He needed to get out.

He regretted not asking Holland about her when he'd had the chance. Now he had to stand in a carpeted and perfumed slaughter-house and piece it together. It wasn't hard to get a feeling for her. Of her. The cats and the neatly arranged bottles and jars on the dressing-table told him enough. He felt behind him for the solidity of the wall, leaned back against it and lowered himself slowly to the floor. The cat that had been sniffing around, a small black-and-white one, ambled over and nuzzled his shins. Thorne reached into his pocket for his phone and held it, dangling between his knees.

He wanted to stay with Margaret for a while before he made the call.

When the cars arrived Thorne was sitting on the doorstep, staring at the woman in the window opposite. The cat, who would not leave him alone, was making itself comfortable on his lap. Holland walked up and hovered. After a few moments Thorne looked up with a twisted smile. He had expected Tughan and was relieved not to see him. He couldn't see anybody he thought might be Brewer either.

'Been promoted, Holland?'

Holland said nothing. Remembering his conversation with Maggie Byrne on the same spot the day before, he was a word, a heartbeat from tears. Thorne watched the SOCOs steaming up the passageway with their equipment. He had felt the same way as Holland fifteen minutes earlier but now a strange calm had begun to settle over him.

'He executed her, Dave. He broke into her house and executed her.'

Holland looked straight back at him and spoke evenly, his face showing nothing.

'He's been busy.'

PART THREE

THE WORD

I'm going to chuck Tim today. Does that sound a bit sudden? Sorry, I know it's out of the blue and maybe I should have built up to it a bit more, but I've been thinking about it for a good while.

Thinking about it.

Like I can do anything else. I'm hardly in a position to discuss boyfriend problems with my best mate, even if I was sure I still had one. Well, I could, but it would be the dullest girly gossip in history. Barley water and blackboards are no substitute for booze and fags and a home-delivery pizza.

And staring isn't laughing, is it?

But I have been thinking a lot about Tim and how unhappy he is. It's a real old line, I know, but it's for his sake rather than mine. Chucking him, I mean. I won't be trotting out shite like 'I love you but I'm not *in* love with you,' or 'I think we should just be friends.' To be honest, I'm not exactly sure what I will say. I say 'say'. Obviously I mean 'blink' and 'twitch' while the poor sod tries to keep the smile plastered to his face as he does his best to work out what the fuck I'm on about.

It's not as if I've got anything to go on, nothing I've ever seen in a film or on telly. Tearful farewells to terminally ill loved ones are ten a penny but this is pretty sodding unique. Never seen this on *EastEnders* or *Brookside*. It's probably only a matter of time, of course. They'll drag it out over a couple of months. Milk it a bit. Probably be the big Christmas cliffhanger with the tragic, yet still very sexy young woman in the hospital bed blinking like buggery while her hunky boy-friend kneels by the side of the bed, sobbing his heart out and telling her that he still loves her no matter what.

Yeah, right . . .

So I don't really know how I'm going to do it, but it's got to be done. I've only ever dumped one person. I was seventeen and he copped off with one of my mates at a party. Had his hand up her bra while I was in the queue for the toilet. Even so, the actual chucking was pretty tricky, and bear in mind, that was when I was vertical with a working gob.

The way I am now, it's shaping up to be a nightmare.

I know that in letting Tim off this very nasty hook, I'm probably coming across like some selfless, saintly figure, but the sad truth is that actually I'm just being a right selfish cow.

Because the fact is that he won't do it.

And I can't stand to see the pain in his eyes any more when he looks at me.

He doesn't know what to do, bless him. He talks, slowly. He talks and he uses the pointer like Anne showed him but I know he can't bear it. He's always been a bit of a girl about hospitals and blood and anything like that.

He said that he wished it had happened to him instead of me, and I know he means it. Before it sounds like this is me setting him free, or some cobblers like that, so he can go off and find someone else, I should say that if I ever get out of here and get myself sorted out, he'd better come running straight back, and I won't want to hear about what he's been up to and who with.

The truth is simple. He can't stand to see me hurt, and I feel the same way about him. And he looks utterly crushed all the time he's with me and it's my fault. I'm five feet fuck-all and I can't move a muscle and I'm squashing all the life out of him. So best to knock it on the head for now. Not the best choice of words probably but that's not something I get a lot of say in these days.

He's not going to like it. He'll cry most

271

probably, big soft thing, or shout. Actually that would be good, there's nothing like a bit of a scene to get the nurses going, but I think that when he goes home and thinks about it he'll be relieved. For Christ's sake, our dream ticket, our magic-island scenario, the best we can fucking hope for, involves wheelchairs and computers and one of us winning the lottery to pay for it all, and me about as much use as one of my two-year-olds and I wouldn't wish that on anybody.

Tim cares about me, I know he does. But I couldn't bear to be pitied. Loved is fine. But not pitied.

And 'cares for' is not 'cares about', is it?

So Tim, think yourself lucky, pet, and I apologise in advance if, at the crucial moment in your posh wedding to some drop-dead gorgeous blonde, when the vicar says that bit about 'just cause or impediment', the door to the church crashes open and some spackhead in a wheelchair trundles in. Just ignore me and get on with it. I'll probably be pissed . . .

Fuck me, did you hear what I said before?

'If I ever get out of here.'

If . . .

CHAPTER 14

The cat had sat and watched, content, unblinking, as a woman who loved her had been smashed across the back of the head and bled dry like a pig. Now she sat staring down at the face of a man who didn't understand any more than she had. Rising and falling with him as he breathed. Rising and falling and watching his eyes. They were closed but she followed the movements of his eyeballs, darting back and forth behind the eyelids like tiny trapped animals. Looking for a way out. Searching for a weak spot. Heads bulging behind the eyes, threatening to burst through the paper-thin skin . . .

. . . and Maggie Byrne smiled and lay back on the bed. She kicked off her shoes and rubbed her feet together. He could hear the nylon of her tights crackling. He said something – a joke maybe. She threw back her head to laugh and the red line beneath her chin started to gape. She blushed and reached for a scarf and he told her that it didn't matter but she was already starting to cry. She shook her head and sobbed and tried to tie the scarf around her neck. The gash gaped wider until it looked like something on a fishmonger's slab. The not-so-slender neck, hacked into sections like tuna. Pink then a darker pink then red.

And his words would not comfort her. And he tried to take her in his arms but they slipped from around her neck. And his hands were stroking her collarbone and his fingers were exploring the damp and clammy interior of the wound.

Testing for freshness.

Maggie Byrne tried to scream but it came whistling from her neck.

He opened his eyes . . .

He hadn't been asleep and it wasn't a dream. Just a mental snapshot, twisted. A memory adjusted and warped by the unwelcome addition of an imagination. Something that lived in the ghoulish and morbid corner of his subconscious having its bit of fun.

He opened his eyes . . .

And waited for the images to blur and become distant. Lying on the sofa, hearing his heartbeat slow down. Feeling the beads of sweat on his face evaporate. Letting something creep back into its corner.

Until the next time.

He opened his eyes and stared back at the cat sitting on his chest.

'Fuck off, Elvis!'

The cat jumped off Thorne and slunk away towards the bedroom. Maggie had been a big Elvis fan and had named the cat before it had been sexed. She'd always thought it was funny. Sally Byrne had taken a couple of her mother's cats back to Edinburgh with her, and the rest had gone to the PDSA, but Elvis had been Thorne's from the moment he'd opened the door to Maggie's bedroom and breathed in the blood. The cat seemed drawn to him, Sally had said. To need him, almost.

Almost as much as he needed her.

Just over two weeks now since he'd opened that bedroom door. Just over twenty-four hours since Margaret Byrne's funeral. Thorne didn't know about the arrangements for Leonie Holden. He was what he'd once heard Nick Tughan describe as 'out of the loop' on that one. Her funeral might well already have happened. They'd found her a few hours before he'd found Maggie Byrne, and if Phil Hendricks had got the bits of her he needed, safely labelled in jars, then the body would have been released back to those for whom it still meant something real. Something in their hearts and in their guts. Then they could say goodbye.

There would have been an official presence at her funeral, of course. It was often just some flowers but he could picture Tughan at the back of a church, in black like an assassin. He wondered if Frank Keable would have put in an appearance. Or somebody higher up. If the body count carried on rising they'd end up having to send the commissioner along. A thin smile and a wreath of white lilies spelling out 'Sorry, doing our best.'

275

Thorne had never made a habit of attending the funerals of his victims . . . the victims of his cases – *on* his cases. He'd go on the occasions when they thought there was a fair chance of the killer turning up. He'd stand at the back then, scanning the mourners, looking for one who didn't belong. There was no chance of the killer attending the funerals of these victims, though. He wanted to forget the dead ones. They were his failures.

It suddenly struck Thorne like a hammer to the chest that he had no idea when Helen Doyle had been buried. Buried, of course, not cremated. Leaving it open for a second post-mortem, should one be needed, or demanded much later by the accused.

Even dead, her body was not her own.

Thorne swung his feet to the floor, sat up and rubbed his eyes. The sweat was making them sting. He was starving. There was a headache starting . . .

It was time to stop hiding.

He'd emerged briefly to pay the respects he felt were due to Margaret Byrne, that he guessed she'd never received when she was alive. He'd hugged the daughter of a woman he'd known only in death. He'd held her close as she wept. He'd laughed as she talked about cats and waved as she climbed into the funeral car.

He'd looked across the all-but-empty church at Dave Holland, who sat stony-faced and stiff, like a sixth-former in an uncomfortable collar. They'd nodded to each other and looked away quickly. It was probably best to keep a little distance with so much accusation still flying around. So much blame to be doled out.

Thorne had given himself a fair bit of explaining to do and hadn't made a particularly good job of it. They knew it was Holland who'd told him about Margaret Byrne and given him her address. They couldn't prove it, but they knew. It didn't change anything. It didn't explain to anybody how the killer had found out. Or how the killer had known that Thorne was close to a positive identification. Or how the killer had been able to pop round to snuff out the threat before calmly going about the business of slaughtering Leonie Holden.

Nothing was easily explained, but what was obvious to everyone was that Thorne had no business being anywhere near Margaret Byrne. He looked unreliable.

He felt responsible.

Margaret Byrne had died because of what she knew and what she could tell him. That was obvious. She'd died because Thorne knew who the killer was and because she could identify him and because somewhere, in an inept operation that he'd once been a part of, there was a leak big enough to sink a battleship.

Thorne had an idea or two about *who*, but was at a loss to explain *how* or *why*. The press getting hold of stuff, which now they had, was never a mystery. The solution was always there, lurking inside the bank balance of a constable with a gambling problem or some sergeant with too much alimony to pay. But this was something else entirely. This leak had led a killer back to Margaret Byrne's door with an iron bar and a scalpel. This was something infinitely more sinister and something to be guarded much more fiercely.

Ranks were swiftly closed. Eyes turned outwards, fingers pointing. And now, for Thorne, everything was in the balance. Keable had just told him to sit and wait. Thorne had little argument. He was in trouble and decisions needed to be made at a higher level. It sounded good, it sounded like a plan of action, but Thorne knew that really Keable just had no idea what to do with him.

And Thorne was already sick of sitting and waiting.

The nagging headache was starting to scream. He stood and walked towards the bathroom in search of aspirin, but his eye was taken by the small red light winking at him from the table near the front door. Messages on his answering-machine.

'It's only Dad. Call me when you get a minute . . .'

'Tom . . . it's Anne. I'll call back.'

Then a voice he didn't recognise. A woman's voice. Quiet. Reluctant. A catch in the throat . . .

'Hello, we've never met. My name's Leonie Holden and I was murdered a week or so ago. I would have been twenty-four next week and now I'm alone and I'm cold and frankly I don't give a fuck about who told who what, or your career, or matching carpet fibres

278

and I'd be grateful if you could try and sort all this out, you know . . .'

He opened his eyes.

A cold shower. And hot coffee. And real messages on a real answering-machine.

Time to stop hiding.

Voices, all of them anxious. His father, twice. Anne, twice. Phil Hendricks, needing to talk. Keable, still trying to save his career, or something. Sally Byrne to check on the cat. Dave Holland . . .

And Thorne needed to get out of his flat and talk to all of them, but in the spaces between the messages was a silence that spoke in a voice more insistent than any other. Murmuring the words that had exploded in his head a week or so before and now buzzed around his brain night and day, like aftershocks. He still heard them as they had been spoken to him, announced to him, with undisguised triumph, in Tughan's cold and oddly characterless accent. Words that still numbed him and would force their way, unspoken or otherwise, into any conversation with Anne Coburn or Phil Hendricks or Frank Keable or Dave Holland or anybody else for that matter.

Jeremy Bishop has a cast-iron alibi.

Jeremy Bishop could not possibly have killed Margaret Byrne.

Lunchtime. A sandwich and an energy drink from

279

a nice deli and a stroll around the choking streets of Bloomsbury to stare at the dying.

He could still feel the shockwave up his arm as Margaret Byrne's skull had cracked. He'd felt it shatter like mint cracknel beneath the blow from the bar. That had shut her up. Silly mare had been squealing and running from room to room from the moment he'd kicked open the flimsy back door. It had only been a few seconds but still he wondered, as he followed her into the bedroom and moved towards her from behind, if the neighbours would be able to hear. As he locked his left arm beneath her chin to keep her upright, and his right hand reached into his pocket for the scalpel, he decided it would be all right. Probably just the TV up too loud. Nothing to get excited about.

He might have been seen too. There had been a noticeable bit of curtain-twitching as he'd walked past the house earlier, but it was all a bonus in the long run, despite the confusion it was bound to cause in some quarters. The jewellery on the floor would probably have troubled them a little as well. They could hardly have thought it was a bungled burglary, but perhaps there'd been a struggle? Perhaps the poor thing had thought he was going to rob her. It didn't really matter.

Whatever they were thinking was wrong.

He could still feel the rush as the blade moved across her windpipe. As the blood spurted and sprayed, soundlessly, on to the thick, ugly carpet, he'd jammed a knee into the small of her back and

280

begun hoicking her towards the bed, wishing he'd had the time to do it all properly.

He could still hear the purring of the cats, the only noise that disturbed the silence as he stood watching the life run out of her. Given the time, he'd have liked to make it look like suicide. That way there would have been no confusion. No problems with the timing of events.

She'd needed dealing with quickly, however, and he'd done what was necessary. He now realised that the rushing, and the way his timetable had become compromised, had probably been responsible for the failure with the girl on the bus.

Leonie, the newspaper said her name was. They hadn't had time, of course, to get to know each other properly.

It hadn't helped, that much was certain. He had not been calm enough during the procedure. The excitement of the earlier events had made him clumsy and thrown his timing.

He'd have done it carefully, of course, the suicide. The layman's way. The slash horizontal across the wrist, as opposed to the vertical cut, wrist to elbow along the radial artery, which is far more efficient but hugely suspicious. Mind you, they might not even have spotted that. Everything else was taking them an age.

But then there was Tom Thorne to consider. There was always him. He hadn't known exactly when Thorne was planning to visit Margaret Byrne, but he doubted she had many visitors, so there was a pretty good chance he'd get lucky. When the papers confirmed the name of the officer who'd discovered the body of 'Mrs Byrne – 43' he'd whooped with joy. The one good thing that had come out of all this was Thorne's . . . marginalisation. Looked at that way, he supposed that the timing could not have been any better. Now Thorne was more isolated than ever.

An isolated Tom Thorne, he guessed, was a very dangerous one.

And that was just how he wanted him.

It was a twenty-minute stroll to Waterlow Park. Thorne had toyed with the idea of meeting at Highgate cemetery, but that was his and Jan's place. Or had been. It was a nice spot in which to waste a Sunday morning. She, desperate to feel like the heroine in some arty black-and-white film, and he, happy to kill an hour or two before a boozy lunch in the Old Crown or the Flask. Both content to spend time doing very little, and laugh every single time at the grave of the unknown Mr Spencer that sat opposite that of the far more famous Marx.

Adjoining the cemetery at its north end was Waterlow Park, a small but much loved green space, which those who frequented it never tired of describing as a 'hidden treasure'. The clientele here was odd to say the least: a mixture of the chattering classes, drugged-up layabouts and community-care cases with a smattering of hugely pregnant women sent here from the Whittington hospital to walk about in the hope of bringing on labour.

Thorne was fond of it, not least because of Lauderdale House, the sixteenth-century stately home at its entrance. Now it housed kids' puppet shows, antiques fairs and exhibitions of hideous modern art. It had a decent restaurant and a nice, if overpriced, coffee bar. But four hundred years earlier Nell Gwynne had stayed there as mistress to Charles II. A snotty woman had once told Thorne that Lauderdale House was where Ms Gwynne had 'received her King'. He told her that it was as good a euphemism as he'd ever heard, but the snotty woman had failed to see the funny side. Thorne decided she could have done with receiving a bit of King herself.

Now the place could always raise his spirits. This lovely listed building had basically been a top-of-the-range knocking shop. For this reason alone, the park had become a favourite place for sitting and thinking, with soundtrack courtesy of Gram or Hank on a CD Walkman, an unexpected gift from Jan for his fortieth birthday.

He walked along the huge curving path that ran towards a pair of ropey tennis courts. Every hundred yards or so he came across a figure made of grass, or carved from a dead tree. Organic sculptures. It was probably some Millennium project. What a waste of time and money that had been. He'd spent 31 December 1999 with

Phil Hendricks, a chicken vindaloo and an obscene amount of lager. They were both asleep before midnight.

It was as good a place as any for a meeting. Thorne took off his leather jacket and sat on a bench, bolted on to the concrete pathway. He stared across the park at the huge green dome of St Joseph's. The weather was warm, considering that October was just round the corner.

A couple walked towards him hand in hand. They were young, in their early thirties, loose-limbed and straight-backed. He wore baggy-fitting beige trousers and a white sweater. She wore tight white jeans and a cream fleecy top. They walked easily together in step, smiling at something said earlier.

As the pair came nearer to him, brash and bullet-proof, Thorne felt envy burn through his body like caustic soda dissolving the fat in a drain. They were somehow so light and so immaculate, the two of them. An advertiser's dream couple, walking off the coffee and croissants enjoyed in some beautifully converted warehouse. Thorne knew that they had good jobs and cooked exotic meals for perfect friends and had great sex. They enjoyed everything and doubted nothing.

They were undamaged.

He thought of himself and Anne, and wondered if the two of them were not just being utterly stupid.

Why was he finding it so hard to call her?

He'd left a message the day after he'd found Maggie Byrne's body, saying that something had come up, but since then he'd ignored her calls. It wasn't just about the connection with Bishop. It was about keeping something of himself back – that shadowy and indefinable part of himself that he'd need if he was going to get through this in one piece and stop the killing. He was willing to risk everything for that, and he knew that if things with Anne Coburn got any more serious, pieces might start to come away. It was armour and it was also camouflage, and he knew that the smallest crack might render it useless. Given time it would probably renew itself. It would harden eventually, but this was still not a good time to be . . . vulnerable.

Yet still he wanted her close. He wanted her closeness. He watched the young couple strolling away from him towards the pagoda, much favoured by those keen on exchanging bodily fluids in the open air. He decided that he was being an idiot. He'd call Anne as soon as he got back to the flat. What the hell was he thinking of, anyway? He was just a copper, at least in theory.

Cracks in armour? Jesus . . .

He imagined himself briefly as a boxer, unable to fuck before a big fight. It was a ludicrous analogy, but the pictures in his head amused him so much that he was still smiling five minutes later when his date arrived.

★   ★   ★

285

There were times when it seemed that a woman deprived of the power of speech was the only person Anne Coburn could really talk to.

Sitting alone in the hospital canteen and pushing a tasteless bit of salad around a paper plate, she contemplated her failings as a professional. The sessions with Alison were going well, but Anne knew that if she wasn't careful there was a danger that they would become fully-fledged therapy sessions.

And not for Alison.

Alison was having problems with her boyfriend and things were coming to a head, yet Anne had spent the large part of their last session together bitching about her own problems.

Problems with her daughter. And her ex-husband. And her lover.

Things with Rachel were not getting any better. At least they were talking but they weren't saying anything. There was an element of walking on eggshells on both their parts, the two of them well aware that the smallest comment could blow up into a major row. It was the work she wasn't doing for the resits and the early nights she wasn't getting and the truth she almost certainly wasn't telling.

It was, Anne had begun to suspect – no, to be *certain* – the boy she was seeing.

Anne had brought it up once, casually, but Rachel's reaction, tight-mouthed and defiant, had left her in no doubt that the subject was off limits. It was so stupid. Anne would have no problems with a boyfriend. Why should she? There had been boyfriends before. It was just the timing that was so bloody silly. Important exams were only weeks away and Rachel was in danger of making a mess of everything and Anne couldn't do a thing about it.

Rachel was stubborn, like her father, and now he wasn't speaking to Anne either. Relations between her and David had been distinctly frosty, bordering on downright venomous, for a while, but since she'd told him about Thorne, things had worsened rapidly. He'd seemingly broken off communication altogether, and at a time when a united front, as far as Rachel was concerned, would have been a nice idea.

What was so strange was that he'd seemed to know about the relationship with Thorne even before it happened. She thought back to the confrontation in the lift. He had been making comments about it even then. That was why she'd told him. She wasn't trying to score points – well, maybe just one or two – but his suspicion was already providing him with ample bile to spit in her direction, so why not simply congratulate him on his prescience? But since she'd confirmed her involvement . . . *was it an involvement?* . . . with Thorne, he'd turned really nasty.

Steve Clark walked past and smiled, and she smiled back and wondered if part of this business with Rachel might not have something to do with Thorne as well. Was Rachel jealous? Anne had made an effort to talk to her about Thorne. Since the big flare-up a few weeks earlier she'd tried to be more open. She'd told Rachel about the case and about her connection with it. She'd left out some of the more grisly details and skirted around Jeremy's . . . involvement, as much for her own peace of mind as anything. She'd kept her up-to-date with Alison's progress and, in general, had made a real effort to build bridges. But perhaps she hadn't explained to Rachel how she felt about Thorne.

Anne pushed away the plate of untouched salad and decided that it was because she hadn't actually worked it out herself.

She stood up and moved quickly to the rear of the canteen and out through the swing doors to the fire escape, where she lit a cigarette and took in the view of large steel bins and heaps of polystyrene packaging.

Thorne . . .

He seemed fairly central to all her problematic relationships. Not least the one with Jeremy Bishop.

She'd barely spoken to Jeremy since the night she and Thorne had ended up in bed. This . . . cooling off had been her decision, but she sensed that he was keeping his distance as well. She couldn't deny the possibility that Jeremy was jealous, and that an element of that jealousy might be sexual, but she also suspected that he was becoming involved with somebody himself. He'd made one or two typically oblique comments in the days before

288

they'd stopped seeing each other. He'd seemed distracted and by something other than work. She hoped that it was a woman. She wished Jeremy happy as much as she wished anything.

She missed him.

But she wouldn't pick up the phone. She'd known this man for more than twenty-five years and despite the stupidity of Thorne's suspicions, to do so would have felt vaguely disloyal to the man she'd known for five minutes.

She resented having her loyalty tested. To anybody and by anybody. And why the hell wasn't Thorne calling anyway?

He'd rung to tell her there had been some sort of serious development on the case. Serious, to her, had sounded like another word for 'death', and two days later she'd read all about it. Then the other stuff. No mention of Alison, thank heavens, but plenty of gory grist to the media mill. The press blackout that Thorne had seemed so anxious about early on was well and truly ended. Outraged leader columns and pictures of five dead women.

She'd stopped looking at the newspapers now. She was living with enough sickness already.

Anne didn't want any involvement in this hideous case bar the one she had already through Alison. She didn't want to know anything else.

Until they caught him.

Thorne and Holland had walked down to the pond next to the park's southernmost exit. They leaned against the railings and talked, occasionally needing to raise their voices above the shouts from the children's playground only a few feet away. A father smoked and read a paper, while two children tried unsuccessfully to clamber up a slide and a third stood on a swing, demanding to be looked at.

While Holland stared out across the water, Thorne watched a large brown rat scuttling about in the dust beneath the low hedge that skirted the pond. There were always a few here, on the lookout for badly thrown bits of bread and Thorne was always excited to spot one. It wasn't a beautiful creature, but while Holland's eye was taken by the variety of ducks and geese on display, Thorne's was naturally drawn to the rat. The scavenger, the chancer, the survivor. The villain.

This city could have no more perfect symbol.

'I hadn't got you pegged for a messenger boy, Holland.'

Holland could feel the redness rising up his neck as he turned to look at him. 'That's because I'm not, sir.'

Thorne instantly regretted his tone. It had been an attempt at dark humour but had just sounded sarcastic. Holland was already past it. 'DCI Keable thought that we might run into each other, that's all. He *had* tried to phone you himself . . .'

Thorne nodded. Lots of people had tried to phone him.

Letting Holland convey this somewhat bizarre

offer was a shrewd move. Frank Keable was not the most inspired or inspiring of officers, but he knew what was going on around him. He could read the troops. He always got a sense of the currents within an operation, which went way beyond who had the hump or who might fancy who.

The rat was standing on its hind legs now, sniffing at a litter-bin attached to the railings. Thorne looked across at Holland. 'So, what do you think?'

Holland smiled, part of him flattered at being asked but the greater part well aware that his opinion would probably be worth less than nothing. 'I think it's a good offer, as a matter of fact. Sounds to me like you'll be pretty much a free agent and as long as you don't get into too much trouble . . .'

'Or mention Jeremy Bishop?'

Holland saw no point in sugaring the pill. 'It could be a lot worse.'

Thorne knew that he was right. Keable had hinted at disciplinary action after the discovery of Margaret Byrne's body, but with that and the Leonie Holden killing, castigating a rogue detective inspector with an over-active imagination had become something of a low priority. That's what Keable had said anyway. Either that or he'd had his own reasons for not wanting to make it official just yet and was giving himself time to think of exactly what best to do with Thorne. Either way, at the end of it all there was probably no more than a wrist-slapping in it.

Holland hadn't told him everything.

'They know about the fibres from Bishop's car boot.'

'Fuck.' Thorne kicked at the ground, the dust and grit sending the rat darting momentarily for cover. Somebody in Forensics with a very big mouth. That would explain the call from Hendricks. He needed to talk to him.

'So I'm in a bit of bother, which, if I accept this offer to become some sort of consultant or whatever bollocks title Frank Keable's come up with, might go away. Is that it?'

'He didn't exactly say that, sir.'

Consultant. He wondered what the catches were. Beyond the obvious one.

Leonie Holden was last seen on a night bus bound for Ealing and her body was discovered four hours later on wasteground in Tufnell Park.

Less than a quarter of a mile from Thorne's flat.

The significance of this latest message from the killer to his favourite detective inspector was not lost on anybody.

Consultant? A better word might have been 'bait'.

'What do you think about Jeremy Bishop?'

Holland phrased his answer carefully. 'I don't think he killed Margaret Byrne, sir.'

'He was supposed to have had a cast-iron alibi for Alison Willetts as well, and we found holes in it.'

'I still don't understand any of it, though. I still

can't figure out how he could have done what he did to Alison and got her to the hospital in the time. Not to mention why. Why did he go to all that trouble just to give himself an alibi that didn't hold water?'

'I'll work it out, Holland. And I'll work out how he killed Margaret Byrne as well.'

'He didn't, sir.'

'A man fitting his description was seen acting suspiciously outside her flat earlier in the day.'

'Coincidence. Got to be. Besides, that woman opposite is a nutter. She thought *I* was suspicious.' Holland spoke calmly, no element of letting Thorne down gently, just stating the facts. 'I've been to the Royal London and spoken to everybody except the patients in deep comas. She was killed sometime mid- to late-afternoon, and Bishop was at the hospital, working through a routine theatre list. There's dozens of witnesses. Whitechapel to Tulse Hill and back without being missed is impossible.'

Thorne was grateful to Holland for having made the effort. He'd almost certainly done it in his own time, and in the knowledge that if Tughan had found out he'd have been in deep shit.

'No alibi for Leonie Holden.' Thorne was thinking aloud now.

'Sir . . .'

No alibi for Leonie Holden. Because he killed her. The fucker killed her and dumped her on my doorstep.

293

'So you think I'm barking up the wrong tree as well, then, Holland? Or maybe that should just be barking?'

Holland sighed. The questions just kept getting harder. 'I *had* been sort of coming round to the idea of Bishop as a prime suspect, sir. There's certainly nobody else in the frame, and even though it's all circumstantial I was willing to . . . go with it as an avenue of inquiry. But Maggie Byrne – her and Leonie Holden had to have been killed by the same man.'

They stood in silence. Thorne had nothing to say. Holland had plenty, but thought most was better kept to himself. Behind them, a child tumbled from the roundabout and began to scream.

Holland cleared his throat. 'All the same, as a theory it does have one thing going for it, sir.'

'Yeah?' mumbled Thorne. 'What's that?'

'It's yours.'

Thorne couldn't look at him. He clenched his jaw. He was scared for a second or two that if he looked at Holland his face would show far too much gratitude. It would be shining and desperate and pathetic.

The face that showed too much of everything.

He turned and began to walk towards the gate. His sudden movement caused the rat to bolt again with a small squeal of alarm. The cheeky little bastard had been sitting on its haunches and cleaning its whiskers. They were so unafraid. Thorne had stood there before now and watched one scamper across his shoes.

He glanced over his shoulder. Holland was half a dozen paces behind him.

Whatever journey was ahead, Thorne had no intention of slowing down but sensed that Holland might be the sort of man, the sort of copper, who would close the gap and walk alongside him.

And perhaps, together, they would bring down Jeremy Bishop.

They reckoned that, in London, you were never more than six feet away from a rat. Thorne knew that you weren't a whole lot further from an altogether nastier breed of vermin.

More diseased. More human.

There is definitely no God. Or if there is, he, she or it is a right sick bastard. Like this isn't bad enough!

The way Anne explained it to me is like this.

They have to keep pulling me about every ten bloody minutes so I don't get pressure sores, even on my lovely vibrating bed. So one of the nurses, don't know which one but my money's on Martina as revenge for the neck-coughing incident, accidentally dislodges the nasogastric feed, that's 'tube up nose' to you and me, as she's moving me. Just an inch or two, but that's all it takes. What happens then is that the feed, which is this tasteless white shite that's supposedly full of proteins and other great stuff, instead of going where it's supposed to go, pours into my chest. Loads of it. Now, you and other people who can cough and splutter, just cough and splutter this crap back up and pull a face, and a few days later you might develop a mild chest infection.

Not me, though. Oh, no.

This feed is like nectar to fucking bacteria. They love it. They swarm all over it and, hey presto, I get bastard pneumonia. This sort of thing was bound to happen sooner or later. I'm prone to infection apparently. Well, isn't that just marvellous?

So, here I am back on the ventilator. Big mechanical bellows doing my breathing and I feel like I did when I'd just come in here.

Everything else stops now until I recover. Occupational therapy gets put on hold. The communication was going pretty well, it has to be said. We'd worked out a pretty good system using an alphabet that's based on how many times a certain letter is likely to be used. So it doesn't go A, B, C, D, E. It's not an A–Z so much as an E–X. We've also got shortcuts for going back, for skipping forward, to repeat words, and Anne has become the human equivalent of that thing on my mobile phone that guesses what I'm going to say. She finishes words for me and most of the time she's spot on. She's just about got used to my swearing as well.

Now all that's got to stop until I'm a bit stronger. Until I'm better.

Yeah, well, when you're like this, better is a relative term.

The blackboard's gone from the end of the bed. I am so fucking frustrated.

To be honest, I say the communication was going well and it *was* compared to a few weeks ago but it didn't make things any easier with Tim. All the things I'd planned to say went out of the window once we got down to it.

He just stood there with the pointer in his hand, looking lost.

Even if you can spell the most complicated words in the world as fast as anything, they're just words, aren't they? You can't spell out feelings with an eyelid and a pointer. I couldn't really make him understand.

In the end all I could do was spell out the one word and say it over and over again.

G.O.O.D.B.Y.E.

Goodbye, goodbye, goodbye . . .

CHAPTER 15

'I shall be glad to have you around, Tom, but having said that . . .'

Keable was behind his desk making a speech. Tughan leaned against the wall, greasy-haired and gimlet-eyed. Ostensibly Keable was welcoming Thorne back to Operation Backhand, albeit in an unorthodox and somewhat undefined role, but in reality he was laying down ground rules. What those rules were, Thorne would need to clarify later. Now he had one eye on his old friend the Exmoor stag.

He saw new things in this dreary piece of ersatz West Country dross each time he looked at it. Today he glanced up from his chair and was drawn by something in the set of the animal's jaw that seemed overtly aggressive. It was probably just fear, or the readiness to charge the photographer at any moment, but Thorne was mentally adding a thought bubble to the side of the stag's head which read, 'We don't like your sort round here.' It was only a matter of days now until the stunning view that encapsulated October would be unveiled. He was sure that Keable looked forward to this moment every month. What riveting image might Thorne find himself staring at next week? 'Badger At Dusk', perhaps. He wondered if he'd be here long enough to see it.

Keable had finished. 'Well?'

Thorne gave Keable his full attention. The DCI's expression seemed open and amenable. So far this had gone a lot better than might have been expected.

'We should make it clear,' chipped in Tughan, 'that nobody's asking if you're interested in accepting this offer, because it isn't really an offer. You don't have any choice.'

Thorne knew he was hooked and landed, but he still wanted to struggle a little. He ignored Tughan and spoke directly to Keable. 'I appreciate you keeping the disciplinary side of recent events low-key, Frank, but I'm still a bit confused as to exactly what you want me to do in return.' *Because I wasn't really listening. Sorry.* 'Consultant . . . secret weapon . . . supersub, whatever you choose to call it, I'll still be the one DI too many. Brewer's still around, I don't think Nick's planning on going anywhere . . .'

He smiled at Tughan. The Irishman smiled back, his face blank.

'. . . so what am I actually going to be doing day to day, Frank?'

Keable took a few seconds to formulate a response. When it came it was spoken gently but the steel was barely hidden. 'It was you who wanted out in the first place, Thorne, and you got what you wanted. You made a bloody mess of it and here you are again. You're not in any position to be questioning anything.'

Thorne nodded. He needed to be careful. 'Yes, sir.' He glanced across at Tughan. This time the bastard's smile was genuine.

Keable stood and walked round his desk. There was a small mirror on top of the filing cabinet in the corner and he crouched to catch his reflection and adjust his tie. 'I want you as an unofficial part of this operation. I know that you're anything but stupid and you realise that while you're here the killer knows where to find you.'

He'd know where to find me wherever I was. He's watching.

'This seems important to him and what's important to him is important to me. There's not a great deal we're sure of, as far as this case goes, but the killer has some . . . affinity with you, which I intend to take full advantage of. If you're unhappy about that, tough.' Keable stood up. His tie was perfect. 'Are you?'

Thorne shook his head. He was anything but unhappy about it. Not that he intended to sit about and wait for the killer to pop by and say hello. The initiative, which he'd had at one point, had slipped away. He'd *allowed* it to slip away. He wanted it back.

Keable was moving past Tughan, back towards

301

his chair. 'Plus, if you're here, *we* know where to find you as well.'

Thorne almost smiled. 'One question, sir . . .'

'Go ahead.'

'Jeremy Bishop. Off limits?'

Thorne saw the look pass between Keable and Tughan. He could almost have sworn that he *heard* the temperature drop.

'I was getting to that. Dr Bishop is quite aware that you turning up at his house a fortnight ago was a charade of some sort. Be thankful he doesn't know that you were illegally gathering carpet fibres from the boot of his car.'

He still hadn't spoken to Phil Hendricks. He'd call him later.

'They got stuck to my briefcase, which *he* offered to put in the boot.'

'Of course they did,' scoffed Tughan.

'Do they match?'

Keable's mouth actually dropped open.

Tughan pushed himself away from the wall. 'I think people are right, Thorne. I think you've fucking lost it. Yes, they match, but so would fibres taken from any Volvo of that colour and model, made since 1994. Do you not think we checked those things? Have you any idea how many cars that is?'

Thorne hadn't and didn't much care.

Keable picked up the baton. 'Dr Bishop has rung several times to complain about anonymous phone calls. He's making accusations.'

Thorne met his gaze, unblinking. Keable was the first to look away.

'These calls are becoming more and more frequent.'

How many times had he called Bishop since the funeral? He could barely remember. They seemed like things he was doing in his sleep.

'Dr Bishop is predictably angry and upset, as is his son, who has been in to complain, and now his daughter is jumping on the bandwagon. She rang yesterday to ask what was being done.'

The daughter rallying to the cause. That was interesting.

'If I ever get confirmation that you know more about this than you're saying, Tom, I won't be able to save you. I won't want to save you.'

Thorne tried to look suitably chastened. Then a smile. Needing to lighten it. 'You've still not answered the question, Frank. Is he off limits or not?'

Things got no lighter.

'Detective Inspector Thorne, are you in any doubt that the person who killed Margaret Byrne is also responsible for the deaths of Helen Doyle, Leonie Holden and the others?'

Thorne thought for a second or two. 'I'm in no doubt that the person who killed Leonie, Helen and the others was responsible for the death of Margaret Byrne.'

Keable stared at him. His thick, unruly eyebrows knotted in confusion. Then he saw the subtle difference. His face reddened in an instant and his voice dropped to a threatening whisper. 'Don't play fucking silly games with me, Thorne.'

'I'm not playing games . . .'

'I don't want to listen to this rubbish again. Psychopaths do not hire hitmen.'

Jeremy Bishop was no ordinary psychopath, but deep down Thorne knew that Keable was right. The alibi had to be flawed. Else?

He didn't know what else.

'So I'm not even allowed to mention his name?'

'You're being childish. If you want to waste your time you can think what you like, but don't waste mine, or this operation's. Tom . . .' Thorne looked up. Keable was leaning forward and staring deep into his eyes. 'It's been four weeks since Helen Doyle was killed, two months since he attacked Alison Willetts, six months or more since Christine Owen was killed, and Christ knows when he began planning the whole, sick bloody thing.'

When he stole the drugs. Something about Bishop stealing the Midazolam still bothered Thorne. It floated about at the back of his head, but he couldn't grasp it. Like a tune he couldn't place.

Keable got to his point. 'Despite the blather in the papers and the earnest faces at the press conferences, we've got nothing, Tom.'

Tughan looked at the floor. Was that the merest glimpse of guilt? Thorne looked back to Keable.

'I just can't understand your refusal to look at this with an open mind. There are no other suspects. So far, this operation has achieved nothing.'

Tughan wasn't having it. 'Every officer on this operation has been working his balls off, Thorne. We've done everything we should have, everything. We found a very credible witness in Margaret Byrne—'

Thorne cut him off. 'And got her killed.'

The words struck Tughan like hot fat in his face. He marched across the room shouting, the spittle flying on to Thorne's mouth. 'Jeremy Bishop has got nothing to do with it. Nothing. While you've been in Cloud fucking Cuckoo Land we've been doing our jobs. Bishop is not a suspect. The only courtroom he's ever going to see the inside of is the one trying the lawsuit for harassment, which he'll be bringing against you.'

Thorne was out of his chair in a second. He casually took hold of Tughan's wrist and began to squeeze. The blood fled from the Irishman's face. Keable got to his feet and Thorne released his grip. Tughan stepped quickly back towards the wall, breathing heavily.

Thorne wearily raised an arm and made a lazy, swatting motion at something unseen by anybody else in the room. He lifted his jacket from the back of the chair and slowly pulled it on, murmuring, 'No other suspects, Frank . . .' He took a step towards the door.

Keable screamed, 'Then get me some!'

Even Tughan, rubbing his wrist in the corner, looked shocked.

Detective Chief Inspector Frank Keable was trying to look hard, but Thorne met his eyes and saw only desperation.

Holland was working at a computer, unaware that anyone was behind him until he heard the voice.

'It's a nice day, isn't it? I thought I might take a bit of a trip.'

Holland didn't turn round. 'Anywhere in particular?'

'Bristol's nice.'

Holland carried on typing. 'Traffic's a nightmare on the M4 on a Friday.'

'I quite fancied the train anyway. Hour and a half each way. Get the papers, patronise the buffet . . .'

'Sounds good. I'll buy a copy of *Loaded* if you buy the tea.'

'You should probably lie about where you're going . . .'

Holland shut down the computer. 'I'm getting quite good at lying.'

Thorne smiled. Holland was closing the gap.

He glanced inside the newsagent and one headline in particular caught his eye. 'Champagne Charlie', it called him. A day or two after the Margaret Byrne killing the papers had got hold of the whole thing.

The multiple killings.

At first he'd been upset and angry. He was no multiple killer. But he saw that it made sense. Obviously the full story was being held back – the truth of it. He guessed that the police had only agreed to co-operate if the press left out some of the key details to avoid hoax confessions or copycats.

They needn't be worried. When he chose to get in touch again, they'd know it was him.

He was enjoying his daily dose of tabloid speculation and chest-beating. The lack of progress on this 'horrific' case was now a matter of national concern. Making the police look stupid had never been what he wanted, far from it, but the hollow-sounding assurances of assorted commissioners and commanders, in papers and at po-faced press conferences, amused him greatly.

Champagne Charlie. Unimaginative but predictable, and ironic, considering he wouldn't be using the stuff any more. With Leonie, the grab and the jab had done the job nicely. Plus the knife to the throat, of course, to ensure silence while they waited. It was all over very quickly. The champagne had always provided forty minutes or so of small-talk. He'd missed that: it had made what came later that much more interesting. But with the needle, the difference in the speed of everything was fantastic. The adrenaline had fast-tracked the drug through the girl's body so rapidly that she was in the car on the way back to his place within a few minutes of getting off the bus. He hadn't even heard her voice properly.

She'd only said the one word, whispered it really.

Please . . .

And then he'd failed again. The distraction of the Margaret Byrne killing only a few hours earlier, was a convenient excuse but he was beginning to realise that the odds were against him. He had elected to perform a horrendously difficult procedure. He accepted that. The success rate would be small. He'd known that all along. Still, failure was deeply upsetting.

But the results when he got it right made it all worth it.

He had enjoyed killing Margaret Byrne immensely. It had been a jolt of unadulterated shame admitting that to himself, but there was little point in self-delusion.

He had imagined being her. He had imagined feeling the cold blade singing on his skin. Holding his breath for the split second between that sweet song finishing and the blood beginning to flow.

It was a feeling he had once known and loved, and had almost forgotten.

The killing had none of the lingering beauty, none of the grace of his normal work. There was some skill needed, of course, but a pale, stiffening cadaver could not compare to what he had achieved with Alison. That was something truly elevated. Something unique.

All the same, the success rate was incomparable.

His work was ground-breaking, of that he was certain, but he had only succeeded once and now doubts were beginning to creep into his mind and squat there like bloated black spiders. Might not the quick kill be the next best thing? Would not this euthanasia be a service in itself? There was no bright, breathing, painless future like the one he'd given to Alison, but it was . . . an ending.

He tried to dismiss the idea. He could not picture himself stalking the streets with a scalpel in his pocket. That was not who he was.

He carried his newspaper to the counter and fished around for change. A woman stood next to him. A puzzle magazine, a lottery ticket and a fistful of chocolate. She smiled at him and he remembered how important his work still was. Yes, killing her would be simple and she would be far better off, no question. But nothing worth having was ever achieved easily.

Death was something medieval. He could offer people a future.

During the short taxi ride from Temple Meads station to the hospital, Thorne and Holland had worked out their plan for talking to Dr Rebecca Bishop. Simply put, they didn't have one. Holland had rung ahead and established that she was working today, but beyond that they were making it up as they went along.

A year earlier, Bristol Royal Infirmary had been at the centre of a damaging public inquiry into an alarming number of babies and toddlers who had died during heart surgery. The resulting scandal had cast a long, dark shadow across that hospital in particular and the medical profession in general, which some believed was well deserved. Doctors could no longer be trusted to regulate themselves.

Rather like police officers.

Since he'd begun working on this case, nothing that happened in hospitals could surprise Thorne. He was becoming used to the strategies employed to get through the days by those who worked in them. All the same, the Bristol Royal Infirmary inquiry had been disturbing. There had been some shocking revelations. One ward had been known as 'the departure lounge'.

Susan, Christine, Madeleine, Helen. Thorne knew how insistent were the voices of those whose lives had been snatched away. He pitied those who still heard the screams of twenty-nine dead babies.

Rebecca Bishop worked in the department of orthopaedic surgery. Sitting opposite them on moulded green plastic chairs, in a corridor just off a waiting area, her manner left Thorne in no doubt as to the strength of the confidence gene in this particular family. 'I'll give you half an hour. After that, I'm assisting at a riveting lecture on the biomechanics of fracture repair. You're welcome to attend.'

She smiled coldly. Aside from the dark, frizzy hair and slightly elongated chin, Rebecca had the features of her father and brother. She was a handsome woman, as they were handsome men. Handsome but not pretty. There was nothing soft about her. Thorne wondered where the influence of Sarah Bishop was to be found. Had she been soft? Or pretty?

Maybe he'd ask Jeremy one day, when they had time to talk. In an interview room perhaps.

Thorne opened his mouth to reply but Rebecca Bishop had her own agenda. 'You could start by telling me why they've sent the man my father believes is responsible for harassing him to talk to me about it.'

Thorne flicked his eyes to Holland. He got back the facial equivalent of a shrug.

'Nobody is harassing your father, Dr Bishop. Nobody we are aware of anyway. The very fact that I've come down here myself should assure you that we're taking his allegations seriously.'

'I'm pleased to hear it.'

'But you must understand we do have other priorities.'

She got up and walked across to scrutinise a noticeboard. 'Like catching Champagne Charlie? I've been reading all about it.'

Holland was content to play the ebullient side-kick. 'Don't believe everything you read in the papers, Dr Bishop.'

She looked at Holland, and Thorne thought he spotted the merest hint of a blush. Did she fancy him? So much the better. He tried to catch Holland's eye but couldn't. Rebecca Bishop turned and stared at Thorne, her hands thrust deep into the pockets of a baggy brown cardigan. 'And is my father a suspect, Inspector Thorne?'

Lying was never pleasant, but it was easy. 'No, of course not. He was questioned routinely and eliminated from the inquiry.'

She looked at him hard. He felt nothing. Doctors kept patients in the dark. Ditto policemen and members of the public.

Holland took over. 'Can we talk about this harassment business? Exactly what is happening, as you understand it?'

She sat down. 'I went over all this on the phone.' Holland took out a notebook on cue. Thorne had to admire the timing. She sighed and carried on. 'Right, well, Dad's been getting these phone calls . . . Oh, and there was somebody taking photos outside his house, but it's mainly the phone calls.'

'Your dad told you about this?'

'No, my brother James rang me. Dad's really upset and angry, and James thought I ought to know what was going on. To add another professional voice of complaint, I suppose. James and I don't exactly chat every day, so I guessed it was something important when I got his message.' She began to chew intently at a fingernail. Thorne noticed that they were all bitten to the quick, some raw and bloody.

It was time to dig a little. 'So you and James are not . . . close?'

She looked up and he could see her considering a reply, and whether to give it. Was this territory she felt safe bringing strangers into? Maybe it was Holland's smile that did the trick.

'We're not a hugely close family. You must know most of this . . .'

They looked at her as if they didn't know anything at all.

'James and I aren't best friends, no. Dad and I don't get on either, if you must know, but that doesn't mean I want to see him upset.'

Holland nodded, full of understanding. 'Of course not.'

She began to speak slowly, but with a detectable relish. 'James and Dad like to think they're close, but really there's a lot of denial flying about. They fell out a bit a few years ago when James went off the rails a little, and now he just sees the old man as a glorified bank manager who's there to dole out cars and deposits on flats, so that good old James can fuck up anything he turns his hand to and not really worry about it.'

Thorne stirred the pot a little. 'I'm sure he does worry about it.'

'Oh, yeah, you've had the pleasure of meeting James, he told me. Christ, how bitter do I sound?' She tried to laugh, but it caught at the back of her throat.

Thorne's voice was quiet, measured. 'And how does your dad feel?'

'Guilty.' An instinctive answer. Word association.

Thorne willed his face to show nothing. Let her carry on dishing the family dirt.

'Guilty that Mum was off her face on tranquillisers and he was too pissed to drive. Guilty that he put her on the fucking tranquillisers in the first place. Guilty that he screwed up both his kids. Guilty that he didn't die instead of her. We're big on guilt, the Bishops. But Jeremy's the top man.'

Tranquillisers. That made a lot of sense. Was the Midazolam doing to his victims in a few short minutes what the tranquillisers had done to his wife over a number of years? Was all this about something as prosaic as revenge? No, not revenge exactly but . . . Thorne didn't know what.

Almost as soon as he'd thought it, he knew that it was too simplistic and, in a strange way, too poetic. The answer to this case wouldn't lie in everyday motives tied up in Christmas cracker psychology.

But he was getting under the skin of Jeremy Bishop.

He gazed across at Bishop's daughter. She looked exhausted. She had been saying something she had not articulated for a while, or so it seemed to Thorne. She was speaking as if he and Holland weren't there. He needed, gently, to remind her that they were.

'And what about you, Rebecca? What are you guilty about?'

She looked at Thorne as if he was mad. Wasn't it obvious? 'That I wasn't in the car.'

While Tom Thorne was questioning Rebecca Bishop, a hundred miles away, her father was having lunch with the woman who, at least in theory, was sleeping with him.

He'd rung the night before. Anne had grabbed at the phone, hoping it might be Thorne, and was more than a little thrown when she'd heard Jeremy's voice. They'd agreed to meet. A pasta place in Clerkenwell, more or less midway between Queen Square and the Royal London.

The hug was perhaps a little forced but the wine soon relaxed them and the conversation flowed easily enough. They talked about work. Stressful – hard to go home and relax. Tiring – when was it anything else? He was starting to think about a change of direction; she was intrigued. She was disappointed and upset about Alison's setback; he was sympathetic.

They talked about children. Was she expecting too much of Rachel? Was she too pushy? He told her not to give herself a hard time over it. He'd always expected the best from Rebecca and James and almost certainly *had* been too pushy. He was proud of Rebecca, and maybe James would work out soon what he wanted.

She told him he should be proud of both of them.

Then a silence, which was just the right side

of awkward, when Bishop broke it. 'Did you not phone because your boyfriend told you not to?'

Anne lit a cigarette, her third since they had finished the meal. 'You didn't call me either.'

'I was worried it might be awkward. I've read the papers and clearly I can't be a suspect any more, but he still seems to have something of a . . . problem with me.'

She flicked non-existent ash into the ashtray. 'I haven't spoken to Tom in over a week.' Bishop raised an eyebrow. More nervous ash-flicking. 'We've never really talked about you, anyway, Jeremy. Best to keep the personal and the professional separate.'

Bishop leaned forward and smiled, interlocking long, slender fingers and resting his chin on them. He stared deep into her eyes. 'I do understand all that, Jimmy, and I know this is hard for you. But what do you really think?'

She held the eye-contact and tried with all her heart and soul to imagine this man the way Tom Thorne did. She couldn't do it. 'Jeremy, I don't . . .'

'I heard a story yesterday about a GP with a morphine addiction. He'd prescribe it to his older patients, then he'd make house calls and steal it back from them. They'd come into the surgery thinking they'd lost it, you know, going doolally in their old age. He'd smile at them, full of understanding, and prescribe them some more. And so on.'

Anne was not hugely shocked. Many doctors had problems with addiction. There was even a rehab centre exclusively for those who worked in the medical profession. Bishop carried on: 'The guy who told me this had known the man for twenty-odd years and had absolutely no idea.'

She looked at him. Holding her breath. His voice was barely a whisper.

'People have secrets, Anne.'

Anne looked down and fixed her eyes on the cigarette she was stubbing out in the ashtray. Carefully and deliberately she removed any trace of burning ember. What did he expect her to say? Was this just a piece of typically theatrical and provocative weirdness or . . . ?

She looked up and signalled for the bill, then turned back to him, smiling. 'Talking of secrets, Jeremy, are you seeing somebody?'

His mood seemed to change in a moment. She saw it, and thought about backing off but decided against it. She wanted to turn the tables a little, to enjoy *his* awkwardness. 'You are, aren't you? Why are you being so coy?' She saw something like an answer in his eyes. 'Do I know her?'

He stared down at the tablecloth. 'It's not really serious and it's probably not going to last very long for all sorts of reasons, but if I talk about it, it will be like I'm cursing it somehow. Condemning it to an early grave.'

She laughed. Why this sudden superstition? 'Come on, since when have—'

'No.' His tone stopped the tail end of her laughter in its tracks. End of conversation.

'It would be like wishing it dead.'

Thorne arrived home fizzing and fidgety. There were people he needed to call. His dad. Hendricks. Anne, of course. But he felt too energised.

It had happened as he'd stepped out of Kentish Town tube station and was wondering which lucky off-licence would have the benefit of his business on the way home. The conversation behind him had gone something like this.

'*Big Issue* . . .'

'Get a fucking job!'

'This is my job, you arsehole!'

And it had gone off.

Thorne had stepped in a second or two after the first punches and kicks began to fly. Wincing as a stray punch caught him on the side of the head, he'd grabbed the get-a-job merchant round the neck and hauled him into a nearby doorway with more force than was strictly necessary. The *Big Issue* seller, having picked up the magazines scattered during the ruck, had moved in close to watch.

Thorne had looked at him, 'Piss off,' then turned his attention back to the one who *had* a home. Drunk, of course, or maybe stoned. A student, Thorne reckoned, with blood from a split lip running on to his white button-down shirt.

Thorne had held him against the door with a stiff

arm at his throat and casually kneed the little tosser between the legs as he removed his badge from the inside pocket of his leather jacket and pushed it into his face. 'Have a guess what *my* job is.'

Now, back at home, opening the first can of cheap lager, he wondered what might have happened if he hadn't been around with a badge in his pocket and some aggression to offload.

If one of them had been carrying a knife.

These were typical murders. Ordinary killings, simple, banal and understandable. People dying because of anger or frustration or a basic lack of space. Dying for a grand cause or a stupid comment. Or a few pence.

Wives and husbands killing with hammers and fists, or men being men with drink and knives, or drug-dealers holding guns as casually as combs.

Thorne understood them, these deaths died in cities. He knew what they were about. Each made its own strange kind of sense.

But not this. Not killing as a side-effect. Bodies as a by-product of some sickfuckingmadness.

He downed the last of the beer, pulled on his jacket, and within forty-five minutes he was standing in a street in Battersea, looking up at the shape that moved behind a light at a second floor window.

He stood for nearly an hour, melting back into the shadows with each twitch of the curtains, real or imagined. Then he stepped back quickly into the anonymous darkness as Jeremy Bishop threw open the curtains and stood looking down at the street.

Bishop stared hard at Thorne, or the place where Thorne *was*, seeing a shape, perhaps, but certainly no more. As Thorne returned the stare, he felt a glacial tremor run through every bone in his body as Bishop's face suddenly changed.

From this distance, Thorne could not be sure.

It might have been a grimace.

It might have been a smile.

I know that I've made jokes before about the NHS and the lack of money and everything. I was taking the piss out of the blackboard when it first appeared, you know, compared with all the flashy stuff they've got in America.

But this?

Anne's been telling me for a while that her and the occupational therapist are going to try to rig up a couple of devices so that I can read and watch TV. Obviously I've been gagging for it, and even more so since I've been back on this bastard ventilator. When a machine is doing your breathing for you, life can get sooo boring, darling! But I didn't realise they literally meant 'rig up'. Honestly, it's spit and fucking earwax.

They've screwed some sort of pivoting arm into the ceiling and the TV now hangs down from there so I'm staring up at the screen. Great. If I was in hospital in Fuckwit, Illinois, or wherever, I'd be able to control the volume and, crucially, *change the bloody channel* with my eyelid. Here, in good old London Town, on the good old National Health Service, those little details seem to have been overlooked. So I have to wait for a nurse to show up, and blink to indicate that I'd like her to turn over. She does exactly that and buggers off again. Leaving me staring at *Supermarket Sweep* or some moronic cookery programme until she puts her head round the door again twenty minutes later and I'm blinking my head off in an effort to get the football on.

I don't want to sound ungrateful, but this is heaven compared to my new reading arrangements.

It's based around a music-stand, I think, though there might be a bit of old coat-hanger stuck in there as well. All right, I'm exaggerating, but not much. I get raised up and this metal contraption is placed across my tits with little clamps that fold down to hold in place my book or magazine of choice. Good in theory. First, I'm hardly in a position to make complex requests on the book front. I'm racking my brains to think of books I might fancy reading with really short titles. Same with magazines, though I'm more or less sorted thanks to *OK!* and *Hello!*. Not too taxing on the eyelids. The problem is the same as with the telly, though. I'm hardly Brain of Britain, but even I can read a page of pretty much anything in twenty minutes, or however long it is until the nurse comes in again. I don't expect them to come tearing in here every ninety seconds to turn my page for me but there must be something somebody can do.

I can't pay for anything, and I haven't got family who can pay for anything or try to raise money, but even so . . .

Everything's fucking half-measures.

Half-measures for half a person.

CHAPTER 16

Thorne and Anne Coburn had spent most of the day in bed together. He'd been up once, for about half an hour. Just long enough to make a few pieces of toast, put on *American Recordings* by Johnny Cash and fetch the papers. *The Observer* for her (he read the sports section). *The Mirror* and the *Screws* for him (she read the supplements). He wasn't planning to get up again until the pubs opened.

He'd woken, alone, several hours earlier with the image of Jeremy Bishop's face looking down at him, captured in negative when he closed his eyes, as if he'd been staring too long at a lightbulb.

He kept his eyes open and did some catching up. The phone lay on the small cupboard by the side of the bed and he propped a couple of pillows up against the headboard. One extremely comfy office. The call to his dad was surprisingly enjoyable. Jim Thorne hated Sundays, and his irascible commentary on everything from garden centres to 'God-botherers' had made Thorne laugh out loud several times. They'd agreed to have a night out the following week.

324

Thorne had arranged to meet Phil Hendricks the day after next but this was a less enjoyable prospect. The pathologist had sounded distant and edgy. The call had taken less than a minute. Thorne wondered what Hendricks wanted to see him about. He was pretty sure it had nothing to do with tickets for Spurs-Arsenal.

Then he'd rung Anne.

She'd been having breakfast with Rachel. The two of them were planning to spend the day together and she told Thorne she'd ring back. Within fifteen minutes she was on her way over. Rachel had not seemed too disappointed at the change of plan, and by the time she was climbing back into bed with her mobile phone, her mother was climbing into bed with Tom Thorne.

After making up for lost time they'd dozed for a while but now, surrounded by discarded bits of newspaper, they lay in a bed dotted with toast crumbs and smelling of sex. And began to talk.

It was a conversation of a very different nature from the one they'd had nearly a month earlier, on the night Thorne had gone round for dinner; the night he'd been attacked and drugged in his own home. Then, certainly as far as *he* had been concerned, there had been a lot of lying. There had been the lies implicit in the flirting and the lies behind his questions about Jeremy Bishop.

There was so much he hadn't told her. So many lies by omission.

Now they talked easily, and truthfully. Two

people the wrong side of forty with little reason to puff up achievements or suck in stomachs. They spoke about David and Rachel and Jan and the Lecturer. Divorces with children versus divorces without. About her grade-seven piano and the work she'd done on her house and the cups she'd won for tennis before she went to university. About how much he hated poncy tea and brown bread, and how he'd been quite a useful footballer until he'd started putting on weight.

About how often she'd saved a life and how many times he'd fired a gun.

They talked about how utterly unsuited they were, and laughed, and then made love again.

For a few hours on a damp Sunday afternoon at the fag-end of September, the case that had changed both their lives – that would twist and warp their lives, and those of others, even more before it was over – might not have existed.

Then a woman picked up a phone in Edinburgh and changed everything.

He'd enjoyed his Sundays in the past. They had been a vital part of the process. It had been the day when he'd selected several of his early ones. He'd watched Christine on a Sunday – she'd had friends round. And Susan – at home alone in front of an old film. Even after he'd stopped working in other houses, Sunday was still a day to take stock. To plan.

Today, he didn't like what he saw. It was all

going to shit. He could feel himself on the edge of a depression that he knew would be crippling if he let it take hold.

The days after Helen had been hard but he'd seen a light at the end of it all. The knowledge that success was possible. That the capacity to achieve success was within him.

And the days after Alison. A happiness he hadn't known before or since.

Today he saw no light ahead. The doubt was taking hold of every part of him and starting to squeeze out the joy and the hope.

It was more than just his own failure, of course. Thorne was failing as well, or at the very least not being allowed to succeed.

Without Thorne there was really no point.

All his channels of information were clear. The news, the rumour, the word. None of it good. He'd made it all so easy for them and they'd screwed it up. They'd missed every marker he'd left so carefully in their path.

He sat and stared at the pristine white wall. Whatever happened, however it worked itself out, he would always have Alison. She would always be a testament to him and his work. The other part of it, *the other half of it*, might not work out exactly as planned but that was not his fault. That was the result of involving others. There were ways of achieving a similar end on his own.

The punishment was not going to fit the crime, but he would see it meted out nevertheless.

It wasn't over, not yet, but he was starting to feel weary.

Twelve days before, with Margaret Byrne's body cooling where he'd left it and his car effortlessly trailing the night bus carrying Leonie Holden towards him, he'd felt bright and invincible. Today, he wasn't sure he'd even be able to drag himself out of doors.

Even though, later, he would have to.

They were laughing about his taste in music. The track was 'Delia's Gone', which involved Johnny Cash tying his girlfriend to a chair and shooting her a couple of times, essentially because she was 'devilish'. Thorne couldn't see the problem.

Then the phone rang. 'Tom? It's Sally Byrne.'

Thorne laughed. 'Hi, Sally. Elvis is fine. He's destroying the place but he's fine.'

Anne, who hadn't met the cat yet, threw him an odd look from the other side of the bed. He grinned at her over his shoulder, shaking his head. *Don't worry about it.* She picked up a newspaper and snuggled down to read.

'It's not actually about the cat, Tom.'

Thorne began to sit up slowly. He could feel the smallest of sensations, a tingle, a burning, an excitement, building between his shoulder-blades. 'I'm listening, Sally.'

'It's just something a bit odd and I probably should have spoken to the Irish officer. What's his name?'

'Tughan.' *Go on . . .*

'Well, I've been going through Mum's things, you know sorting stuff out for the charity shop or whatever, and I was looking through her jewellery and I found a man's ring.'

Thorne was already out of bed and wandering into the living room, trying to pull on a dressing-gown.

'Tom?'

'Sorry. Which jewellery are we talking about?'

'This is what I'm saying, it's the stuff you lot took away. The scene-of-crime people. They let me have it all back after the funeral, said they didn't need it any more. I don't know where they found this ring, on the floor with the rest of the stuff, I suppose, and they obviously thought it belonged to my mum, but it doesn't.'

'It's definitely a man's?'

'Definitely. It's plain gold. Looks like a wedding ring.'

'Not your dad's?'

'Are you kidding? That bastard would never have worn a wedding ring. Might have spoiled his chances of pulling.'

Thorne was starting to miss what Sally Byrne was saying. A melody was pouring into his brain and filling every corner of it. A classical melody. Mournful and haunting. He couldn't remember what it was called. Something German. But he could remember where he'd heard it. And he could remember a rhythm, a tempo, marked out by the clicking of a wedding ring against a gearstick.

'I mean, I'm sure it's nothing, Tom, but . . .'

When Thorne came back into the bedroom a few minutes later, Anne knew in a heartbeat that something had changed. He was trying to sound casual. He asked if she wanted tea.

She got up and began to dress.

Whatever it was that had actually happened wasn't important. She knew that murder and suspicion were back in the room with them and she needed to leave. They moved around each other awkwardly now, embarrassed, and they froze for half a second as each caught the other's reflection in the long wardrobe mirror.

Thorne saw something like accusation and hated himself for wanting her to leave so that he could ring Dave Holland.

Anne saw the excitement that was running through Thorne like voltage.

She saw a hunger in him.

She saw the face of Jeremy Bishop and the dark sadness that had settled around his eyes as he'd whispered to her.

'People have secrets, Anne.'

They sat at a table towards the back of the room, not in total darkness but close to it. It seemed to be the way he wanted it. He'd led her to the table, avoiding the empty seats near the stage. It was probably a good idea considering that they didn't want to get picked on and she was under-age.

Rachel looked around. She wasn't the only one.

Actually she had had no trouble in getting away with it. The club was dimly lit and the woman on the door had barely looked up from her cashbox when the two of them had come in. She'd spent a long time on her makeup. She'd even stood beneath the lights at the bar and bought them both a drink, staring at herself in the mirror that ran along the back wall behind the optics. She looked eighteen easily. Twenty, probably.

This small comedy club below a pub in Crouch End was, he'd told her, one of his favourite places. It was a mixed audience. Nobody cared what you looked like or how old you were. It wasn't exactly the Comedy Store, but you could see some of the same comedians that you were likely to see at the bigger clubs without having to struggle into the West End.

Rachel had liked the sound of it straight away and asked him if he'd take her. He told her about another night at the same club when they did what were called try-out shows or open spots. He came to those as often as he could, if he wasn't working. A dozen or more hopefuls would get up and do a couple of minutes. None of them was any good. It was clearly just therapy for most of them, but it was riveting to watch. Like a car accident. Watching them struggle, watching them 'die', was an amazing experience, he assured her.

The comedian on the tiny stage was a sneering Scotsman with red hair and a loud suit who shouted a lot and swore too much. He talked about sex in graphic detail and Rachel sat blushing in the darkness. She looked out of the corner of her eye at the man next to her so that she could laugh when he did. She didn't want to seem young, or stupid, or unsophisticated.

He was enjoying himself, she could tell. He'd seemed a little tense when he'd picked her up outside the Green Man, but now he looked more relaxed. She watched him far more than she watched what was happening on stage. He stared, engrossed, at the comedian, or at other members of the audience. He was a ferocious watcher, critical and unblinking. She loved that about him. She loved how he lived every moment to its fullest, taking everything in and savouring it. She loved his intensity, his refusal to compromise.

The comedian was telling some joke about his parents and Rachel thought about her mother. Anne had been in a strange mood when she'd come home – from the policeman's place, Rachel guessed. It had definitely been him who'd phoned that morning. Probably at it all day, the pair of them.

She thought quite a lot about Thorne fucking her mother.

She thought quite a lot about fucking.

There had been a bit of an atmosphere when she'd announced that she was going out, but her mother had hardly been in a position to say anything after the way she'd changed their plans earlier.

Around her people started to applaud and she joined in. The compère was coming back on again to introduce another act. He said that there'd be an interval afterwards. She wondered if they'd go out for a meal when the show had finished; there were loads of great restaurants within walking distance. Then they could sit in his car for a while before he drove her home.

The next comedian was a woman. She was gentler and did a really funny song about men being crap in bed to start off.

Rachel took a sip from her half of lager and smiled at him, feeling a little light-headed. He smiled back and squeezed her hand. When he'd let go she slid her arm between his back and the chair.

She was as happy as she could ever remember being.

She rested her hand on his waist . . . the audience laughed . . . he had on a really nice linen shirt which he wore out of his trousers . . . the audience groaned at a corny line . . . he always wore gorgeous clothes . . . the woman on stage started another song . . . Rachel wanted to touch his skin . . . a drunk at the other side of the room started to cheer and clap . . . she moved her hand under his shirt and her fingers crept round to stroke the flesh of his stomach . . .

Then he screamed.

In that split second when everything fell apart, and he was standing up, and her drink was in her lap, and the woman on the stage was pointing at them, it *seemed* to Rachel that he had screamed. Christ, he had. He'd bellowed. As if he'd been scalded . . .

His face was a mask and she reached up to grab his arm, but he called her a stupid little bitch and grabbed for his coat and he was away, moving quickly away, pushing between the tables and knocking over empty chairs.

And the woman on the stage was laughing and saying something to him as he marched out, and he turned and shouted and told her to fuck off, and people in the audience started to boo, and he looked like he wanted to hurt them.

He crashed out through the door, and she could feel the beer soaking through her thin skirt, and the eyes of everyone in the room burning into her. The door slammed shut with a bang, and the woman on the stage leaned in close to her microphone and put a hand over her eyes to stare into the lights and beyond, to where Rachel was sitting and wishing she was dead.

'Bit of a domestic, love?'

A few people in the audience laughed. And Rachel began to cry.

Holland was listening to the sports round-up on Radio 5 Live for the third time in as many hours, when headlights swept across his rearview mirror and he turned to see Jeremy Bishop pulling up outside his house.

Thorne had called at around six and Sophie was not best pleased. She'd known immediately that it was Thorne. She knew *everything* immediately. She'd have been pissed off at his having to go out anyway but Thorne, as far as she was concerned, represented an unhealthy future for him in the force. A future he should run from at all costs. A future without promotion, without stability, without certainty.

By implication, without her.

He couldn't argue with her. Everything she said made complete sense. But they were words from beyond the grave. His father's words. Sophie was mouthing the sentiments of a man he had loved but had never admired.

It was hard not to admire Tom Thorne.

He couldn't argue with Sophie, so he didn't bother. He left the house in silence and conducted the argument with her in his head as he drove to Battersea and sat waiting. In truth, he was arguing with himself as well.

Thorne was clutching at straws, of course he was.

Jeremy Bishop, who, Holland knew, had been at work in the Royal London hospital at the time, had dropped a ring in Maggie Byrne's bedroom as he was murdering her. Right. Looked at rationally, these were the ravings of a man popularly thought by many of his colleagues to have gone over the edge. But there'd been something in Thorne's voice. Yes, desperation possibly, but more than that. An excitement, a zeal, a *passion* that had Holland reaching for his coat and wondering what he was going to say to Sophie before he'd put down the phone.

He stepped out of the car and crossed the road.

Bishop, who had just locked the Volvo and was about to head towards his front door, saw Holland coming. He sighed theatrically and leaned back against the car, his hands thrust deep into the pockets of his trousers.

Holland was ready with an apologetic shrug and all the appropriate phrases. Just a few more questions. Investigating a fresh lead. Grateful for all your help and co-operation. As he approached he could see that Bishop remembered him. He didn't care. He had his badge in his right hand with the other politely outstretched. 'Detective Constable Holland, sir.'

Bishop pushed himself away from the car and took a step towards him. 'Yes, I know. How's your girlfriend's hand?' The tone impatient, the smile saying he knew it was bollocks.

Holland was thrown, but only for a second. 'Fine.'

'How long is this going to take?'

It wasn't going to take very long at all. As Bishop had started speaking, he had proffered his left hand in return for Holland's. They'd shaken, and with a quick downward glance, Holland had got what he'd come for. What Thorne had sent him for.

No wedding ring.

I've been reading a lot. The same page usually, over and over again, but what the hell? Early on, there was a bit of a scramble to find some interesting reading matter and while they were looking, to sort of test out their new-fangled device, the occupational therapist gave me some official hospital literature to read.

Yawn . . .

Well, that's what I thought until I started reading. Fascinating stuff. This is a quote, and I can remember it very accurately having stared at it for twenty minutes: 'The National Hospital for Neurology and Neurosurgery, incorporating the Institute of Neurology, is a unique resource for teaching, training and research in neurology and the neurosciences. The work of academic staff and their research is closely integrated with the hospital's care of its patients.'

Well, that all seems clear enough to me. The 'care' bit is very much an afterthought, you know, tagged on at the end when somebody remembered that it was supposed to be a hospital. The rest seems to be all about research and training and, frankly, they can just fuck right off.

I'm a patient. Trust me, I'd really rather not be here at all, but if I am then my job description is 'patient', mate. I'm nobody's resource. Nobody's fucking teaching aid.

'Let's have a look at this poor young woman here, utterly buggered thanks to brainstem trauma. Can you try and blink for us, dear?'

No thanks.

All right, I'm being a bit over the top but when I first read that I was really upset. I lay awake all night wondering if anybody here was making any effort at all to help me get better.

I'm still wondering.

Am I more use to them the way I am?

CHAPTER 17

Keable and Tughan had questions ready, and Thorne had plenty of answers. First, there was the small matter of another complaint from Jeremy Bishop.

'He claims there was somebody watching his house on Saturday evening.' Keable looked at Thorne.

Thorne shrugged and turned to Holland innocently. 'Did he say anything about this to you last night?'

Tughan spoke before Holland had a chance to answer. 'You are on such thin ice, Thorne.'

Thorne smiled. He was feeling elated and no amount of sniping from Nick Tughan was going to alter his mood. One day soon they would have it all out. For now, he was best ignored.

Tughan was seated in a chair against the wall beneath the calendar, and Holland stood with his back to the door. The office felt crowded. Thorne placed both hands on Keable's desk and leaned down to him. 'So what are we going to do, Frank?'

Keable slid his chair away from the desk,

retreating. He held up a hand. 'First we're going to think about what we've really got here. How on earth can she be sure the ring isn't her mother's?'

'She's sure.'

Tughan snorted. 'She lives in Edinburgh, she never *saw* her mother, for fuck's sake. The ring could be anyone's. Who knows how many men she had round there?'

Holland spoke quietly. 'I don't think Margaret Byrne had any men. Sir.'

Tughan turned round and glared. Holland refused to look away.

'SOC got no prints off the body . . .'

Thorne slammed a hand down on the desk. 'If SOC hadn't fucked up and catalogued a vital piece of evidence as one of the victim's possessions we wouldn't even be here. This would be over by now.'

'No prints on the body, Tom. The killer wore gloves, so how the hell does he lose a ring?'

Thorne took a deep breath. *Answer the question. Nice and calm.* 'I think he put the gloves on once she was unconscious. Surgical gloves. He put them on to handle the scalpel. To make his incision. The ring could have come off anytime before then. There was obviously some sort of struggle.'

Keable looked over at Tughan, who shook his head. 'What does Bishop say?'

Holland stepped forward, placed a hand on the back of Tughan's chair. Spoke over his head. 'He claims to have lost it a few weeks ago.'

Tughan was still shaking his head. Not having any of it. 'How do you "lose" a wedding ring?' He began twisting his own. 'I couldn't get this fucker off even if I wanted to.'

Holland had answers as well as Thorne. 'His comes off quite easily, he told me. He takes it off at work. Takes all his jewellery off. Claims somebody took it out of his locker.'

Keable seized on this. 'Anything else taken?'

'His wallet and a watch. A Tag Heuer.'

'Did he report it?'

'No point. He says stuff goes missing from lockers all the time.'

Thorne's eyes flicked from one face to the other. Holland was doing well. Keable would not go for this without facts. He needed a weight of facts in support, and Holland was supplying them.

'When was this?'

'Nearly three weeks ago. The eleventh.'

Keable nodded. 'The day before Margaret Byrne was killed.'

Thorne said nothing. *The day he'd conned the lift into town. Bishop had been wearing the ring then.* Letting Keable make the decision. It was important he felt that it was his. He was still nodding.

'What do you want, Tom?'

'I want a warrant.'

Tughan stood quickly, his chair shooting back behind him. Keable raised a hand. 'Let's get this ring down here first, and over to the forensic boys. We'll talk about warrants if and when. Nick, get on

342

the phone to Lothian and Borders. I want it driven down here. Understand?'

Tughan was first out of the door. Holland held it open for him. As Thorne went to follow, Keable stopped him. 'There's a press conference scheduled for midday, Tom. I'd like you on the platform, please.'

Keable's tone implied that he would brook no arguments. He wasn't going to get any. The adrenaline was pumping round Thorne's body. He was high as a kite. He'd have happily agreed to appear on *Stars In Their Eyes*.

Thorne . . .

Walking into the operations room. Avoiding eye-contact with nobody. Acknowledging the kind words and approving looks. Putting a hand on Dave Holland's arm and savouring the smile he gets in return. Relishing the scowl on the face of Nick Tughan as the Irishman runs fingers through his thin blond hair and grabs at the phone.

And enjoying the relief in the voices of the girls.

'It's going to be over soon, isn't it?'

'Tommy? Is this it?'

'You going to get him, Tommy?'

'Get the fucker . . .'

Christine, Madeleine, Susan. And Helen at the end. Spitting out enough hope for all of them. It was a hope he was no longer afraid of dashing.

'Yes, I'm going to get him. Very soon.'

And somewhere in the background, the laughter of Leonie Holden.

He watched it twice. He watched it on each edition of the lunchtime news, BBC and ITV. Both times he was entranced. Both times he laughed out loud, and applauded at the end.

He was in a much better mood anyway. Things were looking up and the despondency of the day before – it had been a dreadful day – had evaporated with one small snippet of news. It was a little overdue, but more than welcome. He still had no great urge to try the procedure again, but it seemed as if things might work out as planned after all.

Commander Sincere, Detective Chief Inspector Eyebrows . . . and Tom Thorne. He'd cheered when Thorne had been introduced, finally, to the nation. So everything was hunky-dory again, was it? Tom was back on the team.

The commander spoke about 'new leads' and 'exciting new avenues of investigation'. And about time too! That said, they were *still* keen to hear from anyone who could supply even a partial number-plate on the blue Volvo, and they were *still* showing that bloody awful e-fit, courtesy of some blind passer-by on the night he'd taken Helen Doyle.

Margaret Byrne would have come up with something far more accurate . . .

Then Commander Sincere introduced the officer who was going to 'make a direct appeal to the man responsible for these terrible killings'. The camera moved along to Thorne. He looked a little nervous. Distracted.

He wondered how Thorne would perform on camera. He must have done this sort of thing before, he was bound to be good at it. The Irishman had been smooth but he guessed that Thorne would bring something else to it. Power, perhaps. Something fuelled by a genuine rage.

Of course he would. Thorne was a man after his own heart.

He wasn't disappointed. There was nothing written down; no need for notes. Thorne looked straight into the camera and spoke calmly, but with precision and strength.

He shuffled his chair forward, his face only inches from the television screen, his mouth open. It was as if Thorne was speaking straight to him.

Which of course he was.

'It's still not too late. You can just stop all of this now. I can't promise anything but if you come forward now, if you come forward *today*, then your case is going to be viewed that much more favourably.

'None of us can even begin to guess why you've chosen to do these things. Perhaps you feel that you *have* no choice. You will get the chance to explain all this if you stop the killing now.

'You know, of course, that we will use any means at our disposal to stop you. Any means at all. I can't guarantee that this will not result in injury of some sort to yourself. Or worse. We do not want to see

345

anybody else hurt and that includes you. You can believe that or not. It's your choice.

'So just stop and think. Right now. Think for a minute. Whatever point you're trying to make, consider it made. Then pick up the phone.

'Let's end this madness. Now. Come forward today and hand yourself over to me . . . to us, and people will be there to help you.'

Then Thorne leaned in towards the camera, his face filling the screen.

'One way or another, this will all be over soon.'

Rachel had forgiven him almost instantly.

He'd called first thing and had sounded so upset about what he'd done. He knew his behaviour had been unforgivable and would completely understand if she wanted to end it.

That was the last thing she wanted to do.

His apology made her feel strangely powerful. It was as if there'd been a sudden shift. He could have just walked away but he hadn't. He'd wanted her forgiveness, and once she'd given it, she sensed that their relationship had moved on to a different footing.

He'd explained that things at work hadn't been going too well. There were a couple of people he was clashing with and it had all got on top of him. Obviously that didn't excuse what he'd done or anything, but he wanted her to know that he'd been under a lot of stress, that was all. She asked why he hadn't told her. She wanted to share things like that with him. She wanted to share everything with him. She could have helped. He told her that he *wanted* to share everything with her and that one day soon he would.

She felt her mouth go dry. She knew that he was talking about sex.

He'd asked if it had been very bad after he'd stormed out of the comedy club. She told him that the woman comedian had picked on her for a bit but then it had been the interval and she'd sneaked out. They laughed, wondering what the rest of the audience would have been saying about them. He said he'd buy her a new skirt to replace the one that got covered in beer. He told her he'd buy her lots of things.

They'd dallied over saying goodbye, but eventually Rachel said that she really had to go. She told him she'd call him later and that she loved him and they hung up at the same time.

And then she'd carried on getting ready for school.

Anne was in a meeting and would be for the next couple of hours. Thorne was not unhappy about it. He'd asked at Reception and now he walked towards the lifts, breathing a sigh of relief. If he had run into her it would have been fine. He'd have handled it and so would she, but it was probably best to leave it a day or two.

He hoped that it would all be over by then.

The day before, after the call from Sally Byrne,

they hadn't been able to talk about anything. Once an arrest had been made, once *the* arrest had been made, they would be able to talk about it all. It wouldn't be easy for Anne but he would be there to help her through it.

If she still wanted him.

He'd seen it lots of times with those who'd been close to killers. He remembered how hard it had been for Calvert's mother and father, though that had been very different.

It was a kind of death and there would be a proper mourning to be done. Anne would need to grieve for the friend she'd lost. She would be losing him in many ways, and she'd need to grieve for all of them. This was without the guilt she was bound to feel, and the shame at having been his friend in the first place, and the guilt she would feel because of the shame.

In all probability, she would also be the first port of call for his children and would need to comfort them and deal with their feelings. Then she would have the press to deal with. If they couldn't hound a killer, they would hound a killer's friends. None of it was going to be easy.

Anne would be looking for someone to blame.

It was probably best, then, to avoid confrontation for a while. To stay out of the line of fire. It still might all turn to shit anyway. He'd known plenty of cases, a lot more straightforward than this one, where a result had slipped away from them at the last minute. A fuck-up or, God forbid, a legal technicality was waiting around every corner to bury cocksure detective inspectors. Thorne wasn't counting any chickens. However, he was buoyant enough to be here in the first place, stepping into the lift and wondering exactly how he was going to explain everything.

Because it wasn't Anne he had come to see anyway.

Going into Alison's room was a shock. Anne hadn't told him she was back on a ventilator, even though he'd known how susceptible she would always be to infection.

The room was noisier again, more cluttered, but the girl at the centre of it still drew his eye and his heart as she had done from the first time he'd seen her. She'd had her hair cut since the last time he'd been here. That was the day he'd brought Bishop's photo in, just before he'd been told about the 'anonymous' accusations and things had spiralled out of control.

Everything was under control again now.

He moved slowly towards the bed, walking past the blackboard, now folded away and lying against the wall covered in a white sheet. Had Alison heard him come in? He knew how limited her field of vision was and didn't want to make her jump.

He caught himself. *Jump? Silly bastard.* He knew so little about what her life was like. What it had become. He'd promised himself he'd look into it and hadn't. He'd heard about people who'd had amputations and could still feel the limbs that had gone. Was it like that for Alison? Could she still feel or even imagine she was feeling what it was like to jump or run or kick or kiss?

He stopped at the end of the bed where he knew she could see him. Her eyeball skittered back and forth for a few seconds. She blinked.

Hello.

He moved to the side of the bed, reaching for the plastic orange chair and looking around the room, casually, as if he were just another visitor fumbling for a suitable bedside pleasantry. He could see no flowers anywhere.

There was nothing to do but begin talking.

'Hello, Alison. I hope you don't mind me just turning up but there are a few things I wanted to explain. Because nobody else *has*, really, and I think you have a right to know. Dr Coburn will have given you all the medical stuff . . . the medical side of things, but I wanted to try and tell you what happened to *you*. After you left the club that night. Obviously we don't really know how much you remember. Probably nothing.'

He helped himself to a much-needed drink from the water jug on the bedside table. He wondered why there *was* a water jug when Alison couldn't drink.

'Exactly what happened between you leaving the nightclub and getting home is guesswork, really, but it doesn't matter. You can tell us about where you met the man with the champagne when you get off this ventilator and get a bit better, but we know that he came into your house, and

350

that the drug in the champagne would have been taking effect, and that there'd have been nothing you could do when he . . . put his hands on you.'

There was a loud crash from the corridor outside. He saw Alison react. A momentary tension in the skin around the eyes. Sounds were obviously so important.

He just needed to get to it now. Stop pissing about. He'd told parents how their children had died. Why should this be so difficult?

'Anyway, Alison, here's the thing. You didn't survive. I mean . . . yes, of course you did, but that was actually what he wanted.'

He patted the edge of the bed, cast an eye towards the machines, the monitors, the tubes, and back to Alison's face.

'*This* . . . is what he wanted, what he was trying to achieve.

'It sounds mad, I know it does, and that's because it is. He wasn't trying to kill you. He might easily have killed you because what he did to you is actually incredibly difficult. He's tried before and since, and not been successful . . . and other women have died. So . . .'

So what? Thorne wondered whether he should ever have started this. What should he tell her now? How *lucky* she'd been?

'That's it. I won't tell you that you were fortunate not to die. That's really something only you can . . . have feelings about. But you were strong

351

enough . . . not to die, so I'm sure you're strong enough to get yourself out of here.

'I have no idea why he did this, Alison. I wish I could tell you I did. I could make something up, but the truth is I haven't got a bloody clue.

'I can tell you one thing, though, and I suppose that's why I've come if I'm honest. He's going to tell me why he did it very soon. I want you to know that. Very soon. He's going to look me in the eye and tell me.'

He took her hand. Squeezed.

'Then I'm going to put the fucker in prison for the rest of his life.'

Really? I see. Well, thanks for popping by and dropping that little snippet into the conversation.

He did this to me deliberately. Wants me like this. Wired up, fucked up.

Right . . .

It's hard to take news any other way than calmly when you're like this. My reactions always tend to look a bit similar. On the outside anyway. I might seem a bit placid. Anybody looking at me would be thinking, Ooh, didn't she take it well?

Inside's another matter.

Raging. Understanding what it means when your blood boils, because I can feel it bubbling. I can feel it moving through my veins like lava. Because I know now. I know for certain.

I'd sort of worked it out anyway.

I've been thinking it had to be something like that.

Something fucking twisted.

I've had a lot of time to think about it and you don't have to be a genius to work out that something strange was going on.

There wasn't a mark on me.

There was nothing sexual. Anne told me.

I thought early on that maybe he was trying to break my neck but there wasn't even a bruise. I reckon it's really quite easy to kill somebody if you want to and I've been wondering why he didn't want to.

Trying to work out what he did want.

So I'm the one he got right? I'm a living and almost breathing testament to this bloke's . . . skill?

While other women died.

Hearing the blood sizzle and hiss through the arteries. Steam coming off my skin.

Thorne sounded pretty confident about getting him. Something in his voice made me think that whoever did this is going to be sorry when Thorne gets hold of him.

Said he was going to make him tell him why he'd done it. I'm not sure that knowing why's going to make me feel better, really. Getting him will, though. Thorne said he didn't know how much I could remember. Neither do I.

But if it's going to help catch this bastard, I'm going to fucking well find out.

CHAPTER 18

1 2 February 1999. His mother died.
3 September 1994. Jan left him for the first time.
18 June 1985. Calvert . . .

As Thorne drove towards Camden this Tuesday lunchtime, he had no idea that the following day, 2 October 2000, would be another date to add to the list. Perhaps the most significant day of them all. Days that he would choose to forget, but that he would have little choice about remembering.

Days that formed him. Long, long days. Painful days. Days that had taught him something about who he'd been up to that point, and dictated who he was going to be from that point on.

What he was going to be.

This day, the eve of it all, had not begun well and would only get worse. The ring had arrived from Edinburgh the night before and had gone straight to the forensic-science laboratory in Lambeth. Thorne was on the phone to Edgware Road first thing wanting an update on progress. There had been none, and was unlikely to be before the following day. All he'd received for his trouble had been another earful from Keable, who was getting very nervous. Jeremy Bishop had rung, demanding to know what was going on. James Bishop had done likewise. As yet, with Rebecca Bishop remaining silent, it looked as though Thorne and Holland had got away with the trip to Bristol.

Thorne smiled to himself now, as he steered the car through Regent's Park, past the unfeasibly grand houses of diplomats and oil billionaires. He smiled at his cockiness with Keable, his bluff-calling, his fuck-you attitude with Tughan.

He knew that he was on safe ground. All of it, the calls, the carpet fibres, the visits to Bishop's house, would be forgotten as soon as Thorne had got what he was after.

As soon as he'd proved that Jeremy Bishop was a multiple killer.

Then Keable would be too busy accepting the congratulations of the commander (who'd be smiling for the press and getting patted on the back by a thoroughly delighted commissioner) to worry about a few late-night phone calls. A slap on the wrist, perhaps. A word about procedure, probably. A warning about his methods at the very worst.

As long as the vital evidence was collected cleanly, Thorne knew that he would get a conviction. He knew that the evidence was there. In Jeremy Bishop's house in Battersea. He just needed the warrant.

Thorne had passed a very dull morning in what a football manager (the one at Spurs was still clinging on to his job) would call a free role. In practice, this meant answering the phone a lot, handing bits of paper to Nick Tughan, and resisting the temptation to drive down to the forensics lab and oversee the examination of Bishop's wedding ring himself. Being part of this ponderous machine again was hugely frustrating, but he was happy to do whatever was necessary. And it wasn't going to be for long.

In Camden, Thorne parked the car beneath the enormous Sainsbury's next to the canal. There was no charge for customers and buying a few cans of own-brand lager was a fair exchange for free parking in the middle of the day.

He walked up past the old TV-am building where a crowd of youngsters was gawping at the recording of a show for MTV inside a tiny glass-fronted studio in the car park. He stopped and watched for a few minutes. The presenters, a girl and a boy, were young and good-looking, and for a second he thought they might be the young couple he'd seen in Waterlow Park a few days before.

Ignoring the strange looks from the teenagers around him, he watched them for a while, jigging and posturing in dumbshow behind the glass. Then he ambled away, supposing that he probably knew more about the music they were introducing than they did and headed towards Parkway where he was meeting Hendricks.

The café was cheap and miserable, which Thorne

far preferred to expensive and cheerful. It was a place where, over a number of years, the two of them had talked about work and football, while indulging their shared passion for fry-ups and stodgy puddings.

When Thorne arrived Hendricks was already there, nursing a cup of tea and looking somewhat less than pleased to see him. Thorne had news that he knew would cheer the miserable bugger up. He signalled to the woman behind the counter for a tea and slid into the booth, picked up a menu and started to read it. Wanting to make it sound casual.

'I think we've got him.' Hendricks looked up but without real interest. Thorne went on, 'I *know* we have, and as soon as we get the forensic tests done I can get a warrant and—'

'Save it, will you?'

Thorne put down the menu. What little appetite he had was vanishing rapidly.

'Well?' Thorne stared at Hendricks. The pathologist looked at his tea, carried on stirring it. 'You've obviously got something to say?'

Hendricks cleared his throat. He'd been rehearsing it. 'Did it not occur to you, even for a second, that when that slimy jobsworth in the forensics lab called up your boss to tell him that a pathologist had just happened to stroll in carrying a plastic bag with carpet fibres in it—'

'Phil, I was going to—'

358

'—that he might also be calling *my* boss as well? Did that not occur to you?'

'What happened?'

'Deep shit is what happened. Because I was stupid enough to do you a favour. And you didn't even have the courtesy to pick up the fucking phone to see what was going on.'

He'd meant to, more than once, and hadn't. 'I'm sorry, Phil, there was another killing and—'

'I know there was. I did the PM, remember? And considering what the two of us do for a living I hardly think a body is much of a fucking excuse, do you?'

It wasn't, and Thorne knew it. Hendricks had every right to be angry, but to try to explain to him exactly what he'd been thinking . . . feeling . . . after Margaret Byrne's murder wouldn't have been easy.

'So what happened?'

'The wanker of a clinical director, who's been looking for an excuse anyway, 'cos I don't look like his idea of a pathologist, hauled me up in front of the chief executive and the personnel director.'

'Fuck . . .'

'Yeah, fuck is right. I was given a verbal warning about inappropriate behaviour and they're still talking about the fucking General Medical Council so don't try asking for any more favours, all right?'

Thorne's tea arrived and he took it gratefully, but Hendricks had no intention of letting him off the hook. 'You're completely self-obsessed, do you know that?' Thorne tried to laugh but nothing came out. 'I'm not talking about this case, I mean all the time. You've got no fucking idea what's going on around you, have you?'

Thorne fixed a defiant smile on his face. 'Am I supposed to be answering these questions or is this a lecture?'

'I couldn't give a toss, I'm just telling you. I'm probably the nearest thing to a friend you've got and we talk about fuck all.' Thorne started to speak but Hendricks cut him off. 'Football and work. That's it. Talking shop or talking shit. We play pool and eat pizza and have a joke and talk about sweet fuck all.'

Thorne decided he should fight his corner. 'Hang on a second. What about you? I spoke to you about Jan when we were splitting up, I know I did. You never confide in me about anything.'

'What would be the point?'

'You've never said a word about family, or girlfriends.' Hendricks laughed harshly. Thorne looked at him. 'What?'

'I'm gay, you dickhead. Queer as fuck. OK?'

For reasons he couldn't quite explain, Thorne blushed deeply.

Half a minute passed. He looked up from his tea. 'Why the hell not tell me then? Worried I'd think you fancied me?'

Hendricks laughed again but neither of them

was finding anything funny. 'I couldn't tell you. Not . . . you. Everybody else knows.'

'What? Why didn't they say something, then?'

'Not at *work*.' Hendricks's voice was raised. Thorne stared past him, ashamed, to the woman behind the counter who smiled at nothing in particular. 'I mean everybody I care about. My family, my real friends . . . Christ, it's fairly obvious to most people. What do I look like, for fuck's sake? You're so . . . shielded. You couldn't see it because it doesn't affect you. You've got blinkers on and I'm fucking sick of it!'

Anne had slammed down the phone and smoked three cigarettes, one after the other. Now she felt nauseous as well as furious. She marched towards the coffee machine in main reception, going over and over it . . .

She'd called Thorne on his mobile, and although she had no idea where he was or what he was doing, it was obviously putting him in an awful mood.

Now he'd passed it on to her.

They hadn't spoken since Sunday. She'd known then that something important was happening on the case and this feeling had distilled into something else when she'd seen him on the televised press conference.

Something like dread.

She could sense something coming. She could feel the chill, as if a vast shadow were beginning to creep over them. Over all of them – herself,

Thorne, Jeremy. She'd reached for the phone needing some reassurance, a tender word. She'd wanted to give those things to *him* too, knowing that he might need them.

And all she'd got was a diatribe. He'd told her, no . . . he'd *ordered* her to stay away from Jeremy Bishop. He assured her it was for her own protection, not that he really believed that she'd be in any physical danger. It was just . . . best. *Best,* he'd said. He explained how he'd tried to keep off the whole subject until now to spare her feelings and to avoid a possible conflict of interests, but now things were coming to a head so he'd decided to get everything out in the open.

Bollocks!

He'd avoided the subject until he'd got into her knickers and now he was laying down the law. She was having none of it and had told him so in no uncertain terms.

The coffee machine was repeatedly rejecting a twenty-pence piece. She carried on putting in the coin, picking it out and putting it in again.

Things had got pretty heated, especially when she'd heard the telltale sound of a can being opened. Wherever he was, he was drinking. This, bearing in mind the supposed gravity of what he was telling her – the seriousness of the situation he was trying to make her aware of – annoyed her beyond belief. How fucking dare he?

Then he'd asked her if she could come over tonight.

She smashed the heel of her hand against the front of the coffee machine . . .

It was then that she'd hung up.

Giving up on the coffee, Anne turned and walked back towards the ITU. She had a good mind to go round to Jeremy's tonight. She wouldn't, of course. She'd spend the evening at home with Rachel, if she was in, and drink too much wine and watch something mind-numbing on television, and wonder what Tom Thorne was doing.

And try to keep warm as the shadow grew larger.

The last time he'd stood on this spot, his face had been hidden and his fist wrapped around the end of an iron bar.

Today he had an altogether more subtle message to deliver. He'd rung several times to ensure that the flat was empty, having taken care to withhold his number. He'd smiled each time he'd punched in 141. It was, of course, a trick that Thorne must himself have been familiar with.

Things could not have been going better. The excitement of the procedure, the surge he felt rushing through him, had been replaced by something else, now that he'd admitted to himself that he might never enjoy another success. A different kind of enjoyment, fuelled by a very different purpose.

The enjoyment of the game with Thorne.

The game had been a part of it all from the beginning. A vital part of it. It had gone cheek by jowl with – he smiled – his more hands-on work. It had complemented it, cast a light upon it, put it beautifully into context.

And he had played the game extremely well.

As he moved towards the front door, he wondered if, secretly, Thorne was enjoying it too. He suspected he probably was. There was something in the man's eyes.

He looked around casually and knocked on the door. Just a man of the world paying a visit to a friend. Nobody in? A note would do the trick . . .

He removed a gloved hand from his trouser pocket and reached into his jacket for the envelope. Yes, a different kind of enjoyment. It was not wrapping fingers around a pulsing artery, but he enjoyed its . . . delicacy nevertheless. Popping open a letterbox provided a different kind of thrill from that he garnered when feeling an ordinary life float away under his touch. But, in context, a thrill nevertheless.

The end of the game was in sight.

One way or another, this will all be over soon . . .

He was enjoying it so much, it was almost a shame to let Thorne win.

The car park was starting to empty. Thorne decided it was time to leave. He'd now been sitting in his car for over four hours, during which time he'd drunk six cans of supermarket-strength lager.

He'd never felt more sober.

After his meeting with Phil Hendricks he'd wandered back towards the car in something of a daze. He'd popped into the supermarket to pick up the beer, read the paper, and then sat, listening to the radio, drinking, and mulling over what his friend had said. *Friend?* Had he got any friends?

He knew that Hendricks was right. Everything he'd said was spot on. So he'd thought about it for a while, let one can of beer quickly become four, then turned a bad day into a fucking awful one by deciding to ring Anne.

Where had the caution of the day before gone? He'd decided then that it was probably wise to steer clear of any confrontation until the case had broken. So why, in God's name, had he rung her and told her to stay away from Bishop?

There had been something almost boastful about it. Some part of him had wanted to flaunt this . . . victory. It was becoming about something more than cracking a case and stopping a killer. It was starting to feel like *defeating* a killer. Like besting a rival. He'd as good as picked up the phone and said, 'Stand back, this isn't going to be pretty.' It was proprietorial.

He wanted her to know how good he was. How right he'd been.

She told him she thought he was pathetic. Fucking pathetic.

He'd hurled his phone into the back of the car, turned up the radio and polished off the last two cans.

Now it was dark outside. The supermarket would be closing soon. The security guard who patrolled the underground car park was starting to give him decidedly dirty looks and mutter into his radio.

Thorne realised that he was starving. Six cans of lager was all that had passed his lips since breakfast. He knew he should leave the car where it was and head for the tube. He was only one stop away from home. Christ, he could walk home in about ten minutes.

Thorne started the engine, pulled out of the car park and pointed the Mondeo south, away from home, and towards the centre of town.

Nobody could say I wasn't comfortable. That's the word hospitals always use, isn't it? When you ring up to ask after someone. They're 'comfortable'. Like they're lying there on feather pillows being massaged or something. Well, I'm certainly comfortable with my state-of-the-art mattress and my remote-control bed and my telly and my magazine holder.

Comfortable.

And all I really want to do is scream until my throat is raw, I want to scream and yell and, maybe it's asking a bit much, but I'd like to punch somebody in the face as hard as I can and smash a few things up as well, if that's all right. Break things. Mirrors. Glass things. Feel blood on my knuckles, anything . . .

Do I sound frustrated? Well, I am. Frustrated.

So. *FUCKING. FRUSTRATED!*

There's stuff I want to say, to talk about and I've got less chance of doing it now than I had even a week ago. Now that I'm wired up to this superannuated fucking accordion again.

Since I found out why I'm the way I am, since I was told that somebody planned this, I've been

367

trying to remember. Trying so hard to remember. Something that might help. Anything that might help them get the bastard.

Now there's some stuff in my head that I know isn't a dream or anything I've imagined. I don't know whether it will help. It'll help *me* for sure.

It's memory and it's fighting to come out.

Memory about what happened after the hen party. It's not so much pictures as words. Actually, not even words. It's sounds. I'm hearing words but it's like they're being spoken to me under water. They're distorted and I can't quite make them out but I can guess the sense of them. I can make out the tone.

Soon I'm going to work out exactly what the words are.

They're the words he said while he was doing it. The man who put me in here.

CHAPTER 19

A quarter to midnight and Tower Records was heaving. Dozens of late night shoppers mingled with those who were just there to listen to the music or read the magazines or kill time.

The young man behind the till didn't even look up. 'Yeahcan'elpyou?'

'Yes, I'd like to pay for these, please,' said Thorne, 'and there's a Waylon Jennings import I'd like to order.'

James Bishop reddened furiously. 'What the fuck do you want? I shouldn't even be talking to you.'

Thorne dumped three CDs on to the counter in front of Bishop and fumbled for his wallet. He stared at Bishop until, with a face clouded by resentment, he began picking up the CDs, removing the security tags and running them through the till. He wouldn't look at Thorne, but instead glanced nervously towards his colleagues, thrusting the CDs clumsily into a plastic bag, trying to get it all over as quickly as possible.

Thorne leaned on the counter, waving his credit card. 'What's the matter? Don't want your workmates knowing you've got a friend who buys Kris Kristofferson albums? I did want to get the new Fatboy Slim single but you've sold out.'

Bishop took the credit card, swiped it, and glared at Thorne. 'You're not my friend. You're just a wanker!'

'I don't suppose it's worth asking for the staff discount?'

'Fuck you.'

Thorne shook his head sadly. 'I knew I should have gone to Our Price . . .'

An assistant with a silver spike through his lower lip ambled over. 'Is everything all right, Jim?'

Bishop thrust the plastic bag at Thorne. 'It's fine.' He looked over Thorne's shoulder to the girl waiting behind him. 'Yeahcan'elpyou?'

Thorne didn't move. 'When does your shift finish?'

The girl behind him tutted impatiently. Bishop looked at him with a defiant half-smile. He glanced at the enormous blue G-Shock on his wrist. 'Fifteen minutes. And?'

Thorne pointed towards the door. 'And I'll see you in Dunkin' Donuts. I'd recommend the cinnamon, but it's entirely up to you . . .'

Twenty minutes later, Thorne was just finishing his second coffee and his fourth doughnut when James Bishop strolled in and sat down next to him. He was wearing a red Puffa jacket and the same black woolly hat he'd been wearing in the shop. Thorne took another doughnut and pushed the box towards him. Bishop pushed it back. 'Suit yourself,' Thorne said. Bishop stared at him. 'I've not eaten all day. Do you want coffee?'

Bishop shook his head. Again the strange half-smile. 'So what is it, then? Do you want to know if my dad's flipped out yet, is that it? If you keeping him awake half the night with stupid phone calls is affecting his work? Maybe costing someone their life? Pretty fucking irresponsible, wouldn't you say?'

Thorne stared at him for a few seconds, chewing. 'So has he?'

'Has he what?'

'Flipped out.'

'Jesus . . .' Bishop took out a packet of Marlboro. Thorne's eyes drifted away to the left and Bishop followed them to the no-smoking sign on the wall. He threw the packet on to the table.

'He's pissed off that you're doing it and even more pissed off that you're getting away with it. None of us are going to let it go, you know. Whatever happens, we'll keep making a fuss until you're back in fucking uniform.'

Thorne considered, for a second or two, the uncomplicated life of the woodentop. Domestics. D and D. Traffic. He wouldn't wish it on his worst enemy.

'None of the things that you and your father are accusing me of is against the law, James.'

'Don't hide behind the law, that's pathetic. Especially when you've got no respect for it.'

'I respect the important bits of it.'

'You're not a copper, Thorne, you're a stalker.'

Thorne took a napkin and slowly wiped the sugar from around his mouth. 'I'm just doing my job, James.'

Bishop was agitated. Had been since he'd walked in. Chewing his nails one second, drumming his fingers on the table the next. One part of his body always moving or twitching. Feet kicking, arms stretching. He was jittery. Thorne wondered if he had a drug problem. He didn't find it hard to believe. If he did it was almost certainly funded by his father. Maybe the doctor prescribed something . . .

Another very good reason for wanting to protect him.

'Your sister thinks that you only pretend to be close to your father so that you can keep sponging off him.'

'She's a silly cunt.' Spitting the words out.

Thorne was shocked, but did his best not to show it. 'You do fairly well out of him, though?'

'Look, he gave me a car and he helped with the deposit on my flat, all right?' Thorne shrugged. 'This is nothing to do with money. He's upset and that makes me upset, it's as simple as that. He's my father.'

'So he's not capable of . . . wickedness?' Thorne had no idea why he'd used that particular word.

While he was wondering where it had come from, James Bishop was staring at him as if he'd just dropped down to earth from another planet.

'He's my *father*.'

'So you protect him at all costs?'

'Against the likes of you, yeah . . . using the law to act out a vendetta because he happens to have treated some woman who got attacked by the man you're after and because you're shagging somebody he once had a thing with. I'll protect him against that.'

'It's my job to get at the truth, and if that upsets people sometimes, then that's tough.'

Bishop scoffed. 'Christ, you really think you're a hard man, don't you? Part misunderstood copper and part vigilante. I'd call you a dinosaur but they had bigger brains . . .' He stood up and turned to go.

Thorne stopped him. 'So what sort of copper would you be, James? What do you think it should be about?'

Bishop turned and thrust his hands deep into the pockets of his jacket. He sniffed, pursing lips that were the same as his father's. Thorne could see the small boy hiding just beneath the arrogant posturing. 'What about justice?' Bishop sneered. 'I had the stupid idea that was fairly fucking important.'

Thorne pictured a young girl, in a bed with a pale pink quilt, trapped inside a body growing frail and flabby from lack of use. He pictured a face, the features partly shadowed, staring down at him from the second floor of a large house. Now he stared back, hard, at those same perfect features, set in the younger face of the man to whom they'd been passed on. 'Oh, it is, James. Very important . . .'

Thorne followed him to the door. 'Can I drop you anywhere?' Bishop shook his head and stared out of the doorway at the huge stream of people still flowing round Piccadilly Circus in the early hours of a cold October morning. Without a word he stepped into it, and was immediately gone.

Thorne stood for a few seconds, watching the red Puffa jacket disappearing into the distance, before turning and heading in the opposite direction to pick up his car.

Thorne stopped when he saw the shape in the doorway.

He froze when it began to move.

He breathed out, relieved, when the shape revealed itself to be the somewhat wobbly figure of Dave Holland. Thorne's first thought was that he'd been hurt. 'Jesus, Dave . . .' He moved quickly, reaching to gather up the DC by the arms, and then he smelt the booze.

Holland stood up. Not paralytic, but well on the way. 'Sir . . . been sitting waiting for you. You've been ages . . .'

Thorne had given up the whisky a long time ago, at the same time as the fags, but it was still a smell he'd recognise anywhere. Instinctively he reeled from it, just needing a second or two. It was

374

a smell that could overpower him. Pungent and pathetic. The smell of need. The smell of misery. The smell of *alone*.

Francis John Calvert. Whisky, piss and gunpowder. And freshly washed nightdresses.

The smell of death in a council flat on a Monday morning.

Holland stood, leaning against the wall, breathing too loudly. Thorne reached into the pocket of his leather jacket for his keys. 'Come on, Dave, let's get inside and I'll make some coffee. How did you get here anyway?'

'Taxi. Left the car . . .'

There was really no point in asking *where* Holland had left his car. They could sort it out later. The key turned in the lock. Thorne nudged open the front door with his foot, instinctively turning the bunch of keys in his hand, feeling for the second key that would open the door to his flat.

There was a white envelope lying on the doormat in the communal hallway.

Thorne looked at it and thought: There's another note from the killer.

Not 'What's that?' or 'That's odd' or even 'I wonder if . . . ?' He knew what it was immediately and said as much. Holland sobered up straight away.

Thorne knew that neither the envelope nor the note inside it would trouble a forensic scientist greatly. They would be clean – not a print, not a fibre, not a stray hair. But he still took the necessary precautions. Holland held down the envelope with fingers wrapped in kitchen towel while Thorne used two knives to improvise as tongs and remove the piece of paper.

The envelope had not been sealed. Thorne would probably have steamed it open anyway, but the killer had left nothing to chance. He'd wanted his note read straight away. By Thorne.

He used the knives to flatten the paper out. The note was neatly typed like the others. Thorne knew it was only a matter of time before the typewriter it had been written on was being wrapped up, labelled and loaded into the back of a Forensic Science Services van.

This would be Jeremy Bishop's last note.

TOM,
I HAD CONSIDERED SOMETHING DIFFERENT, AN E-MAIL PERHAPS, BUT I'M GUESSING THAT YOU'RE SOMETHING OF A LUDDITE AS FAR AS ALL THAT'S CONCERNED. SO, INK AND PARCHMENT IT IS.
CONGRATULATIONS ON THE TV PERFORMANCE BY THE WAY, VERY INTENSE. DID YOU MEAN WHAT YOU SAID ABOUT IT ALL BEING OVER SOON, OR WAS THAT JUST HOT AIR FOR THE CAM-ERAS? THERE'S NOTHING LIKE CONFIDENCE, IS THERE? OR ARE YOU JUST TRYING TO MAKE ME JITTERY IN THE HOPE THAT I'LL MAKE A MISTAKE? ONE QUESTION . . .

WHAT I WAS WONDERING IS, WHAT WAS IT LIKE
FINDING HER? BEING THE FIRST ONE THERE?
WAS THAT YOUR FIRST TIME, TOM? YOU GET
USED TO BLOOD, DON'T YOU?
ANYWAY, IF YOU'RE RIGHT, I SUPPOSE I'LL
SEE YOU VERY SOON.
REGARDS . . .

Holland slumped on to the settee. Thorne read the
note a second time. And a third. The arrogance
was breathtaking. There seemed no great point to
it. There was no revelation or announcement. It
was all . . . display.

He went into the kitchen, flicked on the kettle
and swilled out a couple of coffee-cups. Why did
Bishop feel the need to do this? Why was he *baiting*
him about Maggie Byrne, when Thorne had so
clearly risen to the bait a long time ago?

He spooned in the instant coffee.

There was something skewed about the tone of
the note that Thorne couldn't put his finger on.
Something almost forced. Maybe the killer was
starting to lose the control he had over everything.
Maybe his latest failure had tipped him over the
edge. Or maybe he was starting to work towards
the insanity plea he would obviously try to cop
when the time came.

And the time was most certainly coming.

He stirred the drinks. There was nothing arti-
ficial about the madness. Nobody sane could do
as this man had done, but still Thorne would

fight tooth and nail to prevent it cushioning his fall.

He wanted him to fall hard.

There would be pressure, of course, from those who would want to treat his illness, to care for him. There were always those. There were always plenty for whom violent death was a hobby, or a study option or a gravy train. The lunatics who would write to him inside with requests for advice, or signed pictures, or offers of marriage. The campaigners. The writers of books – bestsellers before the bodies had started to decompose. The makers of films. The old women with pastel hair hammering on the side of the van, spitting . . .

And the policemen who remembered the smell of the blood.

Was that your first time?

Thorne carried the coffee into the living room, but stopped in the doorway the second he looked at Holland, who was sitting on the settee and staring at the wall opposite. It was not the faraway look of drunkenness, or tiredness, or boredom.

Thorne felt his heartbeat increase.

He hadn't asked why Holland had come here in the first place.

Holland turned to him. 'We were trying to get hold of you . . .'

Thorne remembered his phone, chucked into the back of his car. 'What's happened, Dave?'

Holland tried to shape an answer and now Thorne recognised the look. He'd seen it fifteen years before, in the bottom of glasses and in shop windows and in mirrors. The look of a young man who's seen far too much death.

Holland spoke, his voice, his eyes, his expression dead. 'Michael and Eileen Doyle . . . Helen Doyle's mum and dad. The next-door neighbour noticed the smell.'

Apparently, the stroke affected only a very small part of my brain. In the brainstem.

The 'inferior pons' this particular bit's called, if you can believe that.

It's just unfortunate that it happens to be the bit that controls things. All the communications pass through it. If your brain's Paddington station, this bit's the signal box. Basically, the signals still get waved or switched on or whatever. When I want to wiggle a toe or sniff or speak, the instruction still goes out. This thing called a relay cell is supposed to make it happen: it fires the signal down the line to the next cell and then the next one. It's like a microscopic version of 'pass it on' all the way to my toe or my nose or wherever. Unfortunately, somewhere in the middle, some of the cells aren't playing the game properly and that's the end of that. In layman's terms, this is me.

Bizarrely, though, as one part of my brain is fucked, it feels like other parts are compensating and changing. The bit that deals with sound. It feels like that bit's been upgraded. I can distinguish between sounds that are very similar. I can place a nurse by the squeak of her shoe and tell how far away things are. The sounds give me a picture in my head, like I'm turning into a bat.

And it's helping me to remember.

Those underwater sounds are getting clearer every day. Words are sharpening up. I can make out a lot of what we said to each other now, me and the man who put me in hospital.

Fragments of a soundtrack.

A lot of it's me, of course, no real surprise there, waffling on about the party and the wedding and stuff. Christ, I sound very pissed. I can hear the champagne going down my throat and I can hear him laughing at my dismal, drunken jokes.

I hear myself playing with the front-door keys. Inviting him inside to finish the drink. Slurred and stupid words. Words that are hardly worth remembering. The last words ever to come out of my mouth.

I'm still groping for the words that came out of his.

CHAPTER 20

As Thorne drove towards the Edgware Road, he found himself fighting to stay awake. The noise of six empty beer cans, rattling around in the footwell, was helping, but it was still a struggle. It had been a long night, and a bleak one. Not even the spectacle of Holland on the phone that morning, squirming and looking pained as he tried sheepishly to explain to Sophie where he'd spent the night, had raised the spirits.

They'd talked long into the night. Holland told Thorne what had happened to Michael and Eileen Doyle. They'd done it with tablets. The police had been called to the house on Windsor Road by a neighbour. She'd presumed they'd gone away to stay with relatives after what had happened to Helen.

A PC found them in an upstairs bedroom. They were holding hands.

In spite of what Holland had already had to drink, Thorne dug out a few cans and they'd sat up talking about everything and nothing. Parents, partners, the job. As the drink met the tiredness head on, Holland had started to drift off, and

Thorne began to ramble vaguely about the girls. About Christine and Susan and Madeleine. And Helen. He didn't say anything about their voices. He didn't mention how strange he found it that he never heard the voice of Maggie Byrne.

Thorne wondered if Holland heard it. He never asked him.

The note lay beside him on the passenger seat, safely wrapped up. He saw himself handing it over in exchange for a warrant. He heard himself reading Jeremy Bishop his rights. He pictured himself leading the good doctor away, down the front path, past his terracotta pots full of dead and dying flowers.

Then he arrived at work and it all fell apart.

'They couldn't get a thing. Sorry, Tom.'

Keable did look sorry. But not as sorry as Thorne. They'd been waiting for him, Keable and Tughan, to fuck him up the second he stepped out of the lift.

'A ring's a difficult enough thing to print anyway by all accounts. A small surface area. This one was just a mess. Dozens of partials but nothing worth writing up. We even sent it over to the Yard. SO3 have got better equipment, but—'

'What about dead skin on the inside? Hairs from a finger?' Thorne was trying to sound reasonable.

Tughan shook his head. 'The bloke I spoke to said it was a forensic nightmare. It's been up and down the country, for Christ's sake, handled by God knows how many people.'

Thorne slumped back against the lift doors and felt fury fighting a battle with tiredness for control of him. 'Did you at least check the hallmark? Check it and you'll find out that ring was made the same year Bishop got married.'

Keable nodded but Tughan was in no mood to humour Thorne. 'Listen, even if we do get something, the chain of evidence is non-existent.'

The fury won the battle. 'And whose fault is that? This has been one huge fuck-up from start to finish. I should have had a warrant by now. I should be tearing that bastard's house apart. This case should be over by now – over.'

Tughan moved back towards his desk. 'It was only ever a slim possibility, Tom. We knew that even if you didn't. What were you planning to do anyway? Slip it on to Bishop's finger like a fucking glass slipper?'

Thorne waited until Tughan's self-indulgent chuckle had finished. 'How are you planning to spend the money the newspaper paid you, Nick?'

The colour rose immediately to Tughan's hollow cheeks. Keable stared hard at him, then back to Thorne, deciding finally that accusations would be best left until another day. 'Listen, Tom,' Keable said, 'Nobody's more upset about this than me and I'm going to crack some heads, trust me.'

And now Thorne felt the tiredness come rushing at him. He could barely keep his head erect.

He closed his eyes. He had no idea how long they'd been closed when Keable next spoke. 'We've got this latest note. It's a significant development.'

'Another press conference?'

'I think it would be a good idea, yes.'

Thorne called the lift back up. Raising his arm and bringing his finger to the button was a struggle. He had an idea now of the effort it took for Alison to blink. He wanted to go home. He had no intention of hanging around and answering phones. He needed to lie down and switch himself off.

One final question: 'Is Jeremy Bishop this investigation's prime suspect?'

Keable hesitated a fraction too long before replying, but Thorne didn't hear the answer anyway, thanks to the roaring in his ears.

He was driving much too fast along the Marylebone Road. The exertion of steering, of concentrating, was leaving him wringing with sweat, which dripped from him as he leaned forward, crippled with exhaustion. It took every last ounce of energy he had to tap out a rhythm on the wheel, as the music exploded from the speakers.

He turned up the volume as high as it would go. He winced. The cheap speakers distorted the sound, turning the treble into shattering glass and the bass into a collision. The music, if it could still be called that, was shaking the car apart, but he would have made it even louder if he could. He wanted to be bludgeoned by the noise. He wanted to be hypnotised.

He wanted to be anaesthetised . . .

He swerved into the inside lane, reached for his phone and pulled up just past Madame Tussaud's.

He flicked on the hazards, turned down the music and hit the speed dial.

A long queue of tourists was standing in the rain, waiting to get in and gawp at the waxy doppelgangers of pop stars, politicians and sportsmen. And, of course, mass murderers: the Chamber of Horrors was always the most popular attraction.

Anywhere.

The violent death gravy train . . .

She picked up.

'It's me . . . I'm sorry about yesterday.'

'OK . . .' Sounding unsure, hedging her bets.

'Look, Anne, everything's changed, fucked up to be honest, and I just wanted to tell you . . .' *Your ex-boyfriend's off the hook.* '. . . the evidence I thought I had hasn't . . . materialised, so just ignore what I said, all right?'

'What about Jeremy?'

'Can I see you later?'

'Is he still a suspect?'

This time it was Thorne's turn to hesitate too long before replying.

'Can you come over later?'

'Listen, Tom, I won't say I'm not pleased because I am. I'm sorry about yesterday too, though . . .'

In the background Thorne could hear a doctor

386

being paged. He waited until it had finished. 'Anne . . .'

'I'll be over about five-ish. I'm on call tonight so I'll sneak away from here early. All right?'

It was very all right.

He'd legislated for some ineptitude. There had been a little *give* built into his thinking. But this was way beyond anything he'd imagined.

Fucking morons. Stupid fucking idiots.

It was stupid to expect any kind of equilibrium, he knew that, but this kind of unpredictability was so *fucking* annoying.

He'd started to feel the depression take hold again the second he'd put the phone down, wrapping itself around him, like a dark, itchy blanket. Making him scratch. Making him smell.

He walked up and down in straight lines. Up one board and down the other. Moving slowly across the room in vertical lines. Up one, his bare feet cool against the bleached floorboards. Down the other, his toes caressing each knot and whorl of the beautifully smooth wood. Up and down, his fingers stroking the straight, puckered lines that ran across his stomach.

Up and down, his breathing slowing, the white walls soothing . . .

He could roll with the punches. He was adaptable, wasn't he? Champagne or IV. His place or theirs. Hen nights or night buses. Whatever was necessary. This would not be the perfect way to end

387

it but it would certainly do the trick. His plan, of course, the magic-island scenario, the beautiful by-product of his medical work, had involved a little suffering spread out over a very long time. A lot of suffering, *quickly*, might prove just as enjoyable.

He picked up the phone to call her back. She'd be happy he'd called. She'd be thrilled with the invitation. Excited at the hint of what the evening might hold in store. Not as excited as he was, obviously, but then he knew just how good it was really going to be.

Time to get proactive.

Time to find a different way of hurting.

Anne managed to get away from Queen Square even earlier than she'd thought, but by the time she got to the flat, around four, Thorne had already spent the best part of six hours bouncing off the walls.

He'd tried going to bed but it was pointless. Every muscle screamed out for sleep but his brain wasn't listening. There was a force in him that was now directionless, an energy desperately seeking an outlet. Though his body felt as weary as it had ever felt, his mind was racing. It roared and rumbled and skidded and slipped from its track, then spun around and roared away again.

He could confront Bishop with the ring.

Tell him that they'd found incriminating evidence.

Plant the fucking evidence . . .

He could beat a confession out of him. Christ, it would be good to feel the bones in that face shatter beneath his pounding fists and not stop hitting until Bishop hovered somewhere between life and death and felt what it was like to be Alison Willetts . . .

'Whatever it takes, Tommy.'

'Helen, I'm so sorry about . . .'

'It's all right, Tommy. Just get him. You can still get him, can't you?'

Part of him imagined that Anne would come and kiss it all away, fuck it all away, and he would go to sleep and wake up cleansed.

And that was almost how it happened.

She bounded into his living room like a teenager, and the first smile of his day made his face ache. She told him to lie down and went to make them both tea.

He'd told her once that he didn't want a mother. Right now he wasn't arguing.

She brought the drinks through to the living room. 'You sounded a bit manic when you called.'

He grunted. When she pulled away the cushion he was holding across his face, she was relieved to see that he was grinning.

'How do you feel?'

'Like I've taken uppers and downers, hundreds of them.'

She handed him his tea. 'Have you ever?'

Thorne shook his head. 'Booze and fags. Honest working-class drugs.'

'The most dangerous of them all.'

He sipped his tea, staring at the ceiling. 'What I need, I reckon, is about six weeks in one of those nice, cosy rooms you've got on ITU. Just drug me up and lay on some nice, sexy doctor to minister to my needs. Is the room next to Alison available? Do they have Sky? I'll pay, obviously . . .'

Anne laughed and lowered herself into the armchair. 'I'll let you know when we've got one free.'

'How is she? I didn't know she was back on the ventilator.' Anne looked at him questioningly. 'I went in to see her the other day. You were in a meeting, I think.'

'I know. She seemed a little distracted afterwards . . .'

He ignored the implied question. 'Is she any better?'

Anne shook her head, and for the first time felt tired herself. 'She's always going to be prone to infections of this sort. Two steps forward . . .'

A dance with which Thorne was all too familiar.

Anne raised an eyebrow. 'What did you say to Alison?' Remembering the last time. The photograph he'd kept hidden.

Thorne laughed. A splutter of self-disgust. 'I went to let her know I was about to arrest Jeremy Bishop.'

The small-talk had lasted about as long as the tea.

The silence that fell between them was in danger

390

of becoming terminal when Anne spoke quietly, not looking at him: 'Why did you think it was him, Tom?'

Did? Past tense. Not for Thorne.

'It started with the drugs theft obviously. Then the connection to Alison and lack of an alibi for the other killings. The physical description, and the car . . .' He sighed heavily, pushing finger and thumb hard into his eyes and rubbing. 'It's all academic. I've got no evidence and no warrant to go and get any.'

'What did you think you'd find?'

'Typewriter maybe. The drugs probably. Unless he kept them at the hospital, which . . .'

Anne was suddenly on her feet, pacing around the room. 'You keep going on about these drugs but it just doesn't make any sense. Why the hell would he need to steal drugs in those quantities, Tom? Jeremy works with this stuff every day of his life. If he'd wanted to, he could have taken as much as he liked without anyone ever getting suspicious. He could pocket an ampoule, even a couple, every day for six months and nobody would ever notice. So why draw attention to himself by stealing a huge quantity all in one go? It's only when drugs go missing in those amounts that it's even registered. Jeremy would not have needed to do that, Tom.'

And boom! There it was. The tune he'd been unable to place. *That* had been what was bothering him all along, lurking at the back of his brain, slippery and elusive. She was right, of course. Why had none of them ever really sat down and spoken to a fucking doctor? How could they have missed it? How could *he* have missed it?

Easy: he hadn't wanted it to be there.

Hendricks: *You've got blinkers on and I'm fucking sick of it.*

He felt like the breath had been taken from him. Beaten out of his body. Christ, it was all coming apart in front of him.

'I'm sorry, Tom.'

He closed his eyes. Screwed them shut. He knew it wasn't Anne who should be apologising. There were people *he* needed to say sorry to.

The first time he'd laid eyes on him, he thought he'd looked like the doctor from *The Fugitive*. *That* doctor had been innocent as well.

'I got *thinking* it was him and *wanting* it to be him mixed up, I think . . .'

'Ssssh . . .' She was kneeling beside the settee, stroking his hair.

'It got too personal. There wasn't enough distance.'

'Tom, it doesn't matter now. Nobody was hurt.'

'I was so sure, Anne. So sure Calvert was the killer . . .' He felt her hand stop moving. Shook his head. Tried to laugh it off.

Slip of the tongue.

'*Bishop*, I mean. Bishop.'

'Who's Calvert?'

Whisky, piss and gunpowder. And freshly washed nightdresses. Oh, fuck, no . . .

392

'Tom, who's Calvert?'

Then the tears came. And he dredged it all up, every heartstopping, malodorous moment of it. For the first time in fifteen years he took himself back completely. Jan never had the time or the stomach for all of it but now he was going to skip nothing. No edited highlights with a warning for those of a sensitive nature.

Thorne fought to bring the sobbing under control.

Then he told her.

CHAPTER 21

Friday, 15 June 1985. Nearly going-home time.

It's a big one. The biggest since the Ripper. Fifteen thousand interviews in eighteen months and they've got nothing. The press are going mental, but not *that* mental, obviously. It's not like he's killing women or straight blokes, after all. Just the right amount of moral outrage with a smattering of self-righteousness and occasional comments about 'the risks inherent in choosing that kind of lifestyle'.

No lurid nicknames, though if the *Sun* could have got away with 'Poof Killer' they would certainly have used it.

Just 'Johnny Boy'.

The fourth victim had told a friend he was meeting a man called John for a drink. This was an hour or so before his heart was cut out and his genitals were removed. An approximation of what might be Johnny Boy's face stares down from the wall of every nick in the country. He's got dirty-blond hair and a sallow complexion. His eyes are blue and very, very cold.

It's a big one.

Detective Constable Thomas Thorne leans against the wall of the interview room at Paddington station and stares at a man with dirty-blond hair and blue eyes.

Francis John Calvert. Thirty-four. Self-employed builder from North London.

'Any chance of a fag? I'm fucking gasping . . .' Calvert smiles. A winning smile. Perfect teeth.

Thorne says nothing. Just watching him until DI Duffy comes back.

'Surely I'm allowed one poxy fag?' The film-star smile fading just a little.

'Shut up.'

Then the door opens and Duffy comes back in. The interview resumes and Tom Thorne doesn't say another word.

None of it is riveting stuff. Duffy is way past his best. It's purely routine anyway. Calvert is only there because of what he does.

A week before he died, the third victim told a flatmate that he'd met a man in a club. The man had said he was a builder. The flatmate made a joke about tool-kits and builders' bumcrack. Seven days and one body later, the joke wasn't funny any more but the flatmate remembered what his dead friend had said.

Thousands and thousands of builders to be interviewed. Some are seen at their home. Some are questioned at their place of work. Calvert gets a phone call and comes into Paddington for a chat.

Later, of course, it will emerge that he'd been chatted to before.

Duffy and Calvert get on like a house on fire. Duffy gives Calvert his fag.

He wants to get home.

Thorne wants to get home too, he's been married less than a year. He's only got one ear on the answers Calvert reels off.

At home with his wife . . . three little girls are a right handful . . . wishes he could go out at night gallivanting about . . . not to those sort of places obviously. Another flash of that smile. He's helpful, concerned. Wife only too happy to talk to you if you want. He hopes they find this nutter and string him up. It doesn't matter what these pervs get up to in their private lives, what this killer's doing's disgusting . . .

Duffy hands Calvert the short statement to sign and that's that. Another one crossed off the list. He thanks him.

One of these days they'll strike it lucky.

Duffy stands and heads for the door. 'Show Mr Calvert out, would you, Thorne?' The DI leaves to begin the tedious process of writing it all up. The investigation is awash with paperwork. There are distant rumblings about the arrival of computers that, one day, will simplify all this. But that's all they are. Distant rumblings.

Thorne holds open the door and Calvert steps out into the corridor. He strolls casually past more interview rooms, hands in pockets, whistling. Thorne follows. He can hear a distant radio, probably in the locker room, playing one of his favourite songs – 'There Must Be An Angel' by the Eurythmics. Jan bought the record for him last week. He wonders what she'll have organised for dinner. Maybe he can go and get a takeaway.

Through the first set of swing doors and a left turn along another corridor, which sweeps round towards main reception. Calvert waits, allowing Thorne to catch up. He holds the doors for him. 'Bet you lot are making a fucking mint in over-time.'

Thorne says nothing. He can't wait to see the back of the cocky little fucker. Past another Johnny Boy poster. Somebody's drawn a speech bubble. It says, 'Hello, sailor.' Thorne's humming the Eurythmics song as he walks.

Then the final set of doors. The desk sergeant gives Thorne a nod. Thorne steps ahead of Calvert, pushes open the doors and stops. This is as far as he goes. This isn't a hotel and he isn't a fucking concierge. Calvert steps through the doors, stops and turns. 'Cheers, then . . .'

'Thanks for your help, Mr Calvert. We'll be in touch if we need anything else.'

Thorne holds out his hand without thinking about it. He's looking towards the desk sergeant, who's trying to catch his eye and mouthing something about a party for one of the secretaries who's leaving. Thorne feels the large, callused hand take his and turns to look at Francis John Calvert.

And everything changes.

It isn't the resemblance to the photofit. He'd registered that the instant he'd clapped eyes on Calvert and forgotten it again moments later. It isn't the resemblance but it *is* the face.

Thorne looks at Calvert's face and knows.

He knows.

It lasts no more than a second or two but it's enough. He can see through to what lies behind those deep, blue eyes, and what he sees terrifies him.

He sees boozing, yes, and football on a Saturday and wolf-whistles with the lads and an incandescent rage that is barely kept in check inside the cosy conformity of a loveless, sexless marriage.

He sees something deep and dark and rotting. Something fetid. Something spilling into the earth and bubbling with blood.

He cannot explain it but he knows beyond a shadow of the smallest doubt that Francis John Calvert is Johnny Boy. He knows that the man in front of him, the man shaking his hand, is responsible for stalking and slaughtering half a dozen gay men in the last year and a half.

Thorne is all but frozen to the spot, not sure how he will ever be able to move. He is rigid with fear. He is going to piss in his trousers any second. Then he sees the most terrifying thing of all.

Calvert *knows* that he knows.

Thorne thinks his face is frozen, expressionless. Dead. Obviously he's wrong. He can see the

398

change in Calvert's eyes as they meet his own. Just a slight flicker. The tiniest twitch . . .

And the smile that is beginning to die a little.

Then it's over. The grip is released and Calvert is moving away through the lobby towards the main station doors. He stops for a second and turns, and now the smile is gone completely. The sergeant is wittering at him about this party but Thorne is watching Calvert walk out of the doors. The look he sees on his face is something like fear. Or perhaps hate.

And, somewhere in the distance, a sweet, high voice is still singing about imaginary angels.

He tells nobody. Not Duffy. None of his mates or fellow officers. What's he supposed to tell them? Certainly not Jan. Her mind's on other things, anyway. They're trying for a baby.

At home with her that weekend, he knows he's distant. On Saturday afternoon as they stroll around Chapel Market she asks if there's anything wrong. He says nothing.

On Sunday night she's keen to make love, but every time he shuts his eyes he sees Francis Calvert, one arm round the neck of the young boy he's kissing deeply, pulling at him, holding the soft mouth against his own. As he groans, and comes inside his young wife, he sees Calvert's other hand, strong and callused, reaching for the eight-inch serrated knife in his pocket.

While Jan sleeps soundly next to him, he lies

awake all night. By morning he's convinced himself that he's being stupid and within an hour he's sitting in his car in a small street off Kilburn High Road. Watching Francis Calvert's flat.

Monday 18 June 1985.

He just needs to look at him again, that's all. Once he watches him step out of that front door he'll see him for what he really is. A nasty piece of pondlife for sure, but that's about all. A slimy little shit who's probably been done for driving without insurance, almost certainly doesn't have a TV licence and maybe slaps his wife around.

Not a killer.

One more look and Thorne will know he was being stupid. He'll know that what happened in that corridor was an aberration. What Jan likes to call a mindfuck.

He's here in plenty of time. People in the street haven't started leaving for work yet. Calvert's white Astra van is parked outside his flat.

For the next hour he sits and watches them leave. He watches front doors open up and down the street, spitting out men and women with bags and briefcases. They climb into cars or hop on to bikes or stride away towards buses and tubes.

Calvert's door stays resolutely shut.

Thorne sits and stares at the dirty white van. Letters on the side: F.J. CALVERT. BUILDER.

Butcher . . .

Stupid! He's being so stupid. He needs to start his car and get himself to work, and have a laugh with some of the other lads and maybe help to organise this leaving party and forget he ever met Francis John Calvert, and instead he finds himself walking across the street.

He finds himself knocking on a dirty green front door.

He finds himself starting to sweat when he gets no answer.

In the respectfully muted euphoria of the days to come, before the astonishing truth that Calvert had been interviewed on four separate occasions emerges, before the resignations, before the national scandal . . . there will be words of praise for Detective Constable Thomas Thorne. A young officer using his initiative. Doing his job. Putting any thoughts for his own safety out of his mind.

Out of his mind . . .

It is as if he is watching himself, like a nosy bystander. He has no idea why he tries the front door. Why he leans against it. Why he runs back to his car and takes a truncheon from the boot.

Calvert's wife looks surprised to see him. Her eyes are wide as he walks into her kitchen, breath held, heart thumping. She lies on the floor, her head against the dirty white door of the cupboard underneath the sink. The bruise around her neck is beginning to turn black. She still has a wooden spoon in her hand.

She was the first to die. She had to be. The children would tell him that much.

Denise Calvert. 32. Strangled.

Thorne moves through the flat like a deep-sea diver exploring a wreck. The silence is pounding in his ears. His movements feel slow and oddly graceful, and there are ghosts in the water all around him . . .

He finds them in the small bedroom at the back of the flat. They are laid out next to each other on the floor, between the bunk beds and the small, single mattress.

He cannot take his eyes off the six tiny white feet.

Unable to fill his lungs, he drops to his knees and crawls across the floor. He takes in what he is seeing but there is a blunt refusal to process the information correctly. Grabbing at a breath he lets out a scream. He screams at the dead girls. He pleads with them. *Please . . . you'll be late for school.*

He is actually begging them to save him.

With that breath he smells the shampoo in their hair. He smells the freshly washed nightdresses and the urine that has soaked them. He sees the stain on the mattress on the floor where he must have taken each of them. The girls have been laid out side by side, their arms across their chest in some grotesque approximation of peacefulness.

But they did not die peacefully.

Lauren Calvert. 11. Samantha Calvert. 9. Anne-Marie Calvert. 5. Suffocated.

Three little girls, who screamed and fought and kicked and ran to find their mummy and then screamed even louder – their mother already dead, the only state in which she will allow this horror to be visited upon her children – then the man they love and trust closed the bedroom door; and they fluttered around in a panic, like moths trapped inside a light fitting. They crashed into walls, and clutched each other and when he grabbed one and pulled her down to the mattress on the floor, they bit and scratched and cried, and went somewhere far better with their tiny fingers clawing at the flesh of those strong, callused hands.

Thorne has to believe that. He cannot accept that they smiled at their daddy as he laid the pillow across their faces.

He will not accept that.

It might be thirty minutes later when he finds Calvert. He has no idea how long he's spent in that tiny box room trying to understand. Thinking about Jan. The child they are desperate for.

He pushes open the door to the living room and his senses are immediately bludgeoned. He smells whisky, so strong he almost chokes on it, and the pungent aroma of gunpowder, which until this moment he has only ever known on a firing range.

He sees the body on the floor in front of the hearth.

The brain caked to the mirror above the tiled mantelpiece.

Francis John Calvert. 37. Suicide by gunshot.

Thorne walks across the grimy mushroom-coloured carpet like a sleepwalker. Not looking down as his foot sends an empty whisky bottle clattering into the skirting-board. Not taking his eyes off Calvert. The outstretched arm is still holding the gun. The underpants are brown with congealed blood. When had this happened? Last night or first thing this morning?

The hands are unmarked by small fingers.

Thorne stands above the body, his arms hanging heavy by his sides, his breathing deep and desperate. He leans forward, knowing what's going to happen, amazed considering that he's had no breakfast. The spasm, when it comes, moves swiftly from guts to chest and then throat, and he vomits, steaming, wet and bitter, across what's left of Francis Calvert's face.

'It wasn't your fault, Tom. I know it must have been horrible, but you can't think it happened because of you.'

Thorne lay on the settee and stared at his dull magnolia ceiling. Somewhere in the distance the siren of a fire engine or an ambulance was wailing desperately.

Anne squeezed his hand, feeling like a doctor. She thought quickly of Alison. 'You were right when you thought it was an aberration. You finding them was just a coincidence. A horrible coincidence . . .'

Thorne had no more to say. The tiredness that had been clutching at him all day now had a firm grip and he didn't feel like struggling any more.

He craved unconsciousness, a blackness that would see everything he'd remembered and described put back where it belonged. The rusty bolts slammed back into place.

He closed his eyes and let it come.

Anne had kept it together while Thorne was telling his story, willing her face to show nothing, but now she let the tears come. Thinking about the little girls. Thinking about her own daughter's tiny white feet.

It was easy to see what drove this man. What had created this obsession with . . . knowing. She hoped in time that he would see his feelings for Jeremy as no more than phantoms. Distorted echoes of a past horror. She hoped they could all move on.

She would be there to help him.

She shivered slightly. The shadow was still moving across them and its chill gathered at her shoulder. She laid her head on Thorne's chest which, within a few moments, began to rise and fall regularly, in sleep.

The pictures are still fuzzy but the words are clearer now. Like watching a film I've seen before, but since the last time I saw it my eyesight's gone funny and it's all a bit jumpy.

We're in the kitchen. Me and him.

I tell him to put his bag down anywhere and I'm still swigging the champagne and asking him if he wants a cup of coffee or a beer or something. He says nice things about the flat. I grab a can of beer that Tim's left in the fridge. He opens it and I'm still talking about the party. About the wankers in the club. Blokes on the sniff. He's sympathetic, saying he knows what men are like, and that I can hardly blame them, can I?

Music comes in for a few seconds as I turn the radio on, and then some static as I try to tune it in to something good, and then I give up.

He says he needs to make a phone call and he does, but I can't hear him saying anything. He's just muttering quietly. I'm still rabbiting on but I can barely make out what I'm saying now. Just gabbling. Something about starting to feel a bit sick but I don't think he's really listening.

I'm apologising for being so out of it. He must think I'm really fucking sad, slumped on the kitchen floor, leaning against a cupboard, hardly able to speak. Not at all, he says, and I can hear him unzipping his bag. Rummaging inside. There's nothing wrong with having a good time, he says. Going for it.

Fucking right I tell him, but that's not how it comes out of my mouth.

I can hear my shoes squeak across the tiles as he drags me to the other side of the kitchen. My earrings and my necklace clinking as he drops them into a dish.

The groaning noise is me.

I sound like I can't actually speak at all. Can't. Like a baby. Or an old person with no teeth in, and half their brain gone. I'm trying to say something but it's just a noise.

He's telling me to be quiet. Telling me not to bother trying.

His hands are on me now and he's describing everything he's doing. Telling me not to worry and to trust him. Talking me through it. He tells me the names of muscles when he touches them.

Stupid names. Medical.

He catches his breath and then he's quiet for a while. A couple of minutes.

And I can't hear myself saying a single thing about it. Not a word of complaint. Just the drip, drip, drip of my dribble as it spills out of my mouth and plops on to the tiles in front of me.

I can make a sort of gargling sound.

There's a couple of grunts but now the sound starts to fade as I begin to slip away from everything.

Then something important. The last thing I can hear. Three words, echoey and strange as if they're from a long way away. Like he's whispering them to me from the end of a long pipe, like my friend saying hello down the vacuum-cleaner tube when we were kids.

I need to tell this, I think.

He says goodnight. Night-night . . .

It's almost silly, what he says. Sweet-sounding and gentle. A word I've heard again since.

A word I heard when I woke up and was like this.

A word that says pretty much everything about what I am.

CHAPTER 22

When Thorne woke up it was already dark. He looked at his watch. Just after seven o'clock. He'd been out of it for two and a half hours.

He had no way of knowing it, but two hours more and it would all be over.

Anne had gone. He got up off the settee to make himself coffee and saw the note on the mantelpiece.

Tom,
I hope you're feeling better. I know how hard it was for you to tell me.
You mustn't be afraid to be wrong.
I hope you don't mind but I'm going to see Jeremy tonight to tell him that everything's all right. I think he deserves to feel better too.
Call me later.
Anne. X

He made himself the coffee and read the note again. He *was* feeling better and it was more than just the couple of hours' sleep. Talking about what had happened all those years ago had left him feeling cleaner. *Purged* was probably putting it a little strongly but, considering that his case had gone to shit, he had no friends and he was headed for all manner of trouble with his superiors, he might have felt much worse.

Tom Thorne was resigned.

It wasn't so much that he'd been afraid to be wrong. He hadn't even considered it. Now he had to do a lot more than consider it. He had to live with it.

Anne was going to see Bishop to tell him that he was out of the frame. That was fair enough. He'd never really been *in* the frame, if truth were told. Only in Thorne's thick, thick head. It was time to face a few harsh realities.

Anne was doing a good thing. Bishop deserved to know what was going on. He deserved to know how things stood.

He was not the only one.

Thorne picked up the phone and dialled Anne's number. Maybe he could catch her before she left. Rachel answered almost immediately, sounding out of breath, annoyed and distinctly teenage.

'Hi, Rachel, it's Tom Thorne. Can I speak to your mother?'

'No.'

'Right . . .'

'She's not here. You've just missed her.'

'She's on her way to Battersea, is she?'

Her tone changed from impatience to something more strident. 'Yeah. She's gone to tell Jeremy he's not public enemy number one any more. About time as well, if you ask me.'

Thorne said nothing. Anne had told her. It didn't matter now anyway.

'How long ago did she—'

'I don't know. She's going shopping first, I think. She's cooking him dinner.'

'Listen, Rachel—'

She cut him off. 'Look, I've got to go, I'm going to be late. Call her on the mobile or try her later at Jeremy's. Have you got the number?'

Thorne assured her that he had, then realised she was being sarcastic.

He tried Anne's mobile number but couldn't get connected. Maybe she had it switched off. She wouldn't have a signal anyway if she was on the tube. Then he remembered that she was on call and guessed that she'd probably be driving. He had her bleeper number somewhere . . .

He picked up his jacket. He'd do what Rachel had suggested and get her later at Bishop's. This time he wouldn't have to withhold his number.

It wasn't even that important; he just wanted to ask her how late Alison Willetts could receive visitors.

He was wearing one of the crisp white shirts he knew she liked so much. He'd stared at himself in the full-length mirror as he slowly did up the buttons. Watching the scars disappear beneath the spotless white cotton.

Now he looked at his watch as the car cruised sedately north across Blackfriars Bridge. He was going to be a little late. She would be on time as always.

She was very, very keen.

He was meeting her outside the Green Man as usual. It was a bit of a slog to drive all the way across the river just to turn round and drive back south again, but he'd rather do it this way than let her get on the tube or bus. He wanted to be in control of things. If she was late or missed a bus or something it could throw the timing of everything off.

When he'd told her that they would be going back to his place, he knew that she was thinking, *Oh, my God, tonight's the night*. He could almost smell the rush of teenage oestrogen and hear the cogs in her silly little brain whirring as she tried to decide which perfume to dab between her tits and which knickers would turn him on the most.

Well, yes, it would be a night to remember for certain.

Back at his place.

It might be a little crowded . . .

On the drive to Queen Square, Thorne didn't really need to think. He'd worked out what he was going to say to Alison Willetts. Now he just needed to be a little more relaxed in order to say it.

He popped out the Massive Attack tape and slid in Merle Haggard.

Getting relaxed enough to apologise.

'Tommy?'

'Yes, and to you too.'

After circling the square for nearly ten minutes, swearing loudly, he double-parked and stuck a dog-eared piece of cardboard with 'Police Business' scrawled on it in the front window of the Mondeo.

The evening was turning chilly. He wished he'd grabbed a warmer jacket on his way out. As he walked quickly towards the hospital's main entrance, he felt the first drops of rain and remembered making this same journey in reverse two months earlier. It seemed a lot longer ago, that day in August when he'd first met Alison Willetts. He'd run through the rain towards his car and found the note. He'd begun to understand the nature of the man he was dealing with.

Today, on the same spot, with the rain starting to fall, Thorne was coming to terms with the fact that he still had no idea who that man was.

Nearly eight o'clock. The latest that Thorne had been inside the hospital. It was a very different place after dark. His steps echoed off century-old marble as he strode through the older part of the building towards the Chandler Wing. There were few people around and those he passed, nurses, cleaners, security staff, looked at him closely. They seemed to be studying his face. He'd never been aware of such scrutiny during the day.

Somewhere in the distance he thought he could hear what sounded like somebody weeping softly. He stopped to listen but couldn't hear it any more.

Even the modern part of the hospital seemed spookier. The lights that normally bounced off the bleached wood in the Medical ITU reception area, had been dimmed. The only sounds were the muted tones of a faraway conversation and the low hum of distant equipment of some sort. It might have been cleaning carpets. It might have been keeping somebody alive.

He looked at the row of payphones in Reception. He'd try Anne again as soon as he'd been to see Alison. He'd forgotten to bring his mobile.

As he walked from the lift, he caught the eye of a woman in the glass-fronted office in Reception. She waved at him and he recognised her as Anne's secretary. He couldn't remember her name. He pointed at the doors and she nodded, signalling at him to go on through. He remembered the three-digit code that opened the heavy wooden doors and stepped through them into the Intensive Therapy Unit.

He let the sister on duty at the nursing station know where he was going and set off down the corridor towards Alison's room. As he walked past the other rooms he realised that he knew nothing about the people inside. He'd never spoken to

Anne about her other patients. He presumed that none were suffering in quite the same way as Alison was, but that all had seen their lives changed in a few short seconds. The time it takes to trip on the stairs or mistime a tackle or lose control of a car.

The time it takes for a brain to short-circuit.

He listened at the door of the room opposite Alison's. The same telltale hum of machinery from within, like the lazy throb of a dozing beehive coming slowly to life after a long winter. Whoever lay in the bed inside that room was here by accident. That was the difference.

Thorne turned and moved across to Alison's door. He knocked quietly and reached for the handle.

He gasped as the door was yanked open from the inside and David Higgins all but pushed him back into the corridor.

'She's not here.' Higgins was in his face.

'What?' Thorne tried to push past him into the room.

'You're out of luck, Thorne. Sorry.'

Thorne looked at him, not understanding. Higgins began to raise his voice. 'My fucking wife. My fucking wife, who you are fucking. She. Isn't. Here.'

Thorne could smell Dutch courage.

'I'm not here to see Anne. Move out of the way.'

'Of course. Have fun.'

Higgins took a step to his left but Thorne didn't move, just looked at him. 'What does that mean?'

415

Knowing exactly what it meant but wanting to hear him say it.

'Well, in the absence of the lovely Anne, who doesn't actually enjoy it that much anyway, you might as well . . . make hay with someone who really doesn't have a great deal of say in the matter. Like a blow-up doll with a pulse.'

Thorne had always thought that the accusations about his relationship with Alison were a little cheap for the killer. A little beneath him. Now he knew who had been responsible. The motivation was obvious but Thorne asked anyway. 'Why?'

Higgins swallowed, licked his lips. 'Why not?'

As his right arm bent and swung at speed, Thorne unballed his fist. A slap seemed so much more appropriate. Higgins wasn't man enough to punch.

The hard flat hand caught Higgins across the jaw and ear, sending him sprawling across the highly polished linoleum. He lay still, whimpering like a child.

Without looking at him, Thorne stepped across Higgins's outstretched leg and opened the door to Alison Willetts' room.

The second he looked at her, she began to blink. Once, twice, three times. Thorne realised that she'd heard the noise from outside and was disturbed. Maybe he should call for a nurse. What had Higgins been doing in her room anyway? Probably just looking for Anne, but couldn't he have spoken to someone at reception?

Thorne's mind was racing. He needed to calm down if he was going to be able to say what he came to say.

Alison was still blinking. One blink every three or four seconds.

'It's OK, Alison. Look, I'll try and keep this short. It's about what I said the other day, about being close to him, the man who did this to you . . .'

She was still blinking.

Please, for fuck's sake shut up, and listen. Get the board . . .

'What's the matter?' His eyes darted across to the blackboard, still lying against the wall and covered with a sheet. He looked back at Alison. One blink. Yes.

Yes!

He moved across the room, whipped off the sheet and dragged the blackboard to the foot of the bed.

He knew roughly how the system worked. He hurried to switch off the main light and then, using the remote at the end of the bed, he raised Alison up so that she was nearly sitting. Then he picked up the pointer, switched it on and positioned the small red laser dot beneath the first letter: E. He began to move the pointer slowly along the letters.

Nothing.

Starting to speed up, studying her face, watching for the smallest reaction.

Come on . . . come on . . .

Then a blink. He stopped.

'S? Was that an S, Alison?'

Yes, for Christ's sake! Of course it was! Hurry up.

Move. Wait. Watch. Move. Wait. Watch. Move . . .

Another blink. Thorne was sweating. He threw off his jacket. 'L. Yes? OK, that's S, L. Right.'

Back to the beginning again and . . . a blink. No, two blinks.

'Is that a no to the E, Alison?'

No, it isn't fucking no. Two blinks is usually no but when I'm doing this it means 'repeat'. Didn't Anne tell you any of this?

'Or do you mean two Es? Yes? Right. S, L, E, E . . . *sleep?* Do you want to go to sleep, Alison?'

Fuck, fuck, fuck . . .

Two strong blinks. One, two.

No. I. Don't. Have you got any idea how hard this is?

He raised the pointer again. Point. Stop. Look. Point. Stop. Look. Point. Stop . . . a blink. No question about it. A big fat positive Y.

'You're *sleepy*? I'm sorry, Alison, I can come back when . . .'

She was blinking quite rapidly now. Repeatedly.

Do I look fucking sleepy? Well, do I? Come on, Thorne, sort it out . . .

The sweat was running off him. He was making a complete mess of it. One more try and then he'd go and get somebody. Back with the pointer. And Alison blinked. And blinked again.

An H. Another E . . .

And the word became obvious.

And a firework went off in Thorne's stomach.

A memory file, a tiny soundbite was pushed forward in his brain and something pressed the button marked 'play' and lit the fuse. The charge began to churn through his guts and the explosions rang in his ears and the sparks were dancing behind his eyes, green and gold and red and silver, and he was squeezing Alison's hand.

And he was scrabbling in his pockets for change for the phone.

Running from the room.

'Bishop? This is Thorne . . .'

'What?' Weary, but also frightened.

'I know what you said to her. I know what you said to Alison before you stroked her out. What you said to all of them.'

'What are you talking about?'

'"Night-night, Sleepyhead." Same thing you said to me when you put me out for that hernia operation last year.'

His tongue heavy in his mouth, his voice growing weaker as he counts backwards from twenty, wondering if it will hurt when he wakes up, and seeing the smiling face of the anaesthetist looming above him. Murmuring . . .

'Is there a point to any of this, Thorne? I'm expecting somebody.'

'The same thing you said to me, Bishop. "Night-night, Sleepyhead."'

'Look, if it helps you, yes, I say that to patients

419

sometimes when they're going under and I say, "Wake up, Sleepyhead," when they're coming round from the anaesthetic. It's a silly catchphrase. A superstition. For God's sake, I used to say it to my children when I put them to bed at night. Is this helping you, Thorne? Is it?'

'I was about to let it go, do you know that? You were so close to walking away. I thought I was wrong, but I wasn't, was I? Now I'm fucking certain . . .'

'You need help, Thorne. Serious professional help . . .'

'You're the one who needs help, Jeremy. I'm coming for you. I'm coming for you right now.'

Jesus . . . Jesus . . . Jesus . . .

I thought he was never going to get it.

I thought maybe it would be important, you know, because I'd heard it when I woke up as well as when he was doing it to me.

That same word.

I thought it was probably significant and as soon as I heard Thorne outside the door I knew I wanted to try to tell him, but I hadn't expected him to shoot out of here quite like that.

Like shit off a shiny shovel, my old man would have said.

He was obviously still worked up after punching Anne's old man.

Like a blow-up doll with a pulse. What a fucking charmer. I hope Thorne knocked his teeth down his throat.

So it has to be that doctor who brought me round. The anaesthetist who came in here with Anne a couple of times is Champagne Fucking Charlie. The one who's her friend. The one Thorne had the photo of. He obviously suspected him all along.

How can you be a doctor and do . . . this?

Jesus, though, I thought that was going to

take for ever. That's the best I've ever done. Anne would have been dead proud, I reckon. I was fucking spot on.

Blinking for England. I said I would, didn't I?

It was so hard, though.

Now I really *am* sleepy . . .

CHAPTER 23

Dave Holland stared at the film Sophie had rented, not taking in a single word. He pushed bits of cold lasagne round his plate, not really hungry.

Thinking about Tom Thorne.

He hadn't been there that morning when Thorne had stormed out of the office at Edgware Road. He was still trying to bring himself round after the night before when he'd drunk far too much trying to forget about Helen Doyle's parents. They'd made quite a night of it, him and Thorne. Even though he'd been pissed, and asleep some of the time, he could remember a lot of what Thorne had been saying. Lying on the settee late into the night, eyes closed, head spinning, while Thorne talked about blood and voices. Things Dave Holland wouldn't forget in a long time.

Now nobody seemed to know where Thorne was, or even if he'd be back at all.

Those who had been there this morning and seen the state of the DI as he'd walked into the lift, *staggered*, somebody had said, had been only too keen to pass on the details when Holland eventually got into work. 'You'll be interested in this . . .' they said sarcastically. It seemed that a line of inquiry, developed by Detective Inspector Thorne, had now been officially discredited.

It sounded like he'd had the shit kicked out of him.

Holland had gone quietly back to work. Every half an hour or so since, he'd checked his mobile, looking for a message.

Suddenly he noticed that the picture on the TV screen was frozen. Paused. He turned to see Sophie, the remote in her hand, talking to him. Was there really any point in her going to the video shop? Or cooking dinner? Or bothering to talk to him?

He apologised and told her that he was still feeling a bit rough, the worse for wear after his drinking session with the lads last night. Sophie had a go at him, but secretly she didn't really mind. She didn't begrudge him a night out on the beer with the lads. As long as he didn't make a habit of it and had worked out which side his bread was buttered on.

As long as he'd finally decided against throwing in his lot with that loser Thorne.

Anne was annoyed. She had a bag full of shopping – food for the dinner she was going to cook for Jeremy – it was pouring with rain, and she couldn't find a single parking spot on his street. She eventually squeezed into a tight space round the corner and ran back, doing her best to avoid the rapidly growing puddles.

She was amazed to see him sitting in the car outside the house.

She tapped quickly on the glass and laughed as he jumped. The electric window on the Volvo slid down and she leaned in. 'What are you doing sitting out here?'

'Just thinking about things. Waiting for you.' The rain was blowing in through the open window on to his face.

Anne grimaced, confused. 'It's a lot warmer in the house.' He said nothing, staring blankly forward through a windscreen running with rainwater. Anne moved the handles of the plastic shopping-bag round in her hand. It was starting to get heavy. 'Are you coming inside?'

'Can you get in here first? Please, Anne, I need to talk to you about something. Just for a minute.'

Anne wanted to go into the house. She was wet, and very cold. She wanted a cup of tea or, even better, a large glass of wine before she got started on dinner. Still, he seemed upset about something. She hurried round to the passenger side and, dropping the shopping bag on to the floor at her feet, got into the car.

It was nice and warm: the heater had obviously been on for a while. He didn't look at her. She began to think something was seriously wrong.

'Is everything all right? Has something happened?'

He didn't answer and instinctively she began to look around her. Was the answer to whatever was going on here with them in the car? There was something on the back seat, covered with a tartan picnic blanket.

She looked at him. 'What's . . . ?'

Instinctively she knew that she wasn't going to get an answer and, with a grunt of effort, she lifted herself off her seat, reached across into the back of the car and pulled off the blanket.

She gasped.

She didn't even feel the needle slip into her arm.

Thorne tried to stay calm. The rain had slowed up the traffic as per usual and it had taken an infuriating twenty-five minutes just to get the half a mile or so from Queen Square to Waterloo Bridge. Now it had eased off a little and the Mondeo was testing every speed camera it passed as Thorne pushed the car south, through the spray towards Battersea.

The clock on the dashboard said eight forty-five and Merle Haggard was complaining about being let down by the bottle as Thorne drove past St Thomas's Hospital.

He thought about a pathologist whose skill, whose observation, whose *curiosity*, months before, had started it all. He might be working late at this very minute, in one of those lit offices, those bright white squares that Thorne could see as he drove

426

past. Getting tired now, probably, as he stared down into a microscope, then excitement mounting as he spotted some inconsistency, some curious detail that might change the lives of hundreds of people for ever.

He didn't know whether, if he ever met that man, he should thank him or spit in his face. What was certain was that, without him, he would not be on his way right now to confront a killer. He had no idea what might really happen between him and Bishop. Confront him, yes, and what else? Arrest him? Intimidate him? Hurt him?

Thorne would know when he got there.

He hit the brakes too late and too hard approaching the big traffic lights at Vauxhall Bridge. The car skidded a little before stopping, the squeal of tyres attracting the attention of the evening's traffic-light cabaret. Those cleaning windscreens in return for a few coins and a great deal of abuse had now been replaced, bizarrely, by street entertainers. One such, wearing a large, multicoloured jester's hat and juggling three balls, stepped jauntily through the rain towards Thorne's car with a broad grin.

The juggler took one look at Thorne's face and backed away again quickly, dropping balls as he went. The light, reflected in the puddles of oil and water, turned from red to green, and the Mondeo sped away.

The lights were with him along Nine Elms Lane and Battersea Park Road. He turned left on amber at the Latchmere pub, put his foot down all the way to Lavender Hill, and a few minutes later was turning almost casually into Jeremy Bishop's quiet road.

He turned down the music and began to breathe deeply. There were cars parked along both sides of the street and Thorne drove slowly, looking for a parking spot. The rain was heavier now, and even with the wipers on double speed he had to lean forward, and squint hard through the windscreen to see anything at all.

Suddenly, fifty yards ahead, lights came on and dazzled him as a large dark car pulled out and accelerated. Thorne's first thought was that he'd got a parking space, but a second later he could see that he was in trouble. The car rushed towards him on the wrong side of the road. With one hand shielding his eyes, which closed at the last second in anticipation of the impact, he yanked the wheel sharply to the right to avoid being hit as the car rushed past him with barely inches to spare.

A car with Anne Coburn sitting in the passenger seat.

Thorne slammed on the brakes and watched in his mirror as the Volvo stopped at the end of the road and turned left. They were heading west.

He might have been wrong but he didn't think that either Anne or Bishop had seen him. Both had been staring straight ahead. Where were they going? He hadn't got room to turn the car round quickly. Without thinking, he ground the gearstick into reverse and put his foot down.

For the first few minutes, past the north side of Clapham Common, Thorne was happy to cruise along two or three cars behind the Volvo, watching for its distinctive rear lights, keeping it close. He was sure now that Bishop had no idea he was being followed. Thorne wanted to keep it that way and was content to maintain a relaxed pace. Let them get where they were going. Following procedure for once in his fucking life. Keep it safe, he thought.

Keep it sedate.

Sedate. As the word formed in his mind, the car in front turned away giving him a clear view through the Volvo's rear window.

There was something very wrong with the picture.

It took half a second and then he got it. He couldn't see Anne any more.

The car hadn't stopped he was certain of that. She had been there a few minutes earlier, her head against the window. There was only one explanation.

She had to be unconscious.

Things began to speed up in every sense. There was another car between Thorne and the Volvo. He tried to get past it as the traffic swung right on to Clapham Park Road, and as he overtook on the inside, he watched the Volvo accelerate away. It looked as though Bishop knew he was there after all.

Thorne had never been good at this. He'd been in plenty of pursuits but he'd never been the one with his foot on the pedal. Forty-five miles an hour, along busy built-up streets at nine o'clock at night in the driving rain was fucking terrifying.

Why would Bishop hurt Anne? Why now? Thorne knew he should call this in. There was no radio in the car. His mobile was back at the flat. He thought about pulling over, using a payphone. By the time a unit picked up Bishop's car it might be too late. He had to keep following.

Fifty miles an hour along Acre Lane. The rear fog-lights of the Volvo blinding, the horns of other cars blaring.

Without taking his eyes off the Volvo for a second, Thorne switched tapes and turned up the volume. One type of music for another. Song replaced by sound. Melody by a pumping rhythm that seemed instantly to be emanating from inside his own head. The noise, the beat becoming a low, almost Zen-like hum, pulsing through his skull like the soundtrack to an arcade racing game.

Focusing. The wheel vibrating beneath his fingers. The car in front. The target. Speeding down the hill now towards the lights and the cinema ahead and pedestrians shouting and the wheels squealing as they turn left much too fast on to Brixton Road.

And suddenly, Thorne knows where they're going.

Brixton. SW2. He remembers the address from a page in his notebook. The page headed 'children'.

Thorne's never been to this address but why on earth would he have?

Thorne knows now that, even with a warrant, he'd have found nothing at the house in Battersea. Where they're going now is Bishop's place of work. It's where he would have brought Helen and Leonie. A place to which he would have a key. A flat for which he helped pay the deposit. Somewhere almost certainly empty late at night if the occupant is working. Easily established with a phone call . . .

The beat and the speed increasing and rain lashing the windscreen, and Thorne's hands on the wheel guided solely by the movements of the two red lights ahead of him. His eyes fixed on those two red lights, which flash as the Volvo brakes suddenly, like the eyes of some sleek, dark monster, which roars and is away from him quickly as the Volvo jumps the traffic lights and he has no choice but to do the same.

From the corner of his eye he sees the blue and red of the traffic patrol car to his left, and a thousand yards further on the second one pulls out in front of him.

The last thing he needs. A pair of fucking black rats, working in tandem.

As Thorne slowed down, hammering his fists on the steering-wheel, he watched the eyes of the dark monster ahead of him get smaller and smaller.

When the constable, a fat fuck with a pockmarked

431

face and a walrus moustache, finally sauntered up to the Mondeo's passenger door, the first thing he saw was an ID pressed hard against the window. The first thing Thorne saw when he removed it was the smug look the constable gave to his colleague in the patrol car: Look what *we*'ve got.

Thorne took a deep breath. This was going to be interesting.

The walrus made a casual winding motion with his forefinger. *Window down.* Thorne counted to three and wound down the window like a good boy.

'Detective Inspector Thorne. SCG West.' There was no reaction. Thorne certainly hadn't been expecting a tug on the forelock and a polite 'On your way, sir', far from it, but this was going to be a bad one.

Age-old animosities. Uniform and plainclothes. *Anyone* and Traffic.

'Fifty miles an hour plus, through a red light, in the pissing rain. Not clever was it?' The estuary accent trying its very best to drip with sarcasm.

'I'm in pursuit of a suspect,' said Thorne, flatly. The constable turned casually to watch the traffic disappearing into the distance and smiled, the rain dripping off the peak of his cap. Thorne tried to keep his temper. 'I *was* in pursuit of a suspect.'

'You *were* driving like a twat.'

Thorne was out of the car, the red mist ready to come down. 'Is this how you normally deal with members of the public?'

Another sly smile, another glance to his mate in the car. 'You're not public, are you?'

Thorne stood, staring straight ahead, the rain running down the back of his jacket. He thought about the killer's first note again. He thought about Anne lying across leather seats, unable to move. Bishop was probably playing classical music . . . Fuck, they'd probably be there by now.

Jesus fucking Christ . . .

'Have you been drinking, sir?'

'What?' Starting to lose it.

'Simple enough question. You fuckers obviously think you're above the law—'

Thorne grabbed his jacket, spun him round, and pressed him hard against the car, sending his cap tumbling into the gutter. From the corner of his eye, Thorne could see the other one step out of the patrol car. Without even turning to look, he shouted through the rain, 'I'm a DI, now get back in that fucking car.'

The walrus's mate did as he was told. Thorne turned his attention back to the man himself, leaning in close, the rain beating down on the two of them, nose to nose at the side of the road. Passing cars honked their approval, the drivers of Brixton pleased to see a copper getting what was coming to him from an innocent motorist.

Thorne raised his voice just enough to make himself clearly understood over the noise of the rain, spattering off the PC's reflective plastic tabard. 'Listen, you fat, scabby arsehole, I'm getting back into my car now and driving away, and if you so much as raise an eyebrow, you'll be pissing blood for a week. That was a threat. The next bit is an order. Are you following this?'

The walrus nodded. Thorne released his grip but only slightly. 'This is an instruction, understand? Get back into your car right now and get on your radio. I want you to contact someone at Operation Backhand out of Edgware Road. You need to get hold of DC Dave Holland . . .'

In my dream I'm running.

It's nowhere dramatic. Not across a cornfield or through the surf on a storm-lashed beach or anything. And I'm not running towards anybody. There's nobody in the distance with arms thrown wide, aching to kiss me. Not a soldier returned from the war or a film star. Not Tim. It's just me.

Just running.

It's funny because I've always hated running, always done whatever I could to avoid it. Skinny little legs and knock knees. I was always rubbish at any kind of sport and I'm totally unfit. Running for the bus, if I absolutely have to, is about my limit, and that will fuck me up for the rest of the day. But here I am . . .

I'm running, sprinting, and it feels easy.

I don't know what I'm wearing or what the weather's like. None of that seems important. I suppose the wind must be blowing in my hair but, to be honest, I don't really notice. What I *do* notice is the wind rushing into my open mouth and inflating my lungs. I notice my lungs pushing the air back out through my mouth.

I'm running.

I notice my legs moving me along and my arms pumping, and I notice that the muscles in my mouth are working overtime, every last fucking gorgeous one of them. Each muscle working in harmony with the others. Meshing perfectly with its neighbour. Forcing my lips to part, raising the corners of my mouth up, pushing my tongue out slightly against my top teeth. Making me smile.

I'm running away.

CHAPTER 24

It was a narrow green door without a window. Easy to miss between a greengrocer's and a shoe shop in a small street behind the busy Brixton Road. Thorne couldn't see the Volvo anywhere. Maybe there was another way to get in. That would make sense, after all. A back entrance that was easier to carry bodies into unseen.

Yes, and maybe he was wrong about the whole thing. Maybe it had just been coincidence that they'd seemed headed for this address and even now as Thorne was standing in the rain, staring at a narrow green door without a window, Bishop was spiriting Anne away to a place where he would never find her.

Was all this just to hurt *him*?

Thorne put his ear against the door and listened. Not a sound.

He was certain that Bishop had known he was being followed. Thorne had half expected the door to be open. Six inches ajar, tempting him inside. Not a trap, nothing so vulgar.

More like an invitation.

He pressed his hand against the door. It was locked.

437

Back off now and wait for Holland to arrive with troops. It wouldn't be long, presuming those idiots in the Traffic car had done as they'd been told. Get back into his car and sit tight, that would be best.

He put the side of his head to the door again and this time added the heft of his shoulder. Not a violent movement. Just a sustained pressure, using his weight.

The door gave as easily as if he'd used a key. There was barely any noise.

Ahead of him, by the light from a shopfront opposite, Thorne could see a long straight hall-way leading to a staircase that climbed away into darkness. Everything else looked to be on the upper levels, above the greengrocer's.

He stepped smartly inside and tried to shut the door behind him. The lock wouldn't catch against the jamb where he'd forced it, so he just pushed it to. Then he turned inside and listened.

Nothing but the sound of his own breathing and the rain outside and the rumble of the traffic from the main road. He felt for a light switch and found one of those press-in jobs designed to save money. He started up the stairs.

The place was messy. Scattered about on the torn stair-carpet were various bits of junk mail and unopened letters. He could smell fast food of some kind, Chinese maybe.

At the top of the stairs was the kitchen. He found the light switch just as the one on the stairs popped out and the light went off.

It was poky and squalid. The brown vinyl floor-ing was cracked and greasy, the walls grubby and sweating. Days' worth of used tea-bags squatted in the sink like turds, and a ketchup stain ran down the side of the once white plastic swing-bin. Fast food would certainly be preferable to anything prepared in here.

Thorne backed out of the room. Another half-dozen stairs led up to the second floor. He could see a door ahead of him and two more off to the left. He moved on slowly towards the rooms on the next level, stopping and listening for a few seconds at every step. His doubts outside the front door had given way to a cold, clammy certainty that he was not alone.

It was ending. He could feel it. Somewhere in this building was the wall he would back himself against.

Thorne moved forward and upward, knowing he must be getting closer to where Helen Doyle and Leonie Holden were killed. The walls of the hallway were bare and dusty, the paper peeling and dry as dead leaves. The carpet was stained and gritty. He imagined he felt it moving beneath his feet.

This was not a place anyone should be brought to die.

The first door on the left opened on to a bathroom no bigger than a large cupboard. Thorne put his head round the door for a few seconds. It was enough. No fripperies. Just grimy white fittings and a bad smell.

Then a bedroom. Maybe a little cleaner but stuffed and cluttered and stinking of stale sweat.

439

There were shoes lined up along a mantelpiece. An ironing-board stood in the corner next to a full-length mirror. Piles of magazines spilled out on to the faded cork floor tiles from beneath the unmade bed and cardboard boxes were piled high against the far wall.

Not in here.

As he stepped back on to the landing he heard a noise from somewhere above him. He froze. The lazy creak of a floorboard underfoot.

Underfoot.

Whether or not he'd heard the noise, Thorne would still have skipped the final room. As he stepped towards it and glanced to his right, he could see the way he needed to go. The stairs leading up to what must be the top floor had been stripped and scrubbed. Each tread, along with the hand-rail, had been meticulously covered in thick, clear polythene.

Sterile.

Thorne looked up. The stairs climbed steeply, at least twenty feet into what had to be an attic or roof conversion. Straight up and into it. Above him, all he could see was a square of light, a hole in the floor of the room above his head. He weighed it up quickly. He knew that he'd be going in blind. He would be able to see nothing of what was in the room above him until the moment his head came up through the floor.

There was nowhere else to go.

'It always comes down to the final door, Tommy . . .'

Above his head he heard a floorboard moan quietly. A second later, he heard a small human voice do the same.

Anne . . .

Thorne raised his head and began to climb.

Despite the attack in his flat and the fact that the man had killed at least six women, Thorne didn't think instinctively of Bishop as somebody violent. As he climbed slowly up, one step at a time, towards whatever awaited him in the attic, he never for a second thought it might be something that could hurt him physically. Bishop would have the advantage of surprise and geography, but Thorne guessed that he would not be waiting for him as his head appeared, inch by inch, above the floor of the attic, with a foot drawn back to kick him in the teeth or an iron bar in his hand.

He was nearing the top now. Just a few more feet.

He felt no real sense of physical danger and yet he was as frightened as he'd ever been in his life.

The last couple of steps.

He was not worried about what he was going to feel . . .

He put his foot on the last tread and pushed his body upwards.

. . . he was terrified of what he was going to see.

His head moved up, through the hole and into bright white light. He blinked quickly to adjust then opened his eyes. Thorne's last thought, before his body turned ice cold and he began to shake quietly, was that he'd been right to be afraid.

He hauled himself up on to floor level, like a drowning man clambering aboard a lifeboat full of holes, and stared in disbelief.

White, white walls and smooth, shining floor-boards. The light from a row of wall-mounted halogen lamps bounced off the gleaming metal of the sharps bin and the instruments trolley. An elegant chrome mixer tap fed two highly polished white basins. To one side a simple black chair, the only piece of furniture in the room. Everything else, cold and functional. Necessary to the procedure.

Bishop was standing in the very middle of the room. He was busy. He raised his head and smiled at Thorne a little sadly.

Thorne was staring at the girl's eyes, bulging as she fought the movements of his fingers on her neck with every ounce of strength she had and without the slightest success. The drug that was coursing through Rachel Higgins had made her limbs as useless and uncooperative as they would become permanently, if the procedure Bishop was about to perform was successful.

From his left Thorne heard a grunt. He turned. Anne lay motionless against the wall, her eyes wide open, drool spilling from her mouth, the Midazolam doing its work on her too, so that she could do nothing but stare helplessly at the hands working on her daughter.

The voice brought Thorne's head whipping back

round. Bishop was caressing the back of the girl's neck. 'Hello, Tom. Come to spoil our party, have you?'

Thorne stood completely still, staring at Bishop. Not wanting to move and spook him. Unable to move even if he'd wanted to. His mouth utterly dry. Voice no better than a whisper.

'Hello, James . . .'

There would be a hundred difficult questions to come, and a complex knot of motivation and psychosis to unravel eventually, but just for a few seconds, in the stark and horrifying tableau in front of him, Thorne saw it all perfectly. Just briefly, for a heartbeat or two, there was clarity, and he knew exactly what and why and who. He saw how he'd been manipulated, how he'd been used. How James Bishop had played him and prodded him and nudged him, exploiting his weak spots and playing to his strengths. How he'd been completely right and horribly wrong. Why Margaret Byrne died and why she might still be alive, were it not for him.

How he'd been led by the fucking nose.

Outclassed.

James Bishop was naked from the waist up. Criss-crossing his stomach were half a dozen straight pink puckered scars, like giant worms beneath his skin. Knife wounds, Thorne thought. Self-inflicted.

Anne: '. . . *he was a bit screwed up about it.*'

Rebecca: '. . . *James went off the rails a little.*'

443

The scars were the least remarkable thing. The short hair was greying. Spray on dye was the easiest explanation. *'Tried being an actor. Anything that pays the rent.'* He was wearing identical glasses and it was easy to see it, even here in a brightly lit room from a few feet away. At night, outside with only the light from a streetlamp, or no light at all, nobody could be blamed for seeing a man ten years older than he really was.

It was Thorne who had seen Jeremy Bishop.

Thorne looked at Rachel and at Anne. 'What's the point of this, though, James? What's *this* got to do with anything?'

Bishop chuckled. Wasn't it obvious? 'Well, as you've so brilliantly failed in your efforts to arrest and convict the wrong man . . .'

'Your father.'

'My father, yes. I'm having to finish things off a little quicker. With a little less subtlety. It isn't what I wanted but it will have the desired effect.'

'Which is?'

Bishop shook his head. 'You're really not the man I thought you were, are you, Tom?'

'I could say the same for you, James . . .'

'Anne's daughter becoming one of her own patients is pretty tidy, though, isn't it? He may not even be able to live with that.' He was running his thumbs slowly up and down the base of Rachel's skull. 'Mind you, he's lived with himself long enough . . .'

Thorne's eyes didn't move from the long, thin

fingers. From the hands encased in the tight surgical gloves. Skilled hands.

James in his flat. Cocky, immature and so easy to read. *'I wasted a couple of years at college, yeah. I'm not the ivory-tower type.'*

The question Thorne had never thought to ask. Four stupid little words.

What did you study?

It was important to keep him talking . . .

'Is that all this has been about, James? Hurting your father? Getting your own back?'

Bishop glared at him. The mask of civility slipping. 'Don't be fucking stupid, Thorne. All this is about?' He looked disgusted at the suggestion. Then his voice softened and changed, becoming almost gentle, concerned, yet with the strength that came from conviction. 'This is about aiming for something like perfection. It's about taking something flawed and weak and rotten and removing the need for it. Eliminating the reliance on it. Letting the brain, which is the only part that's worth anything at all, flourish without the handicap of the body. It's about freedom.'

Thorne threw a quick look to Anne. A look to tell her it would be all right. He put his hands in his pockets, trying to appear relaxed as he turned slowly back to Bishop. Casual, enquiring. 'The frailty of the human body. Something your father taught you?'

'One of many things . . .' The voice had changed again. Casual, disinterested.

'And framing him for it?'

Bishop removed a hand from Rachel's head and ran it slowly across the noughts and crosses scar tissue on his stomach. The other hand stayed where it was, kneading the muscles at the back of her neck. Thorne considered running at him – he could be on him in a second. But a second was all Bishop would need to hurt Rachel. Instead Thorne offered him an answer to the question: 'Killing two birds with one stone.'

'Close enough. Except for the killing bit, obviously. Not very appropriate.'

Thorne disagreed. 'You did plenty of killing, James.' Bishop shrugged.

A weapon would even things up a little. Thorne's eyes flashed to the instrument trolley, to the gleaming tools lined up in a row. Clamps, forceps, a scalpel.

Bishop caught the look. 'Please don't compromise this procedure, Thorne.' He smiled, glancing at the scalpel. 'I think I could reach it before you.'

Thorne nodded slowly. He could feel Anne's eyes on him. Begging.

Bishop stroked the muscle at the base of Rachel's skull. 'The sternocleidomastoid, Tom. Are you familiar with it?'

Thorne was familiar enough. He knew what Bishop was looking for. Feeling for. 'Why the attack on me, though, James? I still don't really understand that.'

'I knew you'd think it was my father. I knew

446

you'd be sure. It was easy. Your relationship with Anne came in very handy. Perhaps your dick clouded your judgement a little. You were so easy to ginger up, Tom, so easy to goad.'

Thorne winced a little at the truth of it: seizing hungrily on every clue Bishop had dropped in front of him; clutching at every straw that had been so deliberately scattered in his path – the drugs, the timing of the killings, the car . . .

'The Volvo?'

'The old man swears by them. When he bought his new one I persuaded him to let me have the cast-off. I gave him a hundred pounds for it, I think, which is obviously less than he'd have got part-ex from a garage but, well . . . he *is* my father.'

That was the key, Thorne realised. Nobody knew Jeremy Bishop better. His son knew his movements, his whereabouts, the words he used. He knew everything his father knew about Alison, about the case. He knew how to steal his wedding ring.

'Sorry it didn't work out with the ring, James. Forensically compromised, I'm afraid.'

'These things happen. *I'm* sorry about the Byrne woman. I'm sorry about all the ones who died, sincerely I am, but I've told you that, haven't I? Of course, she wouldn't have needed to die were you not planning to go charging in there waving your stupid photographs. Have you thought about that, Tom?'

James in his flat. Seeing Margaret Byrne's address

on a piece of paper next to the phone . . .

Thorne had got it so completely wrong. Margaret Byrne hadn't died because she could identify Jeremy Bishop. She had died precisely because she could say for certain that Jeremy Bishop *wasn't* the killer.

They stared at each other, across six yawning feet of gleaming white space, the rain hammering on the roof above their heads.

Thorne jumped, and they both turned their heads when the bleeper went off.

He remembered that Anne was on call. The bleeper was inside her handbag, dumped on the floor next to her.

By the time the bleeping had stopped Thorne had worked something else out. The phone call that Margaret Byrne had seen him make: Bishop had been calling his father, to see if he'd been called in to work. Checking his availability. 'You bleeped your father on the way to the hospital. That night with Alison. You were probably sitting outside, waiting for him to arrive, giving him an alibi that was almost watertight, putting his name on a list.' Bishop smiled modestly. 'Same with the drugs in Leicester—'

Bishop cut him off. 'Yes, a mistake of a sort, obviously. Had you even worked that out?'

Thorne looked across at Anne. *Everything was going to be fine.* 'Anne worked it out.'

Bishop smiled. 'I'm impressed. But it did, as you say, put my father's name on a list. That was the hook. It got you interested . . .'

It had certainly done that.

'But it would never have worked, James. It was all circumstantial. There wasn't any real evidence.'

'That never seemed to bother you, though, did it, Tom?'

Thorne could say nothing, his tongue sticky against the roof of his mouth.

Suddenly Bishop grinned. Thorne could see that his fingers were locked in position, as was the look of something approaching rapture on his face.

'This is my favourite part, Tom. It all begins here.'

The muscles in Bishop's chest flexed as he began to squeeze Rachel's carotid artery. Thorne remembered Hendricks with his hands on his neck, taking him through it. They had about two minutes until she stopped breathing.

Thorne glanced at Anne. The look on her face was desperate. A snarl came from somewhere deep down inside her.

Save my daughter.

Thorne had no idea how. Bishop killed when he needed to, that much was obvious. The hands that were squeezing away Rachel's life in front of them were as dangerous as any weapon. He could snap her neck in a heartbeat . . .

Thorne felt leaden, useless. Mummified.

Ten seconds gone already. Her tongue lolling out.

'How does this hurt him, James? How does this make him suffer?'

Bishop said nothing. His lips moved soundlessly as he counted away the time in his head.

'This won't bring your mother back, James.' Thorne was shouting now. Anything to get a reaction, to make him stop. James was lost in concentration, readying himself for the difficult part, once the girl had stopped breathing. The manipulation.

Time ticking away. Thorne felt the seconds hurtling past him, Rachel's breath rushing past him as he stood frozen and useless.

'Please, Tommy . . .'

'Helen?'

'She's a child . . .'

'What can I do? WHAT CAN I DO?'

Then suddenly, a voice from below them. 'James?'

A reaction from Bishop. A reaction to the *voice of his father*. Fear maybe? Certainly a tension in his body and in his face. Tension in his fingers . . .

'James? I saw you driving away with Anne – what's going on? Is everything all right? Somebody's forced open your front door.'

Half a minute gone . . .

There was no way of knowing what James would do with his father here but Thorne had little option.

Ninety seconds left. Rachel was nearly half-way dead. Thorne shouted, 'Bishop. We're up here!'

Jeremy Bishop appeared in the attic like a ghost rising up through the trap in a stage. The image was completed instantly as the blood deserted his face and the light vanished from the eyes.

Thorne knew what he would look like when he was dead.

'My God – James?' He leaned forward and for a second Thorne thought he was going to pass out. At the last moment Thorne realised he was moving towards his son and reached out an arm to stop him. Bishop glared angrily at him and then, as if woken from a dream, nodded slowly, taking in the full, horrific implications of what he could see around him.

Anne. Rachel. James.

Thorne watched the son glare at the father. Couldn't be much more than a minute now . . .

James's voice was childish, taunting. 'What is it, then? Horror? Outrage? Or just surprise that I know how to do it? A pretty advanced procedure, all in all, considering that I couldn't cut it. Considering what a major disappointment I was . . .'

'Please—'

James screamed, 'Shut up! Fucking shut up, will you?'

Rachel's eyes were rolling up into her head. Sixty seconds, if that . . .

'I always meant to ask you something. When exactly did you start believing the things you do? There must have been a time when you thought the same as the rest of them. About the human body, I mean. All that bollocks about a miracle of design and efficiency. Christ, I'm grateful you taught me what crap *that* was. Your belief in technology was inspiring, did you know that? Truly inspiring. I'm just sorry I couldn't repay the faith you had in me academically. But even when I was fucking it all up, even when I was failing so brilliantly to become the doctor you wanted me to be, I still believed in all the things you did.' He started to cry. 'I still remembered everything you taught me.'

The tears stopped as suddenly as they had started and the voice regained its edge. 'So, when was it? When did you start thinking that the human body was just a worthless piece of shit? Was it when you saw how easily it could be manipulated by drugs? How a body could be slowed up and shaped if you filled it full of tranquillisers? Was she the wife you wanted then? Afterwards? Me and Becks used to call her Snow White – did you know that? Becks said that every time she saw Doc, she went Sleepy and Dopey . . .'

Rachel's breathing was starting to slow. Half a minute . . .

'No, I bet I know when it was. It was when you saw how easily it got damaged, wasn't it? How fragile it was. How easily the skin could be torn by flying glass, or how little it took for a torso to be crushed or twisted. Or perhaps it was both those things. How the body softened up by tranquillisers reacts that much slower in an emergency, in an accident, and becomes a bigger target. Yes, that would make sense. I'd call that a road-to-Damascus sort of moment, wouldn't you? From then on you just saw patients decomposing in front of your eyes. Breaking down, rotting, *dying,* faster than you could stitch them together or prop them up or overhaul them.

'You'd learned a valuable lesson. A powerful lesson. Once you'd learned that, it was about teaching us. Then pushing and pushing . . .'

Rachel had stopped breathing in. Just the last few messy exhalations.

'I would so like to have seen you in prison. Watched your skin go yellow and your bones turn powdery and your hope evaporate. You're soft and vain, and prison would have killed you very slowly. Then you'd have found out just how frail the body really is. Just how frail, Daddy . . .'

Thorne couldn't hear Rachel breathing any more.

James Bishop closed his eyes and whispered, 'Night-night, Sleepyhead . . .'

Anne Coburn screamed. A roar from somewhere down in her guts, and suddenly the room was full of noise and movement. Jeremy Bishop rushed forward, shouting his son's name as if ordering a dog to drop and play dead. James moved with the instinctive obedience of a frightened child, recoiling, taking his hands off Rachel, letting her tumble helplessly forward on to her face.

Thorne ran to turn the girl over and began searching for a pulse.

Come on . . .

He got one. She was still breathing. He picked her up, carried her across to Anne and gently laid her in the recovery position next to her mother. Anne's eyes turned up to him, the spark still strong, the relief evident in every tear that rolled down her cheek and dropped on to her daughter's face.

There was a moment of calm.

Just the noise of the rain coming down, like six-inch nails on to the tiles a few feet above them.

Thorne turned to see Jeremy Bishop moving slowly towards his son, his arms outstretched, his face a deathmask.

James backed into the instrument trolley, which clattered and rolled away from him. He stopped and smiled, his head cocked to one side, and then his arm rose gracefully into the air.

Almost as if he were about to take a bow.

It was a movement so casual that he might have been reaching to scratch a shoulder-blade. Thorne saw the glint of steel at his fist a second before the blood began to spout from the artery in his neck.

'No . . .' Jeremy's voice was a whisper that could have blown down a house.

Thorne leaned against the whitewashed wall and watched as James dropped to his knees and was followed by his father. Jeremy clamped a hand across his son's neck, but the blood gushed between his fingers, running down his arms and pooling across the bleached white floor-boards.

Up one board . . . down another.

Jeremy turned to Thorne, his face already spattered, his hair slick with it. 'Get an ambulance – call somebody.' His voice was thick with desperation. His face implored.

But so did his son's.

James Bishop looked at Tom Thorne and his eyes asked to die. They asked permission to look into his father's face and watch it contort as the blood emptied from the body. He wanted to die watching his father suffer.

Thorne was tempted to let him.

Jeremy's voice was hoarse between the sobs. 'For pity's sake, Thorne . . .'

Then, as Thorne thought about sitting and watching James Bishop bleed to death, he pictured Maggie Byrne, and Bishop watching as her life poured out on to a cheap duvet.

And he remembered a promise he made to Alison Willetts.

Dying would be easy. He was going to see the fucker tried and put away. He was going to watch James Bishop's hope evaporate.

Jeremy was sobbing uncontrollably, his arms, wrapped tightly around his son's neck, slippery with blood.

With a last look at Anne, Thorne stepped down, out of the white room and on to the stairs, hurrying back towards the street, where he hoped Holland would be waiting.

PART FOUR

THE SILENCE

Don't get me wrong, I'm delighted he's dead.

Thrilled about it. Prison is all well and good but I wouldn't want to lie here thinking about him writing his life story, cock of the fucking walk, probably out before he's fifty. Or else in some hospital somewhere, convincing them all he's mental while he pads around in comfy slippers, making model aeroplanes and remembering the women he killed.

Remembering what he did to me.

Sod that, I'd much rather he was dead. If I could get taken somewhere for the day, you know, loaded up into some special van and taken anywhere I want, I'd like to see his grave. Obviously dancing on it isn't really an option but I'd be happy just to be laid across it. Lifted up and laid down on top of him. And I'd lie there with my face on the ground and think dark thoughts that would seep down into the earth and eat into his box like poison.

I'm glad he's dead. Stiff and still, like me.

No, not like me. He's not scrabbling like a madman at the lid of the coffin, is he? Not tearing his fingers to stumps to try and get out. Not fed. Not wiped. Not breathed for.

On the subject of which – no improvement. No response to the antibiotics and no chance of coming off this ventilator in the near future. Apparently the pneumonia in my lungs has been complicated by a fungal infection. Viruses and fungus. It's like I've become a breeding ground . . .

What I really can't stomach is that it was his choice.

He chose this for me and he chose death for himself.

I'll tell you what's really ironic. I'm actually a dead positive person. I really am. You may not believe that and I know I've been a bit up and down but you can't blame me for that. Try this for a while. Lie on your back and stare at the ceiling until your eyes start to water, and imagine it. Imagine being half dead and half alive, and the two halves not adding up to anything. Cancelling yourself out.

It's not easy to be happy all the time.

I am a positive person. But, lying here, I don't think of myself as a person at all any more. Not even a person alone, without anyone close. I wouldn't feel sorry for myself anyway because of that, but I can't even feel it. I just feel like something in a museum.

I just feel like the thing he created.

And I don't believe in God or anything afterwards. I'm sorry but I just don't, I never have. I believe in the way things are. The way I am. I believe in the capacity for people to do terrible things like he did and I believe that some people can do good.

I'd like to do something good. I want to do something.

Most people don't have a choice about a lot of things. They don't choose to be unhappy or poor, and they don't choose to lose children or get cancer. That's just life, though, that's just the lottery, isn't it? It's the same for all of us. But he chose to kill people and he chose to do this to me, to take away my life and give me the one he decided I should have. And then, when he was good and ready, he chose the manner of his own death . . .

Anne's coming back to work next week, I think. We need to talk.

I can't do very much, but I can choose too. I want to have a say.

I don't want to let him win.

CHAPTER 25

Thorne hadn't been able to make good on his promise of a box. Hendricks wasn't pleased, but they were showing the game on Sky anyway, and he agreed to settle for half a dozen cans of cheap lager and a home delivery from the Bengal Lancer.

There had been no great making up, no moment of acceptance or forgiveness. Hendricks called as soon as he heard what happened and they'd talked for a while. It was all that was needed.

Nearly a month now.

When James Bishop died on the operating table, Thorne had blamed himself. Then the post-mortem revealed the drug, and he knew that, even if he'd reacted quicker, the outcome would have been the same. Warfarin. A drug prescribed to treat certain heart and lung disorders and, ironically, used to prevent strokes. An anticoagulant. A drug that prevents the blood clotting.

They couldn't be certain but they guessed he'd been taking it for at least a couple of weeks. Had he been planning it all along? Or had he been taking the drug just in case it ever came down to

463

it? Down to him and his father and a scalpel.

They'd never know for sure.

They'd never know for sure, though Thorne felt pretty certain, that Bishop had been the one who'd gone to the press. Leaking the story to free up the channels of information. Once a few decent holes had been torn in the veil of secrecy, he was able to learn so much more about what was happening on the case. The pipeline that fed Bishop information had been a complex one, running back and forth, in many directions and at different speeds from Thorne himself, via Jeremy Bishop, Anne and, of course, Rachel, who James had been seeing for some time.

She never resat her exams.

Anne wasn't sure when Rachel would go back to school or when she herself would go back to work. That's what she'd said a few weeks ago. Thorne had spoken to her frequently in the days following that night in Bishop's attic, but not since. He thought about her a lot, but never without wondering if his stupidity had somehow contributed to what had happened. Had he been responsible for Anne and Rachel being in that attic?

One of many unanswerable questions with which he liked to torture himself.

It wasn't as if he'd done anything that night to make Anne feel inclined to think better of him. There had been no heroics. Just those who died, and those who nearly did.

Perhaps one day she'd call. It needed to come from her.

He knew it would take a while for the bruises he couldn't see to fade, but he *was* starting to feel better. He had got it wrong, and he knew he would do so again. It was a comforting thought. He had been wonderfully, horribly wrong, and in truth, it felt as though a curse had been lifted.

Fucking-up might just have saved him.

And Helen and Susan and Christine and Madeleine and Leonie? The girls had gone rather quiet. Thorne knew this wasn't because they were 'at peace' or 'avenged' or anything like that. He didn't believe in that sort of crap. He was pretty sure that the silence was only temporary. They would make enough noise when the time came. Them, or others like them.

Right this minute, they just didn't have anything to say.

He watched, confused for a few seconds, as Hendricks jumped from the settee and began to dance around the living room. He glanced at the TV in time to catch the replay. Arsenal had scored. Three more points out of the window and another nail in this season's coffin.

Just one more thing to which Tom Thorne was resigned.

EPILOGUE

A lison and Anne had decided to speed things up.
The process was set down and not open to question. It was ponderous, but that was the way of things when those who took the decisions had to be sure. There was no room for clouded judgement or woolly thinking or, God forbid, overdue haste. The agreement, the rubber stamp of a second consultant, and then, finally, the hearing in front of a judge. These were necessary stages in the process.

Divorce, the custody of children, domestic violence. The High Court Family Division held sway over a great many lives and Alison did not get priority. If anything, her case might be judged less important than some others. So, it was taking time. Alison had first spoken to her over two weeks ago now, and after the tears, the arguments, the doubts, had come a determination on Anne Coburn's part to do what she'd been asked.

To help a friend.

She'd set everything in motion, but it was all too slow for Alison.

469

Anne walked towards ITU, willing one foot to go down in front of the other and keep moving. Steeling herself.

Jeremy was doing a lot better but it was going to take time. The relationship he'd been having with a junior doctor had ended only a few days before James's death, but even if there had been someone around for him to lean on, to take comfort from, Anne would have wanted to be there as well. As it was, he was alone and desperate, and the twenty-five years she'd known him meant that she would always be nearby, ready to help.

Equally, she could never see Tom Thorne again.

It was as if the two of them had survived the crash of a plane Thorne had been flying. Relieved, but unable to look each other in the eye. Guilt and blame and bad memories were not the stuff of a future.

Her future was Rachel.

Alison had been moved to a side room a couple of weeks earlier. It could not be watched directly from the nurses' station, and they wouldn't disturb her.

Anne opened the door. Alison was awake, and pleased to see her.

She moved across to the window and closed the blind. If anything, the room was even more sparse and functional than the one she'd been in before. Anne remembered the half-dead flowers that Thorne had brought from a garage and wondered for a moment where he was and how he might be feeling. She closed her eyes, wiped away the image of him and turned back to Alison.

They spent a few minutes laughing, and crying, before Anne went to work. Her movements were quick, quiet, professional. She removed the oxymeter peg from the end of Alison's finger and clipped it, at a ninety-degree angle, to its own cable. It was unspoken, but most doctors knew that this would short-circuit the alarm and prevent it sounding when the ventilator was switched off. In twenty minutes or so, she would reattach it, when it was over, and she had turned the ventilator back on again. That had been Alison's idea. Take no risks, make it look natural.

Don't fuck about with your career, pet . . .

Anne moved across to the ventilator and flipped back the plastic cover that protected the switch, as if it were the button that launched nuclear missiles. She looked over at the bed.

Alison had already closed her eyes.

Whatever the quality of the strange, laughable life that Alison had lived these last months, it had been lived to a permanent soundtrack of humming, hissing, beeping, dripping. Twenty-four hours a day. A life defined by noise.

James Bishop had condemned her to that, but Alison had refused to let herself be his victim.

Now, finally, the noise had stopped.

More than anything, Anne Coburn hoped that Alison might hold on to life just long enough to enjoy the silence.

471

AUTHOR'S NOTE

My research into locked-in syndrome has made one thing abundantly clear: there is no such thing as a typical case. There is certainly no such thing as a typical recovery, if one is made at all.

That said, any liberties that might have been taken with timeframes, procedure and so on have been taken purely in the interests of the story or else are simple, honest mistakes.

No aspersions as to the efficiency, dedication or commitment of medical staff at any hospital mentioned in this book are intended. Any comment on the parlous state of the National Health Service is meant to reflect badly *not* on the workers within it but on politicians and bureaucrats who, while they happily purchase private healthcare, consistently refuse to fund the NHS adequately in the hope that it will die a nice quiet death.

Mark Billingham, 2000